CORPSEMOUTH
AND OTHER AUTOBIOGRAPHIES

Other Books by John Langan

Novels
The Fisherman
House of Windows

Collections
Children of the Fang and Other Genealogies
Sefira and Other Betrayals
The Wide, Carnivorous Sky and Other Monstrous Geographies
Mr. Gaunt and Other Uneasy Encounters

CRITICAL ACCLAIM FOR JOHN LANGAN'S *CORPSEMOUTH*

"John Langan's enviable range encompasses the whole panorama of horror, from the psychological to the cosmic, the monstrous to the deeply and movingly human, the insidiously disturbing to the thoroughly nightmarish. His imagination never falters or flinches, and his flavoursome prose is a literate pleasure to read."
—WHC Grand Master Ramsey Campbell

"In his masterful new collection, John Langan puts cosmic horror back where it belongs: in our basements, on our crumbling streets, in the crevasses that open in our relationships with our loved ones. These stories don't just pay homage to the Old Gods: they give them fresh lives. Meaning ours."
—Glen Hirshberg, author of *Infinity Dreams*
& the Motherless Children trilogy

"There are certain writers who go straight to the top of my reading list, and John Langan is in that company. One of the finest and most surprising writers working in the tradition of the uncanny."
—Kelly Link, author of *Get in Trouble* and *Magic for Beginners*

CRITICAL ACCLAIM FOR JOHN LANGAN'S *CHILDREN OF THE FANG*

"Langan (*The Fisherman*) draws inspiration from Stephen King, H. P. Lovecraft, David Lynch and other masters of the strange and horrific to create an impressive collection of 21 tales as terrifying as they are mysterious. […] This well-crafted collection will delight fans of dark, literary horror."
—*Publishers Weekly*

"Langan is my standard by which all other short stories are measured. There is something in this collection that will stand out as your favorite, relish your time in these Genealogies to find it."
—*Cemetery Dance*

Critical Acclaim for John Langan's *The Fisherman*

"*The Fisherman* is an epic, yet intimate, horror novel. Langan channels M. R. James, Robert E. Howard, and Norman Maclean. What you get is *A River Runs Through It*…Straight to hell."
—Laird Barron, author of *Worse Angels*

"In this painful, intimate portrait of loss, two damaged men take steps toward redemption, until the discovery of an obscure legend suggests a dangerous alternative. Can men so broken resist the temptation to veer away into strange, unfamiliar geographies? *The Fisherman* is a masterful, chilling tale, aching with desire and longing for the impossible."
—Michael Griffin, author of *The Lure of Devouring Light*

"Reading this, your mouth fills with worms. Just let them wriggle and crawl as they will, though—don't swallow. John Langan is fishing for your sleep, for your soul. I fear he's already got mine."
—Stephen Graham Jones, author of *The Only Good Indians*

"Whenever John Langan publishes a book I am going to devour that book. That's because he's one of the finest practitioners of the moody tale working today. *The Fisherman* is a treasure, the kind of book you just want to snuggle up and shiver through. I can't say enough good things about the confidence, the patience, the satisfying cumulative power of this book. It was a pleasure to read from the first page to the last."
—Victor LaValle, author of *The Changeling*

"John Langan's *The Fisherman* is literary horror at its sharpest and most imaginative. It's at turns a quiet and powerfully melancholy story about loss and grief; the impossibility of going on in the same manner as you had before. It's also a rollicking, kick-ass, white-knuckle charge into the winding, wild, raging river of redemption. Illusory, frightening, and deeply moving, *The Fisherman* is a modern horror epic. And it's simply a must read."
—Paul Tremblay, author of *The Pallbearers Club*

CORPSEMOUTH
AND OTHER AUTOBIOGRAPHIES

JOHN LANGAN

WORD HORDE
PETALUMA, CA

Corpsemouth and Other Autobiographies © 2022 by John Langan
This edition of *Corpsemouth and Other Autobiographies*
© 2022 by Word Horde

Cover art by Matthew Jaffe
Cover design by Scott R Jones

All rights reserved

Edited by Ross E. Lockhart

First Edition

ISBN: 978-1-956252-01-9

A Word Horde Book
http://www.WordHorde.com

TABLE OF CONTENTS

Introduction by Sarah Langan 1
Kore 3
Homemade Monsters 11
The Open Mouth of Charybdis 27
Shadow and Thirst 39
Corpsemouth 71
Anchor 105
Outside the House, Watching for the Crows 163
What Is Lost, What Is Given Away 187
The Supplement 205
Mirror Fishing 227
Caoineadh 251
Story Notes 275
Acknowledgments 295
Publication History 297

For Fiona

INTRODUCTION

Dear Reader,

 Corpsemouth and Other Autobiographies might be the best title of any collection of gothic short stories ever written. Has the author stumbled on a body? Is the author that body? So cheeky, John Langan! You're such a cheeky monkey!

 Not surprisingly, the title's reflective of an excellent and macabre body of work. If you're new to Langan, this is a good place to start, because what's clear from the start, is that there's something very personal happening here. *Families in Peril* is the theme of the day. We've got families that can't remember their own histories, or who are searching in vain for accurate memories, having to suffer through monsters, and possibly death, to find them.

 When a work is personal, a reader can feel it. The work comes alive, pulsing and beating and breathing. An empathetic mirroring happens, where we cannot help, as readers of Langan's work, to think about our own histories, the narratives that sustain us, and those that haunt us. As characters are haunted, our own haunting stories come to life, too. It's an incredible sleight of hand—this empathy Langan builds between author and reader, and I think it comes from the calm, patient way he tells a story, as if always making clear that he wants us to come along. He's thinking of us, even as he

Sarah Langan

tells a story about someone else. Because aren't we all struggling with these universal questions of existence?

And so, as we read, and monsters come to life on the page, we bring our own narratives with us, so that the monsters bang on our windows, too. They lurk in our forests. They lock us in caves, trapping us with mirror versions of ourselves, loops of alternative histories, of possible histories, and possible futures from constantly moving trajectories.

In *Corpsemouth*, familial ties both transcend the monsters in the world, and bind us to those monsters, sometimes in the same story. This kind of friction is the basis for any good horror. What else is horror, but the thing we loved, turning against us? Or worse, what if there's a bad thing inside us, that we had no idea was there?

The characters in this living, pulsing, heartbreaking collection are often under the impression that they survived the struggle, only to attend a high school reunion, or get a phone call from an old family member, and discover that the room they're standing inside, the clothes they're wearing, this entire life they're living, is a scaffold to a lie. Perhaps it doesn't even exist. We are still back in the haunted place. The monster has never left us, and we survived nothing.

What's fun about reading a Langan story, particularly those in *Corpsemouth*, is that he knows his horror literature. We get a little Lovecraft, a little Poe, a little Straub. He's playing with the form, while maintaining its integrity. The stories in *Corpsemouth* read like old-fashioned ghost stories, only not boring. In fact, riveting. There aren't any tricks. They're straightforward, with main characters on journeys, and endings that are, every time, mind-blowing and so goddamned smart.

I expect you'll love this book as much as I do. And if you're holding it in a bookstore—Boo! Also, buy this book.

Wishing you well, from the places where monsters live,
Sarah Langan

KORE

Annie, my wife, started the Halloween Walk when our son was three. We were renting a house on a quiet street. She'd learned that several of the kids in his preschool didn't go trick-or-treating because their neighborhoods weren't safe enough for their parents to take them out in. "We could do something, here," she said to me. "We could make a haunted walk for the kids behind the house." I agreed. Every kid should experience Halloween, right? Together, we set up a course for the kids that took them through the passage between the house and its garage, up the hill behind the garage, and along the terrace cut into the hill. We strung the cottony spider-webs we'd bought at Walmart around the back passage, then populated them with our son's collection of rubber spiders; for a finishing touch, we hung his enormous tarantula puppet in the center of the alley and told the kids they had to duck under it. We filled yellow dish-gloves with bubble wrap, dabbed streaks of red paint along the fingers, and jammed them into the wire fence that extended beyond the end of the garage. The paint dried pink, but the effect was more surreal than ludicrous. "Don't get caught by the hands of the dead," we said to the kids. At the other end of the terrace, on a white plastic chair, we sat the dummy we'd made from filling an old pair of my jeans and one of my old shirts with straw and tying the ends of the arms and legs closed. I had fashioned its head by turning a gallon milk-jug upside down and painting a green-skinned face on it. I'd given it large, baleful eyes. Annie placed half a watermelon that had slid past ripeness on the ground in front of the dummy and jammed a dozen keys she'd bought at the dollar store into the liquescent fruit. This, we told the kids, was Frankenstein's monster. He was asleep but might wake at any moment. His old, used-up brain was lying at his feet. Each of the kids had to poke around in his rotten gray matter until they found a key, which they had to extract without disturbing him. Once everyone had a key, they had to run as fast as they could to the front of the house. There, Annie was waiting on the porch in an old-fashioned witch's costume (although, the pointed hat was bright orange, its brim composed of netting). Each kid presented their key, which she inspected, then instructed them to drop into the plastic kettle before her. In exchange, the child received a brown paper lunch-bag decorated with spiders and skulls, and full of candy. After the last bag had been distributed, we escorted the kids up and down our street, where the trick-or-treating was plentiful and safe.

So big a hit was our first Halloween Walk that it became an instant tradition. A few years later, when we left that rental house to move to one we'd bought, there was a single question on the lips of our son's friends: "Are you still going to have Halloween in your new house?" Of course, we said. While smaller than our previous place, this house had a large, dry, mostly-empty basement. It was, Annie declared, the perfect place for the Walk. Once the sun had slid from the sky, I gathered our son and his friends at the back of the house, where the ground sloped steeply down, exposing the northeast corner of the basement and the door set there. Addressing the kids in the big, over-the-top voice of a circus ringmaster, I described what lay in store for them within. One year, it was Dr. Frankenstein's laboratory. Another, it was the halls in which Dr. Moreau kept his worst experiments confined. A third time, it was the caverns under Count Dracula's (supposedly) abandoned castle. As with that first Walk, each journey presented a goal for the kids to accomplish. They had to steal the batteries Dr. Frankenstein intended to power his next monstrous creation. They had to rescue the (stuffed) animals slated for Dr. Moreau's forthcoming round of vivisection. They had to locate and retrieve the magic rings that would permit Dracula to be resurrected. Flashlight in hand, I led them counter-clockwise around the basement, directing the light at mason jars stuffed with rubber

KORE

eyeballs, at buckets brimming with plastic snakes, at cryptic graffiti on the cement walls. Our destination was always the same: the small room off the southeast corner of the basement. When the real estate agent had shown us the house, she had described the space as a sauna. There was an improvised metal basket full of large, round stones across from the door, so it seemed possible the room had been used for steam. But the open drain in the center of the floor had looked wider than what you would have expected in a sauna. It was deep, too, beyond the range of the flashlight we shone into it. Some kind of drywell, we decided, and covered it with a square of plywood. As I led the kids into the room, I positioned myself at the cover, to keep them clear of it. After the group had fulfilled its annual task, I sent the kids upstairs, where Annie, in some variation of a witch's costume (but always with that orange hat), was waiting for them with bags of candy.

This past Halloween was our most elaborate, yet. We had settled on an archaeological theme, Indiana Jones meets the Mummy, so to speak. There was a big bag of sand left over from one of the aquariums; we scattered it over the floor. We placed plastic snakes, rubber spiders and scorpions, around the room. I chalked the most sinister hieroglyphs I could find on-line onto the basement walls. A friend provided us with a six-foot cardboard box that I spray painted gold then hand painted a pharaoh's mannered features onto. We propped our handmade sarcophagus against one side of the sauna and strewed plastic human bones about the floor. For the first time, I incorporated the drywell into the night's events, removing the cover and filling the floor surrounding it with more malevolent sigils. Also for the first time, Annie took a more active role in the actual Walk. About a month before Halloween, we had attended a birthday party for one of our son's friends. The party had had a classical mythology theme and had climaxed with the gathered party-goers taking turns smashing a huge piñata in the shape of Medusa's head. The rubber snakes with which the piñata was adorned flew off during the attempts to open it, but the head itself was largely intact, and Annie, already thinking ahead, had asked our hosts if she could take it home. "What for?" I'd asked. "You'll see," she'd answered. By trimming the ragged opening at the base of the neck, she transformed it into an oversized mask. She added a pair of long, gray gloves and a pale green gown she'd picked up at the Salvation Army, and *voilà*, she was a goddess. "Which goddess?" I said. "That's not important," she said. Her plan was to sit in the corner of the sauna opposite the sarcophagus. The kids would see the mask and assume it was just another prop; when she stood, it would scare the bejeezus out of them. "What if we use the drywell?" I said. "What if the kids have to throw something into it in order to propitiate you?" "Not me," she said, "the goddess." But we agreed that I would give them each a piece of bite-sized candy that they would have to drop into the well to appease the goddess.

By and large, the Halloween Walk went well. I was concerned that our son and his friends, all of whom are around eleven, might be too old for another Walk, that our props might be too amateurish for them, but both our son and a couple of his friends bought into the scenario with real gusto, which helped to sell it to the rest of the kids. Even the boy who kept insisting that he wasn't afraid of any of this, it was all so *fake*, was looking fairly unsettled. And when I had them gathered in the sauna, which I re-christened the Chamber of Souls, and Annie slowly rose from her seat, the kids gave a collective gasp. "It's Robbie's mom," someone whispered. "Is it?" someone else replied. Playing along, our son said, "That doesn't look like my mom." "She's in a costume—duh!" the first kid hissed. "My mom's upstairs," our son said, managing to sound genuinely nervous. For all its simplicity, I suppose the costume was effective—maybe because of its simplicity. The face on the oversized head was stylized, more department-store mannequin than classical portrait. Its blank eyes were too large for the other features, the narrow, almost pointed nose, the pouting lips. The left cheek was wrinkled, a memento of its previous existence as a piñata. Annie held her head at such an angle that those empty eyes seemed to stare at a point directly above the kids' heads. "Oh Ancient Power," I said, "we bring offerings for your honor. Accept them, and do not drag us down to the darkness where you reign." Considering it was improvised pretty much on the spot, I thought my supplication sounded pretty good. Two and three at a time, the kids darted forward and flung the pieces of candy I gave them into the drywell. A couple of the girls shrieked as they did. The resident skeptic tossed his Hershey's Kiss into the hole with a motion that was probably intended to be dismissive but that came across as full of dread. (I'll admit, I was more pleased by that than I should have been.)

The only part of the Walk that didn't go according to plan involved the younger brother of one of our son's friends. He was seven, and a particularly

Kore

wide-eyed and tremulous seven at that. I wasn't sure that the Walk would be appropriate for him, but he insisted with all of a younger brother's desire not to be left out of his older brother's fun that he wanted to take part in it. His mother offered to accompany us, which I thought would reassure him should he find anything too intense. For most of the Walk, I was right. While I elaborated the terrible history of the latest stop on our tour, I heard the boy's mother murmuring to him, and while his eyes retained their shocked expression, he appeared to be tolerating the event. However, when it came his turn to step out and add his candy to those already cast into the drywell, he refused. "Come on," his mother said lightly, "it's no big deal." The boy shook his head violently. In fact, his entire body was trembling, as if he were freezing. "Come on," his mother said, "it's just Ms. Annie." That loosened his tongue. Through chattering teeth, he said, "How do you know?" "What do you mean?" his mother said. "How do you *know?*" he said. "*How do you know?*" I half-expected Annie to remove her mask, show the boy that his mother was right, it was only her, but she remained still. "*How do you know?*" the boy said over his mother's calm insistence that this was all a game, we were just playing, it was Halloween and that was Ms. Annie in her costume. "*How do you know?*" Finally, I stepped in and announced that it was time for the kids to go upstairs, to receive their bags of candy. I herded my son and his friends to the staircase, cautioning them to watch their steps. As soon as my son opened the door to the kitchen, lighting the stairs, I turned back toward the sauna. But the younger boy and his mom were already on their way out of it, and although his eyes were still wet with tears, he appeared more embarrassed than frightened. Nonetheless, I stopped to talk with his mom, who assured me her son was fine. "Your wife," she said, "is some actress. She had me creeped out." "Me too," I laughed. I ducked my head into the sauna to check for Annie, but she had already left, exiting the basement door to circle around the front of the house and in the front door. By the time I climbed to the kitchen door, she was in the midst of the kids, dressed in her usual witch's costume, this one consisting of a plain black dress the ends of whose sleeves and skirt had been pre-cut to appear ragged, a heavy necklace, and the orange hat. I wound my way through the kids to where she was pouring cups of apple cider and kissed her on the back of the neck. "You are something," I said. "You have no idea," she said, and passed me a cup to hand to one of our son's friends.

It's strange how quickly such an event recedes into your memory. Not until a month later, the weekend after Thanksgiving, did I think about it again in any kind of detail. It was late Saturday night—early Sunday morning, technically. I clawed my way out of the thick folds of a sleep that had wrapped around me like a blanket. I wasn't certain what had awakened me. To be honest, I had the sense that it was because I'd been so profoundly asleep that I'd woken, as if my body had dragged me back into myself from some other state. There was something different about the house. It was like when the power goes out while you've been asleep and you wake to the air colder, the chorus of noises that fills the nighttime hours silent. I glanced to my left, but Annie's side of the bed was empty. Was that what I'd registered, her rising to visit the bathroom? I listened for the sound of her moving downstairs but didn't hear anything. Of course, she might have retreated to the guest room futon to escape my snoring. Only when I was rolling over to return to sleep did I register the figure standing in the corner of the room, to the right of the door. Instantly, I was sitting upright, my heart hammering as if I'd been doused with a bucket of freezing water. The shadows were particularly thick where the form was, away from the windows, but I could make out the oversized head, the dress. I opened my mouth to say, "Honey?" but stopped, overwhelmed by the certainty that, whoever was in the room with me, it was not Annie. For what couldn't have been as long as it seemed, the figure stood in place, its head tilted towards me, while I sat where I was, that little boy's question looping in my mind ("*How do you know?*"). The darkness seemed grainier in that part of the room, as if the air were different, somehow; I had the impression of tremendous distance and age. At last, the figure turned to its right and walked out the door. I waited for the stairs to the living room to utter their creaks and groans, but they remained mute. There was nothing I wanted to do less than leave the bed to see what had become of the intruder. But my son was asleep in his room, and my wife was somewhere else in the house. With as much stealth as I could muster, I slid out from between the sheets and padded to the door, regretting that I'd never gotten around to hiding that baseball bat under the bed. The landing outside the room was empty. My son's door was shut. I opened it, anyway, to check on him, but he was soundly asleep, unaccompanied by any weird visitors. Could the figure have descended the staircase in silence? It seemed unlikely yet appeared the only possibility. I

KORE

followed it down, my heavy footsteps announcing my passage. The first floor was empty of both the intruder and Annie. At this, I felt a momentary surge of panic, and, sliding one of the long knives from the butcher block beside the coffee maker, headed for the basement stairs.

I found Annie in the sauna, crouched over the drywell. She was naked, her hair hanging down around her face. She'd preserved the hieroglyphs I'd drawn on the floor around the hole and added a few of her own. In her right hand, she held an assortment of candies. With her left, she was picking them up one at a time and casting them into the well. I set the knife on the floor beside the door and walked toward her. I didn't know what to say. Without looking up, without speaking, she held out a candy to me. I took it. It was a bite-sized Charleston Chew. I'd lost a tooth to one of these when I was a kid. The tooth had been loose but not that loose and had torn free of the gum with a sweet, sharp pain that had flooded my mouth with the taste of blood and sugar. I gazed at the drywell, at the circle of blackness that dropped who knew how far to who knew what destination. "You have no idea," Annie had said to me Halloween night. I didn't. I tossed my offering into the darkness and reached to my wife for the next one.

HOMEMADE MONSTERS

Was my childhood happy? I'm sorry, I—I don't know how to answer that.

If by happy, you mean, were my physical needs met, for food, shelter, medical care, then yes, without a doubt. That I can recall, I was never hungry (outside of, "Where's dinner? I'm *starving*," complaints). My father provided the money, and my mother made certain I was dressed in the latest fashions (however much the photographic record of those outfits makes me cringe). Whenever I complained of any ailment, I was whisked off to the pediatrician's office posthaste (apparently, I had had numerous emergency visits when I was too young to remember, for everything from a fall during which I smacked my head on the garage's concrete floor, to a small but mysterious bump that my mother found between my eyebrows).

If, however, happiness implies contentment, satisfaction with one's family and surroundings, then I'm less sure. I loved my parents as feverishly, as desperately, as only a small child can, but that love was threaded with fear. I wasn't afraid of them physically; while I'm sure they swatted my butt or slapped my hand when I was a toddler, I don't remember them lifting a hand even in threat until I was a teenager, and, in all fairness, my father's warnings of violence were mostly a rhetorical device to stop me arguing with him. I was their oldest child, the product of seven years' effort at conceiving, and their love surrounded me. Perhaps because I lived in such close proximity to their affection, though, I was sensitive to its daily fluctuations, which, as I grew older and first my younger brother, then each of my sisters, appeared, grew more pronounced. My feelings about those siblings were shot through with ambivalence, the fierce, animal love I had for them alloyed with jealousy and frustration—and guilt, at my conflicted response to them. While our family expanded, our house grew steadily smaller, a structure that had been built for three straining to accommodate twice that number. My parents did their best with the space, converting the original living room into their bedroom, transforming the garage into a new, larger living room, doubling up me and my brother in their former room and my sisters in my old room. But there was nowhere in the house to go for privacy, except the bathroom, and even there, it wouldn't be long before someone would be knocking on the door, telling you to hurry up. It's funny: for all that my siblings and I have gone our separate ways in things like religion and politics, each of us lives in a house that has an upstairs and a downstairs, a place where there's room to be alone.

I'm digressing. The fact is, all the emotions I experienced seemed enormous, much too big for my body. It was as if they roamed the space around me, and every now and again, depending on the situation, stepped into me, filling me to overflowing. I might have been a city in one of the giant-monster films I watched on the *4:30 Movie*. One minute, everything was peaceful and calm, the next, a three-hundred-foot-tall reptile was shouldering buildings aside, crushing cars and buses underfoot, breathing jets of flame at the hordes of people fleeing it. Afterwards—especially if I had been angry—I felt wrecked, hollowed-out by what had inhabited me.

My toys—yes, you're right. I did say that what I wanted to talk about concerns a toy. I was pretty well-off, in that department. Most of my toys were what they call action figures, today; though I don't remember the description attaching to them at the time. First I had G.I. Joe, twelve inches tall, articulated, with a crew cut and beard made of a soft, fuzzy material that came out clumps after you took him in the bath with you. I had Eagle-Eye, whose eyes moved from left to right and back again—scanning the horizon, I guess—when you slid a lever set in the back of his head, and Kung-Fu Grip, whose curled hands were cast in a flexible plastic that started to tear along the palms after a little bit of play. They were succeeded

Homemade Monsters

by the first generation of *Star Wars* figures, who were a third their size, not half as pose-able, but infinitely cooler. They and their vehicles and playsets soon occupied the top positions on my birthday and Christmas lists. What I most wanted, however, was something that, for years, was nowhere to be found outside of the movies. This was a figure of Godzilla, the king of the monsters, whose rampages and battles had been a staple of my imaginative diet since at least first grade, when I first learned of his existence via several of my classmates, who recounted what I later discovered was an extremely inaccurate version of *King Kong vs. Godzilla* to me. From the start, he interested me much more than his smaller American cousin, Kong. Perhaps it was because he resembled the dinosaurs with which I, like every other boy in my class, was fascinated. That he didn't die—at least, not permanently—but continued on in a series of adventures that gradually recast him in the role of hero, also appealed to me. I was never much good with tragedy; although, in all fairness, what child is?

In *Godzilla vs. the Smog Monster*, which must have been one of the first Godzilla films I saw, the little boy who was one of the (human) protagonists' son had a number of Godzilla figures ranged amongst his toys. The instant I saw them, I coveted those figures as I had no toy before. There was nothing like them at either of the local Kay-Bee Toy & Hobby's, and it would be another decade until the first Toys R Us appeared in the area. In those pre-internet days, I knew of no other way to search for a toy I didn't possess. I had a sickening suspicion that the Godzillas were unavailable outside of Japan, or, worse, that they were only props, commissioned for the movie, then taken home by the child-actor.

So desperate did I become for my own figure of the giant monster that, when I was in the fourth grade, I fashioned one, myself, repurposing an eight-inch Captain Kirk whom I'd never found all that interesting in the first place. After stripping him of his accessories, uniform, and boots, I colored him with a green magic marker whose ink dried in long smears. Next, I used scotch-tape to affix a row of dorsal plates I'd painstakingly scissored from a piece of cardboard to his back, then to fasten a tail I'd rolled from a piece of aluminum foil to his butt. I'd tried to construct a Godzilla mask out of a couple of cardboard tabs, a pen, and still more tape, but it required a concentrated effort of the imagination for me to view the head as a success. All the same, the figure was the closest I had to an actual Godzilla toy, and I made the most of it.

Using cardboard tubes, the cardboard backs of the legal pads my father brought home from IBM, aluminum foil, and roll after roll of tape, I built playsets for my monster to trample. I borrowed one of my mother's brownie pans, lined it with foil to represent the Hudson River, and put together a passable replica of the Mid-Hudson Bridge. A cookie sheet beside it supported a model of the Mid-Hudson Civic Center, and several of the tallish buildings I remembered from trips into the city of Poughkeepsie. The scale was off, of course, between the monster and the metropolis, but there was something deliriously terrifying and delightful in the image of Godzilla striding through landscapes familiar to me. In my most elaborate creation, I took over half the dining-room table to build a model of my house and the houses in its immediate vicinity. I cut up sheets of construction paper into the shapes of our various yards and taped them together at the margins. The trees that grew thickly around our homes were toothpicks I'd found in the kitchen junk drawer, left over from one party or another. I broke off pieces of an eraser to hold each toothpick upright and raided the hall closet where we kept medical and cosmetic supplies for a bag of cotton balls, which I separated, dabbed with my green magic marker, and slid on top of the toothpicks for the trees' crowns. The houses themselves were a mix of boxes I'd scavenged around the house and ones I'd put together from cardboard and tape. I went so far as to include the elementary school where I'd attended kindergarten, five houses up the road, and the swamp behind it. My mother was sufficiently impressed with the final result of a long afternoon's work to insist on photographing it with me standing beside, holding my improvised Godzilla. My brother, who came and went as I worked, standing silently at my elbow until I told him to get lost, pronounced my work cool, but that was mostly because Mom was there, and he wanted to participate in her approval. Neither of my sisters paid my project any notice. By the time my father stepped through the front door, I was well on my way to leveling the neighborhood, much to my mother's regret, but, like my brother, he joined in her praise.

I barely heard him. I was caught up in a private movie so vivid it might have been a memory. I was standing in my driveway. To the north, beyond the wide, overgrown field across the road from my house and those of my neighbors, Godzilla occulted the sky. Skyscraper-tall, he appeared to move

Homemade Monsters

slowly, ponderously, yet each of his earth-shuddering footsteps brought him fifty yards nearer. All around me, birds rose from the trees in panicked flocks. Behind me, my house creaked as the ground continued to tremble; from inside it, I heard my mother's good glasses ringing as the vibrations jostled them. Trees cracked and splintered as Godzilla's feet pushed through them. He lowered a splayed foot the size of a barn onto the field across the street and paused. Eyes burning with white light swept the half-dozen houses, the school, that comprised my little neighborhood, as if they were a row of strange growths. I could hear the monster breathing, inhaling and exhaling hurricanes of air, and alongside that sound, a low, steady rumble like the earth's plates sliding against one another. Heat poured off Godzilla's corrugated hide, wilting and blackening the tall grass next to him, and raising sweat all over me. A smell of burning metal wrinkled my nostrils. When he opened his mouth and roared, I clapped my hands to my ears and dropped to the ground, as if I could slip under the noise that radiated from him, bursting the windows of my house and all the houses on the road. Once more, Godzilla was on the move. The earth shook so hard it bounced me onto my back. He'd corrected his course a few degrees to his right, and was making straight for Eddie Isley's house, which was separated from mine by old Mr. Warner's. The monster's left foot swept the front of Mr. Warner's gray farmhouse, shearing it off and causing the rest of the building to sway backwards, half-fallen. His right foot came down squarely on the Isleys' two-story blue colonial, bursting the house like a balloon. Siding, sheetrock, wood flew in all directions. Nor was that enough. A segment of the back wall and the deck remained standing, as did the small barn behind the house in whose neat interior Mr. Isley kept his tools and his car when the weather was bad. That giant foot raised again, and drove down once, twice, with sufficient force to pulverize what was left of the Isleys', not to mention, to send the Warners' house crashing the rest of the way to the ground, and to bounce me around as if I were on a trampoline. Godzilla stepped forward, and kicked the Isleys' barn, most of which disappeared in a cloud of splinters; although I watched part of its black roof arc high into the sky. He snorted and continued up the street.

How did I feel? I felt *great*. What I was watching—and I swear, that was how it seemed to me, as if I were actually there, witnessing all of this, and not imagining it—the scene playing out exhilarated me. The sheer terror the presence of this gargantuan monster evoked from me was balanced, maybe exceeded, by the profound delight, the joy, it also produced. For once, my emotions were in proportion to my surroundings. It didn't hurt, either, that Godzilla had visited such utter destruction upon the home of Eddie Isley.

Eddie. I guess he's the reason I'm here talking to you—him and what happened to him. We were the same age and had been in school together since Eddie and his family had moved into their house when we were in second grade. I'm pretty sure they had come from Arizona; though what had brought them to upstate New York, I don't know. Possibly his father's job: he was with IBM, as was my dad, as was the father of every other kid you asked. (At that time, the Hudson Valley was IBM country, from Wiltwyck down to Ossining, with stops along the way for Poughkeepsie and East Fishkill.) Eddie was shorter than I was by a couple of inches, but he was better-proportioned; even before the adolescent growth-spurt that would raise the top of my head above first my mother and then my father, I was long arms and longer legs, as if my body were laying in plans for the changes to come. Where my hair was a fine, dirty blond that I wore in no definite style, Eddie's was a thick, shining black that he parted on the right with military precision. A pair of heavy, square glasses defined his face, while my own glasses would wait until I was in fifth grade.

Because we were neighbors and the same age, not to mention, students at the same Catholic elementary school, the assumption on the part of our parents was that we would be friends. Our interests were similar enough to place us within the same social group at school, where the more athletically-inclined kids and the more academically-inclined kids were continuing the process of differentiation and separation that would reach its culmination in high school. Not only did Eddie and I like to read, we liked to read the same types of things, books about older cultures, the Greeks and the Romans, the Vikings and the Samurai. I was fascinated by their myths and legends, Eddie by their history, especially the battles they'd fought. Both of us liked to draw, but my artwork was influenced by the styles of the comic books I pored over: its figures were big, bold, either engaged in a dramatic act or posed in the immediate aftermath of one. Eddie's pictures showed the effect of the military histories he read: their figures were small, almost miniature, and there were a lot of them, usually wearing the same uniform,

Homemade Monsters

and in the midst of an enormous undertaking, usually a battle. I loved the wealth of detail with which he loaded each of his drawings. He ignored my work, except to pass an occasional snide remark about it.

From the distance of three and a half decades, I can recognize that Eddie's dismissal of my artwork was driven by jealousy. He was intensely competitive—in class, each of us tried to have his hand up first when the teacher asked a question—and he resented anything that was done better than he could, whether a drawing or an essay that the teacher invited you to read out loud. For the three years of school we shared, there was no success I could have, but Eddie had to mock it. Also from this length of time, I can't help wondering where he had learned such behavior. He had an older sister, Yvette, but she was five years his senior, and from what I observed, as uninvolved with her little brother as she could manage. I don't recall much about his parents, except that they had a house rule that you had to remove your sneakers upon entering their house, and that they served celery sticks smeared with peanut butter as a snack. His mother did—she brought them downstairs to their basement, which was furnished and served as a family gameroom. She was pleasant enough to me, but I have the impression of her as distracted, as if always listening for the phone to ring, or someone to knock on the door. I saw Eddie's father much less frequently; he worked what struck me as much longer hours at IBM than did my dad. I remember him as distracted, too, or, not so much distracted as detached. It's difficult for me to picture either half of that distant couple unleashing the same withering vitriol on their son that he used on me. But maybe they did.

Whatever its source, from time to time, Eddie's verbal nastiness was accompanied by a physical expression of his sentiment. This never happened at school. Even during recess, when the location of the playground monitor might allow you to raise your hand against someone, Eddie did not risk the shoves or sloppy punches of the rest of us; instead, he stalked away from confrontation, a scowl darkening his face. If you ran after him, grabbed hold of his arm to stop him, he flung your hand off with a windmill of his arm and continued on his path. Outside of school, which is to say, in his basement or my room, or either of our yards, or the schoolyard down the road, where we sometimes went to explore the swamp behind it, things were different. Eddie's disdain for a drawing I had completed would be followed by him sweeping his hand across the table at which we were seated, catching the sheet of paper I'd labored over and crumpling it, sending it onto the floor along with a dozen of the magic markers we'd been sharing. His envy over a new toy my grandparents had sent me—say, the Colonial Viper from the first *Battlestar Galactica*, which fired a red missile from its nose—would lead to him pleading for me to let him play with it, just for a minute, *please*, and, once I gave in and handed it to him, finding the quickest way to break it—in the case of the Viper, jamming the missile in so far it became stuck, and could not be fired. Any reproach on my part was likely to be met with a sarcastic, "Sorry," and a remark about how my drawing hadn't been any good in the first place, or what cheap junk my toy had been.

It's funny: it's not only that I remember how I felt at those moments—a mix of anger, frustration, and resentment that enveloped me in a fiery sphere—but, when I revisit them, I still feel the same emotion, incandescent around me. No matter how much I think I've grown, matured, no matter how many white hairs the mirror shows have infiltrated my beard, the instant I recall that crumpled sheet of paper, that damaged toy, there's a direct route in my mind to my younger self and the feelings that rampaged through it. It's as if I'm still there.

I know, I know. Why didn't I cut ties with Eddie, at least, in those locations where he could do most harm? There was a part of me that recognized this as the most sensible course of action. That level of resolve, however, was beyond me. No matter how egregious Eddie's act, it wasn't long before I was at the back door of his house, asking his mother if he could come out to play. When he emerged, he wore a slight smirk that said he knew what he'd done wasn't that big a deal. For a time, he would be on what for him was good behavior, restricting any hostility to his comments to me.

If I couldn't keep away from Eddie, over time, I learned to keep anything that was precious to me out of his sight. This included my improvised Godzilla figure, which seemed guaranteed to arouse the full measure of his contempt. I have yet to work out how he found it. We were in my room, playing Stratego with my younger brother. Eddie and I faced one another, first, while my younger brother looked on, then, after I had defeated Eddie, my brother and I played. Irritated by his loss, Eddie prowled the undersized room. Three moves into the game, I heard him saying, "What's this?"

He was holding my handmade Godzilla. The expression on his face was blank; he might have been trying to identify what the figure in his grip was

Homemade Monsters

supposed to be. I opened my mouth to say I don't know what, something that would distract Eddie, call his attention away from the toy, back to me. My brother spoke first. "Hey," he said, "he's got your Godzilla." The name completed a circuit. Eddie's face brightened. He said, "Godzilla?" and with a wrench of his hands, tore the figure's rubber head off and flung it across the room. I scrambled to my feet, one of my sneakers lashing out and striking the Stratego board, clearing it. Eddie shifted his grip to the toy's waist and snapped it in half. He opened his hands and let the pieces of the figure drop to the carpet. "Doesn't seem like the king of the monsters to me."

My brother, in a move both brave and reckless, had wrapped his arms around my legs. Had he not, I would have crossed the room in a heartbeat. I could see myself leaping onto my bed and using the mattress to trampoline into Eddie. I was beyond angry, beyond upset; I was the center of a fury so transcendent that, for an instant, it seemed as if I could stretch out my hand and it would pour from me in a white blaze that would burn Eddie Isley to a shadow on the wall. As it was, my brother held me in place, and said to Eddie, "You'd better leave."

How I would like to be able to report that the sight of me in my rage unnerved Eddie, registered on his face as the slightest faltering in the sick smile that had crept onto it, the faintest lowering of his bows with concern. It did not. He opened the door to my room, stepped out into the hallway, and departed the house, all without another word. My brother held me until we heard the back door shunk closed. Then he released me. I wanted to kick him for what he'd done, but I was more concerned with sprinting to the back door, hauling it open with enough force to rattle the venetian blind hung on it, and rush onto the porch. Eddie had moved fast, himself, crossing the field between my house and Mr. Warner's, reaching the pair of enormous evergreens whose needled skirts marked the edge of the Warners' yard. I don't know if he heard me throw open the door; he didn't look back, anyway. I considered tearing after him, but with this much of a head start, he'd likely outpace me to his house, and if I caught, tackled, and started pounding him, I'd be doing so in his backyard. I knew how that would look, to his family and to mine. So I waited until Eddie was out of sight behind the evergreens, then returned inside, closed and locked the back door, and returned to my room to plan my revenge.

There wasn't much to it. The next day, after I returned from school, I went into the backyard to the spot behind the garden shed where my father piled the tree branches that the winter snow and ice had stripped from the trees. He would build that heap as the spring and summer thunderstorms brought down more limbs, until the fall, when we would pile the leaves we'd raked on top of the wood and my father would set the whole thing ablaze. I sifted through the branches gathered there until I found one that was a little taller than I was, mostly straight, and not too heavy. I snapped what smaller branches remained from it, and carried it to the porch, where I set it on the picnic table there. I went into the house for a roll of duct tape and a pair of scissors. Outside again, I dug my pocket knife out of the right front pocket of my school pants. My father had bought it for me last summer vacation, at the gift shop at Fort William Henry, in Lake George. Its side panel was decorated with an image of the fort in vivid green and brown. I unfolded the blade and taped the hilt to the narrower end of the branch. I used enough of the duct tape to secure the knife reasonably well, and by the end of my efforts, had a decent spear. I didn't bother trying to bring it inside; my mother wasn't fond of the mess such imports made. Instead, I carried the spear to the white metal garden shed, inside whose right-hand door I positioned my new weapon.

No, I wasn't plotting to kill Eddie; this isn't a murderer's confession. I was as furious with him as I had been the moment he'd destroyed my improvised Godzilla; there appeared to be no danger of that emotion fading anytime soon. Yet my rage was mixed with a terrible grief that threatened to send tears flooding down my cheeks every time I looked at the ruin of the figure I had devoted so much time to crafting. My brother had suggested I could repair it, borrow the Krazy Glue and restore it to what it had been. For once, I hadn't told him to shut up, only shook my head from side to side. The pieces of the figure seemed charged with the contempt Eddie had visited upon them. When you're a kid, you internalize the violence that's done to you; you don't know how not to. Someone calls you a name, and it hurts, and part of the reason it hurts is because you fear it might be true. A toy that I had fashioned had been ruined, and I was afraid that it had deserved to be. What I wanted now was to assert myself against Eddie, and in so doing, to refute the scorn he'd inflicted on me.

Yes, it is pretty sophisticated reasoning for a ten-year-old. Of course I didn't frame what I intended to do in those terms. My thoughts were more

Homemade Monsters

concrete. In another couple of days, I would tell Eddie I was going on an excursion into the swamp behind the elementary school down the road and ask if he had any interest in joining me. I had no doubt he would accept my invitation. For one thing, while I hadn't had him back to my house, at school, I'd kept a tighter lid on my emotions than at any point in the past; even when Eddie asked me how Godzilla was doing after his defeat by the Hands of Isley, I smiled tightly and looked down, as if embarrassed. For another thing, Eddie was inordinately proud of his skill at orienteering; I say inordinately because, on our previous voyages into the swamp, he hadn't impressed me as any more competent a navigator than I was. Spear in hand, then, I planned to lead Eddie deep into the swamp, much farther than we'd been, until everything around us was unfamiliar. Once we were good and lost, I would demand that he apologize for destroying my homemade Godzilla, for all his acts of wanton violence. I would brandish the spear to reinforce my demand. That I might have to put it to use was a possibility I rejected. Eddie behaved like a bully, and the knowledge I'd aggregated from a host of comic books, TV shows, and movies that dealt with such types told me that they were, finally, cowards, who, if confronted convincingly, would back down. I wish I could convey the trembling pleasure with which I contemplated my plot. Lying in bed at night, on the verge of dropping into sleep, I would picture Eddie, standing knee-deep in the swamp's brackish water, glancing from side to side at the strange trees fencing us in, his lip quivering as he struggled to keep from crying.

That vision was closest I came to my plan's success. While the early stages went smoothly, by the time we were in the swamp, my design had unraveled with surprising speed. From the moment we stepped onto the dirt ridge that served as a pathway through the swamp's outer reaches, Eddie had kept well ahead of me. Though he hadn't commented on it, he'd registered my spear with a slight widening of his eyes, a jerk of his head. Our previous journeys into the swamp, I hadn't carried anything with me, afraid to lose it in the murky water. For me to have changed my behavior, and to have done so by bringing a weapon with me, had raised Eddie's suspicions—not enough for him to refuse to accompany me, but sufficiently for him to maintain a cautious distance between us. I had anticipated we would travel with our usual, leisurely pace; instead, Eddie moved briskly, leaping from the end of the dirt ridge onto the first of the chain of small hummocks that formed the route into the swamp's interior. He hopped to the second while I was still on the ridge. I was well-practiced at traversing the network of dirt mounds that thrust their grass-covered peaks above the dark water, but the addition of the spear upset my balance. I miscalculated a couple of my jumps and paid for it with a sneaker full of cold water. The deeper into the swamp we pushed, the thicker the air became, humid and heavy with the stink of the skunk cabbages that populated the hummocks to either side of us. Sweat glued my T-shirt to my back. Clouds of tiny insects drifted through the air, and when I landed on one of the diminutive islands, the insects swarmed my eyes and nose. Already, we were in new territory. Eddie launched himself onto the trunk of a huge, fallen tree whose trunk he ran along until he reached the wreckage of its crown, where he dropped onto the first of a new line of hummocks leading further into the swamp. I struggled to keep up with him. Ferns of prehistoric size sprouted from the soil of this latest archipelago and flailed against me when I landed on their hummock, as if trying to force me off. Great trees whose trunks were wrapped with ivy and patched with moss enclosed us; from somewhere in their ranks, a bird uttered a stuttering cry like a monkey's call. Throughout, I maintained my grip on the spear, but I was more worried about the object in the right front pocket of my jeans. I had stuffed the decapitated head of my handmade Godzilla into my pocket with the intent of confronting Eddie with it during my demand for his apology. The problem was, the pocket was shallow, the jeans a fraction too small, and the figure's head felt constantly on the verge of falling out into the swamp. Nothing was happening as I had imagined it. The fury I'd worked to contain, to channel into my plan for revenge, was leaking from the growing cracks in that plot like radiation from a damaged reactor. It seemed to spill out over my surroundings, making them ripple like a sheet in the wind. In that rage—through it—I was aware of something, a kind of presence, an attention, waiting just out of sight. It was vast as the swamp, alien.

Once Eddie reached a hummock that was sizable enough to host a pair of slender birches, he paused. This, I thought, was my chance if I could take it. I sprang from hummock to hummock, unconcerned when one of my sneakers splashed the water. *Here I come*, I thought. *Here I come.*

He punched me at the moment my feet touched the mound on which he was waiting. It was a shot to the gut that drove the air out of me and sent

Homemade Monsters

me backwards, my arms flailing as I sought and failed to keep my balance. Butt-first, I fell into the swamp's water. For a terrifying instant, I was sure I was going to go under the water's surface and continue dropping, down into inky darkness. The water, however, was only two feet deep. I was soaked up to my armpits, but I was safe. "Eddie!" I shouted. "What the hell, man?"

"Shut up," he said. He was crouched at the edge of the hummock, his hand outreached to where my spear was floating. I dove for it, but Eddie was faster, snatching it out of the water. As I struggled to my feet, Eddie inspected the spear, his expression somewhere between interest and disdain. "Eddie," I said. He grabbed the spear at either end and brought it down onto his knee. The wood broke with a flat crack. "Hey!" I shouted. He flung the base of the spear to his right, and the top, my pocket knife still taped to it, to his left. The pieces spun off between the trees, each plunking somewhere out of sight.

"What did you expect?" Eddie said. "Good luck finding your way home." He turned and strode to the opposite end of the hummock, where he leapt between the birch trees to another hummock, and the one beyond that, ignoring my cries for him to wait, wait, come on, until he was lost amidst the trees.

The fury that burst from me was made worse by the realization that my jeans pocket was empty, the head of my Godzilla figure lost. Big—the emotion dwarfed anything I'd felt, before. I was suspended in it, and it extended for miles around and below me, an ocean. For a second time, the swamp rippled, and I was conscious of that vast presence, at the edge of my perception.

What happened next began as a thunderclap, a cataclysm of sound that rushed across the swamp toward me, blowing a wall of debris, of leaves and sticks and bark, ahead of it. I ducked to the water's surface, but I already had seen what was following close behind, a wave that rolled through the water and the ground underneath, making the trees shake like grass in a breeze, snapping their trunks. The ground beneath me flexed like the hide of some great beast twitching at an irritant, vaulting me into the air. For a long moment, I hung in space, water around me, and then I struck the hummock on which Eddie had been standing. Winded, terrified, I lay there while trees continued to crack and splash into the water, which slopped and slapped against the hummock.

I was still there hours later, when the first firefighter stumbled across me. Before the earth had ceased shaking, my mother and Eddie's were on the phone to one another, each asking if the two boys were at the other's house. They knew we were bound for the swamp and were horrified at the thought that the ground had started to move while we were within it. This was well ahead of the seismologists' determination that the epicenter of what they would describe as a substantial seismic event was located in the swamp—by my later estimates, about a hundred and fifty yards south-southeast of where I'd been standing. In short order, our fathers were called, and not long after that, the police. Although damage to the buildings in the immediate vicinity of the event was in many cases substantial—the ceiling of the elementary school's gym fell in—injuries were remarkably few and mild, allowing the police to devote more resources to a pair of missing fourth-graders than might otherwise have been the case. One look at the wreckage that had been the swamp, and the cops called for whatever backup was available. A steady flow of firefighters, paramedics, and concerned men and women who'd heard the news on their CB's responded to the request. Someone laid their hands on a map of the swamp, and the people who'd gathered in the school parking lot, including my father and Eddie's, were divided into groups and assigned an area of the swamp to investigate. This was how I was found.

Eddie was not. The portion of the swamp I'd watched him heading toward fell, the ground in some places dropping as much as fifteen feet. Apparently, there had been a network of caves immediately beneath the swamp, and when the earth shook, they collapsed, birthing a sinkhole that sucked down whatever was above it, including Eddie. Or so the theory went. Despite ten days of searching that included the use of backhoes to excavate select areas of the sinkhole, no body was recovered.

The Isleys moved a couple of months after the search was called off and their son declared missing and likely dead. During that time, they made no effort to contact me, to ask me about Eddie's last moments. I lived in dread they might and had invented a tale of Eddie running off for help after I twisted my ankle, in case I needed it. But I didn't have to use it, which was a relief. I wasn't certain I'd be able to maintain the requisite deception.

How did I feel? Relieved…and satisfied…and guilty. The last of those emotions was the only one to which I could admit. Without the other two, though, it was diagnosed as the survivor's guilt typical of a child who had undergone the experience I had. My parents, our parish priest, the therapist I was sent to, all offered versions of the same counsel: what you're feeling is normal, but what happened was not your fault. Only I knew how true and not true that statement was, and since I couldn't find a way to explain that to anyone, I buried it in my memory.

Time passed, years, decades. I continued to draw, continued to improve at it, made connections, and eventually got a job drawing comic books. I married, had a daughter who's almost finished college, now. I left the publisher I'd been working for to join some people I knew who'd formed their own company. Eventually, we secured the rights to do a new Godzilla book. I'm going to draw it. Talk about a childhood dream come true, right? I made sketches, planned the first few issues with the writer. I had this idea it would be fun to sneak a few of the locations I'd grown up with into the comic, so that when the monster's wading out of the ocean, it's onto my favorite beach, that kind of thing. I sat down in front of the computer, called up Google Earth, and started typing locations into the search bar. I haven't been by the house I grew up in since my parents retired to North Carolina, and one of my sisters told me that the old neighborhood had changed to the point she barely recognized it, anymore. I entered my childhood address and waited.

My sister was right, the old place was different. The field across the road had been replaced by a sprawling storage facility. Mr. Warner's house had been expanded to the rear, until it was almost twice its former size. There was a large, round pool behind the Isleys' former house. And so on. What drew my notice, however, as I scrolled up the satellite photo, was the swamp behind the school. Following Eddie's disappearance, it had been fenced off, at no small cost to the local taxpayers. But there was no way it was going to be left open, especially when it was right behind an elementary school. No doubt, kids snuck in there; no doubt, stories sprung up about the boy who'd been lost there, consumed by the swamp. Do you know the official description of what occurred that distant afternoon is that it was an atypical seismic incident? Maybe the scientists never studied the satellite images of the area. Or maybe they did and didn't notice anything: when I called my wife in and asked her what the picture on the monitor looked like to her, she leaned in, squinted, and said it didn't look like anything, just wetlands. She didn't distinguish the shape in what had been called a sinkhole. Thirty-five years later, its outline was still visible, the broad base, the three long channels branching off its top, the shorter channel angling forward on its left. It was the imprint of a foot, the foot of a creature whose head would have towered above my old neighborhood the way mine rises over the garden. I told myself I must be imagining things, imposing design on random destruction. But I could not unsee it, no matter how hard I tried. I leaned back in my desk chair, the head of that old, homemade Godzilla in my hand, and contemplated that shape for a long time.

What? Oh, that's right—I didn't tell you. When the fireman carried me out of the swamp, I had the head I was sure I'd lost clutched tight in my left hand. I have no idea how it came to be there. Afterwards, I kept it with me as a kind of talisman, I guess. A few days after I bought my first car, I drilled a hole through the head and threaded it onto my keychain, which is where it's been ever since. Whenever I'm upset, agitated or angry, I squeeze it. The green marker has long worn off, and the flesh tone underneath has faded to a dull color that my wife says resembles bone. Sometimes, if I'm dealing with a particularly annoying person at work, or if my wife and I are at loggerheads over something, or if my daughter is aggravating me as only she can, I clench that relic of distant catastrophe with such force, I half-expect it to push through my skin. I can almost feel what I did that day in the swamp, a vast presence, waiting.

THE OPEN MOUTH OF CHARYBDIS

You know how the story ends before it's even begun. No one had any memory of my brother, Edward, except me. Instead of five children, three boys and two girls, my parents had an equal number of sons and daughters. Photos in which Edward was sandwiched between our brother, Henry, and our sister, Jane, now showed Henry and Jane smiling beside one another. Drawings for which he had won the CYO art contest year after year, their accompanying gold medals, were gone from their position in the hallway, with no difference in the paint to mark where they'd hung. The silver maple in the backyard, whose trunk Edward had attempted to saw through, as revenge for Jane falling off one of its lower boughs and breaking her arm, showed no grooves at its base. Henry and I shared a room in which each of us had a single bed, not the bunkbed and single bed the three of us had argued over for years. Our room was still too small for all our possessions, but without Edward's drawing table filling one of its corners, there was space for a bookcase for me and a desk for Henry.

More had changed, besides. It seemed I was the artistic one, now; while Henry was the academic prodigy. Jane was suddenly famous for her stubbornness at the dinner table, and Victoria, the youngest, was known for her intense Catholicism. Gone were my years as a wide receiver for my high school's junior varsity and varsity football teams. Gone was Henry's ability on the guitar. Gone was Jane's facility with foreign languages, Victoria's knack for the mechanical. Our parents were different, too. Dad was no longer a manager at IBM, which meant he was home earlier, but the family budget was tighter. Mom was prone to more and worse migraines, spending her days behind a pair of large sunglasses. Four kids still meant a busy household, but there was a current of melancholy threading through our relations, impossible to account for, almost as if it was a collective response to an absence no one was aware of.

My younger brother vanished from existence while the family was on a trip to a place of which there is also no trace. Ask the rest of them where we passed the last week of July, the first of August, during the summer of my senior year of high school, and they will tell you Maine, a town called Bucksport, on the Penobscot River. They'll describe day trips to Bar Harbor, to Acadia National Park; they'll talk about the night our parents took us to dinner at Jed Prouty's, the nicest restaurant in town. None of them will have anything to say about spending the same two weeks north of Boston, in and around Gloucester. They won't recall taking the train into Boston to visit the Aquarium. They'll have no recollection of driving through Newburyport to the village of Mason, on the northeastern end of Plum Island.

But we did, all of it. We went on a whale watch out of Gloucester, and Mom became seasick, and had to take a Dramamine and lie down on one of the ship's benches. We followed the walkway that wound up and around the Aquarium's enormous cylindrical fishtank, waving to the divers floating within, feeding the fish. We parked in Mason's single municipal lot, which was located next to its dilapidated docks, and Edward, Henry, and I set off in search of the Marsh House, the museum Edward had asked to visit, because it had a small painting by Paul Gauguin, with whose art he was obsessed. Our parents, who elected to browse the waterfront's abbreviated row of shops with our sisters, told us to meet them back at the car in two hours, which seemed like more than enough time. The village was little more than a few dozen narrow streets, and the museum was not far. At seventeen, I was in charge of Henry (fifteen) and Edward (fourteen), a position I made certain to verify with our parents. "Just behave yourselves," Dad said.

Although open to the public, the Marsh House was a private museum. It

The Open Mouth of Charybdis

had been founded by the family who had given what was actually a mansion their name. Four stories tall, red brick with white trim, the residence had been built in the Federal style. It stood, simple and austere, amidst a scattering of large trees on the ocean side of the island, at the dead end of a cobbled street whose sidewalks had buckled with the decades' weather. A threadbare lawn stretched from the house's back door to the short drop off to the shoreline. The three of us walked to its edge. Amidst the rocks crowding the sand, a half-dozen posts, broken and weatherbeaten, marked points on a line receding into the waves. The remains of the family's private dock, Edward said. According to him, the Marshes had been one of the major families in Mason during the nineteenth and early twentieth centuries. That was when the village had gone by a different name, Innsmouth.

"Why'd they change it?" Henry said.

"Some kind of disease broke out in the early thirties," Edward said, "or maybe it was the late twenties. Whatever it was was pretty bad, virulent. The place was quarantined; there were actual soldiers stationed on the road to keep people out."

"Or in," I said.

"Yeah," Edward said. "Something else went on, too, about the same time. Government raids—like, the FBI. The village used to be a lot bigger. The docks extended pretty far over the water. There were a lot of warehouses built on them—houses, too, like half the village. The federal agents were interested in the warehouses. Supposedly, they arrested a lot of people."

"Smugglers," I said. "Had to be."

"Could be," Edward said. He turned, and Henry and I followed him around to the front of the house and the museum's entrance. A kid somewhere in our age range, wearing an oversized Red Sox jersey and perched on a tall chair, raised his eyes from the swimsuit issue of *Sports Illustrated* he was lingering over and asked how many. I said, "Three." As I did, I heard a tremendous crash, as if two enormous gears had clashed together. The kid, his chair, the wall behind him, were suddenly clear, transparent, as if made of glass. Through a series of ghostly layers, I glimpsed the lawn behind the mansion, the ocean. Head wheeling, I jerked my hand to my eyes. Behind me, Edward said, "What is it?"

"Nothing," I said, because what else was I going to say? I lowered my hand, hoping I'd spoken truthfully.

It appeared I had. The kid, the house, were once more solid. Whatever had just happened to me was, to put it mildly, disorienting, but Edward gave me no time to dwell on it. Pushing in front of me, he asked where the Gauguin painting was. The exhibit was on the main floor, the kid said, in the dining room, which was located on the ocean side of the museum. He pointed us to a stack of photocopied guides sloping on top of a low table across from him. Next to the folded sheets sat an undersized caricature of a pirate's treasure chest with a slot through its lid and the word DONATIONS stenciled on its side. Henry extracted a couple of crumpled dollar bills from the front pocket of his jeans and pushed them through the slot, which guilted me into doing the same. Edward was already off ahead of us, making his way into the house.

Though high-ceilinged, its rooms were smaller than its exterior implied. Each one was crammed full of what I assumed was its original furniture, plus a selection of objects associated by a common theme. The first room we entered was decorated with a dozen ships in bottles, the containers ranging in size from a small, green-tinted medicine bottle to a large, clear bottle whose contents would have served a sizable dinner party. All of the model ships were sailing vessels, two and three masters. I didn't see their names anywhere on the bottles. The bottled ships went with the harpoons leaning against one corner of the room, the cutlasses laddered on the wall opposite. An assortment of sextants and compasses covered the top of one side table, while a collection of carved pieces of what I thought were bone had been laid on top of another. "This was how the Marshes made their fortune," Edward said, "on the sea. They did some piracy during the Revolution, and some whaling later on, but mostly, they were into trading."

Neither Henry nor I doubted Edward's information. Especially when he wanted to go someplace, do something, he researched it as thoroughly as if he were going to present a lecture on it—which he often did, to Henry and me, and sometimes our sisters. Henry said, "What did they trade?"

"All kinds of stuff," Edward said. We followed him into the next room. Sitting on its high-backed chairs, a pair of complete suits of samurai armor greeted us. A sheathed katana spanned the knees of each one. A folding screen whose panels were painted with koi had been positioned slightly behind the chairs and their armor. More swords were displayed on the room's walls, alongside elaborately-embroidered kimonos whose flattened sleeves

THE OPEN MOUTH OF CHARYBDIS

reminded me of pressed flowers. Clusters of side tables held sets of china cups, saucers, and plates. "All right," Henry said, "this is pretty cool."

"Yeah," I said.

That room opened onto a hallway which ran left toward the back of the mansion. Sneakers squeaking on the floor's polished wood, the three of us passed portraits of old and old-looking men and women, wearing the fashions and expressions of a century or more in the past. "Hey," Henry said, "you didn't finish telling us why they changed this place's name."

"Oh," Edward said, "no big mystery. The village never recovered from the epidemic and the government raids. Did I mention the fire? There was a big fire—maybe in 1942? Burned almost all of the docks, the warehouses, pretty much everything over the water. People thought the Germans had set it—you know, saboteurs, on account of the war. There was some kind of massive chemical spill—something that had been stored in one of the warehouses. It poisoned the sea pretty far out. Things kept going downhill until the late sixties, when there was a move to revitalize the area, bring it back to prosperity. As part of that, the local officials decided to change the name to Mason, which was what the English called it when they first wrote about it. They cleaned up the shore, which was full of wreckage from the fire, and knocked down pretty much all the remaining piers, which weren't in great shape. I guess it worked for a little while, but there wasn't anything out here you couldn't find in Newburyport. Unless they have a specific reason to visit here, people don't."

"Like a ghost town," Henry said.

"A ghost town that can't disappear," Edward said. "Although, there's a story—"

The rest of the sentence stayed in his mouth, kept there by his first sight of the painting that met us when we turned right at the end of the hall. The picture had been propped on an easel, set up near the French doors that gave a view of the back lawn and the ocean. The mid-afternoon light pouring through the glass was the only illumination in the room; though I noticed a row of track lighting on the ceiling whose lights were all turned in the painting's direction. A pair of short brass poles held a thick purple rope to mark the limit of our approach. Despite them, the effect of the display was casual, as if the artist might have stepped away from the canvas only a moment or two before.

The painting itself was smaller than I was anticipating. Since it was a work by a famous artist, I assumed the piece would be at minimum the size of the portraits we had just passed, three feet or so high, two feet or so wide. This picture was half as large. It showed a beach scene, done in the simple lines and rich colors that defined Gauguin's later style. At its center, a figure executed in dark blues and black stood on a slight sandy rise, its thin arms held to either side, palms out. Its head was an exaggerated oval, the eyes blank, the features heavy, and was crowned with a pair of wings that swept down behind its torso. At its feet, a trio of figures lay on their sides, their backs to the viewer, their arms and legs tucked in front of them in what could have been positions of birth or death. Their skin was pale white, ruddy in places. Below them, a pool of water, possibly an ocean inlet, was busy with dark green and yellow reflections that suggested forms swimming beneath its surface. In the distance behind the blue figure, the ocean rolled in white waves from left to right, toward a yellow shore curving to receive them.

What drew the eye, however, more than the strange blue form, which I assumed was either an idol or a priest, or the patches of green and yellow, which appeared to outline figures whose arms and legs were long, serpentine, was a patch of canvas to the right of center. There, what had been a tall figure rendered in dark greens and yellow-white had been smeared until unrecognizable, apparently by someone who had taken a cloth soaked in turpentine or a similar fluid and done their best to rub out whatever had been painted there.

Almost simultaneously, Edward said, "There it is," and Henry and I said, "What happened to it?"

"It was defaced," Henry said.

"No duh," I said. "Who did it?"

"I don't know," he said. "No one's sure. Gauguin himself never said that much about the picture. He was living in Tahiti when he painted it. He had finished this huge painting, one he called, *Where Do We Come From? Who Are We? Where Are We Going?* It was supposed to be his magnum opus, his crowning achievement as an artist. He told a couple of friends he was going to commit suicide once it was done. According to Gauguin, he kept his pledge. He went into the mountains, took some arsenic, and lay down so, he said, the ants could have him."

The Open Mouth of Charybdis

"Obviously," I said, "he didn't."

"Or the poison didn't work," Edward said, "which was what he said had happened. Supposedly, when he realized he wasn't going to die, he wandered down to the beach and saw...something."

"What?" Henry said.

"He didn't say," Edward said. "But he returned to his home, located a piece of canvas, and set to work on this painting. He was done in a week. In part, that was because he recycled elements from an earlier painting, *Day of the Gods*. That one has the same composition, the idol in the middle of the beach setting. *Day of the Gods*, though, is full of people, mostly women, and they're all part of a celebration of the blue idol, the god. There's all kinds of symbolism in it, but it's basically a happy painting. This one..." He shook his head. "Not so much."

"What's it called?" I said.

"*What the Sea Gave.*"

"Who's the blue guy supposed to be?" Henry said.

"Gauguin called him an image of the Beyond," Edward said. "I read one critic who said he represents a Polynesian god whose name I can't remember. I read another guy who said Gauguin had transplanted the figure from a Buddhist temple he'd seen somewhere. He's some kind of divinity."

"Why is he holding out his hands like that?" Henry said.

Edward shrugged. "Beats me."

"It looks like he's separating things," I said, "keeping them apart."

"Could be," Edward said.

"What about the damaged part?" Henry said.

"There's no mention of anything wrong with it in Gauguin's letters," Edward said, "which you'd think there would be if anyone had defaced it while he was still alive. Although...most of the stuff he painted, he sent to Paris to be sold. It doesn't seem like he did that with this picture."

"Could he have rubbed out the spot?" I said.

"I guess," Edward said, "but you wonder why he wouldn't paint over it, or trash the painting, if he felt that strongly about it."

"How did these guys get hold of it?" I said. "The Marshes?"

"Their ships were pretty busy in that part of the world. Somehow, after Gauguin died, the painting found its way onto one of their vessels. It had been wrapped in brown paper, with no destination written on it. It ended up in one of their warehouses here, where it stayed for years, until someone decided to take a peek under the wrapping. The family wasn't sure what to make of it; a few more years passed before a guy from the Museum of Fine Arts in Boston came to examine it and tell them what they had. For a long time, they kept the painting to themselves, until they decided to turn their old home into a museum and realized the picture could be an important part of it."

"Huh," I said. For a moment, the three of us stared at the canvas. I was struck by its physicality, by the brushstrokes visible at the edges of the figures, by the minute rises and falls of the paint's surface, by the furious spiral someone had rubbed into the picture. "What do you think was there?" I said to Edward.

"I don't know," he said. "Maybe another idol, like the one in the middle."

"Huh."

We didn't stay much longer. On our way out, we checked the closet-sized gift shop, where the kid in the Red Sox shirt sold the three of us cheap plastic samurai swords and Edward a postcard reproduction of the painting. As we meandered toward our rendezvous with our parents, Edward said, "It's funny: when the Marshes were sailing all over the globe, there were crazy stories about them having made a deal with the Devil—but, like, a sea-Devil. Wouldn't it be weird if that was what Gauguin had painted, a sea-Devil?"

The reply I was about to offer was cut off by a blast of sound. The same grinding noise I had heard in the museum roared in my ears. At the same time, everything around me, the flat-faced houses, the narrow sidewalk, the potholed main street, lost its color, draining to transparency. I looked for my brothers, and saw Edward beside me, translucent, the distant ocean visible through him. A feeling of immense helplessness swept over me, as if something crucial had buckled within me. I knew Henry must be behind me, but I didn't want to turn around, in case he too was fading, and in case, in the time he was out of my sight, Edward disappeared completely. Already he, the surrounding buildings, the street, were filling with light, as if the sun had reached the exact position in the sky necessary for its rays to catch on them. My ears, my skull, rang with the slow clashing and crashing of titanic gears, of machinery vast enough to turn the sky above. Edward blazed with a brilliance that forced tears to my eyes. I fought against clos-

The Open Mouth of Charybdis

ing them, because I knew, with terrible certainty, that were I to do so, the instant I opened them, my brother would be gone.

In the end, I did close them. They shut themselves, despite my best efforts, the pain overriding my intentions. The enormous sound continued for what felt like hours, concluding sharply, as if those gigantic gears had locked into a new position. I waited with my eyes closed until the echoes of the noise had subsided enough to admit other sounds, the boom and hiss of the surf on rock, the cries of gulls overhead, the murmur of distant voices. I opened my eyes to the great rocks of Acadia National Park jutting out into the Atlantic's waves, to white birds hanging in the breeze, to families and couples picnicking on the rock around me. Along with the new surroundings came knowledge of the new life of which they were part. I call it new, but I apprehended this existence as the unbroken record of my experiences to that point. Except that, layered beneath this life was another, which intersected it in some places, diverged from it in more, the most significant of which was Edward, who had been erased from my family completely.

That night, I dreamed about him. I had been quiet the long car ride back to the house my parents had rented, which I explained with an appeal to too much time in the sun. After dinner, I sat with my (diminished) family while we played cards at the kitchen table and listened to WBZ out of Boston on the radio. I lost a couple of hands of gin rummy before excusing myself. My face was flushed. I felt feverish and took the ibuprofen my mother recommended. For a short time, I lay in my bed, listening to my parents and (one) brother and sisters continuing the game, then dropped into unconsciousness.

My dream occurred within the painting we had viewed in the Marsh House. Edward was there, but he appeared as one of the figures in the picture, his features simplified, stylized, his hair a mass of shifting color. Behind and to his left, the blue god held its hands to either side, palms-out. Behind and to his right, a dark smear in the air occulted something whose eyes were too big and a deep, fiery yellow. The joy that rushed through me at the sight of my brother—however strange that sight might be—was tempered by unease at the veiled form.

Smiling, Edward said, "You're here."

"Of course," I said.

"They hid it," he said.

"What?"

"The town, Innsmouth. Changing its name wasn't enough. The problems were too extensive. They decided more drastic measures were called for."

"Who did?"

"The Marshes. And others." He gestured at the dark patch in the air.

I kept my gaze from it. "What—"

"You don't need to know. They helped, that's all."

"Helped with what?" I said.

"Shifting the village. They excised it from this space and hid it in others."

"Others? What others?"

"Stories, mostly, although a couple of novels and some comics, too. A few paintings, movies. They used the zones that are created when you're reading, or watching a movie, those imaginative locations. They figured out a way to align enough of them to hold the village and its residents. There's a lot of higher math involved; I don't understand most of it."

"But what about you? You didn't live there."

"I got caught in the process. It's like these guys created a whirlpool in space and time, and I was standing too close to it. The same thing happened to a lot of people—to a lot of things, too. All of us dragged out of our old lives and washed up in a new one."

"I'll save you," I said. "Hang on. I'll work something out."

"It's too late," Edward said. "At least, I'm pretty sure it is. Reality—your reality—has already been rewritten. I bet you have a whole new set of memories—a whole new life, don't you?"

"Yeah, but—"

"Is everyone okay? Mom, Dad, Henry, the girls? Are you okay?"

"Yes," I said, and knew it was substantially true—as true as it had been in our previous existence, the one Edward had shared. The statement's truth, of course, depended on me ignoring the fact of my brother's disappearance.

"Well," Edward said.

"Where *are* you?" I said. "I still don't understand. Are you all right?"

"It's different," Edward said. "There are things, here…"

"What?" I said. "What things?"

He nodded toward the form obscured behind him. "It's awful," he said, his voice flaring with anger. "It's worse than anything I could have imagined. And I think I love it. God forgive me, but I do."

The Open Mouth of Charybdis

Those were his final words to me. He did an about-face and started walking in the opposite direction. As he drew up next to the disturbance in the air, a hand stretched out of the tumult. The fingers were long, with too many joints, capped with talons. The skin was rough, dark green spotted with whitish patches like blooms of algae. I thought it was trying to grab him and went to shout a warning. But without looking at it, my brother, my now hopelessly lost little brother, raised his hand and took hold of the monstrous one, much as he had caught my hand when we were younger, and he was afraid.

SHADOW AND THIRST

The tower was there when they returned from their early-morning dog walk. August saw it first, squatting in the meadow at the foot of the hill behind his father and stepmother's house. It was round, dun-colored, maybe ten feet high, ten wide. "Hey," he said, "what's that?"

Tony, his father, looked up from Orlando the pit bull, who was rolling in the damp grass, grunting happily. "What?"

"Down there." August pointed. "That's still your property, right?"

"All the way to the stream and halfway up the other side." Tony squinted; he wasn't wearing his glasses. "That looks a bit too elaborate for your little brother to have built by himself. Huh. Guess I'd better have a look at it. You want to come, Officer?"

August had yet to decide whether his father's use of his job title was ironic or conciliatory, a sign of displeasure at his decision to drop out of college and join the Newark city police department, or an indication of Tony's acceptance of his choice. "Sure," he said, "let's check it out."

"It's probably something the neighbors' kid put up," Tony said. "The boy's quite the budding filmmaker; we've let him shoot a couple of his movies here. I played King Arthur in one of them. I bet this is connected to his latest project. Come on, Orlando." He tugged the dog's leash. Orlando snorted, and twisted to his feet.

When they started down the hill, however, the dog planted his feet firmly and would not move. "Orlando come," Tony said. "Come on, big guy, move." Orlando whined and pulled backwards. "Orlando," Tony said, more sharply. "Orlando come!" In response, the dog's whines were succeeded by a chain of high-pitched barks, almost yelps.

"Man," August said, "he does not like that thing."

"Apparently," Tony said.

"You want me to take him inside?"

"If you wouldn't mind," Tony said, passing him the end of the leash. "I'll go check out the round, squat turret."

"The what?"

"It's from a poem by Robert Browning, 'Childe Roland to the Dark Tower Came.'"

August nodded at the dog, who was straining toward the house. "Doesn't look like this Roland read it."

Tony laughed. "Just as well. Things don't turn out so well for the guy in the poem."

"Give me a minute and I'll come with you."

"Don't worry about it. I think Rebecca said she was making waffles. Get started and I'll join you in a minute."

"All right, Professor," August said. He watched his father start toward the prop, a heavy-set, middle-aged man wearing white karate pants and a white T-shirt, his bald spot pinkly visible through the hair he kept long to conceal it. Unexpectedly, August's throat was tight, his eyes burning. *What the hell?* But before he could answer his own question, Orlando lunged in the direction of the back door, almost yanking him off his feet. "Okay, okay," he said to the dog, "we're going."

Inside the house, Orlando didn't wait for his leash to be unclipped; instead, toenails clacking on the tile floor, he scrambled through Tony's office to the kitchen. Dressed in a fuzzy purple robe and pink pajamas, her curly hair gathered in a bun, Rebecca, Tony's second wife, was whisking batter in a white ceramic bowl. Orlando danced around her. "Good morning, baby," she said, craning her head toward him. "What was all that barking about? Did you see a squirrel?" Orlando dropped at her feet. "Hi, August," she added.

"Good morning," he said, moving past her to the refrigerator, from whose top shelf he removed the orange juice.

Shadow and Thirst

"Where's your dad?"

"He went to check out something at the foot of the hill. Actually, that was what set Orlando going. Someone put up a building down there." August stepped to the other side of Rebecca and took a glass from the cupboard.

"A building?"

"It's for a movie. That's what Tony thinks." He placed the glass of orange juice on the kitchen table and returned the carton to the fridge. "He said one of your neighbors shoots his films on your property."

"Nate, yes." She nodded. "Last summer, he constructed a small castle in the meadow."

"Well, maybe he's making a sequel, because he built a tower, this time—not much of one, really—just a single story. Tony called it a round, squat turret."

"That sounds like your father." Rebecca wiped the whisk off on the rim of the mixing bowl and placed it in the sink, then plugged in the waffle maker. "Ever the teacher."

"He said it was from a poem by Robert Browning."

"One of his favorite poets. He taught a special topics course on him a couple of years ago."

"Who's one of Dad's favorite poets?" Forster said. At ten, August's half-brother had already left behind pajamas for gray sweatpants and a red Minecraft T-shirt.

"Robert Browning," August said.

"Oh." Forster went to the cupboard for a plastic cup.

"So how do you like police work?" Rebecca said. She opened the waffle maker and ladled batter into it.

August shrugged. "It's okay."

"You're keeping safe?"

"As much as I can."

"August," Rebecca said, "those kinds of statements do not fill me with confidence. I know Newark's a dangerous place; I want you to tell me you're being careful in it."

"Have you shot anybody?" Forster said.

"Forster!" Rebecca said.

"What?" He finished filling his cup with white grape juice. "I was only asking."

"My firearm has remained in its holster," August said. "Fortunately. Which is not to say there haven't been a few times I thought I might have to draw it."

"Really?"

Rebecca's frown stalled the anecdote forming on his lips. "Nah, not really."

"Awww," Forster said.

"I figure I'll stay in Newark for a few years, then see about going federal."

"The FBI?" Rebecca said.

"What's the FBI?" Forster said.

"Or the U.S. Marshals," August said.

"FBI stands for the Federal Bureau of Investigation," Rebecca said to Forster. "They're like the police, only, they work for the government in Washington, DC." To August, she said, "I imagine the benefits are great."

"Oh yeah," he said, "but you may have to move around a lot, which I'm not sure how I feel about. It's the same thing with the Marshals."

"You're young. You should see the country. Besides, it would give us the excuse to visit you wherever you're stationed. Is that what they say, stationed?"

"I think it's assigned."

"Right. So make sure you're assigned somewhere nice."

"Okay," August said. "Any requests?"

"I'm still lobbying for your father to take me to Hawaii," Rebecca said.

"Can you go to Wyoming?" Forster said.

"Wyoming?" August said. "What's in Wyoming?"

Forster shrugged. "I don't know. I just want to go to Wyoming."

"Fair enough," August said. "I'll see what I can do, buddy."

Forster smiled into his juice.

Throughout their conversation, as the smell of warm vanilla threaded the air, Orlando had remained at Rebecca's feet, his eyes lifted to her while she prepared breakfast, his tongue darting out to lick his lips and nose. All at once, he was up, his eyes on the back door, a growl rumbling his chest. Rebecca looked down at him and said, "What's—" but the rest of her question was drowned out by the barks that burst from the dog. These were not the anxious yelps Orlando had voiced earlier; these were deeper, louder, full of the same aggression that was evident in the dog's stance, legs

Shadow and Thirst

squared, quivering, chest out, heavy head forward. He'd positioned himself between Rebecca and the back door, which, August saw, his father was pushing open. There was just enough time for him to register something different about Tony, something off, and then Orlando sprang from his position and in one snarling bound was on the man.

Rebecca and Forster screamed simultaneously, she, "Orlando! Tony!" he, "Dad!" She stepped toward the back door, which Tony had been forced most of the way out of by Orlando, who scrambled up him, tearing his clothes with his claws, snapping at his neck and face. August ducked in front of his stepmother, trying to work out how he was going to haul eighty pounds of pit bull off his father. Maybe the dog's collar...

His hand was almost at the blue band when he heard a pair of sharp cracks, like wet branches being snapped, and Orlando's snarls gave way to howls. Something was still growling—*Tony?* It wasn't the dog, whose wails continued as August's fingers hooked his collar. Before he could pull Orlando away from Tony, there was a tearing sound; the dog's cries were swallowed by a liquid choking, and Orlando flew against August with sufficient force to knock him off his feet. His head smacked tile. Stars flared in front of his eyes, dissipated in time for him to see his father leaping over him into the kitchen. Rebecca said, "Tony?" and screamed.

August rolled Orlando off him, noting as he did the splintered bones protruding from the dog's forelimbs, the great, bloody hole in Orlando's not-inconsiderable throat. Tony was standing with his back to him, bent forward, his arms out. Rebecca had retreated to the other side of the kitchen table, where she'd grabbed Forster from his chair and had pulled him against her. Her face was bloodless white, Forster's wide-eyed, tearful. "What happened to Dad?" Forster said. His mother answered with a groan.

Tony clearly heard the scrape of August's sneakers on the floor behind him but didn't turn fast enough to evade his son's tackle. The impact carried both men stumbling across the kitchen, Tony's right arm sweeping the waffle maker and bowl of batter into the sink. August caught the shoulders of his father's T-shirt and wrenched them to the left, steering Tony into the refrigerator with a crash. Tony rebounded into August, forcing his left hip into the kitchen table's nearest corner. Though dimmed by adrenaline, the pain was enough to loosen August's grip on his father, who twisted around, swinging his left hand in a sloppy backfist that scraped August's ear. Now that it was plainly in view, August saw that there was indeed something wrong with his father's features, beyond the blood and bits of flesh smeared around the mouth. It was as if he were looking at Tony's face in a smashed mirror, the particulars arranged in cubist angles. He was sufficiently startled not to track Tony's left hand coming back the other way for a punch to the jaw that jolted August's head. He released his hold on Tony entirely, striking his hip against the table a second time as he stepped back. *Who knew the old man could hit so hard?* For that matter, who knew he could rip out the throat of the family dog with his teeth?

August's hand trailed over the plate set out for him as Tony rushed at him. One of the good plates that Rebecca brought out whenever he visited, it shattered against Tony's head, driving him to August's right. August pivoted, and snapped his right fist into Tony's solar plexus. With a hoarse gasp, Tony collapsed against the sink, his eyes stunned. August considered a follow-up chop to the neck, to the vagus nerve, but the combined plate to the head and the shot to mid-section appeared to have quieted whatever had animated Tony. His legs had given out, and unable to prop himself up on the sink, he sagged to the floor. His face was still different—wrong—but August needed to call 911 before worrying over it.

Obviously, his father had suffered a psychotic break, and required immediate medical attention. The cordless was in its cradle on the other side of the refrigerator. He lifted the phone with a hand suddenly trembling so violently the device almost slipped from his fingers. In an instant, the shaking spread to the rest of his body, accompanied by a combination of nausea and dizziness. He leaned against the fridge, closing his eyes to keep from vomiting at the bloody mess that was his father, the ruin of Orlando beyond him. The coppery stink of blood mixed with the vanilla odor of the waffles. From somewhere behind him—the bathroom, he guessed—he heard Forster murmur, Rebecca hush him. August swallowed, called out, "You guys okay?"

"We're all right," Rebecca answered. "Are you?"

"I'm okay," August said. "A little shaken up, but all right."

"Is Tony—" She let the remainder of the question hang.

"He's..." August glanced at his father, slumped at the base of the kitchen counter, his pants and T-shirt torn and soaked with blood, his chest heaving as he struggled to breathe. "I have to call 911," August said. "He's okay, but we have to get him some help. I want you guys to stay where you are for the moment."

"Did you kill my dad?" Forster's voice was high, frightened, full of tears waiting to spill.

"No," August said, "I just…subdued him. But he's okay, buddy, I promise. I'm going to phone for an ambulance, all right?"

"All right," Forster said. "What about Orlando?"

August grimaced. "I'm not sure. He's hurt pretty bad."

Forster wailed, his cries ringing on the bathroom's tiles. "Shhh," Rebecca said.

The 911 operator was brisk, efficient. There would be help at the house shortly, she said. August was reasonably certain he remembered a firehouse nearby; all that remained was for him to keep an eye on his father and offer what assistance he could to the EMTs when they arrived. He returned the phone to its cradle, thinking that the remainder of his visit was going to be radically different from what he had anticipated. Once Tony was on his way to the hospital, August would have to tend to Orlando's remains, carry the dog outside if he could, cover him if he could not, in either case, do what he could to ensure that Forster was not confronted with the sight of his dog's mutilated corpse. No doubt, Rebecca would want to be at whatever hospital accepted Tony, even if, as August suspected, his father was headed for a locked ward. He couldn't imagine she would want Forster with her, but neither could he picture her leaving his younger half-brother here, amidst the bloody wreck of Tony's rampage. Something else that would have to be seen to—

Faster than August would have predicted possible, Tony heaved himself onto his feet and ran for the back door. He was through it by the time August was halfway across the kitchen. *Son of a bitch.* The old man was full of surprises today, wasn't he?

At the threshold, at the top of the four stairs that led down to the back lawn, August paused, sweeping his gaze from side to side. If Tony still had his sights set on Rebecca and Forster, then he might feint, lead August outside while he circled to the front door and gained re-admittance to the house that way. But no, there he was, racing down the hill behind the house, in the direction of the neighbor kid's prop. Had he been in uniform, standard procedure would have dictated August remaining where he was until help arrived. He weighed doing so. Through the woods beyond the meadow at the foot of the hill, wasn't there another house? Hadn't Tony and Rebecca complained about its owners allowing their dog to roam off-leash, provoking Orlando? By the time the help August had requested appeared, Tony could be done with his neighbors and their wandering dog.

Cupping his hands around his mouth, he turned toward the kitchen. "Tony just ran out of here," he called. "I'm going after him. There's help on the way; someone should be here in a minute. Don't come out until they arrive."

Without waiting for an answer, he leapt down the stairs and sprinted after Tony.

His third week in the academy, one of August's instructors—Officer Bennett, a tall, sparse man in charge of the recruits' daily exercise—had delivered a speech about running. *The first time someone runs from you*, he had said, *and they* will *run, because they see you're new, or because they panic, or because they are, in fact, guilty of something—that first chase, you* must *catch them. If you do not, word will get around—word will* fly *around—that you can be outrun, and in short order, every time you approach anyone, they will take to their feet. You cannot permit that to happen.* August had taken the instructor's words to heart, adding a two-mile run—the last fifty yards of which he sprinted—to his daily workout. In the seven months since he had graduated the academy, the extra training had served him well: in fourteen foot-chases, including one through the aisles of the enormous IKEA near Newark-Liberty, he had not been beaten, once. Even with his father's head start—even with his hip throbbing from its collisions with the kitchen table—August had little doubt he would catch him, and quickly, at that.

Tony, however, proved to be fleeter of foot than August would have predicted of a man his age and physique. Already, his father was two-thirds of the way down the back hill, his apparent destination the short tower in the meadow. How was the old man doing it—any of it? The blows he'd taken should have kept him on the kitchen floor. Conceivably, he could have regained his feet, but to cover ground like an Olympic sprinter seemed beyond the realm of possibility. Yet there Tony was, drawing closer to the prop while August barreled downhill in pursuit. Whatever had broken in Tony's mind, it had opened reserves of fearsome strength. August thought of the tube of pepper spray clipped to his car keys, lying on top of the

Shadow and Thirst

dresser in the guest room, and wished he'd brought it with him.

As Tony approached the tower, he veered left. Once beside it, he turned right and plunged into the structure. August slowed, waiting to see whether his father would come hurtling out of the prop the same way he'd gone into it, crashed through the opposite side, or remained within. Tony had to know he was behind him, didn't he? How could he not?

While he was still a good ten yards from the tower, August circled right. From the top of the hill, the prop had appeared amateurish, if ambitious, a frame wrapped with heavy brown paper whose surface had been covered with hundreds of rectangles executed in black magic marker. Seen up close, the structure was considerably more substantial and impressive. It consisted of at least one layer of actual bricks, laid together with a neatness that suggested extensive work days for something this size. The bricks were composed of reddish-brown material that gave the impression of incredible age, an effort August guessed might have been produced with the use of certain tools, which added to the amount of time it must have taken the neighbor kid—and his assistants, surely—to build it. How could Tony and Rebecca have missed it for so long? How could Forster have failed to notice it?

Coming around to the place where Tony had disappeared into it, August saw a narrow entrance in the brick. No doubt it was a consequence of the morning sun, which saturated the air with hazy brilliance, but the doorway to the tower appeared too dark, as if the kid had draped it with a thick black cloth. August walked all the way past the opening, but no matter what angle he surveyed it from, the aperture remained impenetrably dark. Had he not witnessed Tony passing through it, he would have been tempted to assume it was painted on. Tony was likely concealing himself to either side of the entrance, seeking to evade, and possibly ambush, August.

If his father was waiting for him to charge in after him, however, his wait was going to be a long one. Standard procedure in a situation such as this one, where Tony was safely contained—alone—within a building with a single doorway, was to remain outside and wait for backup, and that was exactly what August intended to do. Once properly equipped officers were on scene, August would apprise them of the situation and they could decide how best to proceed. He had not yet picked a spot at which to station himself when the screaming started.

It poured from the doorway, a single, ragged note that extended long past the limits of what August would have judged possible. August jumped as the scream was succeeded by another, and another, the cries echoing on the tower's brick, lingering, so that each new scream overlapped the ones that had preceded it, a strata of pain. He couldn't discern whether all the screams were Tony's. He recognized the tones of his father's voice in certain of the cries, but others sounded different, distinct. *Oh, Christ, is there someone else in there with him?* If there was, then S.O.P. did a one-eighty and you entered the building in question immediately.

Of course there was something wrong with it, with all of it. The time span didn't work. From the construction of the tower in the first place, to Tony's abrupt and catastrophic psychic collapse, to his father's bringing a third party into the tower and hurting them sufficiently to drag the screams of the damned out of their throat, the last thirty minutes' events should have required much longer to happen. Tony and Rebecca should have been walking to the top of the hill to watch the neighbor kid build his tower for weeks on end, and Tony's mental break should have been forecast by warning signs for at least as long. (Shouldn't it? August was no expert in the psyche; that was his mother, and at the moment, he could not consult with her.) As for Tony kidnapping someone and dragging them to the tower—that, too, should have been a lengthier process.

Unless this had been occurring for more time than August had realized. Perhaps his father had been sliding into madness for all this time. Tony could have put up the tower on his own, with the neighbor kid available as a convenient explanation. After the structure was done, he could have brought someone to it...no, none of that worked, either. Rebecca was on sabbatical this semester, making it difficult for the kinds of activities he was imagining Tony engaged in to have escaped notice.

Whatever explanation arranged the morning's details into coherence, it would have to wait. The screaming was now a chorus, blending its agonies. Although he had assumed Tony was lurking to one side or the other of the door, the screams called into question that assumption. Wherever the old man was waiting, August was going into the tower.

For a moment—an instant—as he was rushing across the threshold, August had the sensation of striking and passing through a liquid, as if the doorway framed a fall of black water. By the time he was reacting, clamping shut his mouth, attempting to conserve whatever air remained in his lungs,

Shadow and Thirst

August was on the other side of the entrance, inside a room whose brick walls and dirt floor were bare, near the top of a flight of stairs that corkscrewed into the earth. A circular opening in the ceiling admitted sunlight into the space; none appeared to have followed him through the door. The knot of screaming wound up the stairs; August hurried down them.

There had been, he thought, a wellhead at the foot of the hill, in the tower's approximate position. During August's first visit here, Tony had pointed it out to him, a concrete tube a foot-and-a-half high, three feet in diameter, with a lid that extended another couple of inches all the way around. There was a spring in that spot, Tony had said. The old guy who had owned the property before them had dug out the spot, gone down ten, fifteen feet, poured concrete walls to keep it from caving in. Once he was finished, he had a well for the garden he planted in the meadow, and for himself and his family, should they ever have need of it. Tony supposed it was a good resource, though it became a hazard during the winter, when a decent snowfall transformed the hill into a sledding course for Forster and his friends. He and Rebecca had not figured out what to do about the thing.

August felt reasonably sure that excavating the well further and installing a set of stairs would not have been among his stepmother's choices. Already, August had descended at least fifteen feet, the air dimming as he went. Where had Tony found, or stolen, the time for such a project? The stairway had been cut into the rock below the shallow topsoil, each step topped with a flat slab of stone. It was difficult to picture his father hefting slab after slab into place; although, was it any more extraordinary than Tony crippling and killing an angry eighty-pound pit bull with his bare hands and teeth?

But that wasn't the point: in truth, neither action made sense in relation to Tony, to the existence he and Rebecca and Forster had here. Yes, that was what the family members of criminals always said, wasn't it? Not my father/son/brother/whatever. This was more than the standard denial, though. The rock of the stairway's walls was smooth, polished as if with the passing of many hands over it, and not the rough surface of recent excavation. The screams below rang off it, almost seemed amplified by it. The air was dry to the point of parched, rather than the heavy damp of a well. All of it was more of the wrongness August had recognized outside the tower, a kind of warp to everything that he felt as a pressure behind his eyes, an ache in his molars.

The stairs ended in an archway cut in the rock. While the light had faded to a faint glow, August's vision had adjusted to it, which allowed him to distinguish the tunnel opening in front of him. From somewhere within the thicker darkness farther down the passage, Tony and whoever was with him continued their screams. August wasn't certain how long they'd been screaming—probably not as long as it seemed—but surely, his father and the other person or people should have screamed themselves hoarse by now.

Trying to move slowly enough for his eyes to grow accustomed to the steadily diminishing light, but quickly enough to reach Tony and his companions, August stepped through the archway and moved along the tunnel. In low light, peripheral vision picked up a lot of the slack: was it Tony who'd told him that? He thought so. It sounded like the kind of quasi-interesting fact with which his father had peppered their phone conversations during the middle stretch of August's adolescence, when he'd been angry at Tony all the time, for not staying married to August's mother, for agreeing to her having full custody of him, for staying in New York while he and his mother moved to Pennsylvania. Tony would deliver some nugget of information, and if August didn't snarl at him, his father was off and running, stretching that nugget into as much more conversation as he could manage. The tactic had served its purpose, which was to keep the two of them talking, and subsequently, August had proved an asset during trivia night at the bar he and a few of his fellow officers frequented.

And here was his peripheral vision kicking in, showing the walls to either side of him carved with a series of unfamiliar characters, each the size of his hand. Most of them were combinations of loops and swirls that wrapped around and doubled back on themselves, forming arabesques whose precise design defeated his passing glance. In their midst, however, he found a pair of simpler characters, a circle, broken at about nine o'clock, and a square whose interior was filled by a line that drew in toward its center in a series of right turns—a maze, he thought. Both the incomplete circle and the maze repeated at irregular intervals. With so little light, and his ears crowded with screaming, it was difficult to be sure, but the characters did not appear recent. He trailed his right hand over the wall; the edges of the figures were even with the surrounding rock.

August was losing track of the number of details for which he was unable to account. Could all of this, the stairs, the passageway, the carvings, have

Shadow and Thirst

been here before Tony and Rebecca had bought the place? Had his father ever verified that what he'd been told was a well was, in fact, a well? Why would he have, though?

Ahead, the tunnel branched left, right, and straight on. Screams poured from each opening. August leaned in each direction, attempting to locate the source of Tony's cries. *Left?* He couldn't decide. *Pick one. Left.* He turned and started that way.

Almost immediately, the air was clouded with a stench that forced him back a step, coughing. He had smelled it previously, when he had assisted a raid on a drug house out near the airport. The three guys who ran the place had suspected one of their regular customers of being a criminal informant. The guy wasn't, but his general twitchiness had appeared to belie his protestations to that effect, with the end result that two of the dealers had tortured him to death with a pair of carving knives. Afterwards, there had been great pools of blood, which one of the murderers had had the inspired idea of using a wet-vac to clean up. This had worked reasonably well, except that the men had not gotten around to emptying the blood, so when August and his fellow officers swarmed the house five days later, the wet-vac was sitting in a corner, full of something that swished suspiciously. That something, as the cops found out once one of them unclipped and removed the lid, was spoiled blood. Already, August had smelled some foul odors on the job, but this was especially vile, rotting meat mixed with copper. It was a point of pride with him that he had not vomited, but he alone knew what a close thing that had been.

That same smell hung around him now. The orange juice he'd drunk earlier boiled at the back of his throat. He swallowed, continuing forward. *Oh Tony*, he thought, *what did you do?* Maybe it was an animal. *Please let it be an animal.*

It was not. Dressed in filthy rags, the man was lying on the opposite side of the modest chamber into which the tunnel emptied. From a small hole in the middle of the ceiling, a shaft of light stabbed the floor. August blinked at its brilliance. Ten feet away, the heat it threw off raised sweat from his skin. August circled to the right, keeping close to the room's brick walls. Undiminished, the screaming continued. The man in front of him had been the victim of incredible violence, his chest split open, ribs broken and pushed to the sides as if for some brutal anatomy lesson. The heart was missing, the object, presumably, of whoever had exposed it in the first place. At some point in that process, the assailant had splashed the man's blood on the walls, from which it had run down into puddles that had darkened and decayed. Estimating time of death was not part of August's job, but it was plain the man had been here for, at minimum, several days.

Which meant nothing good, as far as Tony was concerned. Not to mention Rebecca and Forster: how would they react to learning that the man they loved had committed such a savage murder? Sick at the prospect, August leaned against the wall to his right. The slight change in perspective this produced brought into focus the dead man's face, tilted up and back, the mouth open in a final cry, the eyes bulging, and August saw that the corpse sprawled at his feet was that of his father.

His heart kicked. Everything in him seemed to rise up, as if threatening to exit his body through the top of his head, then to drop, carrying him to the floor. His mind was a blank, all other thoughts blown to its margins by Tony's ravaged body. That blank, he understood a moment later, was a grief so immediate and profound it doubled him over, flooding his eyes with tears, forcing sobs from his lips. No matter that one part of his brain had resumed the this-doesn't-make-sense complaint (as the blood demonstrated, the man in front of him had been dead for days, at least; even if there were another explanation for that detail, August should have heard the sounds of his father's murder, despite the screaming that vibrated the air). Tony's corpse made all of that seem inconsequential, irrelevant.

August had wondered, upon occasion, what his response to the death of a family member would be. It was the catalyst in so many of the crime and police dramas he had watched growing up—the hero's wife or husband or mother or father is killed, often in a horrifying manner, and in response, the hero seeks out and has revenge upon those responsible. While it was possible that, later on, he would be overcome by the desire for vengeance, all August wanted right now was to remove his father's remains from this strange and terrible place. He wiped his eyes, his nose, used to wall to help himself to his feet. His legs wobbled. If he crouched, he could slide his hands under Tony's back to his armpits, hoist him up from behind and half-carry, half-drag him out that way. Not the most graceful method, but it would allow for the gaping wreck of Tony's chest.

The arm slipped around August's throat and was dragging him backwards

Shadow and Thirst

almost before he knew it. Strong—it was monstrously strong, its muscles tight against his neck as it squeezed. August didn't bother grabbing for the hand. His feet were still on the floor. He backpedaled hard and fast, going with the choke, overbalancing his attacker. His assailant's feet slipped and he went down, pulling August with him. August twisted as he fell, gripping his left hand with his right to brace the left elbow he drove into his attacker's ribs. He heard a grunt, another when he brought the elbow in a second time. His assailant's grip had slid, placing its right hand in easier reach. August seized it with both of his hands and twisted it off him, maintaining his hold on it as he scrambled to his feet, yanking the arm straight and torqueing the wrist into a lock. His attacker cried out. August kicked him in the ribs he hoped were already broken. "Who are you?" he shouted. "Why did you kill my father?"

The man moaned.

August applied more pressure to the joint lock. "I will snap your goddamned wrist," he said.

"August," the man said.

"How do you know my name, huh? Did he," he flicked his head toward Tony's body, "tell you before you cut out his fucking heart?"

"August," the man said.

"Do not say my name," August said. "Who are you? Why did you kill my father?"

"August," the man said, "it's me."

Though it was hoarse with pain, some note in the man's words caused August to stare at his face more intently. Both the man's long beard and ponytail were white, and his nose looked to have been broken at least once, but August recognized Tony looking up at him; albeit, a Tony from twenty, twenty-five years in the future. The room around him appeared to shimmer, but August retained his grip on the man's wrist. He stole a glance at the dead man. As surely as he could tell from where he was standing, it was Tony lying there. August looked at the man who had choked him. The resemblance was uncanny. "Who are you?" he said.

"It's me, Tony," the man said.

"Sorry," August said, "you're about two decades too old for the part. Try again." He pressed the man's wrist.

The man grimaced. Voice tight, he said, "The last big fight your mother and I had—the two of you had moved. I came down for the weekend to see if we couldn't work things out. We couldn't. She told me she was going ahead with the divorce. I accused her of lying to me, of leading me on. She was standing at one end of the dining room table. I was near the front door. You ran out of your bedroom, which was on the other side of the kitchen. How long you had been listening, I'm not sure. You were in your short pajamas. Your face was red; you were crying. You screamed at the two of us to stop it, which I guess we did. Afterwards, I came to see you in your bedroom before I left. You were inconsolable. I kept telling you it was nothing to do with you, I just had to go, but you knew better. You knew everything had changed."

"Jesus." August released the man's hand, stepping away from him.

"I know." The man he could not yet think of as his father struggled to stand. Clothed in a loose, gray shirt and black pants, the slight curve in his spine worse, he was thinner than August had ever known him, as thin as he'd been in some of the old photos he'd shown August. His eyes, though—his eyes were the same, steel blue. Rubbing his side where August's elbow and foot had found it, he said, "I've thought about how I would explain all of this to you if I had the chance. There was a quotation I was going to use, from Stevenson, *Dr. Jekyll and Mr. Hyde*: 'I hazard the guess that man will be ultimately known for a mere polity of multifarious, incongruous, and independent denizens.' It seemed perfectly applicable to me, but I wasn't sure if you'd agree on the relevance."

"Oh my God," August said, "it is you." His vision doubled, blurred; he swayed drunkenly. The screaming seemed to be happening inside his head as much as outside it.

Tony's hands were on his shoulders. "Hey," his father said, "hey." August's mouth opened, but there were too many questions, tripping over one another in their haste to be asked. "I understand," Tony said. "It's a lot to absorb. Nor is this the worst of it."

"I don't understand."

"Would you come with me so I can show you something?" Tony dropped his hands from August's shoulders.

"What?"

"It's better if you see it for yourself." Already, Tony was backing toward the doorway. "I'm not going to try to hurt you," he added. "I only did that

Shadow and Thirst

as a, a...precaution. You'll have to forgive me. I've been down here a long time."

"You didn't recognize me?"

"It took me a moment," Tony said. "I'm sorry. Come this way." He spun on his heel and exited the room.

Staying in place was hardly an option. August followed Tony out of the room into darkness and cool, the short distance to the junction of the four passageways. There, Tony turned left, August's original direction. This tunnel sloped steeply down. Whatever faint remnant of the sun's glow had accompanied August's initial progress was long gone, despite which, he could discern the general details of the passage, whose walls bore the same weird graffiti he'd observed earlier. In fact, it was these markings—the Möbius characters, the broken ring, the maze—which were responsible for what illumination there was. They didn't glow; rather, so black were they that they caused the surrounding darkness to appear lighter, as if they were drawing it into themselves. The air was dry, and full of screaming.

"Who is that?" he said.

"Who's what?"

"Doing all the screaming."

"Oh. That's me. And others."

On the right, the tunnel wall was interrupted by a succession of rough openings, each about five feet high by three wide. Tony stopped at the fourth and ducked into it. Mindful of his head, August went after him.

The space into which they emerged was more cave than proper room. Approximately circular, it was illuminated by a series of holes drilled in the center of its high ceiling, through which beams of phosphorous-white light slanted to the floor. The odor of dust mixed with that of rotten blood. The cave's circumference was studded with ledges and outcroppings, a dozen of which supported human bodies. As far as August could discern, every one of the figures was in the same condition as the one he'd discovered in the smaller room, the chest wrenched open, the heart taken.

Nor did the resemblance end there. "Come." Tony waved him to the right, where the nearest corpse lay prostrate. Were Tony not standing in front of him, he would have identified the man dead on the rock shelf as his father. Dressed in worn and bloodied karate pants and a torn white T-shirt, he appeared far closer in age to Tony as August had last seen him than did the white-haired figure watching for his reaction. August cleared his throat and said, "If I checked the other bodies in here, they'd all look like this one, wouldn't they? Like you."

"They would."

"You realize how fucked up this is."

Tony frowned. "Language."

"Seriously?" In spite of the body broken and violated before him, of the ever-increasing horror of the entire situation, August laughed. "Since when did you become such a prude?"

"Since I spent twenty years in here," Tony said, flinging his hand to take in the cave and what lay beyond it, "in the tower."

"How is that possible?" August said. "How is any of this?"

His father leaned against the outcropping that held what appeared to be the corpse of his younger self. "This place, the tower, is a prison. Except it's also the prisoner. Never mind that part. The point is, it contains an extremely dangerous man. To be honest, dangerous doesn't begin to cover it. Nor does man, for that matter. The tower houses a monster, and I mean that in the most literal way. It was a man, once, a long, long time ago. Now, he's more shadow than flesh, shadow and thirst. As long as he thirsts, he suffers terribly. Whenever he satisfies his thirst, he earns a respite from his pain."

"What's he so thirsty for?"

"Blood—human blood."

"You make him sound like a—"

"Like a vampire, yes."

"Fuck," August said. "No fucking way. I mean—just—fuck."

This time, Tony did not reproach his cursing. "After everything you've seen—after me..."

"Jesus, Dad," August said. "Why—ahh, shit." He could feel his lip quivering, his eyes growing moist.

"I'll take the 'dad,'" Tony said.

The chorus of screaming went on. After a moment, August said, "You were saying."

"The...prisoner can't leave the tower, so he has to wait for someone like me to come blundering into it. Complicating matters for him, the tower doesn't remain in one place for any length of time. It shifts, changes location

Shadow and Thirst

every few minutes. Based on what I've learned, I believe it moves through time, as well as space. Thought I may be mistaken. Regardless, what this means is, the prisoner's victims are few and far between. He has to find a way to…prolong each one. To this end, he employs a device. It resembles a full-length mirror, but its surface is black. The prisoner positions his victim in front of it, and the mirror splits part of them off. Not an arm or a leg, but a self. One of that multitude of selves Stevenson wrote of, a constituent of the aggregate that is each and every one of us. That new self serves the prisoner's immediate needs. Once he's…calmer, in better control of himself, he cuts more selves away, and sets them loose inside the tower."

"What for?"

"To hunt them. It's a form of amusement for him. The original, the prisoner keeps alive for as long as he can, recapturing them when he needs to slice more selves away from them, until the person is little more than a husk. Unless, that is, a new victim wanders in, in which case, he drains the previous one immediately."

"Why?"

"What do you mean, why?"

"I mean, why not have a couple of food sources available?"

"I'm not certain, but I believe the prisoner is afraid they would find a way to overpower him, destroy him. He's powerful, but not all-powerful. Together, a dedicated pair of individuals might be able to accomplish what one could not."

"But what about the copies, the other selves the guy sends off into this place? Isn't he worried about them ganging up on him?"

"Have you encountered any of them yourself?"

"As a matter of fact, I have. That was what brought me here, actually. He got into the house and killed Orlando. He looked like he was going for Rebecca and Forster, next, but I stopped him. He ran, and I chased him here."

"Orlando's dead?"

"Yeah."

"But your stepmom and little brother are okay?"

"Pretty freaked out, but they're all right."

"Poor Orlando!" Tony said. "He was such a sweet dog. Not a mean bone in his body, I swear."

"I don't know if it'll make you feel any better, but he was protecting

Rebecca and Forster from you—your double."

"God, how awful for them."

"They're okay, really. What about the other selves?"

"Yes, yes. I'm sure you noticed that that version of me was somewhat less articulate."

"To put it mildly."

"That tends to be the result of the mirror's process. Occasionally, one is produced who's capable of coherent speech, but they're mad in a different way. In either case, the prisoner doesn't have anything to worry about from the mirror's children."

"Is this what your vampire does when he catches one of them?" August nodded at the corpse.

"No," his father said, "that was me."

"You did this?"

"I did all of this." Tony glanced at the room's grisly contents. Was the screaming louder in here, more concentrated?

"Jesus Christ."

"You know how savage the creatures are."

"I get that," August said. "Believe me. One of these guys jumps you, you have to do whatever's necessary. It's," he waved his hand at the broken ribs fencing the chest cavity, the missing heart, "this seems a little premeditated, you know?"

"It was." Before August could respond, he said, "I'm trying to starve him."

"All right," August said. "I can understand that. Why remove the hearts, though? Does the vampire eat them?"

"No," Tony said, "I do."

"What?" August's stomach lurched. "What the fuck are you talking about?"

"I read about it. There's a library in the tower. I was looking for a way out of here, and I thought I might find information about it there. The books on its shelves…they're what you'd expect to find in a monster's keeping. They're full of…darkness. I found what I was looking for pretty quickly, but I kept reading. It had been so long since I had held an actual book in my hands, turned its pages, let my eyes take in its sentences, its paragraphs. Imagine having been without running water for a month, and then being able to sink into a hot bath. Or, picture sitting down to a filet mignon after

Shadow and Thirst

a year of stale crackers. I luxuriated in the act of reading. When the contents of the pages under my scrutiny became clear, I didn't credit them. Isn't that ridiculous? Eventually, I learned that there was something to them."

"You ate someone's heart because you read about it in a book?"

"Not someone's heart," Tony said, "*my* heart. My heart sectioned and sectioned again, grown coarse with the use. I've lost count of the number of times I've faced the black mirror, watched another set of me step forth from its darkness. Frankly, I'm amazed there's any of me left. Consuming the heart was supposed to be a way of taking what I'd lost back into myself."

"Christ," August said. "You make it sound so reasonable."

"It isn't," Tony said, "not at all. It's insane and obscene. But so is the tower. And the prisoner."

"Has it worked?"

"I'm still here."

"You said you found a way to escape this place."

"I did. It took me some time to map out the directions to it, but I should be able to get us there fairly quickly. My God, August, how I've missed you. How I've missed all of you."

"I—"

"I know. It hasn't been that long for you. However, we need to start moving, or you're going to find out how much time it's possible to spend in here." Tony pushed himself off the ledge on which he'd been leaning and strode past August, toward the cave entrance.

With a last look at the carnage his father had wrought, August followed. Tony turned right. After the room's beams of light, the passageway was dim to the point of blackness. August fell into step beside Tony. "The tower," he said, "the prisoner: do you know where they come from?"

Tony nodded. "I do. I have to tell you, though, that none of this was what I planned to talk to you about. Were we to meet again, I had a list of things to say to you."

"Oh yeah?"

"Yes. We weren't going to spend our time on the origins of the tower and its occupant. We were going to discuss…important things."

"Well, it's a bit late for the sex talk, so you don't have to worry about that one."

"Very funny. I assumed your mother and stepfather saw to that."

"They did. There was a book."

"A book?"

"It was pretty horrifying."

"I'm sure it was."

"So. Why didn't you try to leave before this?"

Tony glanced away. "I was afraid to. What I told you about the black mirror—there's a reason the prisoner kills the first of its creations right away. He does it to intimidate his captive, which it absolutely does. Long before the books I read in the tower's library, I knew about vampires; I taught 'Carmilla' and *Dracula*. I had a good idea how to destroy one. Yet there's a difference between theory and praxis, isn't there, especially when a monster is involved. Thus my plan for starving the prisoner until he became weak enough to risk confronting."

"All right. Well, what about the prisoner?"

"His name is Mundt," Tony said, "Edon Mundt. He's from a very old city that stood on the shores of a black ocean."

"You mean, like the Black Sea?"

"I mean an ocean whose water is black. It isn't anywhere on earth; it's on another plane of existence…another dimension."

"But there are people there."

"More or less. Mundt was a member of the city watch, the police force. He was good at his job, excelled at it, in fact. His performance came to the attention of his superiors, and he was offered a position on the night watch. This was a group tasked with safeguarding the city's libraries and cemeteries. It was no ceremonial post. The books in the libraries were of the same nature as the ones I discovered here; while the cemeteries were full of all manner of strange things. Mundt accepted the offer, and was made part of the night watch, a process that involved his transformation into a vampire. I'm not clear on all the details, but it involved his having to walk out into the dark. Not the night, or a dark room, but something like death, if death were a place. Mundt entered the dark, and this allowed the dark to enter him. There's a passage about a vampire in one of Byron's poems:

"And fire, unquenched, unquenchable,
Around, within thy heart shall dwell;
Nor ear can hear nor tongue can tell
The tortures of that inward hell!

Shadow and Thirst

"From what I've been able to learn, that seems a fairly apt description of his state."

"Makes you wonder why he did it, in the first place."

"Power. The price he paid bought Mundt enormous power."

On their left, a gap in the wall: the entrance to another tunnel. Tony took it. Carved from rock, this passage was shorter, and curved to the left. Its walls were inscribed with the broken circle and the maze, set one after the other. The tunnel ended in a shallow cave, against whose back wall August distinguished a pale form slumped. At the sound of their approaching footsteps, the figure raised a head that was too long and said, "Help me." August slowed, but Tony caught his elbow and hustled him to the left, into the next passage. August cast a glance back at the white form, but could not make out any details. "Who was that?"

"Not who," Tony said, "but what. I told you the tower jumps around in space and possibly time. Although a person doesn't always wander in, other things do. Animals, mostly, which helps anyone alive inside it to survive. Sometimes, other…creatures show up. That," he gestured behind them, "is one of them."

"What does it do?"

"It hollowed out one of the mirror's children. Left him looking like an old, empty costume. I'm not sure how."

Shorter than the last, this tunnel's walls were also marked with the repeating maze and broken ring. It, too, curved counter-clockwise, until it met bare rock face. August saw the passage on their left before Tony could guide him toward it. "You never told me what happened to the prisoner, to this Mundt guy. I mean, after he became a vampire."

"He committed a crime," Tony said. "I don't know what it was, but obviously, it was severe. The penalty was imprisonment in the tower, which was cast loose through the cosmos. The tower is…Mundt and the tower are connected, in the most fundamental of ways. Its contains all of him, all of his pain. It traps all the pain of his victims, too."

"The screaming."

"It's supposed to heighten his punishment; though I'm not certain how well it's worked."

"That sounds pretty harsh."

Tony shrugged. "He's a monster."

As had been the case with the previous tunnels, this one's walls were carved with the broken circle and maze, and bent left. "How is it that we can keep going this way without running into the other tunnels?" August said.

"The spatial relations in here are not always consistent," Tony said. "It's the same with the passing of time. Depending on your location, time runs more slowly or more quickly. You've been down here for what? An hour?"

"Roughly, yeah."

"Yet for anyone standing at the tower's door, I'd guess no more than two or three minutes have elapsed."

The passage ended in a narrow archway, through which, a flight of stairs led up. Tony halted at its foot. The blended screams of Edon Mundt and his victims poured down it. "These," he said, "will take us to the tower's central chamber. Directly across from the top of the stairs, there is a doorway out of the tower. It has a black frame. That is our destination. The chances are excellent that Mundt will be somewhere in the room. As far as I know, he hasn't fed in some time. He should be weak enough for me to occupy while you make your escape."

"While I—what are you saying?"

"At the door, touch the frame with your right hand and concentrate on where you want to go."

"Where we want to go," August said. "You're coming with me."

"We'll see."

"'We'll see?' What do you think I am, five? I am not leaving you here. I—I didn't realize how long I'd lost you. Shit, I didn't know you were missing to begin with."

"You know I love you, right?"

"Stop," August said. "Do not say that. You think I don't know what you're doing? That's the kind of shit you say when you're preparing for the big sacrifice. No. You are not doing that. No way."

Tony smiled. "Here we are, arguing again." With his left hand, he reached behind his back and withdrew a sizable knife from the waistband of his pants. "But we're wasting time."

"Where did you get that?" August said. The blade of the knife was a foot and a half long, grooved up the center; its handle was bone.

"One of the mirror's children. I'm not sure how he obtained it. There are

Shadow and Thirst

still parts of the tower I haven't explored. It's possible it was in one of them."

"You know how to use it?"

"Did you think I killed my doubles with my bare hands?"

"I guess not. Lucky for me you didn't stab me before you knew who I was."

"I almost did," Tony said. "At the last minute, something stopped me."

"Well that's reassuring."

"All right: we'd better get a move on."

Here, the walls were cut with a single character, the maze, repeated every few feet. The lines of the symbol shone, as if they opened to a blackness more total than August had known. He was overcome with the desire to speak to Tony, to tell him he loved him, too, he enjoyed their intermittent phone conversations, he no longer held his divorce from August's mom against him, all the platitudes brought shuffling to the fore by extremity. However, the words could not find their way out, because they were drowned by the almost-visible wave of fear that swept through the stairway and over him. The temperature might have dropped fifty degrees. His legs shook; goose bumps roughed his skin; the hair on the back of his neck stiffened. Worse, it was as if the cold has passed into him, freezing his heart, his gut, his balls. The screaming seemed to be his own, except his mouth would not open.

On the job, August had experienced moments of intense fear. His second month on duty, he'd been part of a three-man team that searched a condo in whose upstairs bedroom an old woman lay a week dead. The death had appeared natural—the woman was lying on her bed with no sign of violence done to her—but the next-door neighbor who'd called 911 in the first place claimed the old woman had taken in a young, mentally-disturbed woman a few days prior to the neighbor's last contact with her. Sidearms in one hand, flashlights in the other, the smell of rot in their nostrils, August and his fellow officers had cleared the condo's surprisingly large first floor and basement. Although he feigned nonchalance later, when the residence had been found empty, during the actual process of opening doors to rooms and closets, he had been certain he could feel the madwoman in the house with them, waiting like a cliché from a horror film to leap out at them, butcher knife in hand. The air had seemed to vibrate around him, the way it does the instant after a loud noise.

Intense as it had been, the fear that had made the beam of his flashlight tremble had been generated from within, the sight of the old woman's cadaver merging with his memories of one too many slasher films. What halted his advance up the tower stairs was the polar opposite, a sensation that assaulted him entirely from without, as if this portion of the tower were subject to its own weather of the emotions. It was forty-below and terrifying. He wanted to move in the worst way, to lift his foot onto the next step, but he was filled with dread that, were he to raise his leg, it would shake so badly that, when he tried to set it down, he would fall on his face, unable to rise, defenseless against whatever used these stairs, against the vampire.

"August."

He raised his eyes. Tony had stopped five steps ahead of him. "August," he said, "come on."

August tried to speak, to say he couldn't, he was too afraid, but his teeth chattered too much for him to say anything.

"Mundt," Tony said. "Your body is reacting to him."

August nodded, his head jerking as he did.

"It's a natural response," Tony said. "He's completely antithetical to everything in you. I'm sorry; I should have thought of this. If you can focus on something else, it helps. Do you know what I do? I remember all the poems I know, all those fusty Victorians I used to teach. Would you like me to recite one for you?"

Why the hell not? He nodded.

"My first thought," Tony said, "was, he lied in every word
"That hoary cripple, with malicious eye
Askance to watching the working of his lie
On mine, and mouth scarce able to afford
Suppression of the glee, that purs'd and scor'd
Its edge, at one more victim gain'd thereby."

The poem was longer than August had anticipated. Much of its beginning, he struggled to follow, the fear continually snapping his attention. From the way his father's voice rose and fell, flowed and ebbed, he had the sense he was overhearing someone talking to himself. As the poem progressed, so did his focus, until with a jolt, he heard Tony describe, *"The round, squat turret, blind as the fool's heart, / Built of brown stone, without a counterpart / In the whole world."* For the remaining lines, all of his concentration was on his father's words. When the old man finished speaking, August said,

Shadow and Thirst

"That's it?"

"That's it."

"But—"

"Can you move?"

He could, if poorly, his leg shuddering madly as he pushed up onto the next step. "Can you recite it again?"

"Of course. Let's try to keep climbing."

"*My first thought,*" Tony began, and August raised his left leg. The speaker of the poem—some kind of knight, from what August could tell—left the road he'd been traveling to cross a gray field, bare of everything but weeds and scrub grass. On the stairway's surface, the images of the maze shimmered, as if full of black water. The knight encountered a starved horse, forded "*a sudden little river*" that was "*unexpected as a serpent.*" Above and beyond Tony, a doorway was visible. The knight came upon ground churned muddy by a savage fight, beheld an "*engine,*" a "*wheel, / Or brake, not wheel,*" a "*harrow fit to reel / Men's bodies out like silk.*" Faint light flickered within the doorway. At last, the knight arrived at the object of his quest, the "*round, squat turret.*" Two steps down from the doorway, Tony paused. He looked back at August.

"That's a terrible ending," August said.

"You aren't the first person to say so. How are you doing?"

"I'm managing. Thanks."

Tony pointed at the door. "Things are about to get worse."

"Great."

"I'd like to ask if you're ready, but there isn't much choice."

"It's okay."

"The door should be across from where we emerge. As I've said, though, the geography of this structure can be rather fluid, so if you don't see it where it's supposed to be, look around. Remember: it'll be the doorway with the black frame."

"What about Mundt?"

"Let me worry about him."

"You're going to take on a vampire."

"Remind me of your experience with the subject."

"What happened to all that overwhelming terror?"

"It hasn't gone anywhere, don't worry. But seeing you…I'd really like to see your stepmother and little brother again."

"A knife's going to be enough?"

"It's what they use to dispatch Dracula."

"I never read that book."

"Neither has Mundt. Don't worry—I picked up a couple of tidbits from the books in Mundt's library that should prove useful. Let's go."

The room into which they stepped was big as a banquet hall. A scattering of torches set shoulder-high cast orange light over plain brick walls, leaving the vaulted ceiling in shadow. Opposite Tony and August, a door with a thick black border opened to a patch of green grass and sunlight, the meadow at the bottom of the back hill. Hope and relief surged through August. Despite his protests to the contrary, he had understood that Tony might not make it out of here with him. August had been trying to work out how he would get his father home should Edon Mundt appear, but the only solution that presented itself—shove the old man through and stay to deal with the monster, himself—was not particularly inviting. Now, though, it appeared no such sacrifice would be necessary for either Tony or him. If only his legs would move faster, he would be on the other side of this chamber and out of this nightmare in no time.

They were less than halfway to the door when the voice breathed his father's name: "*Anthony.*" It rustled around the room, a breeze rattling dead leaves, somewhere beneath the screaming. "*What have you brought me?*"

"Don't stop," Tony said.

"Don't worry."

"*Is that little Augustus?*" the voice continued. "*Your son? Your firstborn? You've brought him here to me?*"

The doorway was farther away than it had appeared. Or had the room grown larger? In the wavering torchlight, it was difficult to tell. One moment, the space was vast as a cathedral; the next, it contracted to the size of a large hall. It was as if he and Tony were inside a great heart made of brick and shadow. Each time the chamber expanded, August had the momentary impression he glimpsed something out of the corners of his eyes, something awful, but when he glanced in either direction, the room shrank, and all he saw was bare brick.

"The door," Tony said. "Keep your eyes on the door."

"*Of course,*" the voice said, "*you never really wanted him, did you? His*

Shadow and Thirst

mother's decision: wasn't that what you said? You couldn't stand that, could you? Couldn't accept the unfairness of it all, of her having so much control over you. So much power. You've never been able to forgive little Augustus for the way his mother used him against you, have you? Never been able to love him all the way, unconditionally. The way a father should. Not like his brother—Forster, isn't it? You wanted that child. Oh yes you did. And now you've brought me this one as what? Payment for your exit from my company?

"Mundt," Tony said, "shut the fuck up."

"Hey," August said, "what happened to 'language?'"

"You don't argue with the Devil; he always wins."

"The two of you have spoken, though."

"I've been in here a long time. So has Mundt. Over the years, he proposed a number of…truces, I suppose you could call them. He'd had his fill of blood, and was interested in other pursuits, in conversation. It was a while before I accepted his offer. Even then, I was fairly certain I was heading to my death."

"Why go, then?"

"Curiosity. A change from the monotony of worrying about evading capture by him and running into the mirror's children. The chance to learn something about my captor that might help me get the better of him."

"Uh huh. So what's it like having dinner with a vampire?"

"Like sitting at the table with a cobra. I think I was even more afraid than I was when I first arrived here, when I watched him slash open my double's throat. Every time we met, I was aware that I was in the presence of a creature utterly lethal. He wears death like a waistcoat."

"Which didn't stop you from telling him all about me."

Tony paused. They had drawn nearer the doorway, though exactly how close they were was difficult to ascertain, as the distance kept telescoping out and in with the shifting light. "August," he said.

"It's fine," August said, pushing past him. "None of it's exactly a surprise."

"None of it's exactly true, either."

"*But true enough!*" the vampire said. "*And that's too true for comfort, isn't it, Augustus?*"

"Fuck off," August said.

The strip of grass visible through the doorway was fading. "What's happening?" August said.

"The tower's shifting," Tony said. "We don't have that far. Run."

Although his legs were not fully recovered from their paralysis on the stairs, August lurched forward. As he did, the air filled with the sound of flapping, as if a great flock of birds were taking wing. From all over the room, pieces of blackness loosened themselves from the surrounding shadow and darted to a point to his and Tony's left. They spiraled into a whirlwind that reached to the ceiling, then shrunk and condensed into the form of a man. Dressed in black robes that eddied about him, Edon Mundt wore a mask shaped to resemble the head of an ebony bird with a long, cruel beak. Without hesitation, he strode toward August and Tony, his robes catching on shadows as he came. The torches flickered, dimmed.

"Almost there," Tony said.

The light flared, and August saw that the floor was crowded with corpses, with dozens of bodies torn asunder. August had the sense that they had always been there, he had simply been unable to see that he could see them. All of them were Tony. Here was his father with his throat torn out. Here was his father with belly opened, his intestines strewn about him. Here was his father with the top of his skull gone and its contents removed. Here was Tony's right arm. Here was his blue eye staring. Here was a scattering of his fingers. Here was his father's mouth open again and again, as if the true source of the screaming that rang the air.

"August!" Tony shouted. "Keep moving."

August was almost at the door when Mundt slid in front of him with a sinuous motion that, yes, called to mind an enormous snake. August staggered to a halt, almost tipping forward into the vampire. "Augustus," Mundt said, as if they were old friends who had run into one another unexpectedly. This close, Mundt was unbelievably tall. His robes were bedecked with long feathers or scales that clacked and clashed as he moved; his mask was sewn of a leathery material that appeared to grow out of the exposed flesh of his cheeks and jaw. His teeth were not visible, but his breath was foul, as if his gums and tongue were diseased, rotten. His presence flooded August with despair immediate and total. How had he thought—how had he *dreamed* he could escape this creature? His father had compared Mundt to a cobra; August suddenly knew what a mouse must feel, watching the hood open, the mouth part, the tongue flick out, tasting the fear in the air.

"Go!" Tony shoved him to the right, away from Mundt. He could see the

Shadow and Thirst

doorway in which the rectangle of sunlit grass had not faded completely from view. Tony uttered something he didn't understand, and white light burst in the room. Mundt shrieked, a pair of knives scraping together. His eyes dazzled, August stumbled in the direction of the exit.

"That will not save you," Mundt said.

"It wasn't supposed to," Tony said.

August stretched out his hand and touched the smooth wood of the doorframe. *Concentrate on where you want to go*, Tony had said. He pictured the meadow, the hill sloping up from it, the yellow Cape visible beyond the crest. "All right," he called, "I'm here. Dad! Come on!"

Tony repeated the strange syllable, and brightness scorched the air. "Go!" he shouted. "Go on! I'm right behind you!"

August stepped through the door, glancing back as he did. In the instant before he passed through the fall of black water, he watched his father drive his knife into the center of Mundt's form, twisting his body to give the blow all of his strength. At the same moment, Mundt's head surged forward, joining with and absorbing his mask, becoming a black scythe that he drove into the base of Tony's throat. Tony's blood hissed over Mundt's flesh.

August's cry accompanied him out the doorway's other side, into the meadow on whose grass he collapsed. He had not moved when the pair of sheriff's deputies charged down the hill, a minute later. While one surveyed the meadow, the trees beyond, the other knelt beside August. "You're August?" the deputy said. "Your father—where's your father?"

He could no longer hear the tower. If he looked, he knew, he would not see it. "He isn't here," August said. "My dad's gone."

CORPSEMOUTH

I

In July of 1994, the year after my father died, my mother, youngest sister, and I went to Greenock, Scotland, from which my parents had emigrated to the United States almost thirty years before. Mom and Mackenzie flew over for a month; I joined them two weeks into their trip. The three of us stayed with my father's mother, who owned a semi-detached house set near the top of a modest hill. From the window of its front bedroom, on the second story, you could look out on the River Clyde, here a tidal estuary, which had allowed the region to become a center for British shipbuilding for over two centuries. Two miles across, the river's far shore was layered with green hills, the Trossachs, long and sloping, the markers of geological traumas ancient and extreme.

I actually arrived a day late, because of a mechanical difficulty with my plane that was not detected until we were ready to pull away from the gate. The pilot's intimation of it in his message to the passengers caused a woman seated ahead of me to start shouting, "Oh my God, I had a dream about this last night. We're going to crash. The plane is going to crash. We can't take off." Fortunately for her—and possibly, for the rest of us—we were removed from the plane and bused to one of the airport's hotels, where we were put up overnight.

I spent part of that time trying to phone someone on this side of the Atlantic who could call my relatives overseas to let them know not to go to the airport for me. I had no luck and passed the remainder of the night restless from the knowledge that I would have to be up early if I didn't want to miss the return bus to the terminal. I wasn't certain why I had taken the time off from the optometrists' office I was managing for this trip. Obviously, it had to do with the loss of my father, with an effort to address the gap his death had left in my life by returning to the place of his birth and early life, by spending time with the members of his family who still lived there, as if geography and blood might help to heal the edges of what remained a ragged wound. Already, though, my plan seemed off to a dubious start.

II

The sleep I managed was troubled. I fell into a dream in which I watched my father as he sat with a handful of other men in the back of a van speeding along a narrow street that ran between high brick walls blackened by age. Overhead, what might have been the gnarled branches of trees peeked down from the tops of the walls. My father looked as he had during my later childhood, slender, his hair already fled from the top of his head. He was dressed in a denim work shirt and jeans, as were the rest of the men. Although he did not look at me, I was certain he knew that I was watching him, and I waited for him to turn to me and say something. He did not.

III

Despite my concerns, I woke in plenty of time, and had an uneventful flight across the ocean, and was met at the airport in Glasgow by one of my older cousins and my mother and sister. They had checked the flight information before leaving for my original arrival, learned of the alteration to my trip, and saved themselves the earlier run to the airport. Although

CORPSEMOUTH

the ride to my grandmother's wasn't especially long, I was still feeling the effects of my night in the airport hotel (I was too much of a nervous flyer to have napped during my time in the air), and I struggled to hold open my eyelids, which felt weighted with lead. I had a confused impression of stone and steel buildings, of cars and trucks flowing around us, of a strip of blue river speeding by on my right. When we arrived at my grandmother's house, I succeeded in greeting her and one of my aunts and a couple of my cousins, but it wasn't long before I climbed the stairs to the front bedroom, assuring everyone that I just needed a little nap, and slept straight through to the next morning.

IV

Somewhere deep in that sleep, I dreamed I was standing at the picture window overlooking the Clyde. It was night, but the sky shone silver-white with the gloaming, casting sufficient light for me to see that the river was dry. Its bed was a wide, muddy trench bordered by rocky margins draped with seaweed. At points further out in the mud, boulders sat alone and in clumps. Thousands, tens of thousands of fish lay on the mud and rocks, their long, silver bodies catching the light. Most of them were dead; a few still thrashed. All along the riverbed, a great line of people walked downstream, toward the ocean. Male, female, old, young, tall, short, fat, thin: they were as varied a group as you could assemble. As was their dress: some were in their work clothes, some their pajamas; some in formal wear, some in hospital gowns; some wearing the uniforms of their professions, some stark naked. The only detail they shared was their bare feet. They trudged through mud that sucked at their ankles, that slurped at their shins, that surged around their thighs. If they were closer to shore, they stumbled on seaweed, slid on rocks. They trod on fish, kicked them out of the way. It seemed to me that there was something I wasn't seeing, a presence weighting the scene in front of me. It was waiting at the corners of my vision, huge and old and empty. Or, not empty so much as hungry. There was no sound from the crowd, but overhead, I heard a high-pitched ringing, like what occurs when you run your damp finger around the rim of a wineglass.

V

The following morning, I came downstairs to the smells of the breakfast my grandmother was cooking for me, fried eggs and bacon, fried tomatoes, buttered toast, orange juice, and instant coffee. She had insisted to my mother and sister that she was going to make breakfast for me, and that she wanted us to have some time alone. Mom and Mackenzie had removed themselves to my Aunt Betty and Uncle Stewart's house, a short distance along the road.

I wasn't certain what my grandmother wanted. While we had seen my father's parents during our previous visits to Scotland, it had seemed to me that we spent more time with my mother's mother, who had come to stay with us in America (though I didn't remember her visits). The most I had spoken to my father's mother was immediately after his death, when I had done my best to console her over the phone, assuring her that he had been suffering and was at least out of pain, and she had said, "It's like it's himself talking to me."

Now, she sat down with me at her small kitchen table and said, "Tell me about your dad, son."

I didn't know what to say. Her question should not have caught me off guard. My father had been his parents' acknowledged favorite—as one of his younger brothers had told me, their mother's golden boy. Although Mom, my siblings, and I had visited Scotland only every few years, for a good part of my childhood, Dad's job with IBM had necessitated regular international travel, to Paris and Frankfurt, and he was usually able to arrange an extra couple of days' stay with his parents. Despite his geographical distance from them, he had been able to maintain a close relationship with his mother and father; whereas myself, my brother, and my sisters knew our paternal grandparents mostly as names Dad and Mom discussed now and again. Occasionally, my father would mention his father as the source of an old song he was singing, or relate an anecdote about my grandfather's days in the shipyards, when he'd argued with his fellow workers against unionizing. He didn't say much about his mother; though his affection for her was palpable. For her to want me to tell her about him now was no surprise. Quite reasonably, she assumed that he was what we had in common, and she assumed that I felt about him the way she did.

CORPSEMOUTH

This was not exactly the case. I loved him, fiercely, the way I had as a small child. For almost as long, though, that love had been complicated by other emotions, ones that, at twenty-five, I was nowhere near reckoning with. There was fear, of him and the temper that could ignite without warning, and for him and the heart whose consecutive infarctions during my eighth grade school year had left me in constant dread of his mortality. There was anger, at his stubborn insistence on his point of view, at his tendency to cut short so many of our more recent arguments by threatening to put my head through the wall if I didn't shut up. There was embarrassment, at the prejudices that had trailed him from his upbringing, against everyone who was not white, Catholic, and Scottish, at his tendency to point out the flaws even of people he was praising. And there was guilt (as some comedian or another said, the gift that keeps on giving), at my inability to love him as simply, as straightforwardly, as did my siblings. In the year or so leading up to his death, he and I had seemed to be moving, slowly, tentatively, toward some new stage in our relationship, one in which the two of us might be less on guard around one another, more relaxed, but his two months in Westchester Medical Center, his death, had forever kept us from reaching that place.

None of this could I say to my grandmother. Eyes wide behind her glasses, lips pressed together, she inclined ever-so-slightly toward me, her attitude one of anticipation, for anecdotes and details that would allow her son to live again in her mind's eye. So that was what I gave her, a morning's worth of stories about Dad. I couldn't not talk about his final stay in the hospital, the open-heart surgery from which he had never fully recovered, becoming steadily weaker, until testing revealed that he had late stage cirrhosis, his liver was failing, and the situation roared downhill like a roller coaster whose brakes had sheared off. But I could balance that story with others, most of them focusing on his pride in my brother and sisters. I told her about the cross country and spring track practices and meets he picked them up from and drove them to. I narrated his help with and participation in their assorted science projects (including letting Mackenzie wake him throughout the night in order to assess the effects of an interrupted sleep schedule on his ability to perform a set number of tasks). I shared with her his delight in my brother's acceptance to medical school, and his pride in Christopher's commission in the Navy. I expressed his admiration for my middle sister, Rita, who managed a schedule that included teaching dance classes at the school at which she was a student, playing guitar with the church folk group, and working a part-time job at an optometrist's office, all the while completing high school. I considered it an achievement that, not once during our extended breakfast, did my grandmother ask about my father and me.

VI

The remainder of the day consisted of a visit to my aunt and uncle's house, a few hundred yards up the road, for a loud and cheery dinner of meat pies, sausage rolls, bridies, chips, and beans, with Irn Bru to drink. We were joined by Stewart and Betty's children and children-in-law, and their grandchildren, who were fascinated by my American accent and kept asking me to pronounce words in it. Uncle Stewart promised to drive me around to see the local sights; one of my cousins and his wife invited Mackenzie and me to watch a movie at their place; another of my cousins said that my sister and I had to come fishing with her and her dad another night. Oh, and there was a fair down by the water next weekend… In a matter of two hours, my schedule for most of my remaining time in Greenock was arranged. I didn't mind. I had grown up without much in the way of extended family nearby; really, it was just Mom, Dad, my brother, sisters, and me. During the months after my father's death, when the flood of calls and visitors that had swept over us in the immediate aftermath of his passing diminished to a stream, then a trickle, then dried completely, I had felt this lack acutely. To be here, taken into the bosom of Dad's family, was like being gathered into an incredibly soft, comfortable blanket. I loved it.

VII

Later that night, though, as I was sitting up in bed, trying to read by the astonishing late light, I found myself unable to concentrate on my book. Had Mackenzie been awake, I would have talked to her, but I could hear

CORPSEMOUTH

my sister snoring in the back bedroom, which she was sharing with Mom. I could have checked on my mother, but even if she was awake, I was reluctant to disturb her with what was on my mind. It concerned my father, and his final stay in the hospital.

The morning after he emerged from surgery, the nurses propped him up in bed and gave him a pen and pad of paper with which to communicate. (He was, and would remain, intubated, his breathing assisted by a ventilator.) Due to the ICU regulations, only three of us could visit him at a time, so my sister, Rita, and I waited and sent Mom, our brother, and Mackenzie in first. Rita and I made small talk for five or ten minutes, then Chris and Mackenzie came out to trade places with us. I had seen my father in the hospital before, many times, and the sight of him in his hospital gown, the top of the white ridge of bandages visible at its collar, below the trache tube, was not shocking. What was strange, off, was the expression on his face, his brows lowered, his jaw set, a look of concern tinted with anger. Rita and I crossed the ICU cubicle to him and embraced him, both of us delivering deliberately casual greetings, trying to act as if everything was fine, or was going to be fine. He returned our hugs, then turned his attention to the pad of paper propped on his lap. He took his pen and carefully wrote a sentence. When he was finished, he held the pad up for my inspection.

The line he'd written was composed of characters I didn't recognize. There was what might have been a square, except that the upper right corner didn't connect. There was a triangle whose points were rounded. There were parallel lines drawn at an angle, descending from right to left. There was a circle with a horizontal line bisecting it, an upside-down crescent, and a square whose bottom line turned up inside the shape before connecting with the line on the left, and which continued to turn at ninety-degree angles within the square, making a kind of stylized maze. I stared at the symbols and looked at my father. My lack of comprehension was glaringly obvious. I said, "Um, I'm sorry—I don't understand what you're trying to tell me."

In response, he underlined the strange sentence several times and showed it to me again.

"Dad," I said, "I don't understand. I'm sorry. I can't read this."

His eyebrows raised in frustration. Although he was on the respirator, I could practically hear him blowing out his breath in exasperation. Employing the pen as a pointer, he moved it from symbol to symbol, as if taking me slowly through a simple statement.

I could feel my face growing hot. I shook my head, held up my hands. He glared at me.

"Let me see," my mother said, leaning over from the other side of his bed. She didn't have any more luck with what Dad had written than had I. He was irritated with both of us—Rita refrained from looking at the pad—but his annoyance with me felt as if it had a particular edge, as if I, of all people, should understand what he was showing me.

After that, it was time to go. When we returned for the next visiting session, two and a half hours later, Dad was surrounded by several nurses, all of whom were focused on preventing him from leaving his bed, which he was trying to do with more vigor than I would have anticipated from a man who had just had his chest cracked open. Mom talked to him, as did the rest of us as we came and went from the room, but though the sound of her voice, and ours, calmed him slightly, it wasn't enough to make him abandon his efforts. This led to him being given a mild sedative, then put in restraints. For the next two weeks, he struggled with those restraints daily, pulling at the padded cuffs buckled to his wrists. His features were set in a look of utter determination; if any of us spoke to him, he regarded us as if we were strangers.

My mother was afraid he had suffered a stroke, one of the possible complications of the surgery about which she and Dad had been warned. In the notes to his chart, the nurses described his new condition as a coma. Neither diagnosis seemed right to me, but where was my medical degree? All I knew was, he wasn't there, in that writhing body—or maybe, we weren't there for him, he was seeing himself in surroundings foreign and frightening. Finally, at the end of fourteen days of watching him wrestle with his restraints, one of the doctors realized that Dad might be having an allergic reaction to a drug they had been giving him (we never learned which one) and ordered it stopped. With the cessation of that drug, he returned to normal within a day. The restraints were removed, and although he only left his room for follow-up x-rays and further surgery, at least he was himself.

Those symbols, though, I had not forgotten. The most likely explanation was that they were an early product of my father's drug allergy. Had any of my siblings, my mother, asked me about them, I would have offered

CORPSEMOUTH

this rationale, myself. Yet on some deeper level, I didn't buy this. He had exhibited too much focus in writing them. Had he ever been well enough to be removed from the ventilator, I would have asked him about them. Since that hadn't happened, they remained a mystery. I might be transforming the scribbling of a mind frightened and confused into a coded message of great import, but I could not forget the expression on my father's face as he showed me what he had set down.

After all, during the surgery, his heart had been stopped, and although a heart-lung machine had continued to circulate and oxygenate his blood, who could say what state he—his self, his soul—had been in for that span of time, how far he might have wandered from his body? Sometimes, I imagined him, waking from his surgery to find himself in an unadorned room with a single chair and a single door, and being told by a man in a drab suit that this was where he had to wait until the operation was completed and the doctors found out whether or not they could restart his heart. I imagined the man offering him a newspaper, its headlines the row of symbols he would copy for me.

To what end, though? I recognized the scenario I had invented, the speculation that prompted it, as magical thinking of the most basic kind, driven by longing for my father to have been involved in something more than the slow and painful process of his death. In his writing, I hoped for clues to another state of being, evidence of the place he had entered when he died.

I set my book down on the nightstand. I eased out of my bed and crossed to the large window that gave a view of the Clyde and its far shore. In the late light, the river was the color of burnished tin, the Trossachs purple darkening to black. My father had not lived in this house—one of his mother's cousins had bought it for her after my grandfather died. But the river it surveyed had shaped his life as definitively as it had the land through which it flowed. The shipyards on its banks had brought my great-grandfather here from Ireland. A younger son of a farming family, disqualified from inheriting the farm by his order of birth, he had booked passage across the Irish Sea to find work as part of the industry building the vessels with which the British Empire maintained its quarter of the globe. Beyond that, I didn't know much about the man. I presumed he had obtained my grandfather's job in the shipyards for him, which I knew had consisted at one point of painting the hulls of ships. I wasn't sure why my father hadn't followed him in turn, unless it was because my grandfather (and probably, grandmother) had wanted something else for him, an office job, which he eventually found with IBM. All the same, Dad had courted Mom on the Esplanade that ran along the Clyde on the eastern side of town, and he kept newspaper clippings about the river that his relatives mailed to him folded and tucked within the pages of his Bible. I wasn't any closer to knowing what I expected from this trip. But gazing out at the river, the hills, felt strangely reassuring.

VIII

That night, my dreams took me down to the Clyde. A chain link fence kept me from a flat, paved surface above which cranes rose like giant metal sculptures. I turned to look behind me, and almost toppled into a chasm that dropped a good twenty feet. The gap ran parallel to the fence, to the river beyond. Maybe ten feet across, its walls were brick, old, blackened; although its bottom was level—a road, I realized when I saw a white, boxy van drive up it. At once, I knew two things with dream certainty: my father was in that van, and there was something at my back, on the other side of the paved lot. The hairs on the back of my neck prickled at it. Old—I could feel its age, a span of years so great it set me shivering uncontrollably. I did not want to see this. I shook with such intensity, it jolted me from sleep. Awake, I could not stop trembling, and wrapped the bedclothes around me. I took a few minutes to return to sleep, and once I did, it was to a different dream.

IX

Once he was home from work the next day, Uncle Stewart made good on his promised tour of the area. Mackenzie came, too. The three of us squeezed into his car, a white Nissan Micra whose cramped interior lived up to its name, and off we went. A soft-spoken man, Stewart kept a cigarette lit and burning between his lips for most of the drive. He worked for a high-tech manufacturer who had moved into one of the old shipping buildings.

Corpsemouth

He was what my parents called crafty, which meant he had a knack for artistic projects. Fifteen years before, when he'd been laid off his job at the shipyards and unable to find another, he had turned his efforts to building doll-sized replicas of old, horse-drawn traveler's trailers. He'd gifted one to my parents, who placed it in their bedroom, where my siblings and I went to admire it. The detail on the trailer was amazing, from the flowered curtains hung inside the small windows to the ornaments on the porcelain horse's bridle. (He bought the horses in bulk from a department store.) Stewart had sold his trailers, first to family, then to friends, then to friends of friends, then to their friends, the money he earned helping to keep his family afloat until he found a new job.

He was also a repository of local knowledge, some of which he shared with Mackenzie and me as he steered the Micra up and down Greenock's steep streets. He showed us the house our father had grown up in, the apartment where our mother had been raised by her mother, the church where our parents had married. He drove us down to the river, to the Esplanade, and along to where a few cranes stood at the water's edge like enormous steel insects. He drove us east, out of town, toward Glasgow, so that he could show us Dumbarton Rock across the Clyde, a great rocky molar whose ragged crown stood two hundred feet above the river. A scattering of stone blocks was visible at the summit. Nodding at the rock, Stewart said, "There's been a castle of some sort there forever," the words emerging from his mouth in puffs of cigarette smoke that his open window caught and sucked out of the car. "Back when the Vikings held the mouth of the Clyde, and the islands, that was the westernmost stronghold of the British. Before that, the local kings ruled from atop it. Like the castle in Edinburgh—Sterling, too. There's a story that Merlin paid the place a visit, in the sixth century."

"King Arthur's Merlin?" I said.

"Aye. The king at the time was called Riderch. They called him 'the generous.' King Arthur's nephew, Hoel, was passing through, and he was injured. Fell off his horse or the like. King Riderch put him up while he was healing. When Riderch's foes learned he had King Arthur's nephew under his roof, they laid siege to the place. Riderch had a magic sword—Dyrnwyn—that burst into flame whenever he drew it, but he and his men were pretty badly outnumbered. There was no way he could get word to King Arthur down in Camelot in time for it to do him any good. It looked as if Arthur's nephew was going to be killed while under Riderch's care. So was Riderch, himself, but you see what I'm saying. It would be a big dishonor for Riderch, alive or dead."

Stewart steered toward an exit on the left that took us to a roundabout. He followed it half-way around, until we were heading back toward Greenock. As he did, he said, "This was when Merlin showed up. He'd been keeping an eye on Hoel, and he'd seen the trouble Riderch was in for his hospitality to Arthur's kin. He presented himself to the King and offered his assistance. 'No offense,' says Riderch, 'but you're one man. There's a thousand men at my front door. What can you do about a force of that size?'

"'Well,' says Merlin. The King has a point. He is only one man, and although his father was a devil, there is a limit to his power. 'However,' says he, 'I have allies I can call upon for help. And against them, no force of men can stand.'

"'Then I wish you'd ask those friends for their aid,' says Riderch.

"Merlin says okay. He tells the King he needs a corpse, the fresher, the better. It just so happens that, earlier that very day, Riderch's men caught a couple of their enemies attempting to sneak over the castle wall. He has his men bring them before him, and right on the spot, executes the pair. 'There you go,' he says to Merlin. 'There's two corpses for you.'

"'Good,' says Merlin. He has the King's soldiers carry the bodies right outside the front gate. It's going on night time, and Riderch's foes have withdrawn to their tents. Merlin instructs the soldiers to dig a shallow grave, one big enough for the two dead men. Once it's been dug, he has them lay the corpses in it and cover them over. Then he sets to, using his staff to draw all manner of strange characters in the soil. He was a great one for writing, was Merlin. If you read some of the older stories about him, he's always writing on things, prophecies of coming events, usually. King Riderch watches him, but he doesn't recognize the characters Merlin's scratching into the dirt.

"When he's done, Merlin steps back from the grave. Pretty soon, the earth begins to tremble. It moves from somewhere deep below them, as if something's digging its way up to them. Over in the siege camp, a few of Riderch's enemies have been watching Merlin's show. As the ground shakes, more of them run to see what's causing the disturbance. The soil over the grave jumps, and a great head pushes its way through the dirt. It's a man's

CORPSEMOUTH

head, but it's the size of a hut. The hair is clotted with earth. The skin is all leathery, shrunk to the skull. The eyes are empty pits. The lips are blackened, pulled back from teeth the size of a man's arm. The arms and legs of the bodies the King's men buried hang out over the teeth, the remainder of the corpses inside the huge mouth. It's a giant Merlin's summoned, but no such giant as anyone there has ever heard tell of. It's as much an enormous corpse as those it crunches between its teeth. It keeps coming, head and neck, shoulders and arms, chest and hips, until it towers above them. You can imagine the reaction of Riderch's foes: sheer panic. The King and his men aren't too far away from it, themselves. Merlin touches his arm and says, 'Steady.' He points to the siege camp and says to the monster, 'Right. Those are for you.'

"The giant doesn't need to be told twice. It takes a couple of steps, and it's in the midst of the enemy fighters, most of whom are trampling each other in their haste to get away from it. It leans down, sweeps up a handful of men, and stuffs them into its mouth. It stomps others like they're ants. It kicks campfires apart, catches men and tears them to pieces. A few try to fight it. They grab their spears and swords and stab it. But that leathery skin is too tough; their blades can't pierce it. Soon, the giant's feet are covered in gore. Its lips and chin are smeared with the blood of the men it's eaten. There's no satisfying the thing; it continues to jam screaming men into its mouth. In a matter of a few minutes, Merlin's monster has broken the siege. In a few more, it's routed Riderch's foes. Some of them flee to the ships they sailed here. The giant pursues them, smashes the prows of the ships, breaks off a mast and uses it as a club on ships and men alike.

"King Riderch turns to Merlin and says, 'What is this thing you've brought forth?'

"'That,' says Merlin, 'is Corpsemouth.'

"'Corpsemouth,' says Riderch. 'Him, I have not heard of.'

"Merlin says, 'He and his brethren were worshipped here many a long year ago. He was not known as Corpsemouth, then, but what his original name was has been lost. He and his kindred were replaced by other gods, who were replaced by newer gods than those, and so on until the Romans brought their gods, and now the Christians theirs. All of Corpsemouth's fellows went to the place old gods go when men are done with them, the Graveyard of the Gods. Corpsemouth, though, refused to suffer the same

83

fate as his kin. Instead, he lived on their remains. If any men stumbled across him, they were his. As later generations of gods came to the Graveyard, so Corpsemouth had them, too. Down through the ages he has continued, losing hold of everything he used to be, until all that remains is his hunger.'

"Riderch watches the giant crushing the last remnants of his enemies. He says, 'This is blasphemy.'

"'Maybe,' Merlin says, 'but it saved King Arthur's nephew, and it saved you, too.' Which Riderch can't argue with.

"Once the last of the enemy fighters is dead, the giant, Corpsemouth, turns in the direction of Merlin and the King. Riderch puts his hand on his sword, but Merlin tells him to keep it in its sheath. He points his staff at the hills behind Dumbarton Rock. Corpsemouth nods that great, gruesome head, and walks off in that direction. That's the last Riderch sees of him, and of Merlin, for the matter. I don't suppose he was too upset about either."

Stewart's story had taken us all the way back to his front door. He pulled the parking brake and turned off the engine. "And that," he said with a grin, "is a wee bit of your local history."

Mackenzie and I thanked him, for the story and for the tour. While we were walking up to the house, my sister said, "Where did Merlin send the monster—Corpsemouth?"

Our uncle paused at the front door. "The story doesn't say. Maybe north, to the mountains. That's where many terrible and awful beasts were said to dwell. I'll tell you what I think. A few miles east of Dumbarton Rock, there was an old burial place unearthed in the 1930s. It was the talk of this part of the country. I remember my father speaking about it. The fellows who dug it up said they found evidence of an ancient temple there. 'Scotland's Stonehenge,' the papers called it."

"What happened to it?" I said. "Can you visit it?"

"They put a pair of apartment buildings over the spot," Stewart said. "The war interrupted the excavation, then, when the war was over, another group of scientists said the chaps who'd discovered the place had overstated its significance. There were a few rock carvings that were of interest, they said, but as long as they were removed and sent to the museum in Glasgow, they saw no reason not to build the high rises there. So the men from the museum came and cut out the pieces of rock to be preserved and the rest became part of the foundation for the new construction. My father was upset about it, about all of it, but especially about the carvings being taken away. 'There's folk put they things there for a reason,' he says, 'and yon men from the museum would do well enough to leave them be. There's no telling what trouble they'll stir.' I suppose he had a point. Although," Stewart added, "I've yet to see any giants prowling the hills. But if you ask me, that's where Merlin told Corpsemouth to go."

X

That night, I lay in bed thinking about Stewart's story, wondering what my father would have made of it. Mackenzie was sleeping over at Stewart and Aunt Betty's house, or I might have asked her. My mother was long since unconscious. I was sure Dad would have enjoyed Stewart's tale as entertainment. He was a great fan of adventure stories of all stripes, with a soft spot for horror narratives, too. Mostly, he watched them as movies and TV shows; although he might read a book like *Firefox* or *Last of the Breed*. Whenever he saw a new movie, especially if it had been on TV too late for me and my brother, he would describe it to us the next day, in a scene-by-scene retelling no less detailed than the story Stewart had told. In this way, I knew the plots to most of the Connery and Moore James Bonds, a number of Clint Eastwood thrillers, and an assortment of films focused on mythological figures such as Hercules. He would have appreciated the way Stewart's tale blended the historical with the horrific; though he might have preferred a different, more dramatic end to the monster, blasted by Merlin's magic, say, or set alight by King Riderch's fiery sword.

I was less sure how he would have dealt with the story's pagan elements, especially, the idea that gods came and went over time. I knew he'd been interested in mythology. Exploring the basement as a child, I had found stacked in the shelves near the furnace a half-dozen issues of a magazine called *Man, Myth & Magic*, whose title had appealed to me instantly but whose pages, full of reproductions of old woodcuts and classical paintings, not to mention articles written in a dry, academic language, left me confused. I'd wanted to ask him about the magazines but had the sense that I shouldn't. There was a reason they were in the basement, after all. Plus, puzzle me though they did, I didn't want to lose access to them, which

I might if he realized I was paging through them. So I kept quiet about the magazines, but I noticed that, whenever I brought up stories from the Greek or Norse myths I was reading, he usually knew them; though he tended to downplay his knowledge.

I wasn't sure to what extent this was because he was a devout Catholic, his faith fire-hardened from having grown up in a Protestant culture of institutionalized religious prejudice. He was leery of anything that might contradict the Church, his faith threaded through with a profound anxiety about Hell. Occasionally, he spoke about the Passionist fathers who visited his local church when he was a boy to deliver terrifying sermons on the fate of the damned. (I wondered if this was part of the attraction horror films had for him, their glimpses of the infernal.) The standard by which a soul would be judged after death was a source of concern, even worry, for him. We had discussed the apparition of the Virgin Mary to the children at Fatima, during which, she had told one of the boys to whom she revealed herself that he was destined to spend a great deal of time in Purgatory. While Purgatory was not Hell, neither was it a place to which you would have expected a young child to be sent. What could he have done, Dad said, to merit such a punishment? With the perspective of the last year, it had become clear to me that his questions about my church attendance during the two years I lived in Albany, his concern about my dating a girl who wasn't Catholic, were rooted in an honest desire to keep me out of Hell, whose smoky fires burned low and red in the corners of his mind.

I didn't believe my father had anything to fear from eternal damnation. I wasn't sure there was anything for him to be concerned about, one way or the other. During my youth, I had been as devout as my father. To be honest, I had loved my religion, which was full of all manner of marvelous stories, those in the Old and New Testaments, yes, and those in the lives of the saints, too. I shared some of Dad's nervousness at the threat of Hell, but I grew up in the post-Vatican II Church, when the rewards of salvation were emphasized over the torments of damnation. Once I entered adolescence, however, the joys of the opposite sex became vastly more compelling than the strictures of faith. If I was hardly original in this—indeed, compared to the rest of my high school classmates, I was the latest of late bloomers—I roamed off the beaten path in my growing intellectual disagreement with the Church. I found its positions on most social matters riven by contradiction; nor did it help that so many of the men who pronounced them did so with an air of self-righteousness that set my adolescent teeth on edge. The ritual of the Mass, and its central conceit, the intersection of the numinous with the mundane, continued to speak to me, albeit, in a more figurative sense than I was sure my father would have approved. Religion in general seemed to me increasingly figurative, less a description of some ultimate reality than, at best, another human invention to help us through the struggle of living. At worst, it was another way for a small group of men to hold sway over a significantly larger group of people, politics with more elaborate costumes. Either way, it had nothing to do with any life after this one.

To be sure, I had taken comfort from the Church and its rituals during the days and weeks after Dad had died. By the following winter, though, my attendance at Mass had lapsed almost entirely. Even when my work schedule permitted me to take my mother and Mackenzie to church, I sat through the service listening with one ear, especially when the priest stood to deliver the sermon. Sometimes, I thought that I could have been a better Catholic if I lived in a country whose language I did not speak, so that I wouldn't realize the priest was summarizing a *Peanuts* comic to explain God's love for us. I missed the faith I'd had in my childhood, and I regretted its loss because it had been so important to my father and had remained so for the rest of my family. Its loss filled me with a kind of terror, because it had taken with it my father, consigning him to a void in which I and everyone else I knew would, in the end, join him.

XI

No surprise: that night, I dreamed of Corpsemouth. I was standing on the shore of the Clyde. It was the same, twilit time I'd encountered in all my recent dreams. In front of me, the river was at low tide, exposing an expanse of waterlogged sand studded with rocks of varying size. Behind me, the Battery Park, Greenock's riverfront park, stretched flat and green. Beyond where the water lapped the sand, a wall of yellowish fog sat on the river, veiling the opposite shore. From within the fog, I heard the slosh of water being parted by something large. Goose bumps raised on my arms as the air chilled. An enormous silhouette loomed through the fog. Fear filled me like water bubbling into a glass. The fog churned at its edge; waves splashed the beach. A leg taller, far taller, than I pushed into view. The color of brackish water, its flesh was dried and wrapped around enormous bones. There were figures tattooed on the skin, but the creases and folds from its withering rendered them indecipherable. A second leg appeared, carrying the rest of the monster with it, but I didn't wait to see any more of it. I turned and ran for the edge of the park, which had receded almost to the horizon. Sand grabbed at my feet. I slipped on a rock and fell into another. When the giant hand closed on me, I wasn't surprised. I woke as it lifted me into the air, my heart pounding, relieved that I didn't have to see the old god's face, its terrible mouth open for me.

XII

The following day, my cousin Gabriel and his wife, Leslie, drove me, Mackenzie, and our mom to Glasgow. Gabriel was Uncle Stewart and Aunt Betty's second oldest, which made him five years older than I was. The times my parents had taken my brother and sisters and me to Scotland when we were growing up, Gabriel had always been the kindest of my cousins, willing to talk to my brother and me as equals about all manner of serious subjects: nuclear war, the fate of the human race, life on other planets. He worked for the railroad, in what capacity I wasn't clear. Leslie was an elementary school teacher; she and Gabriel had been married for eight years.

After we found a parking spot, Leslie, Mom, and Mackenzie set off for Sauchiehall Street and its assorted shops, Gabriel and I for the West End Museum, a sprawling, Victorian extravagance in red stone whose center was crowned by a selection of turrets that suggested a fairy tale castle full of treasure. The museum, I had learned from a follow-up conversation with Uncle Stewart, was where the engraved rocks removed from the burial site east of Dumbarton Rock had been sent and were currently on display. I wasn't sure why I wanted to see them; it might have been for no more complicated a reason than that my uncle had told me about them. I hadn't shared my objective with my cousin, but he was happy to accompany me across the museum's wide, green lawn.

Inside, we traversed a large, echoing gallery to the stairs to the third floor,

CORPSEMOUTH

where the exhibit on Scotland's Ancient Cultures was located. The display was at the far end of the level. It had been organized around a half-dozen modest display cases, each of which contained a handful of relics of the country's oldest-known inhabitants. Large photographs of the Scottish countryside, each seven feet high by five wide, had been hung in the midst of the cases. Gabriel strolled over to a display case showing the rusted blade of an old sword. In front of a picture of a shallow brook running at the base of a snow-topped mountain, I found what I had come to see.

The only thing in its case, the piece of grey stone was rectangular, larger than I had anticipated, the size of a small table. The white lettering on the glass cover identified it as having been unearthed in 1933 on Gibbon's Farm in Dunbartonshire. The description pointed out the pairs of concentric circles visible on the stone's upper right quadrant, as well as the u-shape directly below them, which I thought resembled a horseshoe. The approximate date given for the stone was 500 ACE. I crouched to get a closer look at the stone, which brought me level with its base. From that position, I noticed a series of marks in the rock. At first, I took them for the scrapes and scars left by whatever tools had been used to extricate the slab. Then they came into focus, and I was looking at a row of characters. A rough square whose upper right corner didn't connect was followed by a triangle with rounded ends, which was succeeded by a pair of parallel lines slanting from right to left. Fourth was an approximate circle with a line through its center, a crescent like a frown fifth. Last was another square, only, this one's edges failed to connect in the lower left corner, instead turning inside in a series of right angles to form a stylized maze.

It was as if I were looking at the figures through a tunnel. Everything except that patch of rock was dark. I could hear the steady click and sigh of my father's respirator, the faster, high-pitched beep of the heart monitor, the intermittent beep of a machine keeping track of some other function. I could smell the antibacterial foam we applied to our hands every time we entered his room. I could feel the thin blanket we helped him pull up because the room was too cold. My heart fluttered in my chest. I went to stand and fell onto my butt. I looked up, and still saw the symbols on the stone. I remembered the expression on my father's face when he showed them to me, the frustration.

Gabriel's hand on my shoulder brought me back to myself. "What happened?" he said. "Are you okay?"

"Lost my balance," I said, pushing to my feet. "I squatted down to get a better look at the exhibit, and I fell right over. I'm fine."

"So you wanted to see this, eh?" Gabriel gestured at the stone. "Let me guess: Dad told you his Corpsemouth story, didn't he? Including the part about the mysterious graveyard whose sacred stones were removed. Am I right?"

"Yes."

"You know he made up all of that."

"Not this." I nodded at the display case.

"No, but it's only a piece of rock with a couple of circles on it. There's nothing magical about it."

I was surprised by his bluntness. "I don't know," I said, "it's kind of cool. We don't have anything like this in New York."

He shrugged.

"What about the figures on the end, there?" I said.

"What do you mean?"

"These ones," I said, pointing to the half-dozen characters on the stone's base.

He bent to inspect them. "Looks like someone was playing with their penknife. What's the display say about them?"

"Nothing."

"That's your answer, then."

I was tempted to tell Gabriel about the last time I'd seen these same figures, but saying that my late father had written them on a piece of paper for me after emerging from surgery during which his heart had been stopped sounded too lurid, too melodramatic. Instead, I said, "I suppose you're right. Why don't we go see what the ladies have been up to?"

XIII

On the way to our meeting spot on Sauchiehall Street, though, past shop windows full of high end clothes, shoes, and liquor, I asked my cousin if he truly believed his father had invented the story of Corpsemouth. "Not completely," he said. "Dad reads all kinds of books; I'm sure he's run across something like his monster in one of them. The king that's in the story, Riderch, he was real, and had his castle at Dumbarton Rock."

"But no Merlin," I said.

"Actually, there is a story about Merlin showing up there," Gabriel said. "What is it they say? If you're going to tell a lie, make sure to fit as much of the truth into it as you can manage."

"It's not exactly a lie," I said, "it's a story."

Gabriel didn't answer.

XIV

For the rest of our excursion, which ended with dinner at Glasgow's Hard Rock Café, and for the return drive to Greenock, which took us past Dumbarton Rock, those symbols floated near the surface of my thoughts. As far as I could remember, my father hadn't taken us to visit the West End Museum during any of our family trips to Scotland. Nor, as far as I knew, had he gone to the place on his own; although this was difficult to the point of impossible to be certain of. He'd never mentioned it, and he'd had no trouble telling us about his visit to the Louvre, while he'd been in Paris on one of his business trips. I asked my mother about it during our dinner at the Hard Rock, delivering my question at the end of a short appreciation of the museum. "There was a lot of fascinating stuff in it," I said. "Did you and Dad ever go there?"

A year past his death, Mom's eyes could still shine with tears, her cheeks blanch, at the mention of my father, of their life together. She reached for her napkin, dabbed the corners of her eyes. "No," she said, returning the napkin to the table. "I think I went on a school trip there—I don't remember how old I was. Just a girl."

"What about Dad?" I said. "Did his school visit the museum, too?"

"I don't know," Mom said. "They probably did, but he never mentioned it to me."

"Oh," I said. "I was wondering. Because, you know, you guys took us to a lot of museums when we were young." Which was true.

"That's what happens when you're traveling with children," she said. "No, in our younger days—BC, we used to say, Before Children—Dad and I went on picnics, or out dancing."

So perhaps my father had been to the museum as a boy, and perhaps on that occasion he had seen the weird symbols carved on the base of the rock. And perhaps his brain had tossed up that memory as his anesthesia wore off. The last perhaps, however, seemed one too many. Yes, the mind was a complex, subtle organ, and especially after a dramatic experience, who could predict its every last response? Yet this felt more like special pleading to me than admitting that something strange had happened to my father, and whatever its parameters, it had left him with a message for me written in characters I couldn't read.

XV

Back in Greenock, we dropped Mom, Mackenzie, and Leslie off at Stewart and Betty's. Gabriel and I drove back to his house, in order, he said, for him to initiate his American cousin into the mysteries of the single malt. He and Leslie lived on a steep street that gave a view of the Clyde. The houses along it sat on a succession of terraces, like enormous stairs descending the hillside. He parked in a short gravel driveway, and led me first into his and Leslie's house, to deposit her day's purchases on the living room couch, then out a pair of French doors, into the back garden. A brick path took us through rows of flowering bushes to a wooden hut whose door was flanked on the right by a large window. A hand-painted sign over the door read GABE'S HORN; under the name, the artist had drawn a simplified trumpet from whose mouth alcohol poured. My cousin opened the door, flicked a light switch within, and ushered me into the building.

To the right, a short bar stood in front of a shelf lined with bottles of Scotch, with some better varieties of vodka and bourbon to either side of them. Behind the bottles, a mirror the length of the bar doubled the size of the room. To the left, a quartet of chairs surrounded a round table. Beyond the table, a chrome jukebox stood against the wall. Posters and pennants of the local soccer team, the Greenock Morton, decorated the walls, with framed photographs of Gabriel and Leslie in assorted vacation settings among them. Gabriel made for the bar, which he slipped behind to survey his selection of whisky.

CORPSEMOUTH

There were a couple of tall stools in front of the bar. I settled onto one of them and said, "This is great."

Gabriel glanced over his shoulder at me. "Do you think so? It's just something Leslie and me put together in our spare time."

"It's fantastic," I said.

"We like to come out here after a day at work, or if we're having friends over."

"It reminds me of a place my dad took me to," I said. "There was a guy who was a friend of his—through work, but he was from Scotland, too. One night, Dad had to go over to his house—to pick up something for work, I think—and he brought me along with him. I was thirteen or fourteen. This man led us down to his basement, which he had set up as a bar—though not as nice as this one. He passed my dad a glass of something—I don't know what it was, but Dad told me afterwards that our host had not been stingy with his booze. I had a ginger ale, which he gave to me out of one of those specialized dispensers you see in real bars, with the hose and all the different buttons on top of it. I was thoroughly impressed. The guy had been in the RAF during the war—he had a couple of big pictures of planes on the wall. The three of us sat around talking about that for an hour. I felt so grown up, you know?"

"Aye." Gabriel nodded. He had picked three bottles and set them on the bar. "I have some ginger ale in the refrigerator, but I think it's time for something a wee bit more mature." From under the bar, he produced a pair of whisky glasses, along with a small pitcher of water. He opened one of the bottles and tipped respectable amounts of its amber contents into both glasses. To each he added a literal drop of water. I picked up the one closest to me and raised it to my nose. The odor of its contents, sharp, threaded with honey, was the smell of I couldn't count how many family parties. It was me playing waiter to my father's bartender, gathering drink orders from whichever guests were there for the latest First Communion, or Confirmation, or Graduation, and conveying them to Dad, who had opened the liquor cabinet in the kitchen and stood ready to dispense its contents. It was me returning to those guests with one or two or three glasses in my hands, delivering them to their recipients, and hurrying back to the kitchen for the next ones. It was me carrying to a particular friend a liquor my father had secured specifically for them, making sure to let them know Dad had said this was something special for them.

"Cheers," Gabriel said, lifting his glass to me.

"Cheers," I said, repeating the gesture to him.

The whisky flared on my tongue and flamed all the way down my throat to my stomach, where it detonated in a burst of heat. Eyes watering, I coughed, and set the half-empty glass on the bar.

"You said you're not much of a Scotch drinker," Gabriel said.

"Not much as in, never," I said. "Which is strange, considering it was the drink of choice at family get-togethers."

"Try sipping it," Gabriel said. "You want to be able to savor a good single malt."

"Okay." I took a more measured drink, and tasted honey mixed with something woody, almost bitter. I described it to Gabriel. "That's the peat," he said. I nodded, trying more. The flavor was not what I was used to: it filled the mouth, asserting itself as did none of the mixed drinks I'd previously had. I'd never been much of any kind of drinker, and I felt the liquor's potency before I was finished with the glass. My cousin's bar and its contents softened, their edges slightly less defined. Something inside me loosened. I said, "All right. What's wrong with your dad's monster story?"

Gabriel raised an eyebrow. "You mean Corpsemouth?"

"Yes," I said, "that. In the museum, I had the impression you were less than enchanted with it."

"Ach, it's fine," he said. "Dad's always been a great one for the stories."

"Mine, too," I said.

"That story—the Corpsemouth one—you know what it's really about, don't you?"

"A giant monster?"

"It's death," Gabriel said. "It's a way of picturing death, of representing the way death feels to us."

"Sure," I said. "It's like—there's a line in one of Stephen King's books—I think it's *Salem's Lot*—this kid is asked if he knows what death is, and he says yeah, it's when the monsters get you."

"Aye," Gabriel said, "that's what I'm trying to say."

The second Scotch my cousin served tasted less of honey and more of smoke, and something peppery. The knot within me that had started to loosen slid away from itself. Gabriel leaned across the bar and said, "So.

CORPSEMOUTH

How're you finding it, being here?"

The row of strange symbols flickered behind my eyes. "It's different than I was expecting," I said.

"It's bound to be."

"Yeah. It's funny. I thought that coming here would let me feel more in touch with my dad. Granted, it's only been a few days, but so far…"

"You don't."

"I don't."

"How could you? You didn't know him here. You knew him in America. It's okay."

"Maybe you're right. If that's the case, then what am I doing here?"

"You're with family."

"Yeah," I said. "I didn't have much of that when I was growing up, you know? It was just the six of us. It's kind of nice."

The third and final Scotch Gabriel poured was thinner, the peat combining with a briny flavor to give the liquor an astringent taste so blunt it was oddly appealing. "Thank you," I said to my cousin, speaking with the deliberation of someone whose tongue was heavy with alcohol. "I appreciate you sharing your expertise with me."

"I'm hardly an expert," Gabriel said.

"Regardless. You know what's funny?"

"What?"

"I can picture my dad enjoying the whole Corpsemouth story. It reminds me of movies we watched when I was a kid, *The Golden Voyage of Sinbad*, *Clash of the Titans*, *Dragonslayer*—these stories about heroes fighting enormous monsters."

"I suppose," he said.

"Well, you two appear to be having a merry time," Leslie said. She was standing in the open doorway to the bar.

"We were talking about monsters," I said.

"I'm sure you were," she said. "Stewart gave me a lift home. I'm not rushing you out, but he says if you want, he can run you back to your Gran's."

"That is probably a good idea," I said. "I'm fairly confident I've reached my limit for alcohol. Honestly, I think I passed it a while ago."

I thanked Gabriel for his generosity with his spirits, and him and Leslie for having squired my mother, sister, and me around Glasgow, today. "We've got to have you back for another tasting before you leave," Gabriel said.

"From your mouth to God's ear," I said.

XVI

Outside, night had fallen, the last of the gloaming retreated to the horizon. Stewart was waiting in his Micra at the end of the driveway. I lowered myself into the front passenger seat. He'd been listening to a news program on the radio; as I buckled my seatbelt, he turned it off. "And how was your education?" he said.

"Great," I said. "Gabriel introduced me to some quality stuff."

"Aye, he's a great one for the single malt, our Gabriel." He released the parking brake and reversed into the street. "Are you up for a wee jaunt?"

"Sure."

"Good man." He shifted into first and started downhill.

"Where are we headed?" I said.

"The river."

"Oh."

The whisky I'd consumed made the steep road seem almost vertical, the Clyde below rather than ahead of us. Retaining walls raced toward us and swerved right and left. The river grew larger in fits and starts, as if it were a series of slides being snapped into view. The car's engine whined and growled as Stewart worked back and forth among the gears. If not calmer, I was at least less terrified than I would have been without the Scotch insulating me.

At the foot of the hill, the street leveled and ran straight to the river. One hand on the steering wheel, Stewart depressed the car's lighter and fished a cigarette from the packet in his shirt pocket. Rows of squat apartment houses passed on either side. Stewart lit his cigarette and drew on it till the tip flared. Exhaling a cloud of smoke, he said, "Did you see that stone in the museum?"

"I did," I said.

"Not much to look at, is it?"

"I don't know. When you think about what it represents—how old it is and everything…I'm glad they have it at the museum, but it's kind of a shame they couldn't leave it where it was."

"Aye."

"The exhibit said no one's sure exactly what the symbols on it mean. Maybe images of the sun."

"They're for binding," Stewart said.

"Binding?"

"Aye, for keeping a spirit or a creature in one place. You bind them by the sun and the moon. That's why there's two sets of circles on the stone. It's a very old rite."

"What was bound there?"

Stewart shot me a sidelong glance. "I told you and your sister yesterday."

"Corpsemouth? For real?"

He nodded.

"I thought that was…"

"A story?"

"Yeah. No offense."

"There was something called up at Dumbarton Rock when Riderch was king. It was older than ancient, and it was terrible. Maybe it was summoned to help the King against his enemies. Maybe it was summoned to fight Riderch. Maybe someone was playing around and opened a door that should've been left shut. It took a powerful man to send the thing back where it belonged and lock the gate after it. That stone was part of the locking mechanism."

"Wait. You're serious."

"I am."

"But…"

"That's impossible? Ridiculous? Insane?"

"I'm sorry, but yeah."

"It's all right. I wouldn't expect you to believe it, even with a few drams in you."

We had crossed the major east-west highway through town and come to a short road, which passed between an inlet of the river on the left, and a couple of apartment buildings on the right. Stewart drove to the end of the road, where a chain link fence sectioned off a stretch of pavement that went another twenty yards to the river. He parked the car and exited it. I followed. This close to the water, the air was cool bordering on cold. While

Stewart popped the trunk, I surveyed the fence, which continued to the right, guarding the edge of a much larger paved area, which was filled with large metal shipping containers, some of them sitting on their own, others stacked two and three high. In the near distance, a trio of cranes faced the Clyde, weird sentinels looking out over the dark water. Tall sodium lights gave the scene an orange hue that made it appear slightly unreal.

Behind me, Stewart shut the trunk. He was carrying a pair of metal poles, each about a yard long, one end wrapped in duct tape. "Here," he said, handing one to me.

I took it. The pole was hollow, but heavy. "What's this?"

"Protection."

"From what?"

"Come this way." He set out to the right. I hurried after. Together, we walked the fence for a good hundred yards, until we came to a wire door set in it. The entrance was locked, but Stewart withdrew a ring of keys from his trousers, which he thumbed through until he arrived at one that slid into the lock and levered it open. The door's hinges shrieked as he pushed it in. I cringed, expecting the angry shout of a security officer. None came. Stewart stepped through. I pushed the door closed behind us, to minimize suspicion.

Keeping to the shelter of the containers, Stewart and I made our way across the paved expanse, he moving quietly, gracefully, I with the exaggerated care of someone contending with too much alcohol. We headed steadily in the direction of the river. A light mist floated around us, waist-high. This close, the cranes were gigantic, monumental. Stewart stopped, raised his hand. "Do you hear that?" he said quietly.

"What?"

"Listen."

Ahead and to our left, on the other side of a pair of stacked containers, something scraped over the pavement. Holding the metal pole in both hands, the tip low, as if it were a sword, Stewart crossed to the metal boxes. I kept a few steps behind, in a half-crouch. He moved right, to one end of the containers. The sound continued in alternating rhythm, a short scrape followed by a longer one. Before continuing to the other side of the boxes, Stewart stopped and ducked his head around for a look at whoever was there. He jerked back. Closing his eyes, he inhaled, then blew out. He murmured something I couldn't hear, raising and lowering the end of the pole while he did. As the light played up and down the metal, I saw writing on it: the symbols I had seen in the Glasgow museum, on a piece of paper in my father's hospital room. Heart lurching, I straightened. I tilted the pole I was holding back and forth, and sure enough, there were the same half-dozen characters cut into it. In an instant, I was sober, the effects of Gabriel's drinks swept away by the sensation of standing within the current of something immense and strange.

"Right," Stewart said. "There's something coming up to the end of this box. When it reaches us, I'll step out and see to it. You shouldn't need to do anything. This one isn't big. If it gets past me, though, you'll have to slow it down. Go for its legs but mind its hands. Here we go."

The scraping was right next to us. Stewart moved out into the alley formed by our containers and one beyond it. As he did, he pivoted, slashing the pole from right to left at whatever was still hidden from me by the edge of the container. There was a heavy crunch, a sharp clang, and the pole flew out of Stewart's hands, ringing on the pavement to his right. A wooden club swung at him from his left. He ducked, but it caught him high on the shoulder with sufficient force to knock him from his feet. He landed hard.

I took a deep breath and stepped out from the container, in front of Stewart's opponent. I couldn't bring myself to strike someone I hadn't seen, but I held the pole up in what I hoped was a menacing fashion. I intended to shout, "That's far enough!" What I saw, however, stilled the voice in my throat.

It was as big as a large man. At first, I thought it was a man, dressed in a bizarre costume. Much of it was mud, thick, dripping with water. Its surface was clotted with junk, crushed beer cans, shards of broken glass, saturated cardboard and newspaper, pieces of plastic, metal, wood. Here and there, rocks studded with barnacles tumored its skin. In other spots, clumps of mussels clustered black and shining. Seaweed draped its shoulders, to either side of a head fashioned from the broken skull of either a cow or horse. The lower jaw was missing, the mouth a hole gaping in the muddy throat. The thing advanced, the scraping I'd heard the debris in its flesh rasping the pavement. I retreated. The club with which it had struck Stewart was in fact its right arm, a single piece of driftwood. Its left arm was a mannequin's, wound in rusted wire and strands of seaweed.

This was not a man in a suit—which was impossible and hurt to think. It swept the wooden arm at me. I leapt back, just out of reach. Stewart was on his hands and knees, grabbing for his weapon. I jabbed at the thing, trying to keep its attention. The wooden arm held straight, like a spear, it lunged at me. I sidestepped, swinging my improvised sword against the arm. With a flat clank, arm and pole rebounded from one another. The creature turned, whipping the wooden arm back at me. I went to duck, slipped, and fell. The arm struck the container behind me with a gong. This close, the smell of the thing, a stink of sodden flesh and vegetation, made my eyes water. Swiveling on my butt, I chopped its right leg with the pole, hammering the approximate location of its knee. The leg buckled inward, tipping the creature toward me. I scrambled away from it. Attempting to maintain its balance, it propped itself on its wooden arm, but Stewart hit its other leg from behind with a blow that sent the creature crashing on its back. Before it could recover, he brought the pole down on its head like an executioner swinging his axe. The animal skull rattled across the pavement. The rest of the thing, however, continued to move, doing its best to raise itself on its broken legs, dropping mud and bits of glass, pebbles, on the ground. My stomach churned at the sight. Ignoring the body, Stewart strode to the skull. He struck it twice with the pole, cracking it into several large fragments, which he stomped underfoot until they were unrecognizable. As if it were an engine running down, the body gradually ceased its motion.

Stewart dropped the pole and crossed to the creature's remains. Careful of its rusted wire sleeve, he caught the mannequin arm at the elbow. "You take the other side," he said.

Leaving my weapon, I did as he instructed. The wood was slimy, as if it had sat underwater for a while.

"Into the river," he said, nodding toward the end of the alleyway.

Together, we hauled the heavy form to where the pavement ended at a concrete ledge. Ten feet below, the Clyde lapped at the wall. "On three," Stewart said. "One, two, three!" I threw so hard I almost overbalanced myself into the water along with the creature's body. Stewart caught my arm. "Steady, lad." What was left of the thing struck the water with a considerable splash. It sunk quickly, leaving clouds of mud in its wake.

"What about the rest—the skull?" I said.

Stewart shook his head. "Leave it there. It's better to keep it separate from

CORPSEMOUTH

the rest."

Adrenaline lit my nerves, rendering everything around me painfully sharp. "I cannot believe I am standing here having this conversation with you," I said. It was the truth. Had Stewart said to me, "You're not. This is a dream," I would have had little trouble accepting his words.

Instead, he shrugged, turned, and started in the direction of the gate we'd entered.

I joined him. "What was that?" I said.

"Corpsemouth," he said, stooping to retrieve his weapon.

"I thought he was supposed to be taller," I said, picking up mine.

"In his proper form, he is," Stewart said. "Fortunately for you and me, enough of the old binding remains to keep him from appearing that way. What he's able to do is put together versions of himself, avatars, out of whatever's lying around. We call them his fingers."

"Who's 'we'?"

"A group of concerned citizens. We came together after the war. That was when Corpsemouth first made himself known, again, once the binding stone was removed. No one knew what they were doing. It had been too long since anything like this had happened. A couple of the founders were able to lay their hands on a few old books that gave hints of how to confront the monster, but a lot of it was learn as you go."

"I'm sure," I said. "Does Gabriel know about any of this? What about the rest of the family?"

"No, that isn't how it's done," Stewart said.

"How is it done?"

"Why? Are you interested in being part of it?"

"No," I said. "No, this was more than enough."

Stewart smiled thinly.

"Was my father part of this?" I thought of those old issues of *Man, Myth & Magic*.

"No," Stewart said. "Though I wondered a few times if he wasn't aware of more than he let on."

"Does this—tonight—does this kind of thing happen often?"

"More than I'd like."

As we walked, the mist thickened around us, rendering the shipping containers, the cranes, faint, ghostly. It didn't affect Stewart's sense of direction.

He continued forward.

"What about this?" I said, holding up the pole. "Not the pipe, I mean, the writing on it."

"That depends on who you ask," Stewart said. "There's some who say that those are connected to old gods. Not as old as Corpsemouth, but not too far off. When they were young and strong, he wasn't of much concern to them. As they grew older, though, and saw themselves being supplanted by newer powers, their strength ebbed and his hungry mouth became a worry. They thought that if they gave up their divinity, the monster wouldn't want them. So they put their godhood into these symbols, and ever since, anyone who uses them has been able to draw on their power."

"Did it work? Did they escape?"

"No one knows," Stewart said. "I doubt it. Corpsemouth eats gods, but he's happy to consume whatever he can get his claws on."

Overhead, a lamp lit the mist orange. Somewhere in the distance, I heard voices, faint, indistinct.

"That's one explanation," I said. "What's the other?"

"You're sure you don't want to be part of this?"

"Is that why you brought me with you?"

"You haven't answered my question."

"Nor you mine," I said.

"Some folk say the symbols come from a fabulous city, one on the shore of a black ocean, where they were the inhabitants' most closely-guarded treasure."

"That's interesting," I said, "but it's not the question I meant."

"I know," Stewart said.

Through the mist, the gate swam into view. Stewart pushed it open and walked out. I went to follow, but before I could, a shout drew my attention to the left. No more than twenty yards away, through a clearing in the mist, a white van was parked. At the sight of it, my heart knocked. I knew this vehicle, had watched it drive through my dreams. For this to be the same van was impossible, of course, but on a night such as this one had proved to be, it could be none other. I was suddenly sick with dread and grief. To walk to the van was terrifying, but to remain in place, let alone, to leave, was worse. Legs shaking madly, I stepped toward it. Stewart said something, but whatever it was didn't register.

CORPSEMOUTH

The mist was full of yells and calls whose locations I couldn't pinpoint. Was one of those voices my father's? I wasn't sure. The mist muffled the sounds, as if I was hearing them from the other side of a thick wall. I was almost at the van. Its interior was dark. Was it empty? Half-expecting my hand to pass through it, I reached for the handle to the driver's door. It was solid to the touch, and when I pulled, it clicked and the door opened. There was no one behind the wheel. Kneeling on the seat, I leaned into the van.

It was empty. There was no evidence of its passengers left behind; although, for a second, two, I caught the faintest odor of dried sweat and laundry detergent, the scent I'd breathed whenever I'd rested my head against my father's chest at the end of the day, when I wished him good night. Then it was gone.

I exited the van, closing the door. Stewart was standing behind me. "Is…" I started, and paused, unable to utter the remainder of the question.

"Aye," Stewart said.

"Where is he?"

He tipped his head toward where the mist was thick. "Out there."

"So if I go there, I'll find him?"

"You might," he said, "or you might not. You could spend an hour searching this lot, or you could wander off someplace else, and be lost."

Without warning, I was crying, tears streaming down my cheeks. I felt every bit as bad as I had the night my father had died, when it seemed a spear had been driven straight through my chest, as if his death were a pin that had fixed me forever in place. To see him one more time, to speak to him, to tell him I loved him and was sorry I hadn't been a better son, was a prospect almost too much to bear. To fail, though, to walk away and not return, was not something I could do to my mother and sister. I turned from the van and headed for the gate.

The shouts and calls persisted. "What's happening?" I said to Stewart. "What are they doing?"

"The same thing we were."

"Corpsemouth?"

"It's not just our world he wants to break into. There are folk on the other side who do their best to keep him out of there, too."

"Can he hurt them?"

"Oh aye, he eats the dead same as anything else." Seeing the expression on my face, he added, "But your dad was always a capable fellow. I'm sure he'll be fine."

XVII

After the night's events, I did not anticipate sleeping. Almost the instant I settled onto my bed, though, my arms and legs grew heavy, my eyelids struggled to stay open, and I slid into unconsciousness. For an indeterminate time, I drifted in a blank, not unpleasant place. Slowly, a long, black cord came into view. It corkscrewed around and around, the way the cord on our old telephone had. It faded and was replaced by the interior of the white van.

This time, it was full of the handful of men I'd seen in it a few days ago. My father was among them. All of the passengers looked worse for wear, their shirts and pants torn and dirty, their arms and cheeks cut and bruised. Dad was leaning forward, a black telephone receiver held to his ear. I couldn't hear every word he was saying, but I understood enough to know that he was saying he was okay.

With a start, I realized he was speaking to me. For the dream's brief duration, he continued to reassure me, while I said words he could not hear. The connection, it seemed, was one way. Then the call was finished, and I was awake—though not before a last glimpse of the white van, speeding along through high, brick walls black with age, carrying my father to the next stop on his long, strange death.

ANCHOR

I

Fire and ruin march on heaven, Surtur
Brandishes his sword, Loki and his awful
Brood come for revenge. Who stands with me now
Stands in my doom.
                      James Ogin "Odin Foresees Ragnarok"

For the rest of what will be a long, long life, every October Will Ogin will dream of this night. It will be one of those dreams so vivid as to be indistinguishable from waking; for all intents and purposes, he'll tell Manda, his wife, when he reveals it to her, he might as well be back at the far end of the driveway to his parents' house, standing beside his father. Although the calendar welcomed autumn a couple of weeks earlier, the trees are still holding onto a few of their leaves; the air is unusually warm. It is nighttime. His father has switched on the green lamppost beside the mailbox, the one they refer to as Mr. Tumnus's Lamp. Its yellow light concentrates around its top in a sphere, as if the surrounding darkness is a physical medium against which it must push. To Will's twelve-year-old eyes, the night seems heavier, somehow, thicker, and not only because he is awake far later than he's ever been up with his dad, sleep-over late. If he cranes his head back, he can see stars overhead without having to squint too much against the lamppost's glow. Tonight, his father told him, is the second night of the new moon, which no doubt contributes to the stars' brightness, but he can't shake the impression that the sky looks different, the figures whose outlines the stars are supposed to mark gone, replaced by other, unfamiliar arrangements. He pointed this out to Dad, who raised his eyes to the heavens, then lowered them without comment.

The two of them haven't been at the end of the driveway for that long, but already, Will's arms are tired from holding the Chinese spear, the *qiang*, out in a forward guard. This isn't the waxwood version of the weapon with which he's trained at his father's studio in Wiltwyck; it's the real thing, nine feet of polished hardwood capped with a sharpened blade. He noticed it leaning against the house, beside the front steps, as Dad led them outside. His father carried it as they walked down and up the driveway, but once they reached the road, he held it out to Will, who said, "Really?" even as he took it. (He *never* got to handle the actual weapons, not like this.)

"Really," Dad said, unsheathing the long, curved sword, the *do*, he'd slid into the belt of his robe before they exited the house. Like the *qiang*, the *do* was serious business, its edge razor-keen, brought out only for cutting competitions at the big tournaments. His father shucked off his bathrobe. He was wearing his usual nighttime attire of old karate pants and worn T-shirt. He took the sword in both hands, squared his stance, and let the end of the blade dip into a middle guard, so that it was pointing toward the woods across the road. Will followed his lead and leveled the spear in the same direction.

He had no idea, could not begin to guess what the two of them were doing there. As a rule, his dad was not prone to much in the way of erratic or unpredictable behavior, his limit being the occasional, spontaneous trip to Boice's in Wiltwyck for a hot fudge sundae or milkshake. He had never roused Will from his bed in the middle of the night. It had been Will, sick or pursued by nightmares, who had hauled him out of his slumber. Sitting up in bed a short time ago, blinking sleep from his eyes, Will asked what was wrong, his voice croaking. In reply, his father told him to find his sneakers, they needed to go outside. More asleep than awake, he did as

ANCHOR

instructed, clomping downstairs to find Dad at the front door, the *do* in its ornate sheath in his right hand. The sight of the sword—of that sword, in particular—jolted Will fully awake. His dad pushed the *do* through his belt, opened the door, and stepped out into the dark. Especially once he saw the spear, Will assumed there was some kind of threat in the yard, an animal, he guessed, though one of the perverts from the boarding house at the other end of their street was also a possibility. He wasn't overly concerned which it was, too excited at being included in the defense of the house.

The longer they've stood with weapons ready, however, the more mysterious their purpose has become. By now, surely an animal would have revealed itself, or fled, likewise, a person. Will feels his father's concentration weighting the space around him, lending the air the same density that fills it in the run up to a thunderstorm. It's not an entirely unfamiliar sensation, but he associates it in general with the studio, when his dad is training in a new form, and in particular during the weeks immediately before his most recent black belt test, the one for third degree. Yet even the longest of those forms didn't last much beyond two minutes, and anyway, there was movement involved. Nor did his father mind if Will interrupted him as he was practicing his *hyung* ("I do Tang Soo Do for you and your mother," his mantra, "the art is for you, not the other way around"). He's less certain how his dad would respond to a break in his focus now.

When he hears the sounds coming from across the street, somewhere deep within the trees that run down the hillside there to the county road, Will is momentarily thrilled, to the point of happiness. Beside him, Dad lets out the briefest sigh, and Will realizes that his father is relieved, that he, too, has had his fill of waiting. A sense of connection, of love so fierce it causes his hands to tremble, the end of the *qiang* to quiver, sweeps him. He readjusts his grip on the spear, readies it for the source of the noise advancing up the hill toward them. Branches rustle and snap. A tree cracks like a rifle shot and rushes to thud on the ground. Another tree groans, as if a great weight is sliding against it. Something grunts, the deep note of a steam engine venting pressure. Bushes hiss as they drag on whatever is pushing through them. The dead leaves and pine needles that carpet the earth make a sound like sizzling as heavy feet shuffle closer. Before it appears between the trunks of a pair of birches, as if framed in a doorway, there is a moment when Will sees the darkness beyond the trees become darker still, occluded by a shape whose outline does not make sense. He glances at his father, whose jaw has tightened. He's on the verge of demanding, "What is this?" when the cause of the clamor passes the birch trees and into view.

It's a bear. Not one of the black bears native to upstate New York, no, this beast is the deep orange of fire overtaking wood. And larger, by several orders of magnitude, than any local species. Its blunt head is the size of the barrel they use for catching rain; the paws it lifts as big as the tires on his mother's Camry. The creature must weigh an actual ton. *A grizzly*, Will thinks. It's the only description that fits; though this bear seems beyond the dimensions of even the largest of that breed. Not to mention, an actual grizzly emerging from the woods across the street raises so many questions, he doesn't know which one to ask first.

When the bear's paws touch the road, it pauses. Its head cocks to the left, as if it has noticed Will and his dad for the first time, which it may have: Will isn't sure how much attention bears pay to their surroundings. Its lips peel back from yellow teeth the length of his palm, and the bear bellows, a long, low wave of sound that Will feels all the way down to his bones. It may be the single most frightening thing he has ever heard. He wants to run, would like nothing better than to cast the spear aside and head for home as fast as his legs will carry him, which he suspects would be far faster than they've run before. He can't, though, can't control any part of his body, from his legs and arms, which won't move, to his lip, which won't stop trembling, to his eyes, which are dangerously close to pouring tears down his cheeks. It isn't only the bear's roar; it's the animal's very presence, which streams at them like heat from a burning building. More than at any point in his life previous to this, Will has the sense of being in a circumstance beyond his ability to handle.

"Will." His father's voice reaches him from a long way away. He has the impression his dad has said his name a number of times. He tries to say, "Yes," but his mouth refuses anything more complex than, "Uh-huh."

"I want you to drop the end of the spear—not the tip, the end—to the ground. Can you do that for me?"

"Uh-huh." To his surprise, he finds he can. He lowers the butt of the spear to the driveway's packed dirt surface.

"Good," his father says. His voice is slightly higher, but otherwise calm. "Now, if our friend over there decides to charge us—which I don't think

ANCHOR

he's going to do, but just in case—I want you to use the ground as a brace for the spear. This way, when he runs up against it, we'll have the earth helping us. Sound like a plan?"

"Uh-huh." Words spill from him in a question: "Where should I aim the point?"

"Anywhere in his middle should do," Dad says. "His neck would be super, but his shoulders or chest would be fine, too. After you do that—after he sticks himself—I want you to get out of the way. It's too far to run back to the house, but you should be able to reach the Smiths' front door."

"What are you going to do?"

"I'm going to see if I can't convince this fellow to head in another direction."

"*No, Dad.*" Panic of a different kind seizes Will, loosens his hold on the spear.

"Steady," his father says. Will re-grips the *qiang*, redirects it at the bear, who is watching their exchange as if it understands them. "Good," his dad says. "Like I said, though, I don't believe our friend is going to do anything, *because what he's looking for isn't here.*"

For an instant, Will has the absurd impression that his father is speaking to the bear. The impression vanishes when the creature advances onto the road. Will digs the butt of the spear into the driveway's dirt; his dad shifts his hands on the sword's hilt ever-so-slightly. "Easy," Dad says, and now Will is certain he's talking to the enormous animal, which has paused in the middle of the street, less than ten feet from them. "Easy," he says. The bear's eyes focus on him. Will aligns the tip of the spear with a point to the right of and slightly below the bear's head, where he feels pretty sure there's a major blood vessel, like the carotid or the jugular in humans. This close, the bear's breath thunders in and out its lungs. Its smell floods his nostrils, a pungent mix of torn vegetation, rotted meat, and urine. If it charges, Will understands, his dad is going to draw its attack, allow him a chance to spear it. "Don't," he wants to say. "Don't worry about me. Move in quick and strike. Do what you're always telling me to do. Don't worry about me." Standing watching his father and the bear stare at one another, the lamp at the end of the driveway casting deep shadows over the road, Will is struck by the absolute certainty that he is seeing his father in the last moments of his life. A combination of dread and acute sorrow washes through him, but he keeps the *qiang* trained on the spot on the bear's neck.

The bear snorts. There's something almost contemptuous in the gesture. It swings its outsized head to the right, the rest of its mountainous bulk shifting in the same direction. Slowly, it ambles up the street, toward the dead-end. Dad turns gradually, tracking the bear's progress with the point of his *do*. Will does the same with the spear. After the bear has been swallowed by darkness, they maintain their positions, listening to the tumult of its passage into the woods bordering the end of the road. Will is exhausted, hollowed out by the confrontation. His surroundings swim in and out of focus. The light from Mr. Tumnus's Lamp burns brighter, as if the darkness has receded. Where the beast stood, the space looks different, the air blacker, as if scorched by the creature's presence.

At some point after the night has grown quiet, the only sound the rush of a car speeding along the county road below, Will's father lowers his sword and turns to him. Dad's eyes are sunken, his cheeks drawn, the short hairs of his beard flecked with white. He looks ten years older than he did at the beginning of the last hour. "Come on," his father says, "I think we can go home now."

Will carries the spear back down and up the driveway. Until they're within sight of the cars parked beside the house, Dad walks with the sword unsheathed, although he leaves the point down. This is the time, Will knows, to ask his dad what just happened, but he cannot summon the energy for any action more complex than setting one foot in front of the other and keeping the spear from striking the ground. His father pauses by their SUV to slot the *do* into its scabbard. Without looking at Will, he says, "I don't think we need to tell your mother about this."

It's a ridiculous statement; as his parents like to say, their household runs on honesty. But Will nods anyway. He stares at the parking space to the left of the Saturn, where, until recently, his dad's friend, Carson, parked his truck while he was staying with them. A connection lights his brain; before he knows what he's saying, he says, "This was about Carson, wasn't it?"

Dad's eyebrows raise. It's confirmation enough, but he nods and says, "Yes, it was."

"Are we safe?"

His father is about to say, "Yes," because that's what dads do, they reassure you, tell you everything's going to be okay, regardless of the evidence.

ANCHOR

Something he notices in Will's face, some difference, stops the word on his lips. Instead, his dad says, "I'm not sure."

II

> The highway is not a symbol, describes
> No mythic transition, is blacktop and miles.
> Carson Lochyer "Driving East on I-90"

When Will Ogin is eighteen and in his first semester at SUNY Huguenot, his Freshman Composition I teacher will assign the class an autobiographical essay, its topic, "A Time of Change." Its purpose, he'll understand, is to ease the class into writing by allowing them to discuss the transition from high school to college, which, while not the only possible response to the assignment, will be the one the teacher discusses with the class with the clear intent of steering them in that direction. After a brief conversation with his mother, herself a professor in the college's English department, Will will decide to write on a different event. He'll seat himself at his computer with a bottle of Dr. Pepper and spend the next three hours in a state somewhere between memory and reflection, his room, the sounds of the house, faint. By the time he's finished with the essay, he's breathing heavily, covered in sweat, as if he's just completed a lengthy workout. Although his mom has advised him always to sleep on his work, he e-mails the essay to his teacher then and there.

The following morning, Will reads what he wrote the night before over breakfast:

> My time of change began when I was eight and a half years old and continued until I was almost twelve. For those three and a half years, my father's friend, the poet Carson Lochyer, stayed with my parents and me, renting a room that had been the office in which my dad wrote his poems. At the time, I didn't realize that Carson living with us was having such an important effect on me, but do you ever recognize the truly significant times in your life while they're happening?
>
> Carson drove cross-country from Idaho to our house in early April. My father, especially, was concerned about him traveling at this time

of year, due to the possibility of snow storms in the mountains and on the plains. Carson told him he had to come now if he was going to come at all. The trip took him three days, and my father had him call to check in every day. After he hung up the phone each night, Dad would announce, "Well, that's him through Montana," and I would look up his day's route in my mother's old Rand McNally road atlas.

Although my parents had gone to great lengths to make sure it was all right for my father's friend to come stay with us, I didn't really understand why he was leaving his home in the first place. In all the time he shared our house, I never spoke to Carson about it, either. It wasn't until a couple of years after he left that I finally thought to ask my parents what brought Carson to us. His marriage had failed, they told me, taking the rest of his life with it. He'd lost his job managing a Home Depot. He'd been asked to leave the school where he taught martial arts. He was seriously past due to turn in the manuscript for his next collection of poetry. He needed a change of scenery, a place to regroup. My parents discussed it, and my mother told my father to tell Carson he could live with us until he was back on his feet.

For three and a half years, Carson was part of our household. He found a job at the Huguenot True Value, which took him out most days. Once he returned home, and on the days he wasn't at the hardware store, he went into his room and wrote. He wrote, and he wrote, and he wrote. Usually, his door was closed, but sometimes he left it open, and I would sneak a look at him on my way to the bathroom or to use the family computer. When I did, I saw him seated in front of his computer, the screen taken up by a page of whatever poem he was working on. He might be reclining in his chair, his chin resting on his right hand. Or he might be bent forward over the keyboard, leaning toward the screen as if he were riding a motorcycle. He liked to listen to music while he wrote, but he wore headphones. During his first six months with us, he was wrapping up *The Broken Circle*. My father loved it, said it was one of the great long poems of the last decade. Carson wasn't too crazy about it. I guess that was because he'd started it when he was still married to his ex, so there was all kinds of baggage attached to it. Dad went ahead and reviewed it for

ANCHOR

the *Los Angeles Review of Books*, and it went on to a better reception than Carson had been expecting. He spent the rest of his time with us writing the poems that went into his next book, *Ardor*. This was the one that won him the National Book Award, though not until after he'd moved out.

I didn't spend a lot of time with Carson. That was my father, who passed almost every night in conversation with him. Dad tried to get him to come to his karate studio, which Carson did a couple of times, but he said that what Dad was doing wasn't for him. My father's *dojang* was a typical American school, family-friendly, the majority of its students kids, classes split between warm up, traditional curriculum, and an assortment of fun activities. If you were a serious student, you could train with the senior students, the red and black belts, whose sessions focused more on traditional material. The goal was student retention, which, Dad said, meant that he had to be willing to come and go with people. Carson had studied with an instructor in Boise who worked with only adults, and whose goal was to teach his students how to survive life-or-death confrontations. It was what the martial arts were originally about, Carson said. If students weren't happy with what his instructor was teaching them, they knew where the door was. I trained at my father's studio, and if Carson heard me complaining about the night's workout, he was ready with a story about the kind of training he'd had to do, most of it a lot of push-ups and sit-ups. There was a kind of purity to Carson's view of the martial arts, an intensity that came from his focus. He told me that he'd spent six months perfecting his middle punch, day after day working on the same technique. I was impressed by his discipline, but I preferred Dad's approach, which catered to my youthful short attention span. I guess you could say that Carson focused on the martial part of the martial arts, and Dad favored the art part of it.

They were like that in their poetry, too. Carson was a fan of James Dickey and Charles Simic. My father loved Robert Browning and Jorie Graham. Carson's poems were direct, concentrated. Dad's were evasive, diffuse. In Carson's work, what you might call rough men and women came up against a Nature that was even rougher, and sometimes beautiful, as well. In my father's poems, there are an awful lot of academics, who confront creatures borrowed from ancient myths, and who spend a lot of time thinking about what's happening to them. The funny thing is, they loved one another's writing. They always said that was why they had become friends. An editor who'd published both of them in her journal sent Dad an e-mail telling him he should check out Carson's poems. Dad did, liked what he read, and contacted Carson. "And thus," my mother likes to say, "was born the bromance of the century." They corresponded; they talked on the phone; they roomed together at conferences and festivals. Eventually, they lived under the same roof.

None of this, I realize, answers the question of what role, exactly, Carson played in my time of change. He didn't cause the change; although it began not long after he arrived at our house. My mother was away for a couple of weeks, visiting her mother in Scotland. I had become obsessed with a TV show called *River Monsters*, which was about an English naturalist and angler who traveled the world looking for rivers where people said they'd been attacked by monster fish. The star of the show, Jeremy Wade, would talk to the locals, do research, then go fishing for the monster. Of course, what he caught were never monsters, strictly speaking, but local fish that could have been responsible for the attacks: giant catfish, arapaima, bull sharks, sawfish, tiger fish, and more.

Inspired by the show, I asked my father if I could go fishing, and to my surprise, he said I could. (Maybe he was running out of ways to occupy me with Mom away; I can't remember.) We went to Walmart, where he bought me my first fishing rod, a Zebco spincast that came with a little plastic tackle box. Dad, who was not a fisherman, had watched a couple of YouTube videos on basic lure tying. We set up the rod and drove to a small pond he'd read online was full of fish and good for beginners. Later, he told me he was waiting to see how I would react if and when I hooked anything.

He found out with my second cast. A good sized largemouth bass took my lure, and suddenly, I was in a situation right out of *River Monsters*, fighting to bring in a fish that was fighting hard against me, splashing the water, jumping out of the pond as it tried to throw the hook. My rod bent. The line vibrated. I held on and drew the

ANCHOR

fish in. Dad was somewhere beside me, murmuring encouragement. As soon as I had the fish close enough to shore, I handed the rod to Dad, kneeled down, and took the fish by the lower lip. He thrashed so hard I almost lost my grip on him. But I didn't, and I guess you might say that the fish never lost his grip on me, either. I knew, as surely as I've known anything, that I had found my life's passion, the same as my father had when he first read *The Ring and the Book*. On the drive home, I was already planning my next fishing trip—was already planning a lifetime of fishing trips.

I have to admit, right from the start, my parents supported my fishing. They took me to all the local lakes and ponds, rivers and creeks, and to some that weren't all that local, too. If they had friends who fished, they invited them to join us so that their friends could give me pointers on my technique. They found instructional videos for me to watch on YouTube. They subscribed to *Bass Pro* for me. But despite all of this, fishing wasn't something either of my parents truly shared with me. No matter how many spots they drove me to, they weren't interested in picking up a rod and joining me in trying to catch something. Instead, whichever one of them had taken me brought a book, which they would sit reading while I fished. Now that I'm older, I can appreciate how much they did for me just taking me out as much as they did. At the time, though, I wanted more of a connection with them over fishing.

This was where Carson came in. He had grown up fishing in Idaho. In fact, his father had been a professional guide in the Salmon River part of the state, leading parties of businessmen along the river for week-long fishing trips. Carson had accompanied his dad on numerous trips, and he had plenty of stories about his adventures trying to hook fish in all kinds of terrain, in all kinds of conditions. He was full of stories about his father's fishing experiences, too, though a lot of these had to do with the characters his dad had contracted to guide, including at least one group of Mafioso who flew in from Seattle. It was Carson who first gave me the idea that I could be a guide, too, and that I could have a good life doing so (which my parents were concerned about; although they denied it). If I returned home having made a big catch, Carson was there to give me his approval, fisherman to fisherman. A "Good job!" from him made me swell with pride, made my head feel as if it was brushing the ceiling. The funny thing was, in all the time he stayed with us, I can't remember him coming to fish with me once. It didn't matter. His praise, his support, did.

Carson left my house with much less warning than I'd had before he arrived. My father was the one who told me Carson was going. It was a Sunday night. I suppose I'd known that Carson would be moving out at some point. After all, from the start, my parents had said he was going to stay with us until he got back on his feet, which implied a time when he would walk off on his own. I did my best not to show how surprised I was (because I was almost twelve and concerned with acting mature). Instead, I asked Dad when Carson was planning to go. "Tuesday, I think," he said. This seemed pretty soon to me. "Where's he going?" I asked. "To our friend, Gaetan's, in Gloucester," he said. This seemed pretty far away, too. "Why does he have to go now?" I asked. "It's time for Carson to move on," Dad said.

That was what he did, setting out for Massachusetts while I was at school on Tuesday. I tried talking to him on Monday night, as I was helping him retrieve the last of the stuff he'd stored in our garage and load it into his truck. He was distracted, as though his mind was already on the road east. I kept making conversation, mentioning fishing spots my father had yet to take me to, the species of fish that were supposed to inhabit them, the lures I planned to use. Carson answered in short, vague sentences. There was so much more I wanted to say to him, a lot of it things I didn't know how to put into words. I'm glad you've been here with us. Thank you for supporting my fishing. Please don't go. I left all of it unsaid, and then he was gone.

My dad and Carson stayed in touch, via e-mail and the occasional phone call. They saw one another at the occasional conference. After almost a year in Gloucester, Carson left for Toronto, where he stayed until this past spring, when Dad said he was on the move again, this time for Iceland. Over the years, I've talked to him a couple of times, when he's called for my father and I've answered the phone. There

ANCHOR

isn't much to our conversations. He asks me how the fishing's going, and I tell him. He might offer a suggestion as to lures. Before I pass the phone to my dad, Carson says, "Sounds like you're doing great. Keep at it. You'll be running your own guide business in no time." Absurd as it might sound, those words never fail to make me feel better, to hope—to believe that someday, I'll be leading men and women into the wilderness to fish. If and when I do, it will be because Carson Lochyer supported me, never stopped encouraging me.

Sometimes, I think it would be nice to have Carson with me when I set out on my first tour. Then I realize, he will be.

III

> The blade burns in the grip of the noble
> Heart. Take it, and your heart be made known.
> James Ogin "Dyrnwyn"

Of course, Will won't mention the incident with the enormous bear in his essay, in part because his father will not have explained how the creature's appearance connects to Carson, exactly. In all fairness to his dad, Will will have avoided asking for such an explanation, on the let-sleeping-dogs-(or bears)-lie principle. On top of that, the event will seem too strange to write down and hope to be believed. Nor will Will mention something that happened a couple of days prior to Carson's decision to leave, but that, with the passage of time, seems to have heralded it. It occurred in the evening, after homework and dinner. He was at the family computer, playing Hungry Games. Due to the unusually warm weather, the windows in the computer room were up, admitting a slight breeze, which nudged the curtains. So involved was Will in surviving to the death match portion of the game and then, once there, in defeating the other finalists, that it took a while for him to register the voices outside the windows: his father and Carson, promenading back and forth along the stone path that ran from the front steps to the driveway. As interested in the conversations of adults as any boy his age, Will rose from the computer chair and moved to the couch, which sat below the windows. Lowering his head to give the impression he'd switched places in order to read, he glanced outside.

His dad was wearing a pair of old karate pants and the black T-shirt printed with the *Famous Monsters of Filmland* cover showing Godzilla and Gamera squaring off. Carson was dressed in long, olive shorts and a faded red T-shirt with the Flash's yellow lightning bolt on it. Dad's hands were clasped behind his back, which, Will had learned, he did to aid the impression he was taking what you were saying to him seriously. Carson's hands were a flurry of motion, in front of him, at his sides, back in front of him, weaving through the air as they did when he was speaking about something that mattered to him. Will looked down at his imaginary book. He couldn't hear much of what his father, who tended to talk softly, was saying. It was easier to distinguish Carson's words, though not what they were referring to. "Absolutely," he said.

Dad murmured.

"The weather, for one thing. It was like this the last time."

Dad said something that ended in, "—incidence?"

"Not with the dreams," Carson said. "Not together like this."

Dad asked another question.

"A sign."

"Where?" Dad said.

"Somewhere close," Carson said. "I don't think there'd be anything on your property, not yet. But somewhere close."

Will couldn't hear his father's next remark, but the nod he gave toward the driveway suggested he was inviting Carson to walk it. "Yeah, sure, that's a good idea," Carson said, and the two of them set off in that direction.

There was fishing gear in the back of the SUV that Will had been meaning to bring in since yesterday. He tugged on his sneakers and hurried outside. While he opened the hatch and unloaded his tackle box, net, and rods, he kept an eye on his dad and Carson. They were ambling up the driveway, pausing every few yards to peer into the woods on either side of it. Whatever they were searching for amidst the maple, oak, and cedar remained elusive, since they continued toward the road. By the time Will had run his equipment into the house and returned to close the hatch, his father and Carson had covered half the driveway's length. Will leapt, caught the hatch, and heaved it shut. Then he took off after Dad and Carson.

The two of them glanced back at the slap of his sneakers on the dirt. His father half-turned to face him. "Hey, wee man. What's up?"

ANCHOR

"Oh, not much," Will said. "Whatcha doing?"

"We are looking for something," Dad said.

"What?"

"We're not exactly sure," Dad said.

"Something…with fire," Carson said.

"Is someone setting fires on our property?" Will said.

"No," Dad said. "We're just checking something out. You can help, if you want. Always good to have another pair of eyes."

"Sure," Will said. He liked being included in his father's and Carson's activities.

"Good," Dad said.

Together, they climbed the driveway as it rose to the street. Will stared into the ranks of trees, their branches stripped by autumn, but saw no tell-tale flashes of orange. This past week, the days had been hot and dry, dangerous conditions should a spark fall on the leaves matting the ground. His father wasn't acting all that concerned, but tension poured off Carson like a fever. Will was aware that his dad and Carson had continued the conversation whose fragments he'd overheard, only stopping when he joined them, and whatever its substance had been hung in the air between them.

They reached the end of the driveway a couple of minutes after the sun had lowered behind the ridge on the far side of their little valley. Like cobblestones, clouds formed a path that led down after the hidden sun, whose glow dyed the clouds a deep, purplish pink. Will, his dad, and Carson scanned the trees around them, on the other side of the street. From the placid expression on his father's face, Will could tell that he considered whatever he and Carson were discussing settled, and in his favor. Dad loved to be right. Once, when Will was younger, he'd run across the expression, "He'd rather be right than President," in an old comic strip he was reading. After his mom explained what it meant to him, he said, "Like Dad." Which made her laugh and tell him not to say that to his father. It was true, though, and one of the qualities he least liked in his father.

"There." Carson pointed across the road—at first, Will thought, to the trees over there, which didn't make any sense, because they'd looked at them already and not seen anything. His vision adjusted, and he realized that Carson had seen something through the trees, near the top of the ridge opposite them. It was a line of fire, as if someone had poured gasoline along a hundred-foot stretch of the hill and touched a match to it. In the evening light, the flames rose and rippled orange. As the three of them watched, the line shifted. Its ends curved, the left lower, the right higher, the left swinging underneath the line, the right arcing over it, until the ends met in the line's center, turning it into a figure-eight. Almost as quickly as they met, the ends whipped out in their original directions. It was as if, Will thought, they were watching a performance, a group of dancers, each one carrying a torch, executing a series of carefully-choreographed steps. Except there appeared to be no breaks in the line, which you would have expected there to be, if it was composed of separate people. Instead, they seemed to be looking at a solid line of flame, behaving in ways Will had never heard of fire acting.

A handful of trees on the ridge had ignited. Will could pick out additional spots where the ground was burning. The flaming line writhed like a snake. Will was waiting for his father, for Carson, to say something, but neither man did, caught up in the distant spectacle. Finally, he said, "Shouldn't we call 911?"

Dad and Carson started, jostled from whatever thoughts the spectacle had kindled in them. The whine of a local siren, followed close behind by those of neighboring stations, announced that someone had notified the fire department first. The three of them witnessed the line of flame curl into a spiral, which tightened into a circle, which fell apart into a dozen smaller conflagrations that splashed themselves onto trees, lighting them. Dad and Carson took this as their cue to turn around and start back toward the house. Will accompanied them.

Later that night, the odor of charred wood drifted into Will's room, through the windows he'd left open because of the heat.

IV

The eyes are difficult.
Carson Lochyer "Taxidermy"

The July after he turns twenty-seven, Will and Manda (then still his girlfriend) will drive to a spacious house outside of Brattleboro, Vermont, for a week's stay. It will be a working vacation. Manda brings books with her so

ANCHOR

she can study for the New York State bar exam. Will brings his fishing rods, tackle, and notebook so he can explore possible destinations for the fishing guide business he's finally started. The house at which they stay is a blended living room and kitchen surrounded by eight plain bedrooms and two and a half bathrooms; in the winter, it rents to ski parties. Will has the idea that, in the summer, it might accommodate fishing groups, which he's shared with the house's owner, gaining a modest discount on the charge for the week.

There's a half-stocked bookcase on one side of the living room, its shelves full of thrift-store rescues. Will flips through them, a habit picked up from his parents, who are unable to enter a room with a bookcase without inspecting its contents. The majority of the books are split between mysteries and spy thrillers, Agatha Christie and Sue Grafton rubbing elbows with Robert Ludlum and Len Deighton. In amongst them, Will finds a thick paperback, its red cover faded to burnt orange. On the spine, he reads *Shardik*, and under it, Richard Adams. He recognizes the name from his mother's bookshelves: it's one of the novels she's taught in her young adult literature class, *Watership Down*. She encouraged him to read the book; he started it, but can't remember finishing it. He slides *Shardik* out for a look. From the center of the cover, a bear's head stares at him. The artist has drawn it mounted on a wooden disk like a hunting trophy, but has left the eyes empty, giving the head the appearance of a mask. Though hardly the most realistic illustration he's encountered, something about it makes him pause, consider it before slotting it back between its companions.

Later that same day, though, after an exploratory trip to a local creek and a dinner of Chinese take-out, Will returns for *Shardik*. Manda is on the living room couch, surrounded by law books. He carries the novel to the easy chair across from her, settles into it, and opens the book. Between the drive here and the afternoon's fishing, he's pretty tired, and anticipates nodding off after the first couple of pages, especially in such a comfortable chair.

To his surprise, he doesn't fall asleep. He stays awake until two in the morning, long past Manda's retreat to bed, unable to stop reading Adams's story of Kelderek, hunter in an invented land, and Shardik, the great bear Kelderek takes as a god. The narrative begins with the bear crashing through the trees of a forest on fire, and that image, of a creature prehistorically large, wreathed in flame, lights his mind's eye for the remainder of the night, and for the next four days, which is how long it takes him to finish the book.

It's been a while since a work of fiction has affected him this profoundly. During his visits to nearby creeks, part of him remains inside the narrative. Or it remains inside him: he isn't sure which statement is correct, only that, were Shardik himself to burst out of the sugar maples, his fur smoldering, and plunge steaming into the stream Will is wading, he would not be surprised. Planning this trip, he was worried that he might be bored after he finished his day's fishing and Manda was still deep in her textbooks, as she had cautioned him she would be. Adams's novel solves the problem before it arises.

Will does not dream of his and his father's confrontation with their own enormous bear, almost fifteen years gone by. If asked about this, he might admit it strange, or might shrug it off. A couple of times as he's reading, that distant night bobs at the surface of his thoughts, but it's swept away by the novel's progress.

When he and Manda leave the house, Will takes the book with him, something he has never done before. For the next ten years, the copy of *Shardik* accompanies him whenever he sets off on a fishing trip of any length. He rereads it on airplanes, on trains, and on ferries. He rereads it by the light of campfires, of ancient light bulbs, of assorted flashlights. Over time, the glue binding the book fails, and he resorts to a heavy rubber band to maintain the novel's integrity. At last, when he's guiding a group of advertising executives up French Creek in Idaho (not that far from where Carson grew up), the rubber band breaks, sending the pages of the novel swirling off on the breeze that's been blowing. Will succeeds in retrieving a few of the pages, but the majority of the book is gone, floating on the surface of the creek, above the trout with their empty gold eyes.

V

> Here, in the combustion of dry wood, may
> The pistoning of creation's engine be
> Glimpsed.
>
> James Ogin "Pyromancy"

February of his thirty-fifth year, Will will be struck by the worst case of the flu he ever has had or will have. It's a direct result of his skipping the

ANCHOR

year's vaccine, which he did for no good reason that he can recall. He was busy: with the guide business that's gone much better than he'd hoped; with Dana, his and Manda's older daughter, whose kindergarten class encourages active parental participation in its curriculum; with Flora, their younger daughter, who's been putting her big sister's record of the terrible twos to shame. Manda, returned to her law firm in Wiltwyck after a long maternity leave following the complications of Flora's birth, had been preoccupied with a defense for which she was supposed to be junior counsel, but which she was pretty much running, and Will has tried to step in to allow her the extra time she needed for the case. He meant to have himself vaccinated—he always does—but the early report pronounced this year's flu neither particularly contagious nor virulent, especially compared to those of the last couple of years, so if he couldn't find the time for his annual inoculation, he figured he'd probably be fine.

The extent of his error becomes clear the moment the disease overtakes him. He's sitting on the couch in his study, reading a memoir of fly-fishing the Catskills one of his mother's colleagues published a couple of years ago, and that he's been meaning to open ever since a copy arrived in the mail, autographed and with a personal message to him. The room is uncomfortably warm around him. He wonders if Manda, always complaining that he sets the thermostat too low, has adjusted it upward. His head is light, the way it is when he's gone too long between meals and his blood sugar crashes. Bookmarking his page with his index finger, he goes to stand, and the shivering starts. It begins as a trembling that keeps him seated, and swiftly escalates to a shaking that convulses his arms and legs as if he's having a seizure. His teeth rattle together with such force, they blur his vision. He loses his grip on the book, which flops to the floor. The sound catches the notice of Manda, on her way into her study. She alters course and enters his room. "Hon?" she says. "Are you okay?"

"Flu," Will wants to say, because that's what it is, he knows, but all he can pronounce is a stuttered "f."

It's enough for Manda, who says, "Oh God, you're sick, aren't you?" While he's trying to nod, she places her hand on his forehead. "You're burning up," she says. "Hang on. We'll get you taken care of."

For the next week, Will spends his days and nights on the pull-out bed in his study. Much of the time, he's asleep, which is fine, because when he isn't, he feels terrible. Every muscle in his body aches, as if he's received the mother of all beatings. If he has to stand to go to the bathroom, his arms and legs seem to be wrapped in lead. When he coughs, his chest is full of razor blades, his temples pound. Worst of all is the fever, which quickly soars to the dangerous heights above 104 and dips only a little with the administering of aspirin. After a day and a half of the highest readings she's seen on a thermometer, Manda phones the family doctor. The nurse to whom she speaks gives her a list of instructions, most of which she's following already, and tells her that if Will's temperature persists at this level through the night, she's going to have to take him to the emergency room. At the nurse's recommendation, Manda fills the bathtub with cool water and empties all the ice trays in the freezer into it. Through a combination of jollying and bullying, she raises Will off the pull-out bed, leads him into the bathroom, and undresses him. Standing this near his bare skin, she feels the fever burning in it. She guides Will into the water, cold and clattering with ice cubes, as their two girls watch from the doorway in wide-eyed fascination.

For Will, the ice-bath happens at a distance, as if he's watching it on the TV on the other side of the living room. He sees himself leaning forward so Manda can scoop water from the bath with one of the girls' bath toys and pour it over his head and neck. The spill and splash of the water sounds faint, as if the volume on the TV has been lowered almost to zero. Ice cubes bob against his legs and back; the contact registers as a faint disturbance. He understands that the water in which he's sitting, which his wife continues to tip over his shoulders, his back, is cool, blessedly so, but his understanding makes scant difference to the conflagration raging beneath his skin. Absurdly, he remembers a phrase from a poem his father read to him, years ago, about a man on fire, consumed by a gift he had not asked for, but had earned. Who wrote that, Dad or Carson? Or someone else?

While the bathroom, Manda, have remained at a remove from Will, another vista has opened for him, as if someone has switched on a second TV, this one closer to him. On its screen, he sees the end of a driveway, the portion of road to which it connects. It's nighttime, the only illumination offered by a green lamppost set back ten feet from the street. Will recognizes Mr. Tumnus's Lamp, the driveway to his parents' house. The trees bare of all but a handful of leaves tell him that it's autumn. At the limit of the lamp-

ANCHOR

post's glow, a pair of figures stand facing the road and the woods across it. One is holding a *do*, a curved Korean sword, in a middle guard. The other has leveled a *qiang*, a Chinese spear, toward the opposite side of the street. Will knows the scene from twenty-three years before, but a number of the details are wrong. His father and he look not as they did then, but as they do now. Dad is thinner, slightly stooped, his beard and hair fully white. Will is wearing the white Joe's Flies T-shirt and grey sweatpants that are his sleeping attire. The woods across from them have changed, the maples and oaks replaced by a thicket like simplified drawings of trees, tall trunks leading up to round crowns of green leaves. From somewhere within the new trees, orange light flickers.

As this scene appears closer to him, its images more distinct, so are its other details more vivid, as if he's drifting into this space. The spear's polished wood is smooth in his palms. His shoulders and upper arms ache from holding the weapon in one position for so long. The night air is warm, threaded with an odor like oranges on the turn. A breeze rustles the weird trees, whose leaves clash together with a metallic sound. His father's breaths are deep, steady. In a low voice, he's reciting a poem he and Will's mom have quoted back and forth to one another for as long as he can remember:

So rested he by the Tumtum tree
And stood awhile in thought.

And, as in uffish thought he stood,
The Jabberwock, with eyes of flame,
Came whiffling through the tulgey wood,
And burbled as it came!

The orange light brightens, tinting the trunks and crowns of the trees. A wave of heat rolls over the road, enveloping Will and his dad. He blinks at the sudden dryness in his eyes. A chorus of creaks and moans issues from the trees. Their leaves crackle and crisp, shriveling brown. Sweat slides down Will's face, soaks his T-shirt, his sweatpants. The wood of the *qiang* is warm in his hands. Orange light floods the woods across the street, joined now by a rushing sound, as if a great wind is sweeping up the hillside. Will's mouth is tacky, his clothes drenched. He removes his right hand from the spear long enough to drag the back of it across his forehead and eyebrows, to wipe the sweat from his eyes. Inside the orange glow, there's something moving, a patch of darker orange mixed with yellow and red. It brushes against a tree, and the trunk detonates with a *BANG!* that Will feels in his chest. The crowns of the strange trees, full moments ago, are naked, each stripped to an intricate weave of branches, their leaves reduced to a fall of dust. The moving form draws closer, gaining definition with each step. The bark of the weird trees blackens, seems to bubble as if metallic and melting. Each breath burns Will's throat, his lungs. Another tree bursts, almost at the road. Will ducks, jerking the spear up in defense. Pieces of sizzling wood fly past him.

"Steady," his father says. "He's almost here." He's panting with the heat himself.

As if to fulfill his dad's prediction, the shape at the heart of the light steps between a pair of trees onto the road. It's a bear, its massive bulk wrapped in flame. Fire runs up its front and rear legs in long, orange tongues. Fire rages along its sides, its back, in flickering sheets. Fire envelops its blunt head, vents from its eyes, its mouth, its nostrils. Despite the inferno surrounding it, the bear is not consumed, nor does it move with the panic and agony of a creature dying. It raises its snout and considers Will and his dad through fiery eyes.

Somehow, Will manages enough spit to speak. "Dad?"

"Uh-huh?"

"What the fuck is this?"

"Language," his father says.

"Seriously?"

"Seriously."

"Fine," he says, amazed to find that even in a situation of such extremity as this, his dad can exasperate him. "What is this?"

"This is our pledge," Dad says, "to a friend."

"Carson."

"Yes."

"I don't understand."

"I'm not certain I do, either."

"Dad?"

"Uh-huh?"

ANCHOR

"I'm scared."

"Me, too," his father says. "Every time, I think it'll be easier. Somehow, it never is."

"What do you mean?"

"Never mind. Don't worry if you're afraid. My sphincter's got all it can do to control itself. Just stand and be true."

"Huh."

"What?"

"That's nice," Will says. "'Stand and be true.' Did you write it?"

"Thank Stephen King."

"If this thing comes any closer, I won't be thanking anyone for anything."

"He won't," Dad says. "*What he's searching for isn't here.* It hasn't been for a long, long time."

The bear narrows its eyes. The flames swirling around it flare, too bright to endure. Will shuts his eyes against the blaze, the insides of his eyelids lit red. This would be a perfect moment for the creature to charge, while the two of them are blinded. Although the *qiang* burns in his hands, he keeps its point aimed at the bear, hoping that, should it rush them, it'll strike the end of the spear before the rest of the weapon bursts into flame.

"Steady," his father says. "*What he wants isn't here.*"

The interiors of Will's eyelids glow white. Heat scorches his face, his arms. His clothes smolder.

"Stand," Dad says. "*Stand*, William."

"WILLIAM!"

Manda's shout is accompanied by a pail full of water dashed in Will's face. A single ice cube smacks his right cheek, directly below the eye. Will splashes backward in the tub, hands raised against the second pail of water his wife is preparing. The bathroom telescopes right up to him. "Okay," he says, "okay, okay."

"Are you all right?" Manda says. "Because for a second there, it looked like you were having a seizure."

A seizure? he thinks. *Is that what all that was?* "I'm okay," he says, lowering his hands. "I'm still sick, but I think the fever's gone down."

"Really?"

"Yeah." He says this mostly to reassure Manda, but the words sound as if they might be true.

They are. The worst of his fever has passed, and while he will continue to feel the flu's effects for days to come, he will not experience the same sense of dislocation—of relocation, of what he supposes must have been a febrile hallucination. (He doesn't believe it was a seizure.) For a couple of weeks after he's better, Will considers phoning his parents, sharing his overheated brain's invention with his dad. *Maybe*, he thinks, *the old man can get a poem out of it*. A couple of times, he has the cell in hand, his parents' number onscreen.

He doesn't, though, for a reason he can't specify. Next year, however, he's first in line for his flu shot.

VI

> Do not run, the Park Service pamphlet warns—instead, turn,
> Raise your arms, make yourself menacing,
> Or the big cat will pounce.
>
> Carson Lochyer "The Puma"

September of the year he turns forty, Will and Manda will take the girls out of school for two weeks for a family trip to Provence. They'll go to meet Will's mother and father, there for a two-day conference devoted to his father's and Carson's poetry, which is being held at the *Université d'Avignon*. There's a chance Carson will join them. After moving from Toronto to Iceland, his dad's friend has continued eastward across the Atlantic, first to the northwest of Scotland for almost five years, then on to Holland, Germany, and now Finland, to a small town in Lapland whose name Will has saved on his phone because he finds it impossible to remember.

Through his father, Will has learned of Carson's rumblings of another departure, this one for a destination still more remote, Nepal or Mongolia. For the foreseeable future, Provence is likely his best chance to introduce Carson to his wife and children, none of whom has met him, since Carson rarely ventures back in the direction from which he came. Even his Pulitzer a couple of years ago could not dislodge him from his log cabin above the Arctic Circle; instead, Will's dad collected it for him. Will himself has not

ANCHOR

seen Carson in person since his departure from his parents' house almost three decades gone by. The desire to do so now grips him. From brief phone conversations and e-mail exchanges he's had with Carson over the years, as well as from what his father has told him, Will knows that Carson is aware of his career as a fishing guide, has read the write-ups on him in *Bass Pro* and *Sports Illustrated*, and has watched the clips of his appearances on a couple of the better fishing shows. But Will wants to see him in person, to shake his hand and thank him for his long-ago support. He wants to show him his wife and children, the best parts of his life. These last few years, there have been a couple of times he's been in close enough proximity to Carson's current address to consider dropping in for a visit, only to be dissuaded by his father. "You know Carson," Dad's said to Will's calls to check his address, "he's funny about his privacy." Will has heeded his dad's words and respected Carson's privacy; now, though, if Carson is joining them, then there's nothing to be concerned about. He even nourishes a secret hope of convincing Carson to accompany him for a little fishing on a couple of the local streams and has packed an extra rod in case that hope becomes reality.

It does not. In fact, Carson does not fly down to meet them after all. In response to the news, Will's parents offer one another a philosophical shrug. Dana and Flora barely register the news, while Manda expresses her regret for Will's sake. His parents know the region, to which they've been traveling since before Will's birth, sufficiently well to take the family on a number of day trips: to Nîmes, Les Baux, Arles, Les Saintes Maries de la Mer, and Aigues-Mortes. Both girls demonstrate a facility with French that surprises and pleases Will and Manda; by the end of their first week there, Dana and Flora are carrying on short, basic conversations in the language with their grandparents. Informed by their previous trips to the area, plus the advice of some of the professors and students from the university, the six of them search out fine restaurant after fine restaurant for lunch and dinner. Even Manda, whose parents ran a restaurant in Wiltwyck and is usually difficult to please in such matters, has no complaints. Will fishes here and there, but not as much as he—or any of the other members of his family—was anticipating. Strange as it sounds, he can't move past his annoyance with Carson for not showing up. *How many more chances*, he thinks, *are we going to have to see one another?*

He talks to his father about it over lunch on a day when his mom, Manda, and the girls are away at the open markets outside Aigues-Mortes. Dad doesn't say anything while he's speaking, eating his *croque-monsieur et frites* with his head cocked slightly to one side in what Will thinks of as his listening pose. The depth of emotion in his voice, the venom with which he treats Carson's peculiarities, surprises Will. Once he's finished, he sits watching his father, half-eager for him to argue with his complaint.

Instead, his dad says, "You're right. Carson can be a real asshole."

"What?"

"How hard would it have been for him to fly here? He could have spent a night and left the next morning. The university would have paid for everything; although, it's not as if he couldn't have afforded it. Trust me: the Pulitzer does wonders for your bank account."

The bitterness in his father's words shocks Will. "Dad," he says, unsure what to say next.

"Never mind," his dad says with a grimace. "You brought another rod with you, right? Let's go fishing."

Will recognizes his father's tactic, attempting to use fishing to distract him from what's bothering him. It's a familiar technique, one his dad has employed to meet any number of disappointments in Will's life, from the end of high school romances to failing his driver's test the first time he sat it. He hasn't used it for years, since a particularly difficult spell he and Manda went through after Flora was born. While his father has written about fishing in some of his poems, he's never been enamored of actual angling. For him to suggest it to Will is an index of his concern and love. "All right," Will says. "Why not? Let's go catch some trout."

No clear destination in mind, the two of them take his parents' rented Renault south, toward the Camargue with its marshes and canals. The afternoon is warm and bright. A French pop song neither of them can understand pulses from the radio. A series of right-hand turns down increasingly-smaller roads takes them, eventually, to a dirt parking lot off the left hand side of the road, next to a canal running between tall, thick reeds. It's as likely a spot as any. Will ties a couple of multi-purpose lures to the ends of their lines, and they set out along the water, following a path through the reeds made, Will supposes, by other fishermen. Within five minutes, the car is out of sight behind them. Were it not for a contrail tracking a jet's progress across the blue bowl of the sky, he and his father

ANCHOR

might have stepped back one hundred, two hundred, five hundred years into the past. On their left, the reeds fall back from a patch of grass sloping to the water. "This should do me fine," Dad says. Will fishes the spot with him for a few minutes, then sets off deeper into the reeds. He isn't worried about his father catching anything; already, Dad's eyes are focusing on that middle distance in which he appears to sight most of his poems. Reeds clatter against one another as Will pushes them aside. Ahead, on his right, there's something beside the path.

It's a piece of stone, rectangular, rising out of the earth like a headstone. Gray-white, its upper left corner worn away, its surface spider-webbed with cracks, the marker gives the impression of considerable age. This feeling is reinforced by the image barely visible on it. Executed in the plain style of a medieval woodcut, a strange animal rears on its hind legs between a pair of simple trees. It's been carved in profile, and at first, Will thinks it's supposed to be a lion. The tail is wrong, though, segmented, insectile, capped with what appears to be a miniature sun. Nor is the head any more accurate: rather than following the line of the back, it rises into what might be a man's head (the wear is especially bad here). Unfamiliar symbols have been cut into the picture's border, a circle broken at about the five o'clock mark, a double arch, a downward-facing crescent, others faded beyond identification. Will glances side to side, on the lookout for other markers. He isn't sure what the purpose of the stone was. Neither its position nor its decoration indicate it stationed a pilgrimage route; nor is Will aware of major local battles it might commemorate. Probably a legend or tradition of the region. His father will know; he'll ask him on the way back.

The two hours Will passes fishing the canal slide by in a dazzle of late-afternoon sunlight and sweltering heat. A couple of times, a fish investigates his lure, only to swim off without taking it. The sun turns the water platinum. Something rattles the reeds across the canal from him, but does not show itself. Random mosquitoes brave the heat and light for a chance at his blood; he crushes them against his arms and neck in red asterisks. Brightness fills his eyes, makes everything around him seem faded, less substantial. ("Easy," his father says, somewhere in the recesses of his memory.) Finally, he decides he's sat beside this stretch of water long enough. He hooks the lure to his rod and heads back toward the spot he left his dad.

On the way, he intends to have another look at the stone marker with its strange creature. He should have taken a picture of it with his phone. He'll remedy that oversight when he reaches it. At the place where the stone rectangle stood, however, there's nothing. Did he misjudge the marker's location? He walks ahead fifteen, twenty feet, doubles back, peering into the reeds. Nothing. Could he have taken another path? It seems unlikely: there's the canal a few feet behind him. He must have passed the rectangle longer ago than he realized. He shakes his head, still fuzzy with the heat.

As he continues on the path to the spot he left his father, Will notices that the landscape around him has fallen silent. There's the clack of the reeds striking one another when he brushes them, the pad of his shoes on the earth, and that is all. No birds chirp or cluck or take flight with a whir. No insects whine or buzz or hum. No cars are faintly audible in the distance. He looks up, and sees no airplanes crossing the sky, the contrail he observed earlier long since blown away. It's as if there's only him, the canal, and the reeds.

And something else, he realizes. A kind of quiet within the quiet, out in the reeds maybe twenty feet to his left. He's spent enough time out of doors—sometimes very far out of doors—to know that there's an animal in the reeds, keeping pace with him. He isn't certain what it could be. A deer? A dog, patrolling the border of whoever's property he's encroached upon? Hasn't he read about an uptick in the number of feral pigs in Europe? No, it's bigger than that. What if whatever it is came upon his father first? He knows he should maintain a measured pace, in order not to provoke a predator to the chase, but the best he can hold himself to is a kind of race-walk.

He finds his dad where he left him, slumped forward: asleep. Will shakes him awake and hustles him to the car before his father completely understands what's happening. He grumbles that Will interrupted a perfectly wonderful nap, but his voice is more amused than irritated. "Thought I'd checked out, did you?" his father says.

"Dad," Will says.

His dad assumes that the tightness of Will's jaw, the speed with which he drives back to the hotel in Avignon, are symptoms of his panic at thinking he'd found his father dead. Not until dinner, when they have met up with Manda and the girls and his mom, does Will reveal the true cause of his agitation, the animal pacing him. Manda, Dana, and Flora find his account of the experience giggle-inducing, and his concern at a possible feral pig pushes them to outright laughter, which his mother cannot restrain herself from joining in. Only his father does not laugh; although his lips grow thin from suppressing a smile. "Well," he says, "what do you think it was now?" "I don't know," Will says. "Probably a rat," an answer which provokes a fresh burst of hilarity from the women at the table. "I'll tell you, though, it felt like whatever was out there was huge. Like, if I had seen a giant head rising out of the reeds, it wouldn't have shocked me."

Dana controls her laughter long enough to ask, "What kind of head?"

"A head," Will says. "I don't know, a person's head."

Over the girls' laughter, his dad says, "What makes you say that?" He is no longer fighting a smile.

"It was just how it felt," Will says. He's tempted to attribute the image to what was carved on the stone marker he found, but the continuing giggles of his wife, daughters, and mother has soured his desire to offer fresh material for their amusement.

"Huh," Dad says.

"You going to use that in a poem?" Will says.

"Could be."

Later that night, while they're preparing for bed, Will tells Manda about the marker. She isn't sure what its purpose was, either. Somewhere in the depths of the night, he dreams he's facing a wall of reeds behind which something enormous is lifting into view. He sees flames. If he sees any more, though, it remains locked in the dream.

VII

>Within this round might two men find friendship,
>The fraternity of shared interest
>In the world's secret language.
>   James Ogin "Rosenkreuz Serves Tea"

Much of the year he turns forty-two, Will will spend away from home. In the late winter, he'll accompany a pair of investment bankers to the Salmon River in western New York state, where he'll instruct them in fishing for salmon.

Throughout spring, summer, and a good part of the fall, he'll be booked solid taking groups of aspiring anglers into the Catskills to try for trout. Early the next winter, he'll fly to Peru with a group of lawyers to a lodge with whose owner he's become friendly, where he'll teach those members of the legal profession to bait a hook for the local fish. It will be the busiest he's been since he started the guide business, in part because he won't feel able to turn away any of the bookings and the money they'll add to the household budget. Dana will tag along on a couple of trips to the Catskills, and both girls will travel down to Peru with him, but otherwise, he won't see a great deal of them.

At the same time, Manda, who made partner in her firm the previous year, will be lead defense counsel for a case in which a local ophthalmologist is being sued for malpractice by a patient whose eye essentially collapsed during routine cataract surgery, which would be tricky enough, were the plaintiff not the mother of the state's attorney general. Her life will be an unending stream of phone calls, text messages, e-mails, and meetings, meetings with fellow counsel, with their client, with expert witnesses of various stripes. Between them, she and Will will joke, they contribute significantly to the local take-out places; though they'll strive for at least one sit-down family dinner every week (or two).

During this time, Will's mother will come for two extended visits, the first early in the summer, when she'll stay for four weeks, the second in the fall, when she'll stay for the five and a half weeks of Manda's trial. While she prepares dinner for whoever happens to be around, it's mostly to be with her granddaughters that she makes the trip from the house out in Bourne to which she and Will's dad have relocated since she retired from the college and he turned his *dojang* over to the black belt who'd been his right-hand woman for years. At twelve and nine, respectively, Dana and Flora still require the presence of an adult (though Dana contests this). Will's mom talks books with Dana, who is an inveterate reader, and listens to the chapters of the novel her older granddaughter is writing. She drives Flora to the farm where her pony boards and assists her in Clover's care. She takes the girls to the movies, on excursions to local parks, and to the art museum over at Penrose College. She makes them waffles for breakfast, grilled cheese sandwiches for lunch, and chicken korma for dinner. When she comes in the fall, she brings her dog, Dinah, with her. A gold and white boxer-bull mix, Dinah licks everyone and everything with her long tongue; the girls adore her and argue passionately over whose turn it is to walk her.

At the end of his mother's second stay, Will takes her to dinner. Manda, whose case has concluded in victory for her client, has taken Dana and Flora for a girls' night out to their favorite restaurant, and though she invited her mother-in-law to accompany them, Will's mom demurred, saying that the girls needed time with their mother. Home from a late-season trip out near Roscoe, Will suggests a jaunt into Joppenburgh for a meal at Widow Jane's, a new-ish restaurant whose smoked fish pie has drawn a number of favorable reviews, including one from *The New York Times*. She agrees, and in short order, the two of them are seated at a small table at the front of the busy restaurant. His mom has a Guinness; he has a Coke with lemon. Much of their pre- and dinner conversation concerns the girls: Dana's struggle with an obnoxious clique at school, Flora's newfound anxieties about death, and the girls' spats and squabbles with one another. As their plates are being cleared, dessert menus produced and considered, Will relates a couple of anecdotes about his most recent client, both of them of the can-you-believe-how-the-rich-behave variety. When his Irish coffee and Mom's apple-berry crumble have been served, Will says, "So: what do you have planned now? A month of rest and relaxation?" His mother laughs. "No, I'm afraid I'm off again the day after I get back. Your father's accepting Carson's Bollingen for him, so we have to drive to Yale. Dad's doing a reading and signing while we're there. He might be visiting a couple of classes, too. At least it's close."

"Dad's accepted so many of Carson's awards, I'm surprised no one's tried to prove they're the same person."

"Once upon a time, someone might have. These days, though, there's enough documentation of Carson online for anyone who wants to verify his existence to do so. Not to mention, every few years, an enterprising young scholar tracks him down to whatever location he's retreated to and flatters an interview out of him."

"When was the last time Dad saw him?"

"They video-chat once a week. They haven't seen each other in person for a few years. The last time...I'm pretty sure it was while we were in Amsterdam for the Tang Soo Do internationals. Carson was renting an old farmhouse on a canal. Your father went out to have dinner with him. He said he might come in to watch Dad compete, but..."

"He didn't."

"He's always been funny about crowds."

"Unlike Dad," Will says.

"Yes," his mom says. "Protest all he likes to the contrary, Dad never met a group of people he didn't immediately try to win over. And succeed, most of the time. It helped him make the karate school such a success. It's the reason people will travel three hours to hear him read his poetry."

"Opposites attract, right?"

"You mean your father and Carson?"

"Well, yeah. It never occurred to me while he was living with us, but afterwards, I remember thinking how weird it was that these two guys should be such close friends. Here's Dad, who grows up in the country, but not that far from the nearest town. Grandma and Grandpa were in favor of education. From what I can tell, they pretty much left him alone to read and write as much as he wanted. He's Mr. Literature, almost all the way to the Ph.D. It seems as if he's read or at least heard of everything.

"Then you've got Carson, who's raised in the middle of nowhere. His parents don't want to educate him any more than the bare legal minimum. It sounds as if they were more interested in putting him to work at their guide business. He works a million odd jobs; it seems as if there's nothing he hasn't learned how to do, from clean a fish to rebuild an engine. I guess the two of them have martial arts in common, but even there, Dad always treated it as a mix of sport and performance, while Carson was more interested in being able to cripple and maim people."

"I suppose all that's true," Mom says. "It's funny. Your father and Carson have been friends for so long, all I see now are the similarities. I don't mean the karate, either. Their lives had more in common than you think. Yes, Dad's parents were in favor of education, but they saw it as a means to an end. You went to school in order to become a lawyer or a doctor, so you could be your own boss. That was what your grandfather used to say to Dad, that he wanted him to work for himself."

"Isn't that what writing poetry is?"

His mother frowns comically. "Not if it doesn't pay the bills. Your father's parents were deeply suspicious of education for its own sake, let alone of a career writing poetry. I'm sorry," she says, shaking her head, "I'm being unfair to them. They had been poor when they were very young—this was during the Second World War—and for them, being financially secure

ANCHOR

was very important. College was great because it allowed you to achieve that security in a way that going out and getting a job after you graduated high school didn't. To use that opportunity for something else was…self-indulgent, and if you had a family, irresponsible. I don't think I ever saw your grandmother as happy—as relieved—as I did at the opening of Dad's *dojang*. She was still nervous about him teaching karate, but as far as she was concerned, it was a big step in the right direction. Had your grandpa been alive, he would have felt the same way. Dad writing poetry made them deeply nervous. Grandpa used to say, 'But how can you know if it's any good? It's all just someone's opinion.' Grandma treated it as a phase Dad was going through, as if he were experimenting with drugs, or voting Democrat.

"On the surface, you're right, Carson's upbringing was completely different. But his parents wanted him to be financially successful in the same way as Dad's family. For them, formal education beyond junior high was a distraction, a delay in earning money. They had a plan to make themselves comfortable, moneywise, and they assumed their son would help them fulfill it. If he talked about anything else, showed an aptitude for reading and writing, that was fine, he could write the brochures and ads for their guide service when he was a little older. Carson wanting to put his talent to other uses made no sense to them. Why would he want to go off and compose poems when there was money to be made at hand? From what I understand, there was some resentment at their son's desire for a life so utterly removed from theirs, as if he was criticizing them with his dream, belittling theirs.

"Both of them had it, though, a…a fire for language, for what you could do with it. Sometimes, I imagined Dad's work as a great library, like the one at Penrose, all Gothic revival, its windows ablaze with light. And sometimes, I would picture Carson's work as a bonfire roaring in the center of a forest clearing, its light falling on redwoods a hundred feet high. They recognized that flame in one another. For as long as he's known him, your dad has said that Carson does what he does with absolute integrity, absolute commitment. Carson's written the same thing about him. So…"

"The bromance of the age," Will says. His mother hasn't spoken of either his father or Carson in such terms before; he's moved, unsure how to respond beyond gentle ridicule.

"Something like that," his mom says. "There's really nothing your father wouldn't do for him."

"I'm just grateful Carson didn't ask him to sacrifice his firstborn son for him."

"Don't be so sure," his mother says.

VIII

> You start with a sharp knife.
> Carson Lochyer "Cleaning a Trout"

Autumn of the year Will's father turns eighty-three and Will fifty, his dad will publish a memoir of his friendship with Carson Lochyer titled *Carrying the Lamp into Darkness*. A mix of essay and poetry, its occasion will be the fifth anniversary of Carson's disappearance and increasingly-presumed death within the wilds of the Kamchatka peninsula in far-eastern Russia. Though he'll bring the slender volume with him on every fishing trip he takes, Will will put off reading the book for an entire year, until a series of ferocious storms will strand him in Seattle's Sea-Tac airport overnight. He'll remember some of the exchanges his father relates, some of the scenes from Carson's time with them his dad describes. The book skips around in time, moving from conversations recent to those of decades prior, and in subject, moving from poems to sports, from family to fellow poets. Dead-center in the book, Will reads:

> There aren't many poems I haven't been able to write. This is not to say all of my work has been of equal success, only that I can count on one hand the number of subjects to which I could not fit an adequate verse-form. One of those was a story Carson told me in the weeks before he arrived to stay with me and my family following his divorce. The split from his wife had been sudden, swift, and merciless, and he came east in rough shape. For the first few months he was with us, he and I spent a couple of hours each night in front of the TV, watching reruns of *Family Guy* and *American Dad*, brightly-toned idiocy whose principle purpose was to kill time, to help move my friend thirty minutes further from his recent catastrophe. Some nights, he would retreat to his room

ANCHOR

afterwards; others, I would remove a bottle of single-malt from the liquor cabinet and pour each of us a couple of fingers' worth. I didn't know many of the particulars of Carson's divorce; strange as it may sound, I hadn't known much about his marriage in the first place. Our conversations and correspondence had focused almost exclusively on poetry: our own, that of our contemporaries, of those who came before us. I expected, though, that at some point he would want—would need—to relate the story of his marriage's collapse, as a kind of therapeutic exercise.

One night in particular, I was certain Carson was about to unburden himself to me. This was in late September, after he had been living with us for five months. Until this moment, all Carson had said on the subject of his divorce was that it was entirely his fault. This declaration, combined with his lack of clarification of it, had led me to wonder if he hadn't been unfaithful to his wife, or guilty of something worse, violence mental or physical. Nothing in his behavior around me and my family gave my suppositions any support, but there are relationships that bring out a unique beast in us, and perhaps this had happened to my friend.

On the night of which I'm writing, Carson had two glasses of Balvenie I served him, a third, more substantial pour he served himself. Revelation trembled the air of the kitchen. He drank half his glass and said,

I ran away from home when I was eighteen. For the last time, I mean. I'd been trying to get away from my parents since my thirteenth birthday. A couple of times, I made it to Lewiston. There's a harbor, there, the furthest-inland seaport in the western U.S. I had an idea I'd play Jack London, sign on board a merchant ship and see the world. Couldn't find anyone to take me before my dad found me. When I was older, I tried jumping trains, but that was harder than I expected, too. The one time I actually succeeded in climbing inside an open boxcar, the train stopped an hour later, and the cops discovered me. Made Dad drive all the way there to get me. You can imagine how thrilled he was to have to do that. Eventually, I turned to hitchhiking, which a lifetime of my mom's warnings about perverts in cars had heretofore caused me to avoid. I encountered a few of them, too, though nothing I couldn't handle. None of my attempted escapes ever took me far enough away from my parents' reach. I might have a day or two in a town, but Dad always seemed to know right where to find me. He never failed to remind me that he knew his way around towns and cities; he'd lived in plenty of them before he and Mom pulled up stakes and headed for the country. I, on the other hand, was just an ignorant hillbilly, ill-equipped for any life but the one he and Mom had raised me to.

How I hated him during those long drives back to whatever hovel he and my mother had christened home that month. The thing was, he owned two large footlockers full of books, a lot of them old hardcovers he and Mom had picked up at library sales and flea markets. There were a lot of the classics, Homer and Dante and Shakespeare, the Romantics, as well as paperback copies of Twain and Hemingway and Steinbeck. I was allowed to read whatever I wanted, as long as it didn't interfere with my chores. I went through every last one of those books, at least twice and in some cases half a dozen times. I could not understand how my parents could own all of these books, could cart them from place to place—and read them, yes, they read a lot of them—I could not understand how they could have this portable library and yet want nothing of what it represented. You know what I'm talking about.

I did.

That was what kept prodding me to get away from them. Sure, there was plenty of physical deprivation, beatings when I misbehaved, unhealthy and inadequate food, outrageous work conditions, and forget a doctor if you got sick, let alone a dentist if you had a toothache. But I sometimes think that, if I had shared their vision, embraced their plan to become the pre-eminent fishing guide service in central Idaho, I might have been willing to put up with those hardships and more, beside. Since I didn't, since I wanted a life completely removed from theirs, the lashes with the belt and the plain spaghetti and the carrying a fifty-pound pack

ANCHOR

fifteen miles upriver—and the strep throat, the bronchitis, and the pneumonia—all of was just piling insult on top of injury.

When I decided to run away the last time, I hit on a different plan. Before, I had always set out for civilization, for town and cities. It dawned on me that if I went the opposite direction, headed deeper into the wilderness, my chances of evading my dad would improve. We were staying in a trailer outside of Stanley, beside the Salmon River. You stepped out the front door, and there in the distance was the Lost River Range, like the teeth of a great, broken saw. I'd been up in the mountains with Dad dozens of times. I knew the course the Salmon River took through them, and I knew the smaller rivers and streams that fed into it. The Salmon's also known as the River of No Return, and that struck me as a good omen.

On a Saturday night my parents were out at a dinner party at a rich client's ranch, I left. I loaded my outdoor gear into an old beater truck I'd bought the past summer, and headed for the mountains. The only thing I took from my parents was a copy of Yeats's Selected Poems. There was no doubt in my mind I was going to fail. My parents would come back early, or just as I was pulling out of the driveway. One of the neighbors we rarely saw would pick this moment to drop in for a visit. My truck would die. I wanted to race up the road with my headlights off: there was a full moon, and visibility was pretty good. But there was a state trooper who liked to ride around Stanley from time to time, and I didn't want to provide him an excuse to pull me over.

There's one major road that runs through Stanley. Smaller roads branch off from it. A lot of them don't go much further than a couple of hundred feet, to a clearing or someone's old cabin. A few of them extend a considerable distance, trails the loggers and miners used. After maybe half an hour, I turned onto one of these. I took the truck as far as it would go into the forest, parked it as best I could on what shoulder there was, so it wouldn't hinder anyone else's passage, and set out into the mountains.

For me, Eliot has it right: "there, you feel free." I was up in them for twelve months. There were a couple of deserted cabins I'd run across during my previous trips to the area. I made for nearest one of those and set it up as my base of operations while I waited to find out if Dad and Mom had worked out my ruse. Once I was satisfied they hadn't, I moved to the second cabin, which was in better shape, better suited for the coming winter. There was a lean-to beside it under which someone had stacked enough firewood to take me a good portion of the way through the approaching season. Tell the truth, I was half-expecting whoever had cut and stacked that wood to show up and take possession of the place. In that event, I didn't know what my plan was going to be.

Nobody appeared to lay claim to the cabin, though, and I remained there for the rest of my time in the mountains. Much of what I did every day related to staying alive, chopping wood to add to the store under the lean-to, setting traps for small game, foraging for plants that were safe to eat, fishing, and making the cabin more weatherproof. I set aside time every day to read Yeats and to write. I'd brought a bundle of legal pads with me, and a handful of pencils, and I used them to write poetry. I'd read somewhere about Virgil writing ten lines in the morning, then spending the afternoon whittling them down to two. I took him as my model.

It was not an easy time. I rarely had enough food. No matter how sick or well I felt, the day's chores had to be seen to. Love Yeats though I did, I was soon desperate for something else to read. My poems were stale, derivative. I could have left, found my way down to Boise, but I was superstitiously certain that, within a day of setting foot in any sizable settlement, I would be found by my dad.

Winter arrived, and everything grew worse. The temperature plummeted outside and in. The warmth my fireplace gave ended about three feet from it. Snow fell for days, drifting to the cabin's roof. One night, a grizzly made a half-hearted attempt to get through the front door. I say "half-hearted" because I'm sure that, had it really wanted to, it easily could have broken in and had me for dinner.

Carson emptied what remained in his glass, tipped another couple of fingers of Scotch into it. He held out the bottle to me; I declined.

ANCHOR

That bear. I don't know why it wasn't hibernating in a cave somewhere. I wish I could convey to you how afraid I was, to have this giant animal on one side of a flimsy barrier and me on the other. This was fear of an almost-entirely physical sort, in the pounding of your heart, the tightness in your balls, the shaking of your legs. The bear snuffled the edges of the door, snuffled them like a dog. It leaned on the door, and the hinges rattled. It pushed against the wood, and the door moaned. I had a rifle in my hands, a .22, but I had little faith in its ability to stop the grizzly before it reached me. I was as certain as I've been of anything that I was not going to survive the next five minutes.

But I did. I made it through the night, and I made it through the winter. That spring was most beautiful, the most astonishing time I'd ever known. Living with Dad and Mom, I had learned to hate and dread the end of winter, because that was when the guide business kicked into gear, and what respite I'd enjoyed while the snow was high was over. Months of frozen whiteness, however, gave me a fresh appreciation for the warmth that trickled into the air throughout the day, for the colors emerging around me. Green—I hadn't realized how many shades of green there were around me, from the emerald of the new grass to the chartreuse of the moss, from the mint of the weeds to the jade of the evergreens. And the wildflowers opening all at once, gold and violet and vermilion and lavender. The air was clamorous with bird song. The streams and rivers were fast and frothing with the spring melt, but I brought my tackle to them and pulled fish bright and fighting from them. I was leery of a return visit from the bear or one of his cohort, but the few grizzlies I saw were at a considerable distance, and uninterested in me.

In late June, around the solstice, I came upon an unfamiliar stream while fishing the Salmon. I was in a spot where the banks were growing steeper, and I was wondering if it was time to turn for home. On my left, a broad stream tumbled down into the river. I didn't remember a stream in this location, but I wasn't overly familiar with this stretch of the Salmon, so I chalked up the discrepancy to poor memory. The stream descended from a canyon a hundred yards back. I couldn't recall the split in the surrounding hills any more than I could the water emerging from it. I decided to investigate.

I had the crazy notion that the canyon hadn't been here, previously, or the stream, either. There'd been a pretty serious earthquake in these parts when I was thirteen. Damaged buildings for miles around, killed a couple of kids on their way to school. Left twenty miles of broken ground. I hadn't felt anything in the way of an earthquake during the winter, but a smaller one could have happened, cracked open this hillside.

From the look of the stream, though, that wasn't likely. The juniper and fir lining its banks were thirty feet high, tall enough to have been growing for a time. As far as I could see, the stream bed was smooth, with no signs of any late upheaval. Where the banks drew up into canyon walls, there were no rockslides, no evidence the hill had been pried apart in the recent past. There was a narrow beach at the base of my side of the canyon. I walked up to and along it far enough to see that the walls opened out again after another twenty yards. Some kind of light was flickering in that area—I thought it was a fire, but the color was wrong, platinum instead of red and orange. Nor was there any sound of trees burning. I continued toward the other end of the canyon. My eyes wandered to the rockface across the stream from me. It was difficult to be positive in the canyon's dim light, but I couldn't pick out any of the striations you'd expect to find in a patch of exposed rock that size. A single unbroken wall of rose-colored stone faced me. There was a patch of shadow at its base, a little ways back from me, which resembled a door, but I figured the similarity was due more to my imagination than what it was acting on.

Where the canyon walls fell off to either side of me, the stream collected in a small lake that caught the rays of the afternoon sun and angled them directly into my eyes. For a moment, I saw nothing but dazzle. I could hear something over the rush of the water exiting via the canyon, a kind of low, irregular humming. Gradually, my surroundings swam into view. Low hills surrounded

ANCHOR

the scene. Directly in front of me was the lake, which collected water that flowed into it from a stream on the right. Beneath the sunlight wavering on its surface, the water in the pool and of its tributary appeared black. I took this as an after-effect of the sun overwhelming my eyes. Across the lake, the light I had seen from the canyon twisted and blazed. By walking the shore to the left of the lake, I soon came to a flat expanse of pale, chalk-colored rock which extended into the water. It was the dimensions of a modest church or auditorium. At the other end of the rock shelf, in the approximate center of the lake, a tower of white fire shone like liquid metal. It was a squat construction, slightly taller than I was, as wide as it was tall. Even at the distance I was from it, a flame of that volume and color should be uncomfortably hot. I felt nothing. I advanced closer to the burning tower and saw that it hovered above a round depression in the rock, which was full of a liquid that did not reflect the fire writhing over it. A stone cup sat on the rock in front of the pool.

I don't know what I was thinking. Or, it was as if my mind was running on multiple tracks, simultaneously. I was wondering if the flame might be the result of some kind of gas vent, and if that might account for its color and its lack of heat. I was also wondering if what I took for fire was water, steam, full of a mineral that was catching and reflecting the sunlight. I was thinking that this was among the stranger sights I'd witnessed and debating the wisdom of being so close to it. If I'm being honest, then I have to admit that I was telling myself, "Dad and Mom might be able to make some real money off this thing." And I was watching myself, too, approach the shining fire, which never grew hotter. Some part of me must have been shouting, "What the hell are you doing?" but I don't remember it. What I recall is the sense of absolute rightness that came over me as I walked toward the fire, as if I were doing exactly what I was supposed to. Shielding my eyes from the glare with one hand, I knelt and picked up the stone cup with the other hand. The surface of the cup was rough, sharp in places, as if recently and quickly fashioned. I dipped it into the liquid beneath the tower and held it up for consideration.

The cup was full of water. Dad's years of warnings about the perils of unfamiliar water sounding in my ears, I raised it to my lips and drained it. The water was cool but not cold, tasting of nothing but itself. I weighed taking more, decided against it, and returned the cup to its place before the pool. I stood and retreated from the white tower. The humming I'd noted earlier had grown louder, become words I couldn't quite make out, delivered in a slow chant by many voices. All around the perimeter of the rock ledge, the air was alive with figures, men and women, robed in pale flames, the ghostly echo of the blazing tower. It was difficult to say for sure, but I thought I recognized a couple of them. There was a man whose fiery beard framed the features of Whitman, another whose crown of flames sat above Dante's aquiline nose and melancholy eyes. I couldn't decipher their chant, but I understood that it was old, far older than even the oldest poems we know. This was what the hunters had sung in celebration after they brought down a mammoth. This was what families keened over their dead after they were done piling stones on them. These words had welcomed the spring and begged mercy of winter. They had named the constellations, enumerated the deeds of the beings they represented. I could feel my lips beginning to move in time to the chant's rhythm, my tongue shaping itself to its sounds.

And then a great brass shout rang off the surrounding hills, a clanging note that drowned out the words of the fiery company and made me clap my hands to my ears. A wind rose from the ground and whirled around the stone ledge. The poets around me faded. Something was approaching. I felt it as a thickening in the atmosphere, as if something vast was pushing a wave of air in front of it. I couldn't judge the direction of its travel; I had the impression it was going to bound out of the very air.

Before it could arrive, I ran. Pack bouncing on my back, I fled that place and its fantastic sights as fast as my legs would go. At my back, the wind roared. I sprinted through the canyon, along the shore that had taken me here, kicking stones into the stream as I went. I shot out of the canyon down the slope to the Salmon, already veering right, in the direction of my cabin. I knew I could

ANCHOR

hike for the better part of a day and cover substantial ground in the process. I hadn't known I could run like this. My legs were in agony, my lungs burning, but I did not slow my pace until I had the cabin in sight. The moment I was through the door, I dropped the pack and went for my rifle. I passed the rest of the day and all of the night, until the sun rose the next morning, positioned at the front door, which I had open a crack, scanning the long meadow in front of the cabin for whatever had been on its way from the wind. Nothing showed. Not then.

I didn't return to the place. That's the question, isn't it? Did you go back? Was it still there? Did you invent the experience, hallucinate it, or did you stumble through a gap in our world to…some other place? I knew what I'd seen, what I'd heard, what I'd tasted. At least, I thought I did. I weighed another trip to the spot on the Salmon, but couldn't make up my mind about it. I wasn't especially worried that I'd imagined the place on the other side of the canyon, the flaming tower, the fiery poets. There was nothing in the rest of my behavior to indicate that I'd suffered a psychotic break. To be honest, I was more, much more concerned that the stone ledge had been real, that by drinking from the pool in it I'd drawn the wrath of…I didn't know what. I didn't want to find out, either.

Anyway, I was busy writing. In the days after my excursion up that stream, I started a series of poems that sounded less like poor imitations of all my reading and more like distillations of it, filtered through a style and a voice that felt like mine. You know, there are times you begin work on something, and right away, you can tell, this is going somewhere. There may be some bumps on the road—let's be frank: there may be blown head-gaskets, and washed out bridges, and sudden thunderstorms—but you can just about see your destination at the outset. These were the sonnets about trout-fishing with Dad. I had full confidence in what I was doing in them, and I was pretty sure that they were going to announce me to the world. I worked on them daily, tirelessly, for eight, ten, twelve hours at a time. Beyond what was necessary for my immediate survival, I neglected everything in favor of the words pouring out of me. Wood lay ungathered, uncut, and unstacked. My traps had not been reset in weeks. The cabin had not received the maintenance it required, rotten boards replaced, gaps in the walls filled. By midsummer, it was obvious that I would not—could not—stay in this place another winter, not if I intended to continue writing. I decided that, come fall, before the weather turned too bad, I would pack my gear and head for Boise.

This was what I did; although I left about a week ahead of schedule. The fall had been and remained unusually warm, summer-like. I was reluctant to depart the location where I had broken through to my own voice, where I had written poems that seemed beacons lighting the way to what I might do, next. I may have been a little anxious about the effect a change of scenery would have on my poetry. The days were getting shorter, though, and I had no desire to be in the mountains when the weather changed.

I kept writing. Each night, I stood from the table where I worked, stretched, and went outside for a walk around the cabin. It was one of those things you do to give yourself momentary distance from whatever you're writing. I brought the rifle; I hadn't forgotten my encounter with the bear. I startled a fox, once, but that was it. A couple of weeks before I was planning to hike down to civilization, I strolled outside to see the top of the peak to my left in flames. Two-thirds of the way to its crown, a belt of red-orange encircled it, lighting the low-hanging clouds. While I knew forest fires were a possibility, the sight of the flames was shocking. I wondered if I'd have to clear out that night. I couldn't see for sure, but the fire appeared to be burning above the tree line. I hadn't heard thunder, seen lightning strike, nor had I noted hikers or climbers in the vicinity, earlier. As absorbed as I was in writing, though, it was conceivable I might have missed any of those.

As I watched, the band of fire rose up the mountain, as if it were a line of climbers carrying torches, ascending the summit. It moved faster than a person could, and with more uniformity. I couldn't figure out what it was, what natural phenomenon I was witnessing. The fire gathered at the very top of the mountain, then leapt straight into the sky. It pierced the clouds and was gone.

How could I not have drawn a straight line between what I saw

ANCHOR

that night and the place beyond the canyon, with its tower of white fire? I tell myself that I must have made such a connection, but if I did, it failed to signify. I thought something to the effect of, Strange things happen in the mountains, but that was all. I did not recognize this incident as a consequence of my actions months before. That came three nights later.

It was after I'd put down my pen for the day and was lying in bed, reading Yeats. There was a sound in the woods at the far end of the meadow in front of the cabin, the crack and crash of a tree falling. I lowered the book and listened. Something big was pushing through the brush. At the same time, light stabbed through the gaps in the walls, beams of red-orange that filled the cabin with a dull glow. I rolled up from my bed, grabbed the rifle, and crossed to the front door. In spite of the light shining into the cabin, I was thinking it was the bear from last winter, come back for another visit. I opened the door the barest sliver, and at first, what I saw prowling the edge of the woods was a bear, the biggest kind I'd seen. It was enveloped in fire, an orange inferno that should have killed it immediately, whose heat I could feel a hundred yards away, but which the animal seemed not to notice. It voiced a roar that was the clashing of a huge bell, and I saw that it was no bear at all. It was nothing I'd seen before. The face was more like a man's, only bigger, and when it opened its mouth, it was full of rows and rows of teeth. I didn't want to look at the rest of it—I couldn't; the sight of it sent a sharp pain through the middle of my head. There was a tail of some kind, arched over its back.

I eased the door shut and stood with my back against it. The light within the cabin brightened as the creature moved out of the trees, into the meadow. I didn't think the .22 would make any impression on what I'd seen, but I didn't dare flee the cabin, lest I provoke it to chase me. There was nothing to do but stay where I was and await the thing's next move. It thrashed through the meadow, voicing its heavy, metallic roar. The air in the cabin warmed. Sweat weighted my clothes. I white-knuckled the rifle. This, I had no doubt, was what had been coming for me after I drank from the pool below the flaming tower—what I had summoned. It was near enough that the interior of the cabin shone with a red-orange light, as if dawn were throwing its rays over the mountains. The structure shook with the creature's roars, dust dropping from the ceiling, lifting from the walls. The door was hot where I was leaning against it. I straightened away from it. There might be a fire raging in the meadow.

Whatever I had come to this place to do, it was not burn to death in a cabin. I caught the door handle, turned it, and pulled the door open. At the same time, I stepped into the doorway, rifle up, sighting along it to the spot where I guessed the beast was. There was a purity to the act that was wonderful, that filled me with elation, even though I was certain I was passing to my death.

Except I wasn't. The meadow was empty. The traces of the creature's presence were in evidence: the tall grass and wildflowers had been burnt down to the baked earth, where scattered flames continued to flicker. The outside of the door, that side of the cabin, were scorched black. Keeping the rifle at my cheek, I retreated inside to pull on my boots. Feet protected, I went outside and made, first a tight circuit of the cabin, then a foray into the meadow to stomp out the remaining fires. Once the last flame had been extinguished, I retreated inside and started to pack.

Carson emptied what remained in his glass. He did not refill it.

The next morning, I hiked out of the Lost River Range. I brought with me fifty-four poems, which I began submitting to literary journals as soon as I was settled in a room in a boarding house in Boise. The first was accepted for publication late the following winter. Days, I worked a succession of odd jobs. I started to take classes in combatives. That was how I met Willa, at my martial arts school. She'd received one too many advances from pushy guys who thought they should be the ones to date Boise's hottest meteorologist. She and I got together. I was promoted to assistant manager at my job, then manager. And while all of this was happening, the pages on the calendar peeling away, I wrote, what had started in the cabin in the mountains continuing to the room in the boarding

ANCHOR

house, then a small apartment, then Willa's condo once we shacked up, and finally to the house we bought in Hayley after she accepted the job there. I published a chapbook with a micropress. Robert Haas said some complimentary things about it. The University of Virginia published my first full length collection of poems.

I know you know all of this. What you don't know is that the creature, the fiery monster, pursued me. It took years for it to track me to my apartment. At first, I didn't know it had found me. I looked out the living room window one night and saw flames on the roof of a building down the street, and assumed it was a normal fire. Only when the flames gathered into a sphere, which hung over the roof before bursting apart like a firework, did I understand that I had been located. The same night, I carried my meager belongings to my car and drove to a motel on the south side of the city. I stayed there for a couple of days while I considered my options. Willa had been asking me to move in with her, and she owned a nice condo in a suburb about a half-hour outside of Boise. I could chance taking her up on her offer, or I could get onto the interstate and let it take me where it would. The second option, I understood, was the prudent, the responsible one. But I loved Willa, loved the life I thought we could have together. I called her, told her I'd decided she was right, it was time for us to take the next step in our relationship.

Well. You see how right I was about that. Funny thing is, the beast didn't catch up with me again until the very end, after Willa had decided it was time for her to move onto bigger and better things, a move that did not require the encumbrance of me. Our marriage had been the axis holding the rest of my life in orbit. When it was over, everything went spiraling off in its own direction. Willa moved out, told me I could keep the house if I could afford it, which I couldn't. I didn't know what I was going to do; I literally could not think of it. I guess I was waiting to see what would happen, how much worse things could get. Then one night, one very late night when I was most of the way through a bottle of Scotch not half as good as this one, I gazed out the window and saw fire dancing on top of a hill about a mile away. This time, though,

I decided I was going to confront the creature, was going to face it and let whatever happened, happen.

What was that?

Nothing. I left before it reached me. I saw it three days after the flames on the hill prowling the woods across the street from the house. For the last two days, I had been loading my truck, not in any particular order, more as it occurred to me I didn't want to leave this book or that blanket behind. I'd been keeping an eye on the other side of the street, which was where I had a sense the creature would appear. I had a rifle, a Remington, better quality and caliber than the gun I'd carried in the Lost River Range, but I was no more optimistic of its efficacy against the beast. In the early evening of the third day, I heard the creature's roar, that metallic clang. I was finishing the second-to-last knot in the tarp I had thrown over my truck's bed. The front door of the house was wide open, as was the garage; all the lights were on inside. The house sat on a rise, which permitted me to look down into the woods opposite to where the air was flooded with orange light. From deep in the trees—from somewhere *deeper* than that—the creature padded toward me, flames twisting around it. Its broad face was blank as a statue's. My keys were in the front pocket of my jeans. I slid behind the wheel of the truck and pulled out of the driveway. I'd like to say I didn't look back, but of course I did.

A couple of weeks at another motel, you and your wife's generous invitation, and here we are. I don't know how long it'll take the thing to find me on the other side of the country. I'd like to think I've given it the slip, but I suspect that isn't the case. When it shows here, I'll throw my gear into my truck and hit the road. I fantasize about striding out to meet it, playing Hercules with the Hydra, Theseus and the Minotaur, but what chance would I have? I'm pretty fond of this life; if I can avoid leaving it too soon, I'd prefer to do so.

Now I reached for the Scotch and poured a generous portion of it into my tumbler. The story I'd sat listening to was impossible, more for the pages of the latest Stephen King than anything resembling daily life. Yet I never doubted its veracity once. I swallowed the single malt without tasting it and said, "Are you positive the creature is hostile?"

"It burned my house to the ground. Willa wanted to pin it on me, but the arson investigator said the fire originated from a point across the road, possibly from a lightning strike. Said it was the weirdest thing he'd ever seen."

"All right. And there's no way to fight it?"

Carson shrugged. "Nothing certain. I've done a little research here and there, but I've yet to hit on anything in the way of a definite solution. Until I do, I'm reluctant to experiment."

"Could you placate it?"

"What do you mean?"

"Obviously, it came in response to your drinking from the pool. Is there any way you can apologize for that, atone for it?"

He shook his head. "Not that I've read. And to be frank, I wouldn't if I could."

"Come again?"

"You're the classics guy. What do you think that water was? It was the Pierian Spring, or something like it. Do you think it's a coincidence I found my voice after I drank from it?"

"As I recall, none of the myths mentions a monstrous guardian."

"That's because this was the thing itself, not some earthly analogue. Taste its waters, and you're trespassing on what's supposed to be the gods'."

"Then why hasn't the creature caught and punished you?"

"I don't know. I ran across something online that said there are very specific ways something like this can intersect our world, our reality. Maybe that's it. I'm not complaining."

"This website, the one that gave you this information, did it offer any suggestions for dealing with the beast?"

"No." Carson stared straight at me as he said this. I had the momentary impression that, within the depths of his pupils, I could pick out twin points of fire, burning white. For the first time that evening, I was almost certain my friend was lying to me.

There is nothing else in the book like this. The memoir, if that's what it is, contrasts sharply with the remainder of the volume's more prosaic contents. It's like finding a shark swimming amidst a school of trout, incongruous, absurd. The reviews of the book he pulls up on his phone express a similar sentiment, with greater and lesser degrees of pique. *The New York Times* accuses his father of having "turned Carson Lochyer into a character in an elaborate fantasy intended to elevate his late friend to mythological status (thereby, one suspects, accounting for his own failure ever to equal Mr. Lochyer's achievement)." *The Washington Post* compliments his dad for "an inspired bit of ventriloquy which makes Carson Lochyer into a kind of Ahab-in-reverse, relentlessly pursued by the same monster that gave his life its purpose."

Will intends to ask his dad about the piece himself. He wonders if it's a kind of stealth tribute to Stephen King, one of his father's favorite writers. (Carson, he remembers, preferred Cormac McCarthy's novels.) He dials his parents' number, but the call is shunted to voice mail. Ah well, it can wait until he's home.

When Manda greets him at the front door the following afternoon, however, it is with tears in her eyes, and the news that his father is suddenly dead.

IX

> Gone the grim gods of my grandfather, who
> Demanded a man meet mortality
> At the stroke of a sharp sword, and arrive
> Among them a fit companion, worthy
> To sing his own deeds.
> James Ogin "The Death of Wiglaf"

There will be a larger crowd at Will's father's wake, and funeral, and the reception after the funeral than he will anticipate. Family will come, of course, his father's surviving siblings, his younger brother and his wife, and his youngest sister and her husband, along with a mass of cousins and their children and, in a couple of cases, grandchildren. Manda's parents will fly

ANCHOR

in from their retirement villa in Arizona; her older brother and his wife and two children will drive over from Boston; and her younger sister and her husband and daughter will rent a car and drive up from Brooklyn. He and Manda will host her parents and Will's mother, who will alternate between stunned acceptance of her husband's death (from a stroke) and torrential weeping. The members of both families will be joined by friends ranging from close to acquaintance. There will be former colleagues of Will's mom's, from when she taught at SUNY Huguenot. A large contingent of his dad's karate students will appear, each of them bowing to Will and Manda as they shake their hands and offer their condolences. There will be white-haired, wrinkled poets whose younger selves stood laughing or talking with his father in photos forty years old. There will be poets Will's age and younger, who will hold his hand too long as they tell him how important his dad's work was to them when they were younger, the possibilities it suggested to them. There will be a few complete strangers, come to pay their respects to a man whose lines signified something to them and some crucial juncture in their lives.

Surprised and pleased by the number and variety of women and men who appear to mark his father's passing, Will has the odd sensation that his dad is slipping away from his private recollection of him to the collective remembrance of the public. Since his teenage years, he's been aware of his father's identity, his persona, as a poet, a literary figure. It's always seemed to him that there was the slightest bit of daylight between who he thought his dad was and who his father's readers thought he was. With his death, already Dad is becoming a Name, which Will supposes he must have wanted but which weights him with melancholy on top of his grief.

Because Carson Lochyer has not been declared legally dead, there has been no formal memorial service for him, nor is one planned for any time in the near future. Due to this, and to their long-time friendship, Will's father's wake, funeral, and post-funeral reception become an impromptu memorial for him, too. Dad, Will supposes, would approve.

The night of his father's funeral, after his mom has taken a sedative and retired to bed, and his in-laws have gone off to the other guest room, and Manda and Flora have kissed him good night, Will sits at the kitchen table with Dana, a bottle of eighteen-year Talisker open between them. They drink the Scotch slowly, allowing it time to loosen their tongues and unlock their memories. The stories they exchange of Dad, Grandpa, aren't all that different from those he imagines most people tell in such situations. Will talks about the time his father dropped everything to drive out to Wood's Hole so he would be in time to meet the afternoon ferry from Martha's Vineyard. On it was the twenty-year-old son of one of Will's mom's friends from college in Scotland. The son, whose name was Lance, had taken a summer job at an expensive hotel on the island for which he had been disastrously unsuited and from which he had been fired in short order. For reasons Will can't remember, Mom's friend was unable to get to her son. Dad volunteered to pick him up from the ferry and bring him to their house, which he did. A couple of days later, he drove Lance to Newark for his flight back to Edinburgh.

Dana speaks of her years studying in Grandpa's *dojang*, of how amazing it was the first time she saw him break a pair of boards with a jumping front kick, this big man leaping into the air, the boards snapping with a sound like a book slapping shut. How old would she have been? Six, seven? Old enough to remember the event. And afterwards, he was still Grandpa, his hair a mess, his face sweaty, his hairy chest visible at the top of his *dobak*. At the same time, he wasn't Grandpa, or not the same Grandpa. It was as if there was all this energy radiating from him, this…fire. Does that make sense? his daughter asks and, Yes, Will answers, it does.

At some point after the kitchen has been reduced to a quasi-cubist backdrop that spins whichever direction Will turns his head, Dana pushes away from the table, mumbles that she has to get some sleep, kisses the top of her father's head, and sways away in the direction of her room. There's a scrim of alcohol coating the bottom of the bottle of Talisker. Will lifts the bottle, pronouncing, "*Slàinte Mhath*," his father's preferred toast, and downs the last of it. He should find his way to his and Manda's room, but the combination of whisky and exhaustion makes this appear an insurmountable challenge. Nearer by far, the living room couch seems a safer bet. Almost knocking over his chair, he stands and, hands out to either side to aid what balance remains him, he wobbles into the living room where the blue and white striped couch is waiting to receive him. Will sinks into its cushions. Briefly, he has the sensation of falling, as if unconsciousness is a pool he's plummeting toward, and then he's asleep.

The dream that envelops him is of the kind so vivid as to be indistinguish-

ANCHOR

able from waking. It begins with him sitting up on the couch. The air around him vibrates the way it does in the immediate aftermath of a great sound. Dim light sketches the contours of the living room's complement of seats and cabinets. He must not have turned off the kitchen light. Rising on stiff legs, he crosses to the kitchen doorway, reaches through it, and flips the light switch. The kitchen darkens, but the living room remains full of a soft orange glow. It's coming from the windows, seeping into the room around the edges of the curtains. Dawn? It can't be: the sun rises on the other side of the house. Will walks to the picture window and parts the curtain veiling it. Through the glass, through the trunk and branches of the cedars in the front yard, he sees flames at the edge of his property. He rushes to the front door, unlocks and opens it, and runs outside onto the front porch of the house in which he grew up.

Startled, he looks from side to side. To his right is the wooden rocking chair his father liked to sit and read in when the weather was mild. To his left hangs the hummingbird feeder in the shape of an oversized strawberry. Before him, the ground runs level for the length of the short yard, dips into a gully, then rises in a steep hill to the road. Fire burns up there, too—or maybe it's the same fire. At the top of the stairs descending to the yard, he sees the *qiang*, the Chinese spear, leaning against one of the posts. He steps forward and grabs hold of it. The haft is smooth to the touch. Does this mean his father...? He hurries down the steps.

Holding the spear at his side, Will jogs along and up the driveway. Red-orange light makes a Halloween scene of the woods to either side. His thighs protest the driveway's grade. Ahead on the left, he spots Mr. Tumnus's Lamp, a black sketch on orange construction paper. There's someone a few feet to the right of the lamppost, a silhouette whose slight stoop causes his heart to pound. Eyes focused on that figure, Will forces himself to sprint the last few yards to the road.

Bathed in red-orange light, his father is waiting for him. He looks much as he did the last time Will saw him alive, his beard in need of a trim, his hair thin but not gone, his brow and the sides of his mouth grooved with deep lines. He's let the robe he was wearing drop to his feet, which are bare. He's dressed in a pair of worn karate pants and his favorite *Famous Monsters of Filmland* T-shirt, the one that shows Godzilla squaring off against Gamera. In his right hand, he holds the *do*, the curved Korean sword, point to the ground. He's smiling, as if he's about to share some groan-inducing piece of humor.

Will stops, says, "Dad."

His father nods, reaches over and pulls Will into a hug. His dad feels real, far more so than the body in the casket against whose still, cold brow he pressed his lips before the coffin's lid was secured. Will steps back, his throat full. "Dad," he says again, because he wants to speak and can't think of anything to say.

"Will," his father says. "I wasn't sure you'd make it. I should have known."

"What do you mean?"

With his left hand, his dad gestures at the other side of the street. Will supposes he must have seen what his father directs his attention to as he crested the driveway, but ignored it, all his attention focused on his dad. Now he sees the half-dozen trees across the road burning, their crowns great torches casting fiery light about them. The trees behind them are aflame, as well, and so are the trees beyond them. Several details strike him at once. Instead of descending the slope on the opposite side of the street, the trees continue back on a level surface. That surface is a white sand rich in crystals, which catch the light and flare like miniature stars, describing strange constellations on the ground. Though the tops of the trees are balls of fire, the trunks below them are unblackened. In fact, Will feels no heat whatsoever from them.

"*Luceo non uro*," his father says.

"What?"

"A private joke." Dad raises his sword, takes it in both hands, and assumes a middle guard. Will grips the spear in his hands and holds it in front of him. "This," he says, "is not what I remember."

"No," his father says, "I don't imagine it is."

"What is it?"

"It's what we actually saw, that long-ago night. Or close enough."

"What are you saying?"

"I'm saying your mind constructed another memory to stand in for this one, because this was too much for it. A bear, wasn't it?"

"The biggest one I ever saw."

"For me, it was a man. He stepped onto the road in hand-tooled leather cowboy boots. He was wearing jeans, a white shirt, and a leather jacket. His

ANCHOR

hair was long and black, and he had no face."

Will shakes his head. "I can't… All right," he says, "if I didn't see a grizzly, and you didn't see a guy without a face, then what did we see?"

His dad tilts his head toward the burning trees. "It's coming."

Squinting against the glare, Will peers into the ranks of trees facing him. Amidst the trunks, something moves, winding its way between the trees toward them. Big as a Clydesdale, bigger, it pads forward, its shaggy head low. Will sees muscular flanks, huge paws, thinks, *Lion?* Its tail hoists behind it, a segmented arc that extends almost to its shoulders. A knob bristling with spikes caps the tail. *Not a lion.* He says, "What *is* it?"

"The guardian," Dad says.

"You mean like in that thing you wrote about Carson?"

His father's eyebrows lift with pleasure. "You read that."

"I did."

"Then, yes."

"It was true—the story?"

"As true as I could make it. Carson found his way to another place, where he drank from a spring and summoned the creature appointed to guard it."

"It doesn't sound any less crazy, hearing you say it."

His dad shrugs. "There are more heavens and earths—and hells—than are dreamt of in your philosophy."

"Great."

"If it's any consolation, I didn't believe Carson's story, either, the first time I heard it. Not as literal truth."

"What changed your mind?"

"A couple of days before Carson left, he and I walked up here—"

"And saw the fire on the other side of the valley," Will says. "I was there, remember? It…moved, danced."

"Yes," his father says. "That's right, you were there. Anyway, watching those flames move on the side of the ridge did the trick."

Across the road, the creature reaches the edge of the tree line and pauses, its armored tail thrashing behind it. Although its body is that of a lion—a monstrously-large lion—the face framed by its heavy mane is a man's, grown to a giant's proportions. Its eyes shine, windows to a furnace. It opens its mouth, and Will sees row upon row of sharp teeth receding down its gullet. Its roar is the metal song of a full complement of cathedral bells.

The fiery tree tops shiver at it.

Will winces, but does not release the *qiang*. He expects the thing to take advantage of its roar's effect to charge him and his father. It does not. Once enough of his hearing has returned for him to hear himself speak, he says, "Remind me what we're doing here, again."

"We're the anchor," his dad says.

"The anchor?"

"Like a distraction, but more lasting."

"How so?"

"The guardian doesn't have the same relation to space and time as we do. What little information Carson had been able to turn up on it told us this much. In order for it to spiral in on its prey, it was necessary for the creature to maintain its focus on them. If you could find a way to draw its notice away from its target, you might be able to split its concentration."

"To what end?"

"Ideally, the beast would become confused, lost, like a dog off the scent. If not that, then the red herring would act as a drag on the guardian, slowing it enough for Carson to maintain his lead on it."

"An anchor."

"Exactly."

"I take it this has something to do with why I dream about that night every October."

His father nods. "You aren't remembering it—it's still happening."

"What do you mean?"

"Having confronted it, you and I became entangled in its time. Not enough for us to be trapped in it, but sufficiently for a part of us to remain in this moment. Carson was not happy with the plan; he said there was too much risk in it."

"It sounds like Carson was right," Will says. "Didn't you think it was maybe a little dangerous to bring your twelve-year-old son with you to confront a Goddamn monster?"

"Language."

"Answer the question."

"Of course I recognized the danger," his dad says. "But we had to make a convincing display to the creature, and you knew how to handle the spear. You thought the world of Carson. I assumed if I'd told you what I was up to, you would have wanted to join in. Plus, I was reasonably sure the guardian wouldn't attack us."

"Reasonably isn't the certain I prefer," Will says. "Though you're right, had you asked me, I would have agreed to help."

"Well, I'm sorry I didn't."

"Don't let it happen again. So did your plan succeed?" Will says. "I assume the thing finally caught up to Carson in Russia, but until that point, he seems as if he was doing okay."

"Look," Dad says, dipping the point of his sword at the waiting creature.

Enlarged, its features are exaggerated. Will sees the deep-set eyes, the high cheekbones, the rounded chin, and recognizes the face as Carson's. He steps back. The tip of the *qiang* drops. It's as if he's been punched in the solar plexus; he can't seem to draw enough air into his lungs. He leans forward. Of all the fantastic sights to greet him tonight, this is one too many, the piece of straw that cripples the camel. He finds enough breath to whisper, "What the fuck?"

His father's hand falls on his shoulder. "Steady," he says. "It's all right. It's okay. Come on. It's all right."

Gradually, his chest loosens, and Will straightens. His dad is watching him. His right hand remains on Will's shoulder; his left keeps the *do* trained on the creature, which observes the two of them with its burning eyes. Will lifts the spear and centers it on the thing's chest.

"Carson finally confronted the guardian and killed it," Dad says.

"What? When?"

"The first time was during his stay in Scotland. He'd rented a house in the Highlands. It sat at one end of a glen to which a narrow valley gave admission. He'd selected it precisely for its layout. He spent a summer digging a deep pit where the valet was at its most narrow. He filled the bottom of the hole with Punji sticks he fashioned from eight foot two by fours. He stitched together three of the biggest tarps he could buy, and secured them over the pit, scattering dirt on them to disguise the trap. The night the guardian appeared, he stood on one side of the tarps, a homemade spear in one hand, an axe in the other. The creature ran at him and plunged into the pit. It heaved and sank, dealt a half-dozen mortal wounds. Carson waited until it was quiet, then lowered himself into the hole and beheaded it. He buried it right there, shoveled all the dirt and rock he'd excavated on top of it.

"He was pretty happy. He talked about returning to the States, coming to visit us. First, he had a book to finish, interviews to respond to, introductions to write. All of it took him longer to complete than he'd anticipated, but what difference did that make? He was free of his pursuer.

"Late the next summer, it returned. There were the familiar warning signs: he dreamed he was back at the pool in the rock; the weather was unusually warm; he heard the faint echo of the creature's voice, somewhere in the surrounding hills. He tried to dismiss them, discount the dreams and sounds as byproducts of stress surplus from years of being chased, the spike in the mercury as a fluke. When he looked out the window one evening to see fire lighting the top of the nearest hill, he knew his previous effort had failed, and the beast was on its way. He considered fleeing, but the success he'd had made him bold, and he decided to stay and fight. There was no time to construct another elaborate trap, so he settled on a simple one. He built a number of rudimentary bombs and positioned them just beyond his prior trap. As the creature stepped into their midst, he detonated them. The storm of shrapnel cut the guardian to pieces. This time, he dismembered it and disposed of the limbs at considerable distances from one another."

"I'm guessing this didn't work, either."

"You're right; it didn't. He spent one more year in Scotland and left after his first dream of the creature. He killed it several more times, once in Germany, once in Finland, twice in Nepal, and once in Mongolia. There may be another I'm forgetting. He used everything he could lay his hands on against it, shotguns and rifles, wolf and bear traps, dynamite. He drowned it; he electrocuted it. The creature died and died and died, and returned and returned and returned, never any less relentless. Had it not been for you and me, restaging our confrontation with the guardian year after year, adding weight to our anchor with each repetition, the creature would have had Carson on a couple of occasions.

"Eventually, he grew tired of running. He had come to Tilichiki, a small town on the northeast coast of the Kamchatka peninsula. When next the guardian came for him, he told me, he was going out to meet it with an axe and a machete. There would be no more traps, no more experiments to discover if this means of death might be the one to slay the beast for good. He had called to say goodbye; he knew his chances of surviving such an encounter, even with our anchor, were slim.

ANCHOR

"There was nothing I could say, not really, but I did offer a suggestion. If he overcame the creature again, this time, maybe he should try eating it?"

"Eating it?"

"It's an ancient means of absorbing your opponent's power. To be honest, what suggested it to me was an essay I'd been reading, in which the writer compared the job of the critic struggling to come to terms with a poem to that of a hero fighting a monster. The only solution, the writer decided, was for the critic to consume the poem. All of this was clever metaphor, needless to say, but it occurred to me as a tactic Carson had yet to employ."

"Obviously, he did."

"He phoned a couple of days after that last fight. Although the connection was terrible, I could hear the severity of his injuries in his voice. He'd lost an eye, an ear, had his scalp laid open. His torso was riddled with puncture wounds, from the creature's tail. He suspected its spines were envenomed, because the wounds had swollen and were leaking pus. His left hand and forearm had been crushed, and his left foot torn most of the way off. But he had done it, he said, had stabbed the beast in two of its three hearts, severed its tail at the base, and split its skull with his axe. As soon as he could move, he bound his wounds as best he could and started gathering wood for a fire to roast it. Its hearts were tough, he said, and he burned them but he'd had better luck with its liver, or what he thought was its liver. What was bizarre was he'd had no appetite at all, but the second he put that first piece of flesh into his mouth, he'd been ravenous.

"That was the last I heard from him. I assumed his injuries had been too severe for him to survive. Apparently, something else happened."

"Apparently," Will says. "What do we do now?"

His dad studies the creature facing them, Carson, or what Carson has become. He lowers the *do* and holds it out for Will to take.

Will does. "What is this?"

"I think I have to go with him."

"You have to?"

"I'm supposed to—it's what makes sense."

"Makes sense? How?"

"Symbolically."

"Are you serious?"

"It's the kind of logic these types of places follow."

"And if you're wrong?"

"Avenge me, oh my son," Dad says, and grins.

"This is not funny," Will says.

"It is what it is." His dad turns to him. "You're a good man, and I'm proud of you. It's been my privilege to be your father, and I love you."

Their embrace doesn't last as long as Will wishes it would. How could it? He doesn't bother wiping the tears that fracture his vision. "Why?" he says. "What made you agree to help him?"

"He was my friend," his father says. "I had to. Not to mention, how could I pass up a chance to see an actual monster?"

And then he's away, striding across the pavement to where the creature that bears his old friend's face waits beside trees whose blooms are fire. As he walks, he calls out, "Hail, guardian of the sacred spring! Hail scourge! Hail psychopomp!"

The beast opens its mouth, full of fangs, and roars its awful welcome.

> Tell me a story.
> Make it a story of great distances, and starlight.
> The name of the story will be Time,
> But you must not pronounce its name.
> —Robert Penn Warren, *Audubon: A Vision*

OUTSIDE THE HOUSE, WATCHING FOR THE CROWS

Dear Sam,
    I know: who writes a letter, anymore?
    I suppose you're used to the mail as a conduit for care packages from your mom and Steve, or Liz and me, but if you're anticipating any written communication from us, you'll check your e-mail, or your Facebook account, or even Twitter. I thought about sending this as an e-mail. Actually, I did more than think about it. In the "Drafts" folder on my laptop, there are a couple of paragraphs I obsessed over for several hours after our last conversation, then for several more hours the following night, before I decided it would be better to sit down at my desk with a pad of legal paper, an extra-fine Precise V5 (black), and compose a letter to you. (For reasons you'll understand later, the social media options never were.) This is the way I plan out a case, spread all my notes around me and arrange the facts they relate into a coherent structure.

    I don't have any notes, now. What I have is your question, "What's the weirdest thing that's ever happened to you—I mean, the *weirdest?*" which (I admit) I speculated might have been prompted by your experimentation with substances I probably don't want to know about. Yet the answer that instantly occurred to me seems to come directly from such an experience. To be honest, I'm almost embarrassed to tell it to you. For one thing, it's so extravagant you may suspect I've finally started the novel I've been threatening. For another, it doesn't show me in the best light, and while I know you've been aware of my clay feet for a long time, I'm reluctant to call attention to them. At the same time, there's a part of me that's been desperate to relate this story to someone since it happened. I thought I had long since learned to control that urge, to suppress it, but your question threw open the doors and let it loose. By writing this, I suppose, I'm giving in to my need to confess; although I'm doing so in such fashion that I still have the option to delete it once I'm finished.

So: it begins with the answer to your question: at the beginning of the summer between my junior and senior years of high school, I attended a concert by a band called The Subterraneans at The Last Chance, which was a club in what I guess would have been called downtown Poughkeepsie. There weren't many other people present. Aside from me and the friend I'd met there, maybe two dozen bodies filled the space in front of the stage. At the beginning of the show, I had positioned myself toward the rear of the open area. About halfway through the band's set, in the midst of a keyboard solo that went on and on, I felt a breeze tickle the back of my neck. I glanced behind me, and saw the section of the club there, under the balcony, had changed. It was completely dark, except for a strip in the middle opening into a narrow alley right through what had been the club's bar. I was not hallucinating—at least, I hadn't ingested anything that would have allowed this to be a possibility. The breeze blew out of the alley against my face, carrying with it the smell of the ocean, brine and baked seaweed. I looked away, but the odor persisted. When I turned around, the alley was still there. I took a step toward it. Around me, the keyboard, sounding like a manic pipe organ, continued its solo. Bright moonlight picked out scraps of paper skittering across the alley's cobblestones. At the far end of the passage, a group of tall figures stood in silhouette. I advanced another step. I didn't like the way the moonlight slid over those tall shapes, but this didn't stop me from continuing in their direction. I was wondering why none of the rest of the audience was noticing this when Jude, the friend I'd met here, shoved past me and walked right up to the verge of the alley, where he stopped—waiting, I realized, for me to join him.

Outside the House, Watching for the Crows

There isn't a great deal more—though there is something—but what I've related is incomplete, devoid of the context that brought me to that moment. If I'm being frank, then I have to admit, I'm not certain how much those details explain the events of that night. But it feels wrong to relate this portion of the narrative without what came before. I need to back up, to an aging manila envelope I've kept for twenty-five years, through moves from apartments to rental houses to my own house. It contains an audiocassette tape, a ticket stub, and a Polaroid faded almost beyond visibility. The tape has been unplayable since it unspooled in my car stereo and became so hopelessly entangled in the deck's mechanisms that I had to snap it in several places to extract it. Although I spent I can't tell you how many hours attempting to repair it, smoothing its creases, gluing its ends together, winding it back onto its wheels, it was too far gone. Nor could I replace it, since it was a copy of a bootleg recording of which, as far as I know, there was only one original. (I'm not even sure about that, since I never saw the tape it was copied from.) And yes, I've searched online for it, and no luck. When it still played, the tape contained fifty-nine minutes of the band I mentioned, The Subterraneans, performing a live show at The Last Chance. The ticket stub is for another concert by the same band at the same place on June 21, 1986.

The Polaroid is not a picture of the band. It's of a group of people I spent Friday and Saturday nights hanging out with during the spring of my junior year of high school. Even with the damage two and half decades have done to it, I can identify everyone in the photo; though my memory supplements details that have deteriorated beyond recognition. Were you to look at it, I imagine you'd see a collection of pale ovals like a talented child's approximation of faces, each one ornamented with a tag screaming "Eighties!" Long hair hair-sprayed into exaggerated pompadours in the case of the guys; short hair spiked and/or dyed purple in the case of the girls. Short leather and denim jackets festooned with buttons displaying the names of bands, the anarchist "A," slogans like "Sticks and stone may break my bones, but whips and chains excite me." Jeans and Doc Martens, or ankle-length skirts and Keds, or leather miniskirts and fishnet stockings with Docs or Keds. Clunky jewelry. It was Punk meets New Wave meets Proto-Goth.

No, I didn't dress like that. However much I may have wanted to, I was far too self-conscious, too much of a conformist, to abandon my Polo shirt, jeans, and Converse, not to mention, my blue-and-yellow varsity jacket, an article of clothing I'd worn in all but the hottest or coldest weather since lettering in spring track my sophomore year. My clothes didn't exactly make me fit in at school—my shirt and jeans were whatever brands were on sale at Marshall's or K-Mart—but they didn't make me stand out. They were like a kind of low-grade camouflage. The jacket drew a few startled looks from the self-identified jocks and their girlfriends; that was all. It might have made me a little less visible as a target for ridicule, which was about as much as I hoped for.

So if I was so obsessed with invisibility, why did I spend my weekend nights in the company of people whose clothes, hair, everything drew all eyes in their direction, right? To start with, there was a girl. Her name was Lorrie Carter. She was my date for the junior prom. When I asked her to go with me, it was as a friend, because she cocked her head to the right, narrowed her eyes, and said, "As boyfriend-girlfriend, or as friends?" and I said, "As friends," the tone of my voice implying, "Of course." Lorrie was attractive. I would have been happy to invite her as boyfriend-girlfriend, but I was reasonably sure she was seeing someone who wasn't a student at Mount Carmel, and I was desperate for a prom date. To be honest, even had I not suspected she was dating, I would have given the same answer. Unlike you, by the ripe old age of sixteen, I had yet to have a girlfriend. I hadn't even kissed a girl. During the games of spin-the-bottle I'd taken part in at the couple of sweet-sixteens I'd been to, the neck of the bottle never seemed to point exactly at me; instead, the guys to either side of me saw their nights improve. Too much information, I suppose. The point is, as far as girls went, my self-confidence was nil.

But Lorrie agreed to go to the prom with me, and about two weeks before the event, she invited me to join her and some of her friends for Chinese food on a Friday night after I was done with work. (I had a part-time job at a Waldenbooks, which I'm not even sure exist, anymore, in a mall that I know doesn't exist, anymore.) Your grandparents were only too happy to give their permission. Until I turned sixteen, they strongly discouraged me from dating anyone. Once my birthday passed, however, they began to inquire and even nag about my romantic prospects. They had looked dubious at my description of my prom date as a friend. For me to be meeting her for a meal was more in keeping with their expectations.

Outside the House, Watching for the Crows

If they'd been there for the actual meal, though, any comfort they felt would have evaporated. I met Lorrie and her friends in the main parking lot of Dutchess Community College, whose location I knew but to which I'd been only once, the time I accompanied Uncle Matt to the County Science Fair there. The parking lot is at the foot of the hill on which the campus sits. I remember being surprised at the lights still shining in the windows of the college buildings, the number of cars in the parking lot at nine forty-five on a Friday night. Lorrie and the quartet of friends with her had already picked up their order of Chinese and were passing the open white containers back and forth, some using the chopsticks the restaurant had provided, others opting for plastic forks. Lorrie had the door to her old Saab open and was perched on the edge of the driver's seat, legs extended, ankles crossed. To her left, a tall guy whose white-blond hair rose above his head in a rooster's comb leaned against the car, while the remaining guy and pair of girls sat in a half-circle on the blacktop in front of Lorrie.

At the sight of me, sporting the ubiquitous varsity jacket over my shirt-and-tie work clothes, a collective tense stiffened the group, until Lorrie's face lit with recognition and she proclaimed, "This is my friend, Michael. He's my *prom date*," and everyone relaxed. One of the girls sitting on the ground held up a carton of food. I took it and the chopsticks Lorrie handed to me. I hadn't seen chopsticks outside Sunday afternoon kung-fu movies on channel 9, but I slid them from their paper wrapper, snapped them apart, and gave it my best try. The container I'd taken was full of large slices of mushroom and green pepper floating in a spicy blue-gray sauce that numbed and stung my tongue at the same time. Mushrooms weren't something your grandmother served on a regular basis, by which I mean ever, and I didn't like the way these ones squirmed in my mouth. I ate enough not to be rude, then exchanged the carton with the sitting guy for one full of fried rice, whose taste I greatly preferred; although I spilled more of it than I ate. I hadn't known to bring anything to drink with me, but no one else had a beverage, either, so I guessed it was okay.

It was a strange night—the hour and a half of it I spent with Lorrie and her friends before I had to speed home to miss my curfew by only a little. I guess it's always a bit awkward when you meet a new group of people, but the few times this had happened to me previously, it hadn't taken long for me to flip through my list of general high-school-related topics and find one that would allow us to pass the time pleasantly if blandly enough. Where do you go to school? How is it? Really? Or, You listening to anything good? Bryan Adams? Yeah, I love the video for his song, "Heat of the Night." (Don't you laugh at Bryan Adams.) These guys, though—it was like talking with people who spoke, not another language, but a dialect so profoundly removed from your daily speech, you could pick out only every third or fourth word if you were lucky. School? With the exception of Lorrie, everyone there went to a different private school I'd heard of but otherwise knew nothing about: Heartwood Academy, Most Holy Temple, Poughkeepsie Progressive School, George Rogers; although, from their conversation, it wasn't clear how much any of them knew about their individual schools, since their days apparently consisted of skipping class, in-house suspension, and blowing off school altogether. If I tell you how shocked I was to hear people comparing notes on the best way to forge a hall pass, I realize how naïve, how sheltered that will make me sound, but I was both of those things. I might have thought about missing Calculus, but fear of being caught—and punished—by your grandfather kept the thought from becoming action. Parents, though, and any reprisals they might threaten, were of scant concern. Even Lorrie talked with cheerful disregard of calling her mother an uptight bitch for asking her why there were so many absences listed on her last report card.

As for music…I liked to think of my tastes as fairly eclectic, extending from Michael Jackson to Prince to Bruce Springsteen to Madonna (although I wouldn't admit the last one), plus a few bands who were mildly off the beaten track: INXS, U2, The Talking Heads. (While I'm sure my examples will seem painfully parochial to someone of your generation, I would make the case that, say, *Bad*, *Sign "O" the Times*, *Tunnel of Love*, and *True Blue* cover a much larger musical terrain than you might grant them credit for.) In fact, when talk turned from school to records, I felt a brief flare of hope that I would be able to break what had become a long and uncomfortable silence. However, except for a nod when the guy with the rooster-comb—whose name was Jude—asked if I knew INXS's *Listen Like Thieves*, I remained outside the discussion. Bauhaus, Love and Rockets, Dead Can Dance, Pixies, Throwing Muses: I had never heard of these bands, let alone anything they'd done. Other bands—Depeche Mode, Psychedelic Furs, Siouxsie and the Banshees—I recognized as names attached to songs

OUTSIDE THE HOUSE, WATCHING FOR THE CROWS

I'd listened to on the radio, none of which had impressed me one way or the other. You know how it is when you're talking to your friends about a shared passion. You speak in shorthand. While perfectly intelligible to you, it leaves anyone unfamiliar with it with the sensation of listening to a radio broadcast clouded by static, so that only the occasional phrase or sentence comes clear. It's the type of thing for which lawyers are constantly criticized, speaking "legalese," but really, there are a multitude of examples.

Two events redeemed the night. When a check of my watch showed it was time to go, Lorrie walked me to my car. After I thanked her for inviting me, I'd had a good time, her friends were cool, she said, "I've been thinking about the prom."

At those words, my stomach lurched. She was about to announce her decision not to go with me, after all. Tonight had been a test and I'd flunked it with flying colors. I wondered if I'd be able to find another date in time.

Lorrie said, "Remember when I asked you if we were going as boyfriend-girlfriend, or as friends, and you said, 'Friends'?"

I nodded. "Sure." She was going with her boyfriend. Was it Jude? The other guy?

"I think we should go as boyfriend-girlfriend."

For a moment, I literally did not understand what I had heard. Then, when the meaning caught up with the words that had delivered it, I said, "Really?" I like to think my voice wasn't too high-pitched and incredulous.

"Uh-huh," Lorrie said, and stepped forward, raised up on her tip-toes, and kissed me on the lips. It was brief, almost chaste. Before I could respond, she said, "See you Monday," and was walking away. Fully twenty-five years, a quarter century, have passed since that night in March, and the soft give of Lorrie Carter's lips is as vivid to me as if she had pressed them to mine this minute past.

All right, all right: once again, too much information. The other thing that saved the occasion occurred as I was nodding to everyone, saying my goodbyes. Jude stepped away from his position on Lorrie's car, his right hand held out to me. At first, I thought he was offering to shake my hand, which wasn't something my friends and I did, but when in the DCCC parking lot...until I noticed the black plastic cassette tape in his fingers. "Here," he said as I took it, "if you like *Listen Like Thieves*, you might get this."

"Thanks," I said, and slipped it into my jacket pocket. There it stayed until the following morning, when I was searching for my car keys. Do you know, I never asked Jude why he gave the tape to me? There were several moments later on when I could have, but the question always seemed to slip my mind until it was too late. And then it was.

The fact I'd been handed the cassette in the first place had vacated my thoughts, pushed out by the memory of my first kiss from my first girlfriend. There have been a lot of happy events in my life since then: your birth, my wedding to Liz, completing law school, opening my own practice—those and plenty more, but I'm not sure any of them made me happy in exactly the same way I was after that kiss. My first impulse is to compare the emotion I experienced during the drive home that night to what I felt as a child at some unexpected pleasure, say, your grandfather surprising Uncle Matt and me with a trip to the Roosevelt to see *Star Wars*. But that's not it. The smell of Lorrie's perfume, floral (lilacs, I think) without being overpowering; the faint taste of the mushroom and pepper dish she left on my lips; the momentary press of her body against mine—obviously, none of this is anything like sitting in a darkened theater as spaceships arc across a starscape, exchanging dashes of red and green fire. What is the same is the quality of the happiness which infused each occasion, a certain…the word that occurs to me is "purity," which is accurate enough for me to set it down; although further reflection suggests "uncomplicated" wouldn't be a bad choice, either.

By the trip to work the next day, my emotion had moderated, though the early sunlight that made me squint and flip down the visor seemed more intense, more charged with raw, unprocessed beauty, than I'd noticed before. I'd brought the tape with me. There was writing on it, a single word I couldn't decipher beyond the extravagant "S" from which it unspooled. The word was repeated on the other side, no more legibly. I slotted the cassette into the tape deck, adjusted the volume, and waited.

Considering how important the tape was to become to me, you'd think my first listen to it would have been an experience to rival Lorrie's kiss. It wasn't. The quality of the recoding wasn't particularly good. A low-level hiss underlay a fuzzy collection of longish songs built around an electric guitar whose heavy reverb kept getting in its own way, keyboards whose pipe organ tones clashed with the guitar, and a singer whose nasal whine frequently disappeared into the competing noise. Neither bass nor drums

Outside the House, Watching for the Crows

were especially clear, and what was audible through the din sounded basic, uninspired. Had I been told this was a garage band playing in an actual garage, I would have accepted the description without question. I left the tape on for the twenty minutes or so of the drive to the mall, not so much because I thought the music would improve—hope springs eternal, yes, but there are some albums, just as there are some books, movies, TV shows, that you know early on will not change. They may become more of what they already are, speed further and faster down the road they're on, but they aren't going to veer off it. I was more curious to see if I could deduce what had prompted Jude to pass this tape to me. Yes, he'd mentioned INXS, but this was nothing like *Listen Like Thieves*. That record was crisp, clear, the band's assorted instruments working with one another and Michael Hutchence's voice to construct each song. At least on a first listen-through—which I completed during the ride home from work that night and the drive back the following morning—I couldn't hear any obvious connections. I wondered if the cassette was meant as a corrective to the more popular album, an example of the kind of music I should be listening to. I entertained the possibility it was some kind of joke; although if this were the case, it seemed unnecessarily obscure. Unless that was the point, to demonstrate to me that I was not part of the group. As far as explanations went, it fell pretty firmly under the paranoia column, but such is adolescent psychology.

When I started the tape a second time, on the way home Sunday afternoon, it was because I was no closer to understanding what I was supposed to take away from this music at its end than I had been at its beginning. To anyone in a similar situation, then or now, my counsel would have been, "Don't worry about it," but this was advice I myself was (and am) unable to accept. If someone tells me a work of art's something special, I will stick with said piece of art until I: a) decide the person who recommended it was right, b) decide the person who recommended it was wrong, or c) decide I need more time with it. If something requires more time, I'll take as much of it as I require, to the point of years. After my first listen to Jude's tape, I was pretty close to option b), but enough doubt colored my impression for me to conclude another listen was in order. It didn't hurt that the guy who'd handed it to me was a friend of my newly-minted girlfriend.

However, the most my repeat play accomplished was to leave the cassette in the tape deck, resulting in a third and fourth exposure on the drive into school, the drive from school down Route 9 to work, and the drive home from work. Nothing clicked. There was no magic "Ah-Ha!" moment when understanding dawned on me. But by the time I was back at the beginning of the tape for run-through number five, a vague sense of what was so significant about the music on it had started to suggest itself to me.

That music. Once you accommodated yourself to the clash of the guitar and keyboard, and could concentrate on the melody they were fighting over, you realized the band's songs were basically the kind of music that had filled the airwaves of 1950's radio, the bluegrass-inflected R&B gathering itself into rock n' roll through the ministrations of Buddy Holly, the Big Bopper, and of course Elvis Presley. In an odd way, The Subterraneans—it would be another couple of weeks until I deciphered their name—were doing something comparable to what a band like the Ramones was—only, where the Ramones were trying to refine the rock song down to its simplest, purest state, these guys were trying to widen it, start with those simple chord progressions, basic melodies, and throw open all the doors and windows. Had I known anything about jazz, then, I would have identified the parallel of starting with a straightforward progression of notes, stretching them into new configurations, and returning to the original arrangement. As it was, I just thought they were addicted to long, strange solos. The more used to the music I became, the more of its lyrics I was able to decode; although large patches of every song remained opaque to me. There were references to feeling like death, and to litter on the street, and to puddles of black water, and to walking around at two a.m. Someone named Jo-Jo lived in an apartment that was a great place to crash at. There were several mentions of standing outside the house, sometimes a church, and the words "in-between" seemed to find their way into every set of lyrics. At least once, the singer proclaimed, "You've got to watch out for the crows."

Looking over what I've written, I realize I've failed almost completely to do justice to the music I listened to constantly, every time I was in the car, and soon when I was in my room—I dug out an old cassette recorder that had a single earplug for quiet listening which practically took up residence in my left ear. I've made The Subterraneans sound like a concept band, an exercise in performance art, and conveyed nothing of their immediacy, of the immanence in their songs, the overriding impression they gave that there was something they were on the verge of saying, a revelation they

Outside the House, Watching for the Crows

were on the cusp of delivering. I went to sleep with their music filling my ear, and their songs followed me into sleep, into dreams where I stood on the streets of a city I did not know while the wind chased paper bags and Styrofoam cups across the pavement.

The following Friday, Lorrie invited me to join her and her friends. If she hadn't, I would have asked to. Of course I wanted to meet her outside of school, where our respective schedules permitted us to see one another in only a few classes, but I was eager to talk to Jude, as well, about the tape whose songs were playing in my head whether I was listening to them or not, which had become the soundtrack of my life—or, I'm not sure if this will make any sense, but it was as if my day's activities had become an extended illustration of the music, a feature-length video for it.

The principal difference between this night and the previous Friday was I spent it sitting beside Lorrie on the hood of her car, my feet resting on the front bumper, hers crossed under her legs, so she had to lean against me to keep from sliding off. I wasn't daring enough to put my arm around her, but I placed my hand on the hood behind her and pretended to support myself with it, when its actual purpose was to allow a maximum portion of me to come into contact with a maximum portion of her as unobtrusively as possible. An hour and half with a pretty girl pressed into me was more than sufficient compensation for the remainder of the night being a virtual repeat of the week before, from another carton of vegetables in a strange-tasting and spicy sauce to further conversation to which my contribution was minimal. In addition, Jude was not in attendance. I asked Lorrie about his absence while she walked me to my car. She shrugged and said, "He's got a lot going on." I wasn't exactly disappointed, especially since the kiss I received at this departure was significantly longer and—more involved, I guess you might say. But when Lorrie suggested I might like to meet with her and her friends the next night, some small measure of what prompted me to say, "Sure, yeah," was the prospect Jude would be present.

He wasn't, and since the weekend after was the prom, I didn't see any of Lorrie's friends. I saw her, and the large house where she and her parents lived, and D'Artagnan, her standard poodle, and her parents, who were younger than mine and glowed with money, and the elaborate royal blue dress she wore. Your grandfather had rented an Oldsmobile to ferry us to the prom, held in the catering hall of the Villa Alighieri, an Italian restaurant.

Later, he chauffeured us to an after-prom party being held at someone's house out in Millbrook, and still later to retrieve us from the smoldering embers of the party and return us home. Lorrie and he hit it off, and the night went as well as these things do. The meal and music were adequate, the company at our table pleasant.

What I remember most about the prom is that The Subterraneans' music colored it, too. In fact, were it not for my subsequent experiences at The Last Chance, I likely would have identified a moment at the dance as the weirdest thing that ever happened to me. It occurred while the DJ was playing the prom theme (for the record, Madonna's "Crazy for You"). Lorrie and I were slow dancing, her head resting on my chest. Underneath the homogenized sentimentality of Madonna's lyrics, The Subterraneans' singer was declaring it was *always* Halloween, here. The space around the dance floor dimmed, as if the lighting there had been lowered almost completely. Where the tables and chairs had been, tall forms moved from left to right in a slow procession. I had the impression of heads like those of enormous birds, with sharp, curving beaks, and dark robes draped all the way to the floor. Then the light returned, and the figures were gone. What I had seen was weird with a capital W, but it also vanished so quickly I was able to blink a couple of times and put it out of my mind. The girl leaning against me, in her stockinged feet because she'd removed her uncomfortable shoes, swaying in time to the theme, facilitated this. For the remainder of the prom, the vision did not return, nor did it during the after-party events, when I was engaged in more pleasant pursuits. The night concluded with a good-bye kiss on the front step of Lorrie's parents' house, after which, your grandfather took me for breakfast at McDonald's.

One month after the prom, Lorrie broke up with me. It was less traumatic than you might suppose. Although I had continued to join her and her friends at the DCCC parking lot for takeout Chinese on Fridays and Saturdays, school, sport, and work commitments kept me from seeing any more of her. Not to mention, one of the girls on the track team, a cute sophomore, had told me she thought I resembled the lead singer of the band, ABC, and he *was* cute. While I had never been quickest on the uptake when it came to such things (a fact to which your stepmother will attest), even my limited powers of perception could detect this new girl's interest in me. So when Lorrie called to say, "It isn't working," I found it easier to sigh

Outside the House, Watching for the Crows

and agree than I might have otherwise. I was still welcome to hang out with her and her friends, Lorrie said, which I took as a formality but appreciated nonetheless. I said I might. After I hung up the phone, I was sad, and briefly angry, at things not working out between Lorrie and me, but I was also more philosophical, more mature about it than I believe I have been about the end of any subsequent relationship, which is a strange thing to realize.

Lorrie and I remained friendly; although I returned to the college parking lot only once to eat with her and her friends. As luck would have it, Jude was there as well, for the first time since the night he had handed me the tape of The Subterraneans. I wondered if he remembered passing me the cassette, but of course he did. Since I was no longer seated next to Lorrie, it was easier for him and me to lean our heads toward one another and talk. He didn't ask me if I'd listened to the tape. He knew. He said, "Well? What do you think?"

"I think I can't stop listening to that tape," I said. "It doesn't matter if it isn't playing: I'm still hearing it, you know?"

Jude nodded. "Anything...else?"

"What do you mean?"

"Have you seen anything?"

"Have I...?" But I had, the robed forms moving past the dance floor at the prom.

Jude caught it in my face. "You did," he said. "What? What did you see? The Black Ocean? The City?"

"People," I said. "I think they were people. They were tall—I mean, seven feet plus—and wearing these costumes, bird masks and long robes. At the prom," I added.

"The Watch," he said. "You saw members of the Goddamned Watch."

"Is that good?"

"As long as they didn't see you—they didn't, did they?"

Did they? "No," I said.

"Then you're fine," he said. "Holy shit. You know you're the first person I've met who actually saw something? Amazing."

"I don't understand," I said. "I'm sorry. I mean, I get that something important has happened—to me—but I don't know what it is."

"It's the music. It thins what's around you, lets you see beyond it."

I had read and watched enough science fiction to think I understood what Jude was talking about. "You mean to another dimension?"

"Sure," he said. "Dimension, plane, iteration, it's all just a way of saying someplace else. Someplace more essential than all of this." He waved his hand to take in the cars, the parking lot, the college, us.

"How—who are these guys? The Subterraneans? How did they do this?"

"I don't know. There are rumors, but they're pretty ridiculous. A lot of bands have messed around with occult material, usually as an occasion for some depraved sex. Fucking Jimmy Page and his sex magic. This is different. These guys are into some crazy mathematics, stuff that goes all the way back to Pythagoras and his followers. What they tried wasn't a complete success. Most of the people I've handed the tape to played it once and ignored it. A few became obsessed with it. Like I said, though, you're the first to see anything."

"Have you?" I said. "You have, haven't you?"

"Twice. Both times, I saw a city. It was huge, spread out along the shore of an ocean for as far as I could see. The buildings looked Greek, or Roman. A lot of them were in ruins, which made the place seem old, ancient. But there were people walking its streets, so I knew it wasn't abandoned. The ocean was immense. Its water was black. Its waves were half as tall as some of the buildings."

"Where is it?" I said. "Do you know what it's called?"

"No." He shook his head. "I spoke to a folklorist over at SUNY Huguenot. He'd heard of the city. He said it was called the Black City—also the Spindle. He thought it was another version of Hell. He was the one who told me about the Watch, the guys in the bird masks. Said you did not want to attract their attention."

"Why not?"

"He didn't spell it out. I'm guessing a fate worse than death."

"Oh."

"They're coming here, you know."

For a second, I thought Jude was referring to the Watch, then I understood he meant the band. "Here? Where?"

"They're playing a show at The Last Chance. Late June, I forget the exact date."

"Are you going to go?"

"Are you kidding? You have to come, too."

Outside the House, Watching for the Crows

"Me?"

"Look at the effect a recording of their material had on you. Imagine what hearing it live could do."

"I don't know." To be honest, I was as worried by the prospect of what your grandparents would say as I was any further visions. Depending on their moods, they had a way of making a request to do something new sound as if it were a personal injury to them.

"You cannot be serious," Jude said. "You're standing on the verge of…" He threw up his hands.

"Of what?"

"Does it matter?" he said. "Really? Does it? Even if this place is a district in Hell, isn't that more than you're ever going to find, here?"

I was religious enough for his example to give me pause, but I understood and sympathized with the underlying sentiment. It was what I responded to in The Subterraneans' music in the first place, in so much of the music I liked to listen to, the sense that there was more, to what was outside and to what was inside me. "Let me see," I said.

As it turned out, your grandparents raised no objection to my attending the concert. They ran through the standard questions: Where was it? When was it? Who was I going with? Who was this band? All of which I answered to their satisfaction. Their biggest concern was that I understood I would still have to wake up for church the next morning. I said I did. Having cleared this hurdle, my principal dilemma was whether to invite Adrienne—the girl from the track team, with whom I'd been going out for a couple of weeks. On the one hand, I wasn't sure what I might be exposing her to. On the other hand, she might be angry at not being invited to a concert with me. Yes, my priorities were not what they should have been. I decided to play the tape for her and let her decide for herself. The expression she made when the first note of the first song burst from my car's speakers told me her decision before the song was done: this was not her kind of music. I could have insisted she listen to the remainder of the cassette, but I was relieved she hadn't liked the band and didn't press the issue. It meant I could attend the show with her consent, and without having to worry about her.

This left Jude and myself to be concerned about. Not only did The Subterraneans' music continue to form the soundtrack to my life, to the extent that whatever was taking place around me seemed to occur less for its own sake and more as an illustration, however obscure, of the lyrics of the moment, but I experienced a second vision. It occurred while I was lying on my bed, reading for school (*Waiting for Godot*.) The earplug was in my right ear, the cassette nearing its mid-point. Beyond the foot of the bed, where my desk was jammed against the wall, the air darkened, wavered, as if a sheet of black water was descending from the ceiling to the floor. I put down my book and sat up. A figure stepped forward, almost through the water. It was one of the Watch. This close, it was enormous, nearer eight feet than seven, wider than my narrow bed. The beak on the bird mask shone sharp as a scimitar; the glass eyes were black and empty. The mask left uncovered the figure's mouth and jaw, white as fungus. Its body was hidden by a heavy cape covered with overlapping metal feathers, or maybe they were scales. A long moment passed, during which my heart did not beat, before the figure and its watery aperture faded from view. Once I could see my desk again, my heart began hammering so hard I was afraid I was going to vomit. Jude's words, "As long as they didn't see you," sounded in my ears, temporarily drowning out The Subterraneans. What if the Watch saw you? What if one of its members stood at the foot of your bed and leveled the glass eyes of its mask at you? What did that mean?

Nothing good, obviously, something Jude confirmed when I called him. I asked him what the SUNY professor had said about the Watch. Not much, it seemed. According to him, the Watch dealt with invaders to the City. Don't worry, Jude said, I was probably fine. I said I didn't feel fine. "They're trying to scare you," he said.

"Well, they succeeded," I said. "I'm thinking maybe we should give the show a miss."

"Are you kidding?" he said. "We have to go."

"Did you not just hear the story I told you?"

"What do you think is going to happen if you stay home?" Jude said. "Do you think everything's going to go back to normal? You are inside the music now. We both are."

"And what do you think is going to happen if we go?" I said. "If the music has us, then how will going to its source help us?"

"Listening to the tape started something," Jude said. "It isn't complete. That's why we're catching glimpses of the other place, instead of seeing

Outside the House, Watching for the Crows

it whole. If we're in the presence of the actual music, it might finish the process."

As far as logic went, Jude's argument left a lot to be desired. But so did the entire situation. In the end, I decided to attend the concert, after all.

It may have occurred to you to wonder why I didn't share any of this with my parents. As your mom and Steve, Liz and I have done with you, throughout my childhood and adolescence, your grandparents routinely assured me that I could always come to them, there was nothing I couldn't tell them, no matter how bad. I think they meant it, too. The times I had taken them up on their advice, though, had gone less than swimmingly. When I struggled with math or science, your grandfather, who was something of a math prodigy, couldn't understand how what was in front of me wasn't perfectly clear, and had trouble finding the words to explain it to me. When I brought home a failing grade, my protests that I had tried my best were dismissed, because if I had tried my best, then I wouldn't have failed. When I complained of being teased by other kids in school, my parents asked me why I was letting it bother me. From the distance of years—not to mention, the perspective I gained raising you and your little brother—I understand and appreciate that they were doing the best they could, as do most parents. At the time, however, it meant there was no serious chance of me approaching them about what was happening to me. What would I have said? I couldn't stop listening to this tape? I was seeing tall men dressed as birds?

So after I signed out at work on Saturday, June 21, I drove up Route 9 to Poughkeepsie and The Last Chance. The moon hung full and yellow in a violet sky. I knew the club from the concert calendar the DJs at the local rock station read off twice a day. It had achieved notoriety as the place The Police had played on one of their early US tours—it may have been the first—to an audience of half a dozen people. (There was a snowstorm that night, or so the story goes.) I hadn't been to it, but this was because the bands and singers I wanted to see were playing the Knickerbocker Arena in Albany, or Madison Square Garden to the south. The club reminded me of my high school auditorium, a long, rectangular space overhung by a balcony for about half its length, with a curtained stage at the far end. There was a bar along the back wall, but the fluorescent green band around my wrist restricted me to overpriced Cokes. Underneath where the balcony ended, the floor dropped six inches. A few tables and chairs were positioned around this abbreviated ledge. By the time I arrived, they were occupied by couples in various states of fascination with one another. Maybe fifteen feet in front of the bar, the sound board was illuminated by its own set of lights. A skinny guy who didn't look much older than I was stood holding a pair of headphones to his right ear while he slid a lever steadily up a slot in the board. Cigarette smoke clouded the air at the bar, where I stopped for a Coke and to survey the club. I was wearing my work clothes; though I had removed my tie; but I didn't stick out as much as I had feared. What audience there was appeared slightly older, college age, and were dressed in jeans and casual shirts. It was easier than I'd anticipated to find Jude, who sighted me at the bar and came over to join me. He was wearing a torn *Anarchy in the UK* T-shirt, camouflage pants, and Doc Martens. His hair stood up like the crest of some tropical bird. I had missed the opening act, he said, but that was no loss. Some guy with long hair whose guitar strings kept breaking; already, Jude had forgotten his name. He guessed the band would be on in another forty-five minutes, maybe an hour.

We passed what was in fact an hour and a half making small talk. Much of it concerned Lorrie and the other people I'd hung out with in the college parking lot. It was gossip, really. Apparently, Lorrie was seeing a guy who'd been a senior at our school. I recognized his name. He'd been in the drama club. I didn't know him, but Jude considered him an asshole. "She should've stuck with you," he said. I thanked him, but told him the decision to break up had been mutual. This was a surprise to him. Yes, I said, I was seeing someone new, too, so really, everything had worked out all right. Despite the music playing in my head, everything seemed normal, mundane. We were a couple of friends out to listen to some live music, discussing our mutual friends. The weirdness that had enveloped me for so many weeks seemed far away, dream-like.

The appearance of The Subterraneans, themselves, bolstered my sense of the ordinary. There were four of them, drummer, keyboardist, guitarist, and lead singer, who strapped on an acoustic guitar which spent the part of the show I saw hanging at his side like a prop. The four of them wore black jeans and plain black T-shirts. Their hair was long, but not so much they couldn't have worked most day jobs. The curtain parted, and they emerged from backstage nonchalantly, picking their way through the cables on the stage to their respective instruments. Without introduction, they started

OUTSIDE THE HOUSE, WATCHING FOR THE CROWS

into their first song.

The cassette had given a fair impression of the band's sound. What it had not conveyed was the intense focus with which they performed. In my car, on my bed, listening to the guitar and keyboard clashing with one another, I had imagined a group whose members were struggling for control of whatever they were playing, and I would have predicted a certain amount of tension, if not outright animosity, amongst them. (Think Oasis.) Everything The Subterraneans did, however, was deliberate and smooth, intentional. The antagonism between the pipe-organ keyboard and the surf-rock guitar, the way the singer's voice overrode and was overridden by them, the drums' steady, almost monotonous beat, all were precisely as they were supposed to be. The band finished their first song, and, before the audience had started applauding, slid into the next one. This was the way they acted, as if the club were empty and they were performing for themselves. Maybe they were annoyed at the low turnout for their show; though I had the impression that had the place been filled, they would have behaved in the same manner.

When the band took the stage, my internal soundtrack was about two-thirds of the way through their tape. By the opening notes of the second song, however, my interior music had synchronized with the concert. The sensation was strange, as if I were the margin where two versions of the same song by the same band converged. I kept to the rear of the space in front of the stage. Jude stationed himself at the stage's foot. In such a confined area, the sound was overwhelming, deafening. As The Subterraneans progressed through their set list, the stage lights went from white to a deep blue that had the effect of rendering everything on stage fuzzy at the edges, as if it had slipped out of focus. At the same time, I seemed to hear the music in a way I previously hadn't. The keyboard and guitar weren't fighting; instead, the keyboard's chords were creating a vast space off whose walls the guitar's notes echoed. The drum buttressed the enormous structure, while the singer was the point around which the great architecture arranged itself. A feeling of the sacred—sublime, terrifying—swept through me.

This was the moment the breeze tickled the hairs on my neck, and I turned to witness the alleyway that had replaced the bar. It seems incredible to me that I should have walked toward such a thing, but I couldn't come up with any other response to it. As my feet crossed the floor, I noted the tall forms gathered at the far end of the passage: members of the Watch, there to meet any trespass. Air moved over my face, filling my nostrils with the damp smell of the sea. My body felt curiously light.

Then Jude shouldered past me and strode to the edge of the worn cobblestones. There, he stopped and glanced over his shoulder to see if I was coming. I wanted to, but it was as if his contact with me had robbed me of my ability to move. Not to mention, the Watch had shifted into the alley proper, and there was something about the way they moved, a kind of liquid quality, as if they were ink rather than flesh, that filled my stomach with dread. I hesitated. Jude did not. He turned to the passage and crossed its threshold. I took one step, two, closer. The keyboard's solo rang off the alley's walls. Jude must have seen the black figures drawing nearer, but he did not alter his pace. The Watch allowed him to reach the halfway point of the alley—it may have been a border they had to observe—before they took him. One second, they were ten, fifteen yards from Jude; the next, they encircled him. It was like watching a group of snakes, of eels, slither around their prey. Jude looked from side to side, his eyes wide, his mouth moving. I couldn't hear what he was saying, nor could I read his lips. The guitar echoed up the alleyway. The members of the Watch raised their cloaks; although it looked more as if their cloaks raised themselves. Their masks rippled, the beaks lengthening, the eyes melting into them. Jude lifted his hand, begging for more time, perhaps, asking them to hear whatever else it was he had to say. The Watch fell on him. His hand kept its position amidst the black swirling around the rest of him. I could swear I heard high, hysterical laughter, worse, it was Jude's. I ran for the alley, but it was already gone.

Instead, I collided with one of the bouncers, who was first annoyed with my clumsiness, then panicked by my shouting about what had happened to my friend. Drugs, I'm sure he thought. He ejected me from the club and told me to get lost before he called the cops. I did, because I couldn't think of what else to do. I'm not sure how I made the drive home. The following morning, after rising for church with my family, I claimed a bad stomach and spent the day in bed. I was exhausted, but I couldn't fall asleep for any length of time. The image of those tall figures lifting their cloaks, their masks flowing into blades like scythes, would not leave me. When I did sleep, I dreamed of crows, hunched around some poor, pale thing, their

Outside the House, Watching for the Crows

beaks poised to strike. I was horrified, by what I'd seen and was certain had happened to Jude, and by the prospect of his parents, or worse, the police, showing up at the front door and asking me what I knew about his disappearance. Alongside my horror, guilt gnawed at me. I wasn't responsible for Jude's fate, not directly, but I hadn't done anything to stop it, had I? Probably a lawyer could argue the case for my innocence, but I knew better. I was complicit in what had befallen my friend.

Secretly, I wanted the cops to ring the doorbell. I wanted to confess my role in the events at The Last Chance and be punished. For all my disagreements with the Church over the years, I have always granted it the power of the sacrament of Confession, and the penance that accompanies the rite. It's what the law provides, or can provide, on the secular side of things. No police appeared, however. If Jude's parents knew he'd intended to meet me at the club, they chose not to follow up on it. I actually went to Confession the next Saturday, but after listening to an abbreviated version of what I've written here, the priest gave me a prolonged lecture on the perils of drug use. Had I attempted the same thing with your grandparents, the result would have been approximately the same.

I considered trying to find my way back to that alley; though I'm not sure what I thought I would find. Jude's remains? Evidence he was still alive, held captive in some alien prison? Whatever I hoped for, the other world was closed off to me. In the days after the concert, I realized that The Subterraneans' music was no longer playing its endless loop in my mind. When I listened to the cassette, the songs refused to stay in my memory. In the weeks to come, as the summer unfolded, I continued to play the tape, hoping the air in front of me would waver, and I would once again see the alleyway opening in front of me. It appeared Jude had been right, though. Whatever had been started by the recording of the band's music had been completed by its live performance. Eventually, the week before my senior year was to begin, the cassette unspooled in my car's tape deck, and was so badly damaged as to be unplayable, its songs lost to me.

For years afterward, every time I was in a record store, I kept my eyes open for a copy of The Subterraneans' tape. At the same time, I was on the lookout for information on the band, itself, who its members were, where they were located. I had no luck with either search. Last year, I spent a couple of days researching the band and its music online, but found little of any use.

As for Jude: at the start of senior year, I joined Lorrie for lunch in the senior lounge. We exchanged pleasantries about our respective summers, the classes we would be taking. I turned the conversation to Jude. How was he doing? I asked. Oh, she said, no one had seen him around for a while. Supposedly, he'd left for Boston, which he'd been talking about doing for years. Boston, I said. Yeah, she said. He wasn't very happy here. He had a lot of stuff going on at home. Well, I said, wherever he was, I hoped he was happier. "I doubt it," Lorrie said. "Some people just aren't, you know?" I said I did.

As I told you at the outset, I've never shared this story with anyone, not your mother, not Liz. Maybe I shouldn't have with you. If it's easier—if I send this letter to you—you can trash it, pretend I answered your question in some other, innocuous way. That might be better. I'm not sure what more there is to say about any of it. That is, except for the questions I still can't answer.

Love,
Dad

WHAT IS LOST, WHAT IS GIVEN AWAY

I

My ten-year high school reunion, held in the fall of 1997, was a disappointment. This should not have been a terrible surprise, but I'm afraid I had bought into the scenarios played out in endless movies and TV shows, the ones where all the old animosities, the divisions between jock and nerd, popular and outcast, are put aside, and the former classmates discover their similarities outweigh their differences—as, of course, they always had. What I found instead was that a decade had not been sufficient time to alter much beyond hairlines and waistbands. I learned other things, too.

The reunion was a two-night affair, with an informal meet-and-greet at the bar of The Castle, a local restaurant, on Friday, and a formal dinner at the Poughkeepsie Tennis Club on Saturday. In between, those who wanted to rekindle their school spirit brighter still could attend Our Lady of Fatima's homecoming game Saturday afternoon. Starting Friday, I had the sense that the weekend was not going to live up to my hopes for it. For one thing, no one recognized me. To be fair, I had changed more than anyone else there. When I graduated, I was six feet tall, one hundred and fifty or sixty pounds if I was wearing a heavy coat. I had gained another sixty pounds in the intervening years, as well as a beard that was the same light brown my hair had darkened to in my early twenties. None of my old classmates had deviated as dramatically from their former appearances, so it was perhaps to be expected that they would not know me. They were not prepared to.

All the same, I found this disconcerting. I walked past people paired and grouped as they had been in the halls of Fatima, and their gazes slid over me without catching on anything. While I had not been the class president, or captain of the football team, or even the class clown, I had been in the drama club, acting the part of the villainous Jonathan in the senior class production of *Arsenic and Old Lace*; I had lettered in spring track (hurdles) twice; I had played an active role in discussions and debates in our English, Social Studies, and Religion classes. Especially since our graduating class numbered one hundred and thirty-two, I assumed I had made some depth of impression on the people I had spent four years with. This did not appear to be the case.

After an hour of sitting at the bar, nursing a Corona and watching the room fill with people exchanging hugs, handshakes, and backslaps, I decided to leave my stool and introduce myself to my former classmates. Standing directly in front of them, I extended my right hand, calling them by their names and reminding them of mine. Yet even so direct an approach did not yield the look of pleased recognition, the firm handshake, the repetition of my name followed by an exclamation of pleasure. Instead, the men and women I greeted took my hand hesitantly, their faces confused, as if, while familiar, my name was not one they could immediately place. After uttering a platitude about how great it was to see me, they resumed the conversations whose breaks had allowed me to make my introduction. The forty-five minutes or so it took to complete my circuit of the room left me disheartened, depressed, and back at the bar. I had come on my own, so there was no point to ordering anything stronger than another beer. I poked the wedge of lime jutting from the bottle's neck down into it and toasted my reflection in the bar's mirror. *Here's to obscurity.*

To my left, a voice said my name. Mood instantly lightened, I turned on

WHAT IS LOST, WHAT IS GIVEN AWAY

my stool, and saw Joel Martin—*Mr. Martin*, I couldn't help thinking of him as. Junior year Chemistry, senior year Physics, assistant coach of the boys' junior varsity football and varsity basketball teams. Disgraced in the closing days of my senior year for an affair with Sinead McGahern, one of my classmates, which left her pregnant and him out of a job at which he had been a favorite. He looked terrible. His hair, thinning when I had sat in his classroom, had largely deserted his head, except for a few spots here and there where he had allowed it to grow long. The lenses of his glasses were scratched and scored, opaque in some places. The heavy five o'clock shadow that had always darkened his jaw had thickened to a heavy beard, which he appeared to have maintained himself, without the benefit of a mirror. Never a big man to begin with—I would have put his height at five five, his weight at one forty—he seemed smaller inside his shapeless black suit, shrunken. A martini glass, full, stood on the bar in front of him.

I was stunned. In the weeks and months after graduation, Joel Martin's situation had gone from scandal to ongoing catastrophe, ending with him in jail, first in Argentina, then locally. During my first couple of years of college, when I still met some of my high school friends at winter and summer breaks, the latest chapter in the ongoing saga of Mr. Martin and Sinead McGahern was among our immediate topics of conversation. As his actions had progressed—or declined—from the questionable to the out-and-out criminal, so had my mental image of him transformed from intense, affable science teacher to something darker, a seducer, a humiliated and desperate father. To encounter him here, looking different, yes, yet more threadbare than sinister, was a scenario I would not have anticipated. Which may have been why, when he held out his hand, I took it. His flesh was gritty, as if he had come directly from the beach without washing. I wondered if anyone else had identified him. Was Sinead here? I wasn't sure. I hadn't seen her, but had I seen everyone?

"How've you been?" he said.

"Good," I said. It was the answer I would have given had any of the people I'd tried to talk to posed the question.

"What're you up to these days?"

"Teaching," I said. "I teach college."

"Oh yeah? Whereabouts?"

"SUNY Huguenot. Across the river."

"That's great," he said, his voice full of its old enthusiasm. "What do they have you doing?"

"English," I said. "Freshman writing, mostly."

"Very nice. Say, you know what I've been sitting here trying to remember?"

"What?"

"The prank you guys pulled when you were juniors. Well, maybe 'prank' is too strong a word. No one got hurt or anything. Do you know what I'm talking about?"

I did. "The 'What the hell is that?' routine."

He snapped his fingers. "That's it! Who came up with that?"

"No one. I mean, someone saw it on TV—*Saturday Night Live*, I think—and we decided to do it in school."

Joel Martin was laughing now, albeit quietly. "What the hell is that?" he said. Keeping his hand close to his chest, he pointed at a spot above the bar's mirror. "What the *hell* is that? What the hell *is* that? *What* the hell is *that?*" He lowered his finger. "You remember the time I joined you guys?"

I nodded. It had been our most successful staging of the bit.

"Long time ago," he said. "Long, long time ago."

With sudden and uncanny certainty, I knew that the man who had gotten me through both Regents Chemistry and Regents Physics was on the verge of broaching topics I had no desire to discuss. An emotion halfway to panic gripped me. I decided to forgo finishing my beer and depart the reunion early. I was pretty much done already, wasn't I? Joel Martin saw me withdrawing a ten from my pocket to cover my drink and tip. His eyes widened, but before he could open his mouth, I said, "I have to go. Have a good night," and slid off my stool.

Excusing and pardoning myself, I navigated the groups and couples standing between me and the front door. The room had grown hot, stiflingly humid. The sports coat and turtleneck I'd opted for were too tight, constricting. I glanced back to see if Joel Martin was still at the bar. I couldn't tell; there were too many people crowding the space.

Outside, the night air was blessedly cool. I pulled off my jacket, tugged my shirt out of my slacks. My car was in front of the restaurant, at the concrete divider separating the parking lot from the main road. I was unlocking the driver's side door when I heard my name shouted. I looked toward The

What Is Lost, What Is Given Away

Castle's front door, and there was Joel Martin holding it open. I raised the hand holding my jacket in what I hoped was a noncommittal wave. From within the doorway, he called, "See you there tomorrow?"

I motioned with the jacket again, ducked inside my car, and almost broke the key off jamming it in the ignition. I was positive I was going to hear a tap on my window and see my former teacher's smiling face leaning toward me. When I stole a look at the front door, however, it was, though still open, empty. It was as if I had just missed Joel Martin stepping away from it to return inside. I had the impression of something within the lighted rectangle, a cloud of dust or sand, but I was too relieved at my good fortune to pay much attention to it. I shifted into gear and drove out of the parking lot.

II

The following night, I spent the car ride from my apartment in Wiltwyck to the Poughkeepsie Tennis Club narrating Joel Martin's fall from grace to Linda, my date for the evening. She was a former girlfriend who had broken up with me in order to pursue a relationship with one of her professors at NYU. They had split when she became pregnant, and now she was the mother of a two-year-old daughter, Elaine, whose father had visitation rights alternating weekends and two weeks during the summer. She managed a bank in Wiltwyck, and lived with her dad, a retired cop who spent his days watching his granddaughter. Long past our post-relationship bitterness, we had lunch every few weeks, trading news about our latest romantic prospects and complaining about our respective jobs. After my most recent relationship petered out, Linda had agreed to accompany me to my reunion dinner as, she said, a psychological investigation into the forces that had shaped me. While she might have anticipated a certain level of pre-event nervousness on my part, she was unprepared for the agitation that had hold of me—that had not released me since the previous night. We hadn't been on the road two minutes when she said, "All right. You better tell me what's going on with you."

The first part of the story was related quickly enough. Having lived her own version of it, Linda was less shocked than she might have been. "I take it things didn't work out between this guy and the student," she said.

"To put it mildly," I said. "From what I understand, Sinead's parents wanted to press charges against Martin—statutory rape, contributing to the delinquency of a minor. The problem was, she had turned eighteen the previous December, and both of them swore nothing had happened between them until the end of January. I think her mom still wanted to go after him, legally-speaking, but her dad was less gung-ho. This was the father of his first grandchild, and Martin was saying all the right things, how sorry he was, how much he loved Sinead, how he intended to do right by her and the baby. Plus, Sinead kept insisting she was in love with him. Eventually, mom cooled off, especially when Martin proposed to Sinead at the end of the summer. That was the news in the fall, when I was home for Thanksgiving break. Mr. Martin and Sinead McGahern were engaged, with a wedding planned for some time in the spring, after she'd had the baby and regained her shape. Martin had a job at a gas station, which sounded like a bit of a come-down after having taught high school, but maybe not. Supposedly, he was saving to rent a house for them."

"I want to say they didn't go through with the wedding," Linda said.

"They did not. Sinead had the baby the day after Christmas, a little boy, Sean. Apparently, Martin was in love with the kid the moment he laid eyes on him. I heard that was part of what broke them apart. One look at his child—his son, right?—and he's all ready to settle down with Sinead and start working on baby number two. Her, not so much. She'd been accepted to Penrose, and they'd agreed to defer her admission for a year. This was something she was not willing to give up."

"Plus," Linda said, "the bloom was off the rose, for him as well as for her. You start seeing someone in secret like that, someone who's off limits to you, who embodies, I don't know, a certain kind of authority for her, a certain kind of youthfulness for him, and let me tell you, it's pretty heady stuff. Forbidden fruit and all that. It doesn't take long, though, for the fruit to spoil. What they had was a fling. Their mistake was in trying to prolong it—which, I understand, they did because of the kid. They would've been better hiring lawyers and drawing up a custody agreement. Did they?"

"Eventually. By that time, things between them were pretty dire. Her second year at Penrose, Sinead moved into an apartment with the kid. It was near the college. Apparently, Penrose offered pretty good childcare for

What Is Lost, What Is Given Away

its students and faculty, and this was where little Sean spent a lot of his time. Too much, according to Martin. He accused Sinead of dumping the kid at daycare or on her parents. Said that, half the time, he didn't know where his son was. On one occasion, he showed up to collect the baby, and Sinead was out; she'd left her new boyfriend in charge of Sean."

"Ouch."

"Yeah. Martin took her to court, but her parents hired a nasty lawyer for her, sicced him on Martin the way Sinead's mom had wanted to in the first place. From what I understand, he shredded Martin into tiny pieces. I guess the judge was pretty sympathetic to Sinead, too. The upshot was, Martin's custody of Sean was limited to every other weekend; plus, he was put on the hook for all kinds of expenses in addition to child support."

"Could have been worse," Linda said.

"I'm sure," I said, "but Martin didn't see it that way. I don't know if he honestly believed Sinead wasn't taking proper care of their child, or if he was stung by losing the court case."

"Or both."

"Or both. Whatever the reason, he couldn't let things alone. So he came up with a plan. He bought a dime bag of weed—"

"He didn't."

"Yeah, he did. Sinead had a habit of leaving her car unlocked in front of her apartment. He intended to drop the bag under the driver's seat. Then, the next time she brought Sean to his place, he would just happen to notice the drugs. He would call the cops on her and, ultimately, gain leverage when it came to the kid. Unfortunately for him, Sinead's boyfriend looked out of the window at the exact moment Martin had her car door open and was bent down inside it. She called 911. There was a police car close enough to show up before Martin had driven away. A big scene ensued. The pot was discovered. Sinead and the boyfriend accused Martin of planting it, said they weren't into that kind of stuff. I gather they told the cops they could search the apartment if they didn't believe them. Martin still had on the gloves he'd worn to ensure he left no fingerprints. Combined with him having been seen inside Sinead's car… The cops took him to the station. I'm not clear what the charges were. Nothing too major. Sinead, though, used the incident to haul him back in front of the judge and have his contact with Sean reduced to one weekend a month."

"Well," Linda said, "this isn't the worst story I've ever heard."

"There's more."

"More?"

"This part I didn't learn about until a few years later. For about a week, it was front page news. One or two of the TV stations out of the City covered it. You would think Martin's brush with the law would have taught him a lesson—scared straight and all that. It didn't. Or, it did, but the lesson he learned wasn't a good one. Since his more modest efforts at rectifying the situation had failed, he decided it was time for drastic action. The legal system had shown it was no friend to him—or that he couldn't manipulate it the way he wanted—so it could be ignored. He started doing research online."

"This isn't some kind of murder-for-hire deal, is it?"

"No," I said. "What Martin had decided to do was take his son and flee the country. He spent months setting it up. Fake documents, fake id's, fake passports, not to mention, enough money to tide him over until he could find a job. Finally, when Sinead needed him to take Sean for a long weekend, he put his plan into action. He left his apartment pretty much as it was, except for his computer. He removed the hard drive, wiped it with a magnet, microwaved it, and dropped it in the dumpster outside the building. He drove to Stewart, where he took a flight to Orlando. He made sure to tell anyone who would listen that he was taking his son on his first trip to Disney World.

"The two of them actually spent a day in Florida, but only so he could make himself up to look like the photo on his new passport. From Orlando, Martin and Sean boarded a flight to LAX, where they passed most of another day before catching a flight to Buenos Aires, via Miami.

"Once they were in Argentina, he hung around Buenos Aires for a week, until he talked himself into a position as a tutor for the children of a cattle baron somewhere in the south of the country. That was where he was when the cops caught up to him, three months later. He had done a good job at disguising himself, and even the kid, but he was still a single man traveling with a young child. As soon as the cops figured out his new appearance, it was mostly a matter of sifting through hours of video from airport security cameras to reconstruct the route he'd taken. The way the papers presented it, he didn't try to escape when the police arrived. He knew they had him.

What Is Lost, What Is Given Away

Sean was taken to Buenos Aires, where Sinead and her parents were waiting for him. Martin was thrown into an Argentine prison; although he lucked out—a little, anyhow. The guy whose kids he'd been tutoring liked him and had enough connections to have his sentence reduced from five years to nine months. The minute Martin was released, however, he was back on a plane to the US, where his actions earned him another eighteen months behind bars."

"Holy shit," Linda said. "What happened to him, after?"

"I don't know," I said. "I assume he got out and went about trying to put his life back together. From the way he looked last night, I don't think that's gone so well for him."

For a long moment, the two of us were silent. On either side of the street, large, well-kept houses signaled their owners' wealth. We were almost at the Tennis Club.

Linda said, "The things we do for love."

"Or revenge."

"You don't think he loves his son?"

"I'm sure he does. I'm also sure he hates his son's mother."

"Hmm. Was she there, last night?"

"I don't think so. I didn't see her."

"Do you know if she'll be at this thing tonight?"

"I haven't the foggiest. We weren't exactly close in high school."

"All of a sudden," Linda said, "things have become more interesting."

III

The second night of the reunion was in many ways like the first, with better food and with everyone in semi-formal wear. At the entrance to the ballroom in which the dinner-dance was being held, the reunion committee had set up a long table on which name tags had been laid in alphabetical rows. In addition to our names, the id's of my former classmates and me bore wallet-sized reproductions of our senior portraits. As I pinned mine to my suit jacket, I let my eyes drift over the remaining badges, but did not see Sinead McGahern's among them. There were also name tags for a handful of former teachers, but Joel Martin's name was not among them.

Linda and I were seated with a group of people with whom I had been friendly during senior year. One of the guys had taken over the family business, a sit-down Chinese restaurant at which his wife had been a hostess. Another guy was not long out of the Air Force, and not long married to the young woman with him, who kept expressing her concern over their daughter, who I gathered was only a couple of months old and being watched by his mother. I asked the restaurateur if he'd kept track of a few of my favorite teachers; he said he wasn't positive, but he thought they were dead. I asked the ex-Air Force guy what he was up to, now; he said he was managing a Radio Shack in eastern Massachusetts. During these exchanges, something that had occurred to me the previous night became clear. Of the people with whom I would have considered myself especially close during my four years at Our Lady of Fatima, not one had opted to attend our reunion. Who knew where they were? (I tried the restaurant guy; to each of their names, he said he wasn't sure, but he thought he'd heard of a number of personal catastrophes including drugs, prison, serious injury, and devastating illness.)

This left me at an event like a restaging of my senior prom, complete with all the songs and dance moves that had not aged particularly well. Linda actually seemed to be enjoying herself. She had managed a Chinese place in Albany at one point, and her father had been in the Air Force, so she was able to maintain conversations with both of my former classmates. About halfway through the event, the DJ—a local celebrity who anchored the morning show on the classic rock station and had been a couple of years ahead of us in school—announced that it was time to read the memories people had written on the slips of paper provided at each table. (I had chosen not to.) In the midst of recollections about specific teachers' classes, and sporting victories, and trips here and there, someone contributed a note that read, "I had sex with one of my teachers." I felt as if someone had thrown a bucket of ice water over me. I'm not certain what response I anticipated from the rest of the audience, but the most the confession received was a scattering of laughs and a couple of approving howls. Linda gave me a significant glance. Had someone else slept with Joel Martin? Or, God help me, had one of my old classmates had an affair with another teacher? Yes, it was naïve to be this shocked, but so what? Apparently, I hadn't left my younger self as far behind as my appearance might have suggested.

I was not expecting Joel Martin to show himself at this night's festivi-

WHAT IS LOST, WHAT IS GIVEN AWAY

ties, not really. It was one thing to chance slipping into a room packed with people busy with one another and sitting with your back to them while you sipped from your cocktail. It was altogether another to stroll into a ballroom whose tablefuls of your former students would have little trouble identifying you. All the same, when I turned from the urinal in the men's room and saw him standing against the door, the phrase that almost escaped my lips was, "Of course." It was as if that anonymous admission had summoned him here. I couldn't imagine what he would want with me. I crossed to one of the sinks and washed my hands.

"Nice place, this," he said.

"Yes," I said, "it is."

"You ever been here before?"

"No. First time."

"I was. Years ago. One of the senior classes a few years ahead of you guys had their prom here. I was a chaperone; brought my girlfriend at the time. This was—you would have been freshmen. Yeah, freshmen."

I finished drying my hands, dropped the paper towel in the trash. "I should be getting back. My date—"

"I guess you heard about my…troubles," he said. "Yeah, you did. Who didn't? Especially after they were all over the front page of the Goddamned papers."

He was right; there was no point denying it. I nodded. "I did."

"Do you have any kids of your own?"

"No."

"Let me tell you, once you do, you will not believe you could love anyone that much. You look at this little wrinkled creature, its arms and legs still tucked up from being in the womb, and it is love at first sight. There is nothing you will not do for this kid. Your entire focus shifts from whatever bullshit you thought was important to making sure this child—your child is okay. All the things you couldn't imagine doing—changing dirty diapers, dealing with spit-up, waking up in the middle of the night to rock them back to sleep—become the order of the day. Do you understand what I'm saying to you?"

"I do."

"Everything I did, every last bit of it, was for my son, to keep him safe, to give him the kind of life he deserved. I have always wanted what was best for him. Always. I never stopped wanting that, even when I was locked up in Argentina, or when I came back here so they could lock me up some more. My son's mother had taken him and left. She didn't leave word where. Didn't ask for child support from me, in case it allowed me to trace them. Was that fair? I ask you, was any of that fair?"

"I don't know," I said. "I guess she felt—"

"It doesn't matter," Joel Martin said. "While I was in prison in Buenos Aires, I met a guy who let me in on something that is going to get my son back and make certain no one takes him from me, again."

"I'm not—"

"Do you know who Borges was?"

"The writer?"

"This guy I met was a friend of his. That's what they called him, the other prisoners, the Friend of Borges, *el amigo de Borges*. He'd hung out with Borges when he was younger, at university. He was a mathematician, into some pretty exotic stuff. There was this one story Borges had written, 'The Aleph'—have you read it?"

"The one about the point that lets you see all other points in space and time."

"Exactly. The guy was fascinated by that story, by the math underlying it. Poincaré theory—how well do you remember physics class?"

"Not at all."

"That's disappointing," he said, "but it isn't important. The conversations with Borges took the guy only so far, but the writer put him in touch with one of his friends at the university, who gave him the name of another person, and so on, until he met with a group who were familiar with the theory underlying the aleph, and a lot more, besides."

"Okay."

"You don't get it. That's all right. Do you recall me telling you guys that everything was just math?"

"Yes."

"You thought I was talking figuratively—if you gave it any thought at all. I wasn't. The group the Friend of Borges met understood this. They comprehended it. They were part of a…tradition of scholars who had been working with this exotic math for a long time. Like, longer than you'd believe."

What Is Lost, What Is Given Away

"I'm not—"

"These scholars had figured out all kinds of applications for the material they were studying. They had worked out how to employ it, using combinations of words and sounds and...mental images, you could call them."

"It sounds like you're talking about magic."

"What you call it isn't important. What's important is that it works."

"Then why was this guy—the Friend of Borges—in prison? Couldn't he just magic his way out of there, teleport or something?"

"He was in hiding," Joel Martin said. "Or, that's not it, exactly. He'd had a falling out with the other members of his lodge, and he had decided to secure himself within Unit 1."

"Couldn't he have found a better place to hide out?"

"That doesn't matter!" he shouted. "You're missing the Goddamned forest for the trees. I'm telling you I met the modern day equivalent of fucking Merlin, and you want to know why he isn't staying at the Hilton. Jesus!"

There was no doubt in my mind that my former teacher had traveled far, far around the proverbial bend. I raised my hands, palms out. "Okay. I'm sorry. You met the Friend of Borges, and he told you about this weird math. Did he teach any of it to you?"

"A little. You can appreciate, the conditions weren't ideal for this kind of instruction. What he did was to tell me where I needed to go, once I was free to travel, again. Which took a while, and I had to work a bunch of shit jobs to save up the money, but in the end, I got there."

I couldn't help myself. "Where was it?"

"Quebec."

"Quebec?"

"Quebec City. That's where the nearest lodge—the nearest school is."

"And they took you in—accepted you as their student."

"They did."

"So now you're one of them, a...mathematician."

"Basically."

"But—why are you here? If you have access to the aleph, or whatever, shouldn't you be using it to track down your son?"

Joel Martin's face drew in on itself, to an expression it took me a moment to name: embarrassment. He looked down at his shoes, stuffed his hands into his jacket pockets. "There's been a slight complication."

Here it comes, I thought, *the escape hatch, the detail that allows the fantasy to exist yet remain ineffectual.* "Oh? What kind of complication?"

"I'm imprisoned. The master of the lodge guards his knowledge jealously. He doesn't introduce you to new material until he's satisfied that you're ready for it. I had passed all the basic tests with flying colors. Everyone said I was one of the best students they'd taught in years. They—the master wanted me to wait before studying anything more advanced. I was sure I didn't need to. I was eager—I could feel time slipping away from me. Every day, and my son is getting older, whatever memories he has of me growing fainter. Have no doubt, his mother and whoever she's with are doing all they can to erase me from his life. I needed access to the aleph now. I pressed the matter with the master. He wouldn't budge. Things got heated between us. I made some…intemperate remarks. The master invited me to act on them. I did. It didn't go well. When the dust settled, he trapped me in a place…it's kind of a place between places. He said if I could figure my way out of it, I might be ready to start learning, again."

"You're in prison," I said.

"Imprisoned," he said. "Again. It's more complicated than the other lock-ups I've been in. There's a limited amount of energy sustaining the cell. I can draw on it, but every time I do, the space constricts. If I had accepted my sentence, I could remain here indefinitely. But I told you, I can't do that. I have to get out of here. I tried reaching out to one of the other students at the lodge, someone I thought was sympathetic to me. I was wrong, and I shrank the prison. I decided I had to think more creatively—outside the box, ha ha. It occurred to me that your ten-year reunion was coming up. I was able to find out the times and locations without making the cell too much smaller."

"Wait," I said. "You're in this cell."

"Correct."

"Yet you're standing here talking to me."

"This," he said, removing his hands from his pockets to gesture at himself, "is a simulacrum. It's as if you're talking to me on a videophone."

"Okay," I said. "Couldn't you appear to your son, then? Why waste time with me?"

"Because I don't know where he is. I was able to draw on your memories—your class's combined memories of me to locate this spot and as-

WHAT IS LOST, WHAT IS GIVEN AWAY

semble a version of myself. I reached out to you in particular because we'd gotten along when you were my student. I hoped you would be willing to help me."

"How could I help you?"

"I have a storage unit on Route 9, down by the malls. There are a couple of things in there, a book and—"

"Mr. Martin," I said. "Joel." At the sound of his name, his head jerked, as if I had slapped him. I said, "I don't know what's going on with you, exactly, but I wonder if maybe you need to talk to someone who could help you with all this."

"What do you mean?" he said. "That's why I'm—oh." His eyes narrowed. "I get it. You think I'm delusional. Paranoid schizophrenia, right?"

"It sounds as if you've been under a tremendous amount of stress," I said. "Things with your son—"

"Don't you understand? There are no 'things with my son.' I don't know where he is. As long as I'm stuck in this prison—"

"Stop. You're in the men's room of the Poughkeepsie Tennis Club. You are not in some kind of magic jail."

"You have no idea," he said. "You have no Goddamned idea. This place is a blank. It isn't a place, properly speaking. It *isn't*, do you understand? It's the white between the letters on the page. Most of the time, it's all I can do to keep myself coherent. And on top of that, it's getting *smaller*. It may have reached its limit. Any more loss of energy, and it's going to collapse, and take me with it. I am not shitting you when I say that you are my last chance. I'm doing everything I can to hold on, but time is running out."

A tremendous pity rose in me. I had been in here much too long. "I have to go," I said. "I'm sorry." I walked toward the bathroom door.

"What? Hey, hang on." He put his hands up.

"Please get out of the way."

"Wait—"

I was expecting Joel Martin to move to the side. If he didn't, I had a good half a foot and probably seventy-five pounds on him. Should it prove necessary, I had no doubt I'd be able to muscle past him.

When his outstretched fingers touched me, however, there was a sound like a houseful of windows shattering. Something like a blast of air shoved me across the bathroom, into the wall. Stunned, I looked at Joel Martin.

The air around him appeared to have dimmed. He seemed to have lost substance, to have flattened. As I watched, he began to crumple, as if he were made of paper and a pair of giant hands were crushing him between them. His mouth was open; he was saying, "No, oh no no no no," over and over again. The words sounded as if they were reaching me from across a vast gulf. He tried to reach out in my direction, but the force that was compressing the rest of him collapsed his arms against him. Eyes wide with pain, he alternated his no's with his son's name. His shoulders gave; his legs folded up to his torso. "Wait!" he shouted, his voice farther away still, "Wait! Wait!" His body bent inward, condensing itself. As his face began to crumple, he screamed, a howl of rage and frustration.

Then he was gone, and the air was full of swirling dust. Coughing, I raised my hands to my face. My eyes teared. It seemed I could hear Joel Martin screaming still, or maybe that was only the whine of the fluorescent lights. I coughed so hard it doubled me over. The dust had triggered an asthma attack. I pulled myself up on one of the sinks and saw in the mirror a man whose scarlet face was streaked with tears and dust. For a moment, I remembered standing beside Joel Martin, the two of us vibrating with barely-suppressed laughter, as we pointed at a corner of the hallway ceiling and said to one another, "What the hell is that?"

Before the dust had finished settling onto the fixtures, the floor, I fled the bathroom, half-running down the dark hallway back to the ballroom. Everywhere except the dance floor, the lights had been lowered. On the dance floor, men and women wearing the disinterested expressions of funeral statuary swayed and shuffled to the Talking Heads' "Road to Nowhere" thundering from the speakers like a demented march. Those seated in the shadows bobbed their heads in time to the beat.

Another round of coughing shook me. No one could hear it over the music. Hand covering my mouth, I stumbled to my table, where I was relieved to find Linda seated. She smiled when she saw me, but her brows lowered as I leaned over for a fresh bout of coughing. My head was spinning. I straightened, listed to the right, and Linda was there to steady me. Leaning close, she shouted, "What is it?"

I managed to say, "Asthma," loud enough for her to hear. She nodded, said, "Do you have an inhaler?"

I shook my head.

What Is Lost, What Is Given Away

"Is it bad?" she said. "Do you need to go to the emergency room?"

I shook my head again.

"Do you want me to drive you home?"

I nodded.

"Okay. Let me tell everyone what's going on."

This Linda did, drawing concerned looks and waves from the rest of the table. I returned the waves, but kept my distance. On the way out of the Tennis Club, we passed a couple arguing. He was severely drunk, seated on the lowest of the front steps, his tie yanked to one side, his shirt half-unbuttoned. She was standing in her stocking feet, using her flat pocketbook to punctuate the points she was making. The two of them had been among the popular crowd at Fatima, not homecoming king and queen, but certainly, part of their court. I was grateful another round of coughing took me as Linda and I walked by them, so I could pretend I wasn't aware they were enacting what appeared to be a fairly regular drama.

By the time Linda pulled into the parking lot in front of my apartment building, the worst of my asthma attack was over. It had prevented much conversation on the ride back, except for me to say that it had been triggered by something in the air in the men's room. As she handed me the keys, Linda said, "Are you going to be okay by yourself? Because I can stay over if you need me to."

"It's all right," I said. "I'll be fine. Thank you."

"Call me if you get worse."

"I will, but really, I'm fine. I'll use my inhaler the second I walk in the door."

"You'd better."

I did. And since I knew there was no chance of me falling asleep anytime in what seemed like the next several days, I took down the bottle of Talisker from the top of the refrigerator and poured myself three fingers whose effects I did not feel. I carried the bottle and glass into the living room, where I set them on the side table and found the TV remote. The night time channels were full of all manner of weird and pathetic programming, but together with the scotch, they were almost enough to keep me from dwelling on Joel Martin's expression while his prison crushed him, on his calling his son's name, on his final plea for a reprieve that was not granted. Eventually, I drank enough of the whisky for it drop me into a black, empty place.

IV

When I received the e-mail invitation to my twenty-fifth high school reunion, I'll admit, I considered responding to it. Enough time had elapsed for me to hope that my classmates and I might finally have moved beyond our differences. Instead, what I discovered, after a couple of messages to old friends found again through social media, was that there were two reunions being planned, one for the former elites of my class, and the other for the rest of us. I was sufficiently disgusted by the news to delete my invitation, washing my hands of the business of high school reunions for at least another quarter-century.

My decision was influenced as well by information which came to me at almost exactly the same time via the same social media connections. One of those old friends sent me a message asking if I'd heard the news about Sean McGahern, Sinead McGahern and Mr. Martin's kid. I replied that I hadn't. She forwarded me a link to a story about the tragic death of the young singer-songwriter whose first album, *Possession with Intent*, had won him critical acclaim and a Grammy nomination. The record chronicled his life growing up as the child of a narcissistic mother, an uninterested stepfather, and a father who appeared to have vanished off the face of the earth. Emotional and psychological difficulties had led him to experiment first with pot, then heroin, to which he had become addicted. For a brief period of time, while he was working on his album, he seemed to have put his addiction behind him. The pressures of touring to support it, however, combined with those of producing his follow-up effort, had sent him back to heroin. He had died of an overdose; there was some question whether it was an accident, or suicide.

After closing the link, I had to stand up and walk away from the computer. I had to leave my office, within the buzz of whose fluorescent light I heard another sound, high-pitched, impossibly distant: Joel Martin, screaming—still screaming—for all he had lost, all he had given away.

THE SUPPLEMENT

I hadn't seen Minerva Baker for six months, since she'd taken an early retirement that left the rest of the library's senior staff several shades of green. At the time of her departure from SUNY Huguenot's Harriet Jacobs Library, our Head Librarian had been a tall, heavyset woman whose brown hair, regularly-dyed and -styled, and fine, caramel features, carefully made-up, gave the impression she had only recently crossed the threshold into middle age, rather than advanced almost to its other side. The illusion was strengthened by the manner of her dress, current while avoiding the trendy, and the matter of her conversation, serious and informed by her morning's read of *The New York Times*. That there had been tragedy in her life was an open secret: an only child, a daughter, dead at fifteen of a heroin overdose in the bathroom of Huguenot High, and a husband who had left the following year, for the therapist they had been meeting. Minerva didn't speak of any of it to us, however, so neither did we to her. In the month before her departure, she softened slightly, sharing with us her intention to spend her looming free time first on a trip to the Jersey shore, then on catching up with some reading. Her farewell dinner was a bland, pleasant hour and a half, where those of us who had worked beside and under her stood to offer generic tributes and toasts to her.

And that was that, until I saw her in the produce section of the local

Shop-Rite, fumbling over a display of plums, lifting one for inspection with a trembling hand. Immediately, I knew who she was, even as I was thinking, *There's no way.* Had twenty, thirty years elapsed since our last contact, I might have believed the woman hunched in front of me was the same one who had been my boss for the better part of five years. Wrinkled, liver-spotted, the skin hung loose on her arms, about her neck. Beneath a dingy Mets cap, her hair was white, wild. A pair of thick reading glasses balanced on the end of her nose. Her lower jaw jutted forward, pushing her lips up and out in a way that reminded me of my grandfather, in the latter stages of his dementia. Everything about her suggested a collapse of catastrophic dimensions, Alzheimer's of terrifyingly-fast onset, or a major stroke, or a devastating injury. Gone were her fashionable clothes, replaced by a sleeveless blue dress speckled with the remnants of recent meals. A clear plastic bag looped around her left wrist contained a wallet and a set of keys. As she was struggling to hold, and dropping, the plum, the urge to flee, to separate myself from this person and whatever calamity had enfolded her, seized me. I might have succumbed to it, had one of the supermarket's employees not coughed and said, "Excuse me," at my back, so that he could push a cart stacked with yogurt past me. I stepped aside, recovered myself, and walked over to my former boss and said, "Uh, Minerva?"

At the sound of her name, she turned her head toward me. The grooves in her skin seemed to cut all the way to the bone. Her right cheek was a forest of skin tags. The whites of her eyes were yellowed, the pupils cloudy. Her jaw worked, and I wondered if her affliction had taken her identity from her, too, if she was here as part of a group from one of the local care facilities. In a voice that had aged as much as the rest of her, she said, "Sam."

The pleased surprise with which she pronounced my name made it clear that she recognized me. Her follow up questions, "How have you been? How are things at the library? How's Hideki doing? Is he running you ragged?" confirmed that her mind remained intact.

"Good," I said, "I'm good. We're good. Hideki's…coming along."

She laughed. "Ever the diplomat."

"What about you?" I said. "How have you been?"

"You mean, What the hell happened to you, don't you?"

"Have you been sick? I meant to keep in touch, but…"

"It isn't as if we were all that close to begin with," Minerva said. "It's fine.

The Supplement

I have not been sick, not really. What I have been is busy."

"That's good."

"Maybe it is and maybe it isn't. What I've been engaged in has taken its toll on me, to the extent that, frankly, I'm surprised you knew who I was."

"You don't look that different."

"Yes I do. It's kind of you to say, but I can still see myself in the mirror."

"Okay," I said, "so what the hell have you been busy with?"

"A book."

"A book? What—like, restoring one?"

She shook her head. "If you can hang around for a couple of minutes while I pick up a few things, then run me back to my apartment, I'll show you what I've been up to."

My wife was teaching her graduate class, which meant there was no need for me to rush home. Not to mention, my curiosity had been raised, as well as pity at the image of Minerva in her diminished state, alone in her apartment. "Sure," I said.

I trailed after her as she filled her basket with the scant necessities of her daily life. Our talk continued, though it focused on me. Yes, Alexa was well. Yes, we had talked about trying for a baby a second time. No, we hadn't done anything about it. "Yet," I added.

"Give it time," Minerva said. "You're young."

Her shopping concluded, mine forgotten, I drove Minerva to the other side of Huguenot, to her modest apartment in the Riverview Arms. While she stored her groceries, I inspected the photographs on her living room walls. Here were Minerva's graduation portraits from high school, college, and graduate school, each surrounded by smaller photos of her, in her robes, flanked by an older man and woman I assumed were her parents, and assorted other people I took for aunts, uncles, cousins. There were pictures of her in a number of foreign cities, London, Paris, and Prague, and seaside shots that could have been taken anywhere. There were more photos of her at work than I would have expected, including a couple in which I identified myself. I was not surprised to find no pictures of her wedding, but I was struck by the lack of any photos of her daughter. Perhaps the memory was too painful, or perhaps she kept those pictures in a more private place, her bedroom or study.

"All right," Minerva said from the kitchen doorway. "I would offer you a beer, but I haven't got any. Would you like a Coke?"

"I'm fine, thanks," I said. "Don't let that stop you."

"It won't." She returned to the kitchen. I heard a cupboard door squeak open, the clink of glass, the *pock* of a bottle being unstoppered. She reappeared holding a tumbler a little less than half full of a dark, honey-tinted liquid. She deposited the glass on an end table beside a recliner. "Make yourself comfortable," she said, waving her hand at the short couch. "I'll be right back." She exited the room down a corridor that led, I presumed, to the bath- and bedrooms. A doorknob clicked, hinges squealed. A moment later, she shuffled back into the living room.

As she did so, some trick of the light made it appear as if there were momentarily two of her, as if her reflection had escaped the mirror and was walking beside her. I shut my eyes, shook my head. When I looked again, I saw one Minerva, carrying a large, framed photograph in one hand and a slender, leather-bound book in the other. She crossed to me and held out the picture, which I took. "My Yvonne," she said. She made her way to the easy chair, into which she lowered herself carefully. Safely seated, she placed the book in her lap and reached for the tumbler.

The photo she'd handed me was a portrait of a teenage girl, the head-and-shoulder shot offered every fall by most schools. Its background, blurry, showed trees in autumn yellow, orange, and red. Yvonne Baker smiled ruefully at the camera, her teeth fenced by braces, her eyes shrunk by a pair of thick, round glasses. A rash of pimples spread across her forehead. Her hair, black, curly, was cut in a bob whose lower ends flared out and away from her chin. She was wearing a blouse whose broad, white and peach stripes made it appear wider than it was. I thought of my own, equally-disastrous high school pictures, the look of long-suffering regret I'd worn for them. "She's lovely," I said, rising to pass the portrait back to Minerva.

"Thank you," she said. She placed it face-up on her end table. "She didn't think so—said she was hideous, a freak. I never took her seriously. That's what every fifteen-year-old girl says, right?"

"And boy."

Minerva nodded. "I trotted out the same clichés my mom had used on me. Ugly ducklings turn into beautiful swans, I said. Just you wait. Anyway, it's what on the inside that counts. None of that had worked for me; I don't know why I imagined it would for her. We offer these platitudes because

The Supplement

we're afraid of admitting the truth. This is a horrible time. People will be more cruel to you now than they ever have been before or are likely to be again. There's little you can do except endure. All I can offer is my love, which I'm afraid isn't enough."

She sighed. "I'm not sure how she got into heroin. I assume the why was to fit in, and for the relief it offered. I don't know who introduced her to it, when she started using, how she afforded it. I didn't pick up on any of the warning signs. How is any of that possible, right? That was what my ex-husband kept saying. 'How could you not have known?' *You*, not *we*. She was found in the girls' bathroom, the week before Valentine's Day, unresponsive. The ambulance was called; they rushed her across the river, to Penrose. She was put on life support, but there was no brain activity. We waited a couple of days, and then we—I made the decision to let her go."

"I'm very sorry," I said.

"Thank you," she said. "After that, everything fell apart. My marriage broke up, and most of our friends went with my ex. His cut-throat lawyer was better than my cut-throat lawyer, so when the house was sold, our assets divvied up, he came out ahead. I'd like to say I didn't care, but I did. I was angry at the way he had made Yvonne's death my fault, her and him collateral damage from my professional ambitions. Can you believe that? When he and his lawyer outmaneuvered me and my lawyer, it was—I knew he would present it as proof that his version of events was true, a kind of updated trial-by-combat. Which was ridiculous, of course, except that the majority of our friends took it that way, too. I guess I did, a little. Or—I was nervous it was true.

"I did not want to be one of those people who are defined by their tragedies. I didn't want the first thing anyone said about me to be, 'Oh, Minerva Baker, she lost her daughter to drugs,' or, 'Her husband ran off with a younger woman.' I threw myself into my work. I lobbied for more funding for the library, expanded the science catalogue, upgraded the film and video holdings. I convinced Veronica Croydon to donate her late husband's collection of Victorian books and artifacts to us. I scheduled lectures, book groups, film screenings. At the risk of sounding immodest, I made the Jacobs Library the premiere university library in the Mid-Hudson Valley."

"Yes, you did," I said.

"It wasn't enough, though. In the end, no matter how much I accomplished during my time in charge of the library, it was a case of the Ronald Coleman room."

"The what-room?"

"Ronald Coleman. It's in the old library building, over by Old Main. Last time I checked, Photography was using it as a darkroom. Ronald Coleman was provost of the college when it was still a teachers' school. After he died, at the age of one hundred and four, a room in what was then the school library was dedicated to his memory. I had noticed the nameplate beside the door one time I was over there, so I researched it, even found a copy of the dedication speech. The room, it said, would serve as a reminder of the provost's relationship to the school for which he had done so much. Every time students saw Coleman's name, they would think on him, and his memory would endure.

"Except it didn't. Nor is he unique. The Huguenot campus is littered with plaques dedicating this tree, that bench, this room, that building, to the memory of former students, faculty, administrators. The only name anyone can tell you anything about is Harriet Jacobs, and that's because she was a writer. The others…you understand they meant something to somebody, but that's about it. Only the sentiment survives. A tree might be planted for me, a classroom designated the Minerva Baker room, but in the end, I would suffer the same fate as the former provost.

"Had Yvonne been alive, I doubt any of this would have mattered as much, if at all. The adage about your child being a kind of immortality is true enough. But she wasn't alive. What remained of my daughter was her death, the space she'd left in the world."

Minerva lifted the tumbler and tasted its contents. "Well," she said, "I guess that was a bit more than you were expecting."

I didn't know what to say.

"A bit more, and a bit less." She drank from her glass a second time. "None of this explains the reason I look the way I do; although you might call it the context. The immediate cause of my decline lies in here," she said, and patted the book in her lap. Beyond noticing that it was oversized, the dimensions of a magazine rather than a hardcover, and bound in leather the soft color of butter, I hadn't paid much attention to it. When the palm of Minerva's hand touched the cover, for the slightest of instants, I would have sworn she vanished, that instead of her seated in the chair, there was a

The Supplement

blank within her silhouette. So quickly was she there again, however, that I discounted what I had seen as a perceptual glitch. She said, "The fellow who told me about it called it The Supplement."

"What is it?"

"He wasn't the one who gave it to me. No, that was somebody else—George Farange was his name. You wouldn't have known it to look at him, but he was old. Much older than I am—than I've become. He wore his years easily, as comfortably as the navy suit he had on when he showed up at the door to my office. This was maybe six weeks before I retired. This man appeared at the front desk asking to view a manuscript from the Croydon collection. Lucille sent him to talk to me. He was pencil sketch of a fellow, the lines of his cheeks, his jaw, his forehead, somehow faint, as if he weren't all the way *there*. The only part of him that was present were his eyes. They were pale, almost no real color to speak of, but they burned in the sockets. If he was a sketch, then the eyes were holes poked in the paper, a blowtorch shining through them. Everything else, the expensive suit and shoes, the neatly-trimmed van dyke, the hair slicked back against his skull, was decoration.

"He had come, George Farange said, because news had reached his ears—that was how he talked, *Word has reached my ears*—that the late Professor Croydon had succeeded in obtaining a letter that the writer, Wilkie Collins, had written to his friend, the writer, Charles Dickens, about a visit to the Parisian catacombs. I couldn't imagine how this man had come by his information. Most of the Croydon collection was still in boxes in one of the conference rooms, awaiting cataloguing. Had Mr. Farange known Roger Croydon? I asked.

"The pleasure had been denied him, he said. He had not learned of the letter's location until after the Professor's untimely end, which was a shame, because he would have relished the opportunity to call on the man in his fascinating home. (Roger Croydon lived in that big place on Founders, the Belvedere House.)

"I still wasn't clear how the man knew about this document. Nor was I sure why it mattered. Assuming I agreed to search for the letter, and assuming I found it and allowed him to look at it, I wasn't about to let him walk out of the library with it. If he tried to take it from me, I outweighed him by at least fifty pounds. Thin—insubstantial as he was, I figured one punch and he'd vanish in a puff of dust. I had a pretty good idea where the piece was, and it wasn't as if I had much else to do: Hideki had already assumed most of my day-to-day duties. I couldn't promise anything, I said, but I would have a look. Farange thanked me.

"As I'd thought it would be, the letter was in the second of four boxes of rare manuscripts and correspondence. It was toward the front, six sheets of paper held in a clear plastic sleeve. There was handwriting on eleven of the twelve sides, tall, careful script, easy to read. I eased the pages from their cover and spread them on one of the room's tables. I was pretty pleased with myself. I returned to my office, and fetched George Farange.

"The sight of the pages impressed him far less than I would have predicted. Hands in his trouser pockets, he strolled over to the table as if he were browsing a display of old flyers. He didn't lean closer to inspect the letter, the way a scholar (or a collector) might. To be honest, he didn't look as if he was paying much attention to them at all. When he turned around, he had a book in his right hand, this book," Minerva nodded at the volume on her lap. "I would have sworn on a stack of Bibles he hadn't carried it into the room with him. He said, 'I wonder if I might impose on you to examine this for me.'

"Right away, I was certain I'd understood his game. When I opened the book, I would find a stack of bills tucked inside the front cover. I would say something like, 'I'll need to examine this in my office,' step out of the room, and return to find the table empty. I'd give the book back to Farange, he would leave, and that would be that. Maybe we would do this again, should he learn of another rarity in the library's possession.

"Of course I wasn't going to accept his bribe. I was curious, though, to learn what the going rate was. I took the book. Already, I was looking forward to the expression on his face when I rejected his offer. Holding the book in my left hand, I used my right index finger to turn the cover," she mimed the action, "to heighten the drama.

"There was no money. In fact, there wasn't anything in the book: its pages were blank. I would have said it was no different from the journals you can buy at any bookstore or stationery shop, except that it had the feel of a much older volume. The cover was smooth with age. The pages were soft, almost oily; I thought they might be vellum. As I turned them, little clouds of cedary dust rose into the air. I went through every last page, but the book

The Supplement

was empty. I looked at George Farange and said, 'I don't understand. What is it I'm supposed to be examining?' I held the volume out to him.

"Would I mind having another look at it? he asked. It was his experience that, as a reader might need to accustom himself to a particular text, so a particular text might need to accustom itself to a reader.

"Had I missed something? I didn't suppose Farange would try bribing me via personal check, but I was new to this world. I opened the book. I lingered on each page, making sure that it wasn't stuck to the next one. Whatever material they were, it was softer, *spongier* than vellum. At the end, though, the book still contained neither text nor money. I was starting to wonder if George Farange and his blank book were a prank, some manner of farewell-tomfoolery cooked up by Hideki; although the point of it was lost on me. As far as strippers went, this fellow was about the last man you would have chosen for the job. I raised my eyes from the book—

"—and Yvonne was standing in front of me, just as real and alive as you are to me and I to you. She was wearing an oversized tie-dyed T-shirt and a pair of new jeans—one of the outfits, I realized, her father and I had bought her when she completed her stay in rehab. Yes, rehab. Instead of overdosing, the girl before me had walked into her guidance counselor's office, dumped the contents of her purse on that woman's desk, and declared herself in need of help. I give Ms. Bowen credit. She didn't panic, didn't rush to call either the school's resource officer or me and Yvonne's father. She left the mess on her desk untouched. She spent the next three hours talking with Yvonne, until my daughter felt ready to phone me and her dad. I *remembered* that call, remembered the shock that had poured through me like cold water, the crumpling sensation in my middle, as if my insides were made of tin foil and an enormous hand was crushing them. When I went to back my car out of its spot, I put it in drive and leapt the barrier, scraped the undercarriage. I met Yvonne's father at the school entrance, and he was that furious way he got when he was truly afraid. We joined hands and entered the school for a meeting with Yvonne and the guidance counselor that ended with her father and I driving her across the river to Penrose, to check her into their residential rehab unit. The next month was full of meetings for Yvonne's father and me: with the case worker supervising her treatment, with a support group for family members of addicts, with Yvonne's guidance counselor, and with my daughter, herself, with and without her case worker. The meetings continued after we took her home; in fact, that was what she and I were talking about, changing the time of her next therapy appointment to allow her to try out for spring track.

"Not only was my daughter talking to me, she was doing so in the kitchen of the house her father and I had sold as part of our divorce. I loved that house. It had big rooms with high ceilings, which made it a pain to heat, but I didn't care. The kitchen ran the back of the house and ended in a window nook where Yvonne used to sit and read when she was younger. The house was one of a pair that had been built, side by side, after the Civil War by a man who made his fortune in the railroad. He lived in our house, and his twin brother lived in the house next door, until they had a falling out, and never spoke again. I could tell you all sorts of thing about that place. Once a researcher, always a researcher, I suppose. The point is, there we were, in the kitchen with its long counters, and there was Yvonne's father, too, at the stove, sautéing a pan of onions and spices for the chili he threw together every couple of weeks. The sight of him in his sweater and jeans and the DON'T MAKE ME POISON YOUR FOOD apron he wore was almost as much a surprise as seeing Yvonne. But it made sense: she hadn't died, so none of the awful consequences of that most awful event had occurred. We were still a family, living in our home.

"I was stunned. I was about cry with joy. I was horrified. Yes, horrified. After someone dies—after someone that close to you, that much a part of you, dies, it takes years to accept their death, to adjust to their absence. Is it Freud who talks about the work of mourning? It is work, a process whereby you move your loved one from the land of the living to the land of the dead, from *is* to *was*. To have them back after all that time, all that effort, wrenches you. Not to mention, you're immediately terrified you're going to lose them again.

"Which I did, when I dropped the book. It thumped on the carpet, and I was back in the conference room. Everything grew dark; I was afraid I was going to faint. I reached out my right hand to the table, to steady myself, and saw its surface bare, the letter gone. As was George Farange. I took a seat. The book lay open on the floor. I leaned down for it. I glanced at the pages, still blank. How had he—

"—and there was Yvonne in her tie-dyed T-shirt and jeans, in the kitchen of the old house, her father pouring the first can of beans into the frying

The Supplement

pan. Well, she wanted to know, what did I think about rescheduling her appointment?

"This time, I slapped the book shut, and was in the library. I started to shiver, in that uncontrollable way you do when the flu is coming over you. Had Farange slipped me some kind of drug? I recalled the dust that had lifted from the book's pages as I turned them. Could it have been a hallucinogen? The idea seemed ridiculous, but considering what I'd just experienced—twice—maybe not. Thing was, I'd dabbled with magic mushrooms during my student days, and while time had dimmed the memory somewhat, my encounter with Yvonne had been substantially different from tripping, more definite, the edges sharper.

"But no matter what Farange had done to me, Wilkie Collins's letter was missing, a not-insignificant part of a legacy for whose integrity I was ultimately responsible, even if I was behind in cataloguing its contents—which I had planned to complete my last couple of weeks before retirement, a pleasant way to pass my final hours at work. In fact, I had yet to record any of the contents of the box which had held the letter.

"Like that, the solution to my dilemma presented itself. Yes, Veronica Croydon had included printed lists of the contents of each box of her husband's papers, but we could only be accountable for what was there when we composed our official record. If a document she listed wasn't present, well, maybe she'd made a mistake. It was entirely possible: there were a lot of materials in those boxes. The likelihood of her poring over the library's breakdown of her husband's effects was slim to none. After all, if she'd been that concerned about them in the first place, the woman wouldn't have donated Roger Croydon's papers to us, would she?

"Yes, I know how all this sounds. I could have gone to the Dean and explained to her what had happened, and her first question would have been, Was I all right? After which, she would have called the campus police, told them I had been the victim of a possible assault, during which important documents had been stolen. No doubt the local papers would find out. That prospect, of my being a victim—a dupe—was not one I welcomed. I did not want my remaining time at the job at which I had excelled to be shadowed by failure, as if by a sign that my departure from the position was happening in the nick of time, if not slightly past it. Vanity, yes, to which, I suppose I would have told you, I was entitled.

"What I really wanted, though, was the chance to spend more time with George Farange's blank book. By the time I had finished putting away the Croydon boxes, it was late enough in the day for me to leave without raising any eyebrows. I drove straight home, made a quick bite to eat, and settled down to find out if the book retained its strange power.

"It did. I turned a couple of its pages, and there was my daughter, right hand on her hip, head tilted to the left, a look on her face like she'd just tasted a piece of fruit that was slightly rotten. It was her, 'Mother, I'm *waiting*,' pose. Here—wherever this was, this past that hadn't been—Yvonne was listening for my answer to her spring track question. Her father was stirring the beans he'd added to the frying pan. I opened my mouth and said, 'I think we can manage that. What does your father have to say?'

"'He said to ask you,' Yvonne said, which made me think, *Typical*, but which also made my heart jump. I had talked to my daughter, and she had responded. However small it was, we had had an interaction. While Yvonne's father continued to add more kinds of beans and a can of tomatoes to his chili, my conversation with her continued. Did she have any idea what events she might want to try out for? Sprints? Distance running? The hurdles? Long jump? Sprinting, she said, she was the fastest in her gym class. Yvonne had never been what you would call competitive. Was she prepared to race against girls from another school and try to beat them? 'Geez, Mom,' she said, 'when did you become one of those sports parents?' 'Yeah,' her father called, 'if she wants to run, let her run.' I wasn't stopping her from running, I said, I simply wanted to be sure she understood what the coaches would be expecting of her, that was all.

"It's funny. After someone is gone, you think, 'If only I could speak to them one last time, I would say all the things I never said, never said enough, while they were here.' I had a litany of such statements, from the big, 'I love you,' to the small, 'On my desk at work, there's a picture of you in the waves at Myrtle Beach. You were five, wearing that green bathing suit with the orange fish on it that you said made you a fish princess. Every time I look at that photo, no matter how bad a day I'm having, I smile.' Yet here I was, granted that extra conversation, or something close enough to it, and already, I had fallen into the habits of a decade and a half gone by. Throughout our exchange, I had not ceased feeling George Farange's book, resting on my lap. I closed it and brought myself back to my apartment.

The Supplement

"I had to locate Farange and speak to him, maybe pay him a visit. I spent the next day sequestered in my office, tracking him down. It took some doing, but I found him on the High Street in Edinburgh, in Scotland. That ruled out a face to face encounter, but his phone number was listed. I wrote it down and then…nothing. I didn't touch the book, which I placed on the desk in the guest room, and I didn't call George Farange. I took no action, but it was one of those cases where not acting is a deliberate choice. What I was waiting for, I'm not certain; although it may have been my last day at the library. Were I to open the book again, I knew I would find it more difficult to shut, and I didn't want that to interfere with my job. Actually, it was more that I didn't want work to interfere with the experience of the book.

"The night my retirement began, after a celebratory dinner at Pesce, I went into the guest room and retrieved the blank book. I lay down on my bed with it and did not leave either bed or book for the next several hours. During that time, I sat with Yvonne on the living room couch in my old house and watched the second half of *The Aristocats* on TV. She loved that movie, had ever since she was a little thing. We watched the cats outsmart the baddies, while the air filled with the smell of Yvonne's father's chili, cumin and garlic and tomato, and when the credits were rolling, we went into the kitchen and ate chili and cornbread for dinner. Between bites, Yvonne said that the film always made her want to visit Paris. Well, her father said, maybe we should, and suddenly, we were planning a vacation to France for the following summer.

"It was all so *ordinary*. We could have been one of a million different families, going through their nightly routine. No muss, no fuss. Only, once all that has been lost to you, the mundane becomes fantastical, a kind of lost oasis of happiness and tranquility. Throughout the evening, I struggled not to burst into tears at the sheer quietness of everything. Yvonne did her homework, went up to bed. Her father retired not long after. I sat up to watch the late news and one of the late night talk shows. Once the talk show was over, I climbed the stairs to Yvonne's room. Her door was open. I peered inside. She was asleep, snoring softly. I tip-toed into her room, slid the chair out from her desk, and lowered myself onto it. Much the way I had when she was a baby, I watched her breathe, as sleep crept over me.

"I came to with a start, unsure where I was. My room, the bedroom I'd laid my head down in for the last twelve years, looked strange, unfamiliar, as if I'd emerged into a dream. I sat up, and noticed the book sprawled on the floor, where it landed when it slipped from my lap. The sight of it brought me back to…my senses, I suppose. My head was splitting, and I was exhausted to the point of nausea. I fetched a glass of water and a couple of ibuprofen, and climbed back into bed.

"The next morning, I didn't feel much better. *It figures*, I thought. *First day of my retirement, and I come down with the flu.* However, being sick gave me an excuse to spend more time with George Farange's book, if I needed one. I breakfasted on weak tea and dry toast and returned to those empty pages. I won't bore you with a recitation of that session's events; suffice it to say, they were incredibly unexciting. As were those of the next day's session, and the one after that, and so on, until a week had slipped by and I hadn't stirred from my bed any more than was absolutely necessary. Despite the extensive bed rest, my sickness hadn't improved; although I wasn't especially concerned. A good flu can knock you down for ten days, two weeks, even. What concerned me was glancing into the bathroom mirror that seventh morning and seeing the streak of white in my hair. This wasn't the color treatment I used starting to lose its hold; this was my hair bleached white. You might have said it leant me a stylish appearance. But the texture was wrong, fibrous, the way I remembered my grandmother's hair feeling. It could have been some fluke of the last product I'd used, but I knew in my gut that it was a direct consequence of the last week with the book. I had a strong suspicion my illness was connected to it, too.

"I didn't waste any time. I located George Farange's number and placed the call to the UK.

"A different man answered the phone. He sounded younger, substantially. He spoke with an American accent, from somewhere in our neck of the woods, I'd guess. No, he said, Mr. Farange wasn't in. He was away on business; the young man couldn't say when he would return. Perhaps he could be of assistance. What was I calling in regard to?

"A book, I said. Mr. Farange had given me a book to examine, and I wanted to speak to him about it.

"What kind of book?

"It was about the size of a magazine, I told him. Bound in leather. Thirty sheets of what I thought was vellum. I estimated it as late eighteenth cen-

The Supplement

tury, but wasn't certain. That I could detect, the cover, the pages, were devoid of any text.

"He drew in a breath, said something like, So you're the one. Then he said, 'What has it done to you?'

"From the tone of his voice, I knew what he was asking. I said I'd been sick, with what I'd assumed was the flu. Now my hair was going white.

"The book was called The Supplement, the young man said. It was also known as Odin's Eye.

"What is it? I said.

"For an answer, he told a story. There is a city, he said, that stands on the shore of a black ocean. It is old, and it has many neighborhoods. In one of these, there is a church. It's not much to look at, a long, low building whose walls are cracked and whose front door doesn't lock the way it should. Anything of value inside, sculptures by famous artists, sacred vessels fashioned of gold, relics of saints long-dead, has long since been moved to a more secure location, or stolen. If you walk up the center aisle to the altar, however, and circle it to the right, you will find a doorway in the rear wall. It's barred by a heavy gate whose lock is in perfect working order. Should you happen to have in your possession the key to that lock, and should you also know a certain sequence of words to utter while fitting and turning the key, you will find yourself at the top of a flight of stone stairs. They descend a considerable distance. At their foot, you will enter a corridor that leads to a large, heavy door, also locked. If you have come this far, then it's likely you'll have the key to this lock, too, and know the proper words to speak as you insert and twist the key. When you open the door, you will confront what appears to be a wall of white material, plaster, perhaps. Touch it, though, and you will feel it soft, warm, almost oily. It glows with a white radiance that overwhelms whatever light you have employed thus far. It is alive—or rather, it's part of something alive. Call it an eye, but such an eye as never was. Do you know the myth of Odin's right eye? He plucked it from the socket in order to gain a draught from the well of Mimir the wise. After Mimir took it, he dropped the eye into the waters of his well. Imagine the eye of a god, floating in dark water. Imagine an eye vast as a cathedral, an organ that can take in the reaches of the galaxy, of galaxies far beyond. Imagine an eye that can view what was, what is, and what will be, as well as what was not, is not, and will not be, that can apprehend all contingencies simultaneously.

"Now, the young man said, suppose you have brought to this aperture a knife of surpassing sharpness. With such a blade, you might shave from the surface of this great eye the thinnest of sheets. Who knows how many you could peel away? Later, after you have returned to your chambers, you might assemble these sheets into a book, bind them between leather covers. This book would allow its reader to participate in what the eye surveys; though to the reader, unaccustomed to the eye's perspective, it would seem as if they were living within that vision. Some might seek the answers to exotic mysteries. Some might venture through time and space. Some might pursue more modest goals, might search out lives in which they had been spared certain tragedies, the untimely death of a loved one, a missed opportunity in love. Rare indeed would be the man or woman who could turn the pages of such a volume and not be drawn out of themselves, into another vista.

"But why the sickness? I asked. Why the white hair?

"Divorced from their host, the young man said, the book's pages required another source of power.

"Me, I said.

"If I were to put the volume aside, never open its cover again, then the likelihood was that I would recover in short order. The white patch in my hair would grow out. If I returned to The Supplement, however, I could expect my condition to worsen. The young man had not heard of anyone lasting more than a year with the book, and if he was to be candid, most were consumed by it in half, a quarter that time.

"Why had George Farange given it to me? What had I done to him or his?

"A trade, the young man said. He assumed Mr. Farange took something from me.

"There was a letter he was interested in… But what the hell kind of trade was that? I had no idea what I was taking from him.

"He wasn't saying it was a fair trade, the young man said. Anyway, would I have believed Farange if he had told me what the book was and what it did?

"It was a fair enough point. I asked what was supposed to happen next.

"Nothing, he said. I had The Supplement. I was free to do with it as I chose.

"He and his friend didn't want it back?

The Supplement

"They would have the book in due time, he said."

Minerva raised her glass and finished its contents. "As you can see, I returned to the book—to Yvonne, to the life we hadn't lived. I would like to make it out as a dramatic choice, but it was more something I fell back into. Oh, I steered clear of it for a good couple of weeks, took that trip to Cape May I'd promised myself, sat on the beach and caught up on my reading, ate at some very nice restaurants. And all the time, I kept thinking, *I wish Yvonne were here: she'd love this*. It wasn't exactly a new thought, but my experience with The Supplement leant it a weight it hadn't had for years. I've always loved the ocean, always found sitting beside it restorative. Watching the waves roll onto the shore by myself, though, hurt. After I returned here, I decided to open the book for a few minutes, just long enough to check on my daughter. Already, I was wondering if I could maybe look at it every now and again, once a month, or once a week. That wouldn't be so bad, would it? Spread out its effects over years, decades, even.

"What was supposed to be a quick visit turned into a much longer stay, almost two days. Something strange happened to the passage of time in the other place: almost a full week went by. There, we had rescheduled Yvonne's therapy appointment to allow her to try out for spring track. She made the team. Her father and I took her out for a celebratory dinner at the Plaza Diner.

"When I emerged from this session, it was to more white hair on my reflection, some serious lines on my forehead, alongside my mouth. The flu feeling was back, bad as ever. I can't say my appearance didn't make me jump, but the surprise didn't last long. I cleaned up, ate a good meal, and went back to The Supplement, to what I had started thinking of as my real life.

"I watched my daughter win races, the four- and eight-hundred meters. I helped her select a prom dress when one of her teammates asked her to go. I went to the high school's varsity breakfast, where Yvonne received her letter. She and her father and I took our trip to France. I sifted through college catalogues with her, helped with her applications. She decided on Penrose, which secretly pleased me, because it was close. At college, she majored in Economics. She graduated and moved to the city to take a job with a non-profit. She left that position to work at the UN. She met a boy from Kenya. Her father liked him well enough; I was never able to talk much with him. He made Yvonne happy, though, so when she called to say they were engaged, I screamed and played the part of the ecstatic mother. For a brief time, I was afraid they would move to Nairobi, where his people were. They didn't, settling in Westchester, instead. They had two children, a girl, Tonya, and a boy, Reuben. The three and then the four of them visited holidays, and Yvonne's father and I drove down to spend time with them as often as they could tolerate us.

"Don't I sound like someone's grandmother?" Minerva said. "I could talk about that life all day. This life…well, it's been less pleasant. The changes to my appearance are obvious: people I worked beside twenty years don't recognize me. Most of the last six months, I've been in pain. First, it was arthritis, lighting my hips and shoulders on fire. Aspirin helped for a time, then I had to schedule an appointment with my doctor. I've been in her office a lot; it seems that, if I'm not with Yvonne, I'm with Dr. Citera. She wrote me a prescription for something to dampen the joint pain, as well as a calcium supplement for the osteoporosis she picked up on. My bones had turned to kindling. Not long after that, my kidneys started acting up, and my blood sugar went on a roller coaster ride. More pills helped with all of that, but there wasn't much they could do about the wasting of my muscles, the weight melting off me. My doctor's convinced I'm suffering from an underlying condition that's the root cause of everything else, one of those rare diseases that spurs rapid aging. When my liver numbers came back bad, she wanted to send me up to Albany Med to consult a specialist. I appreciated her concern; to tell the truth, I felt bad not being able to tell her that she was right, my maladies did share a common source. What good would it have done, though, to have explained that my physical decline was the result of continued contact with a book whose pages had been razored from an unimaginable eye? She would have added dementia to my list of symptoms. As kindly as I could, I declined the trip to Albany Med, uttered the old-lady cliché about it being my time to go when it was my time to go that I'd heard my grandmother use in her final months. The doctor wasn't happy, but she respected my decision.

"Now…now, it's a question of how much more time I can manage with my daughter before my body gives out. I'm hoping to see my granddaughter graduate high school. If not…" She shrugged. "Pain has become a constant, to the extent that it follows me into the other life. Yvonne's noticed me gri-

THE SUPPLEMENT

macing, had me consult a doctor over there. He's running tests for cancer. I can't tell him the truth, either. Or Yvonne, for that matter: the last thing I want is for my time with her to be spent with her worrying I've lost my mind.

"It occurs to me," Minerva said, "here at the end, that there were other routes my life might have traveled, other possibilities the book might have shown me. Maybe if I'd known how to use it properly, I could have lived some of them, too. You know, when I was in high school, there was a time I thought I was going to be an Olympic fencer? I competed nationally, won more than I lost. Could I have witnessed that life? Or was the time I missed with Yvonne always going to be what I saw?"

"Bit late to worry about it now, I suppose."

Whatever the expression on my face was, it caused Minerva to laugh. I blushed, looked down. "I'm sorry," I said.

"Don't worry," she said. "I'm not so far gone I don't know how all of this sounds. I appreciate you listening to me. I think I needed to hear myself tell the story to someone before—while I still could."

"Do you—"

"There's nothing for you to do—nothing you could do. Even if I never open this book again, my days have reached their limit. I'd just as soon spend them with my daughter."

"But—"

"You can let yourself out. Give my best to your wife."

Already, her gaze was drifting to the book in her lap. I stood, said, "I'll see you," and walked toward the apartment door on legs stiff from sitting so long. My skull felt tight, full past the brim with Minerva's delusion. Fascination at the scenario she'd constructed competed with raw sadness at the crumbling of a fine mind. Hand on the doorknob, I paused, overcome with guilt at leaving someone in such a state on their own. I turned and hurried back to the living room, an apology forming on my lips.

The sight of Minerva dried my words. She was holding the book in both hands, tilted upright, her neck inclined toward it. From my position, I could see that the pages open before her were indeed blank. They trembled, as if composed of a substance less solid than paper. From the page to Minerva's right, a slender white tube extended to her right eye, plunging into it. From the page to her left, another such tube rose to the base of her throat, piercing the skin there. While I watched, Minerva faded, growing steadily less distinct, and the white tubes, the pages of the book, filled with pale light. Through her silhouette, I saw at a distance a space like a garden, its myriad of paths branching one from the other, forming a design too vast and complex to take in, each path trod by a version of Minerva Baker.

I stumbled backward. I had to do something, had to save Minerva from this impossible fate. But this imperative sat somewhere high above, divorced from the rest of me, and when I acted, it was to run to the door, throw it open, and rush out without closing it behind me.

***

Two weeks later, Minerva Baker died. At her request, her wake was closed-casket. Her funeral was held at the Huguenot Reformed Church on Founders' Street. I attended her wake, but not the funeral. I had not returned to her apartment since fleeing it, my heart pounding.

A week and a half after that, the mail carrier delivered a large, padded envelope addressed to me in Minerva's spiky script. I knew its contents before I sliced open one end and peered inside. Without removing The Supplement, I set Minerva's last communication to me on the kitchen table and walked into the living room. Alexa wasn't home, wouldn't be home till later this evening. The past months—the past year, really—she hadn't been spending a lot of time at the house. To be fair, when we were together, our conversation didn't go much past what we were having for dinner, what bills were due, occasional gossip about work. She had miscarried at five months, and while we had clung together desperately in the immediate aftermath of our loss, the further we went from it, the further we went from one another, too.

I wandered from the living room down the hallway to the door that what was supposed to have been the nursery. Antonia: that was the name we'd picked, Antonia Rose. I opened the door and stepped into the room. We'd talked about doing something else with the space—it was one of the few discussions we still had—but our plans had remained that.

The gliding rocker we'd bought was in its place beside the empty crib. I sat in it. I considered the crib, the stenciled animals decorating the walls. I thought about Minerva's book, safe in its padded case, about what it could

The Supplement

show me. I thought about the child whose cries, never voiced, I'd never stopped hearing.

MIRROR FISHING

Four feet tall by a foot and a half wide, framed in blond wood, the mirror hung on the inside of Patrick and his younger brother's bedroom door. His father had positioned the glass rectangle a couple of inches from the bottom of the door, which for the longest time had allowed him and Davis to check their school uniforms in it each morning. During the past year, however, Pat had started a growth spurt that had left him six inches taller at the end of seventh grade than he had been at the beginning. Now the top of his reflection's head was no longer visible unless Pat bent his knees. Dad had been talking about adjusting the height for the last couple of months, but had yet to act on his plans.

Lisa grasped the mirror on either side, a bit above the halfway point, and lifted it free of the nails supporting the heavy wire strung across its back. She stepped away from the closed door, toward Pat's bed, pirouetting to navigate the foot of the bed. With the room's lights off, the only illumination was slices of late-afternoon sunlight that slid around the edges of the drawn blinds, picking out random details on the posters hung on the room's walls, the Bionic Man's gleaming left eye, a glittering sleeve on one of the Bee Gees' Sergeant Pepper jackets. Pat opened his mouth to tell Lisa to be careful, but she maneuvered through the dim space without difficulty. She lowered the mirror, glass-side up, onto the carpeted alley separating his bed from his brother's, straightened, and climbed onto Davis's bed, seating herself in the middle of it, cross-legged.

Pat was already sitting on his bed in the same fashion. Beside him lay the simplified fishing pole his older cousin Carol's friend had handed him, a slender stick stripped of bark to whose end a length of string had been tied. Pat had followed Lisa's instructions and secured the other end of the fishing line to an object of importance to him, the three and half inch metal figure of Dangard Ace, which he was too old to play with but which he kept on his side of the nightstand for good luck. Lisa raised the fishing pole on Davis's blanket. Squinting, Pat saw that its lure was a plastic ring in the shape of a wolf's head. She caught the ring, held it up for him to examine. The color was faded halfway to white, the plastic worn.

"I got this at a fair when I was a kid," she said, pronouncing each word in the careful accent that Pat thought of as English, and that Lisa referred to as BBC standard. "My parents bought it for me. My sister was there, too, and she also got a ring. Hers was an ape's head. I think it was. Its forehead was high and bald. It almost looked like a man, a horrible old man. Sara's ring was mustard-colored. Did I tell you my sister's name was Sara? She wanted my ring; I could tell. But I had seen it first and asked my parents if I could have it. It was the only one of its kind, so Sara had to pick her old, mustardy ape. She pretended she was happy with her choice, but I knew better. I knew she would find a way to make a try for my ring.

"She waited until the car ride home, when there was no chance of us returning to the fair. Her ring broke, she said. The lower part of the band snapped. *How did that happen?* I wondered. She made an awful fuss. My father glanced at me in the rearview mirror. My mother looked over her shoulder at me. Neither of them spoke a word. Eventually, I sighed and twisted the ring from my finger. *Oh thank you thank you thank you,* Sara said. *Are you sure it's all right? Yes,* I said, because what else was there for me to say? My parents made approving noises.

"Can you guess what happened next? You can, can't you? You've got siblings. A short while later—it couldn't have been more than two or three weeks—I found the ring, *my* ring, in the drawer of Sara's desk. I can't recall what I was searching for in there. It was a repository for junk, where my sister tossed things in which she's lost interest. Including the ring she'd made such a fuss to gain from me. Really, I shouldn't have been surprised. My

Mirror Fishing

sister always was a bit of a magpie, flitting from one bright, shiny object to the next. But the sight of the ring lying there made me furious. I snatched it up and ran back to my room with it. I hid it in a wooden box behind the encyclopedias on the lower shelf of my bookcase. (This was where I kept my most precious possessions.)

"Probably, I could have waited another couple of weeks and started wearing it, and Sara wouldn't have noticed. My parents would have, though, and they would have forced me to return the ring to my sister, no matter how much I protested. Sara would have taken it all over again, just to make a point. So I kept the ring hidden. Sometimes, I took it out and wore it if I was by myself and unlikely to be disturbed, which generally meant when I was doing homework. I found it deeply satisfying to lie on my bed wearing my ring, while the next room over, my sister went about her business, unaware that I had taken back what was mine.

"And when I learned about mirror-fishing—what I want to show you—I had my lure right at hand." Before Pat could ask her the circumstances under which she had been taught this game, Lisa said, "Now, what about you? What have you got on the end of your line? A robot?"

"It's a Shogun Warrior," Pat said, hating how juvenile the name sounded. "They were toys when I was a kid. From Japan. They were supposed to be giant robots who protected the Earth. Each one was hundreds of feet tall. They could fly, shoot rockets and lasers, even change into other forms. They were the biggest toys my brother and I ever got, like, two feet tall. There were three of them, to start with, then the company brought out more. There was a comic, too. It was about three people who got picked to pilot the robots by the last survivor of the group that built them. There was a guy from America, a guy from Madagascar, and a woman from Japan. You could tell the American was supposed to be the favorite. He was a stuntman, a real devil-may-care character. I preferred the guy from Madagascar. He was a scientist, a marine biologist. His Shogun Warrior was named Dangard Ace. Not only did his robot look cool, it could transform into the Dreadnought, which was a kind of heavy-duty attack ship.

"The only problem was, Dangard Ace wasn't available in large size. The only way you could get him was as part of a line of smaller die-cast figures. They came in these boxes that were about the size of a deck of playing cards. Davis got one for his birthday, and there was a piece of paper folded up with it that showed all the Shogun Warriors that came in that size. Dangard Ace was one of them. I looked everywhere for him, every toy store we went to, every store that had a toy section, but I never found him. Maybe it was because of the comic; maybe lots of people wanted a Dangard Ace. Then the comic was cancelled. I don't know why. I liked it. My friends liked it. For a while after, you could still find the toys, but not as many. Eventually, you couldn't find any.

"This past May, though—it was after my Confirmation. I had some money; my family had given me a lot when I was Confirmed. My parents made me put most of it in the bank, but they let me keep a little out to spend. I was at the mall. I guess I assumed I'd buy something at one of the bookstores, but I wanted to look around. There's something about walking through a store, knowing you have money in your pocket...I don't know. Anyway, I went into KayBee Toy and Hobby, and what did I find on the end of the action figure aisle? A whole bunch of the die-cast Shogun Warriors. The boxes were battered, torn in a couple of cases. They had bright orange discount stickers on them. What must have happened was, someone found a crate of the figures in the warehouse that was supposed to have been returned a long time ago; they panicked and sent the toys out to be sold cheap.

"There was just about a complete set of them. For a moment, I wanted to buy all of them. I could have, too. I had enough cash. But I didn't. I could imagine what my parents would say if I told them I'd spent my money on a bunch of toys. The exception was Dangard Ace. I couldn't resist getting him, not after all that time searching for and not finding him. It was only one toy, and not a very big one. My dad gave me a look like he couldn't believe I'd spent my money on *this*, and my mom smiled in a way that said I wasn't so grown-up, after all. I didn't care. Well, I did, but not enough to return Dangard. I keep him on the nightstand. He's...I tell people he's for good luck."

"But he's more than that, isn't he?" Lisa said. She held the tip of her fishing pole out over the space between the beds, above the mirror, and released the ring. It swung out toward Pat, back toward Lisa, out to Pat, the arc of its swing rapidly diminishing. Pat watched it twist as it pendulumed. "He's a sign," Lisa said. She dipped the rod, lowering the ring to its reflection. "An emblem of desire." The ring tacked on the glass.

Mirror Fishing

"Desire?" Pat said. His mouth was suddenly dry. His cousin's friend was attractive: her fine features always made up, her slender limbs tanned bronze, her choice of clothes tending in the direction of short-shorts and crop-tops. At the same time, she was nineteen, older than the babysitter his parents continued to employ for him and his siblings when they went out for their monthly date night. She and his cousin, Carol, occupied a position that, while not quite equal to that of his parents (to whom both visitors were respectful, deferential), was decidedly removed from that of Pat, Davis, and their sisters. To think of Lisa as anything other than remote as Farah Fawcett smiling down from the walls of his friends' bedroom walls felt vertiginous. Especially since his parents, Davis, and his sisters had taken Carol to the mall, leaving Lisa in charge of him. She had mentioned this activity, mirror-fishing, that she wished to share with him, and he had assumed it was a game from her pre-teen days she wanted to revisit. Which was fine. He enjoyed her company and was willing to indulge her nostalgia. That she might have something else in mind—he wasn't sure what, only that it involved desire, one of those words which wasn't quite dirty, but which dragged the corners of his parents' mouths down every time it was pronounced—was a prospect that filled him with a trembling emotion either terror or joy or both.

"Wanting," Lisa said. Before Pat could say that he knew what the word meant, she pointed at his fishing rod and said, "Your turn."

He leaned forward for a better view of Dangard Ace as he brought the figure to the mirror. "You wanted," Lisa said. "You wanted the toy—*this* toy—and you cast that desire out into the world. Like a fisherman, casting a lure to attract the fish he wants. And what happened? You caught your fish. You got what you wanted."

The Shogun Warrior clinked on the glass. Although arguing with her was the last thing he desired, he couldn't help saying, "Eventually," as he laid the fishing pole on the bed.

"Well, yes, that's the problem, isn't it? We fling our wanting away from us—it's as if we're using children's poles to fish the ocean. Or something. I don't know that much about proper fishing, actually. Do you?"

"Not really."

"You understand what I'm getting at, though? We want, and sometimes our wanting brings us what we want. But we don't know how it does—if it does. Suppose we could? Suppose there was a way to focus your desire, to make it more effective. What would you do then?"

"How would that work?"

"To start with, you need a mirror."

"And then?"

"You call on Auld Glaikit."

"Owald—what?"

Lisa laughed. "That's what my grandfather called him. It. Auld Glaikit. It's Scots, like your parents. It means Old Silly, or Old Stupid. Not very nice, is it? It sounds like the name of what you're calling—close enough. You don't want to pronounce its actual name, so you use Auld Glaikit, instead."

"Why don't you want to say the real name?"

"Because it would get you hanged as a witch, back when such things still happened."

"What—is it another name for the Devil?" The possibility that Lisa wanted him to participate in some kind of occult activity—something Satanic, like a Black Mass—hadn't occurred to Pat. He knew kids at school who had played around with Ouija boards, a few of whom claimed to have felt a presence sliding the planchette across the board. His religion teacher had frowned at these reports, reminding the class that *The Exorcist* movie was based on a true story, and warning them that Lucifer and his angels were always on the lookout for an opportunity to seize control of a soul insufficiently cautious. The excitement fizzing in him flattened.

"No," Lisa said. "No, it's not the Devil. It's more of a—like a spirit."

"A ghost?"

"More like a fairy."

"A fairy?"

The tone of his voice drew a laugh from his cousin's friend. "Not like Tinkerbell. Fairies were beings of extraordinary power and beauty. They resembled angels, except, they lived in their own kingdom and went about their own affairs. Most of the time, what we, women and men, did was of no concern to them. Every once in a while, though, one of them would become interested in us, and then, there was no telling what would happen."

"So Auld Glaikit is one of these fairies."

"Kind of. A fairy from far, far away."

Mirror Fishing

"Another country?"

"Another universe."

"How?"

"I don't know. My grandfather said it came through the Big Bang, but he couldn't explain it very well. Or I couldn't understand it. It traveled in a beam of light."

"Like a transporter."

"Could be. The people who saw it arrive here, on Earth, thought it was a meteor. They were wrong."

"Where did it land?"

"A lake in England. Only, it didn't land in the lake."

"What happened to it?"

"It went into the reflection on the water's surface. Into that…space."

"That's why you wanted the mirror."

"Exactly," Lisa said. "You are a smart one."

Pat felt his cheeks redden.

"All reflections open on the same territory. You can reach Auld Glaikit through any of them."

"With these," Pat said, nodding at the fishing pole.

"Look," Lisa said, gesturing at the mirror.

Dangard Ace was moving on the glass, slowly rotating, head down, feet up. The angle at which the figure was positioned didn't make any sense, until Pat's eyes adapted and he understood that he was seeing the toy within the mirror. It was as if the surface had been composed of transparent ice, which had melted, dropping his improbable lure into the water underneath. He inhaled sharply, saw that Lisa's blue ring was submerged inches away from the robot. Below the pair of objects, the mirror's depths were full of flickering silver light. Pat had the impression of gazing into liquid not quite water, more viscous. He raised his eyes to Lisa, who was grinning. "How are you doing this?" he said.

"The things you want—I mean really and truly desire—fill up with that wanting. They hold it, like a charge. Under the proper conditions, this allows them to cross into the mirror."

"What happens next?"

"We wait and prepare ourselves."

"For…?"

"For Auld Glaikit."

"What do we do when it shows up?"

"If it answers our call, then we can ask something of it."

"Like, a wish?"

Lisa nodded. "What is it you want, more than anything? Not another toy, surely."

"No," Pat said. "What do you want?"

"Haven't you ever heard, you're not supposed to tell your wishes, or they won't come true?"

"Yeah," Pat said, although he'd thought the prohibition confined to birthday cake candles and shooting stars.

"Concentrate on what you'd like the most. Close your eyes. See it. Feel it."

Self-conscious as it made him, Pat shut his eyes. What did he desire more than anything else? His mind's eye was blank. Across from him, he heard Davis's bed creak as Lisa adjusted her position on it. The coconut odor of her sun-tan lotion filled his nostrils. The hair on his arms, his legs, tickled.

"Can you picture it?" Lisa said. "Can you imagine what you want?"

"Yes," Pat said. A toy? That sounded pretty juvenile for what was happening in front of him. Diane Abbot? She was the girl on whose desk he'd left a heart-shaped box of chocolates on Valentine's Day, and a chocolate Easter Egg a couple of months later, but to whom he'd been unable to utter a single syllable. Should he wish for her to like him? What about Clark Figg and Joe Weisskopf? Of all the kids in his class who teased him, which was most of them, Clark and Joe were the worst, the ones whose taunts combined venom and delight most cuttingly. Often enough, he'd fantasized punching Clark in his smug, self-satisfied face, kicking Joe in the nuts hard enough to drive them halfway up his chest. Would a wish best be spent revenging himself on them? Or Lisa—she was willing to share this secret with him: maybe there was more she would share.

"Look!"

He opened his eyes. Lisa had flattened onto her stomach, to allow her an unobstructed view down into the mirror. Pat did likewise. "What is it?"

"It's coming," Lisa said.

"Really?" He peered into the mirror's shimmering vista. Shadowy shapes rose and fell and tumbled around one another, tricks of the shifting light.

Mirror Fishing

In what appeared to be the middle distance, long black threads drifted from right to left. "I don't see anything. What does it look like?"

"There."

"Where?"

"*There.*"

She was talking, Pat realized, about the black lines, which curved and looped as if caught by invisible currents. "Those?" he said. "What are they?"

"They're like fishing lines."

"It's fishing for us?"

"No," Lisa said. "Not exactly. They're searching out our desire."

"What do you mean?"

"Isn't it obvious?"

Actually, it was. "They're Auld Glaikit."

"They are. A part of it, anyway." She glanced over at him, her eyes shining with the mirror's pale light. "We did it. We brought it here."

"We did," Pat said, wishing the affirmation filled him with more confidence. "What happens now?"

"Now," Lisa said, "we go swimming." She pushed herself to sitting, then extended her legs over the side of the bed, scooting forward until she was balanced on the mattress's edge, her toes inches above the mirror. Using her elbows for support, she eased her feet, then her shins, then her knees, into the glass, as if she were lowering into a pool of cold water, allowing her skin to adjust to the temperature. "Come on."

Pat was far from the world's most able or enthusiastic swimmer, the consequence of a number of dunkings he'd received from his father and one of his uncles when he was younger. The prospect of submerging in a pool of who-knew-what was enough to set his heart racing, slick his palms with sweat. "How do you breathe?" he said.

Lisa was in to her shoulders. "It's not really swimming," she said. She raised an arm to view. It was dry. "See? It's more like floating. Come try it."

Already, the situation had moved from shared childhood memory to nowhere Pat had imagined being, let alone been. While the supernatural was not unfamiliar, conceptually-speaking, his practical experience of it was limited to the consecration at Sunday mass, where, to be frank, you had to take it on faith that the host had been transubstantiated. This...Lisa moved to the other end of the rectangle, to permit him more room to enter it. He maneuvered off his bed until he was standing on the carpet at the mirror's head. He lifted his left foot and placed it on the wood frame. By raising his heel, he could dip his toes into the glass. He was aware of the slightest resistance, and his foot was through. The medium didn't feel like water; it didn't feel like much of anything. Cooler than the air in his room, maybe, though not by much. He bent his right knee so he could immerse the rest of his foot. Below his foot—he couldn't say how far, exactly: fifty feet? a hundred?—a trio of the black threads was spiraling upwards in slow motion. He looked at Lisa, who was watching him, expectantly. "I can't believe this," he said.

"I know," she said, "isn't it amazing? The first time my grandfather showed it to me, I was sure he was playing a trick on me. He wasn't. This isn't all of it, either."

"All right," Pat said. He sat on the carpet, letting both his legs drop within the mirror. Bracing himself on his arms, he swung his torso inside. Now that he was almost entirely surrounded by the medium, he was aware of a slight buoyancy to it, as if it was supporting him. Holding onto the frame, he descended to his chin. The sensation of floating was more pronounced. To his right, Dangard Ace rocked from side to side. Maintaining his hold on the frame with his left hand, he reached out his right to the figure. His fingers brushed the smooth metal, the braided clothesline knotted around it.

"Careful," Lisa said.

Pat withdrew his hand. "What?"

"That little robot and my ring are keeping this doorway opened. Remove either one of them, and it closes."

"What happens then?"

"If we're on the other side of it, we're stuck there. If we're in it..."

"Part of us is stuck there."

"And the rest remains here. Rather messy, you can imagine. So let's not let that happen, shall we?"

"Agreed."

"Good. Now that's out of the way, let's go say hello to our visitor." With that, Lisa ducked her head under the glass. Pat watched her drop into its silver depths with the slow motion of a leaf traversing the gap between branch and ground. She turned her face to him, calling a, "Hurry up!" that seemed to reach him from far away.

There was no way for him to talk himself into this. If he was going to join Lisa, he had to release his grip on the frame and fall. Before he could second-guess the decision, he opened his hands.

The surface of the mirror contracted over the top of his head, and it seemed to be this motion that propelled him into the place on the other side of it, as if he were a seed being squeezed out of a slice of orange. Around him, wisps and ribbons of silver hung like decorations. Further off, thicker patches of whiteness drifted in slow schools. Further still, huge, fantastic galleons of platinum and white crashed and dissolved into one another. A sharp, antiseptic smell stung his nostrils. Pat had the sensation, not so much of falling toward a fixed point as of simply moving, as if, were he to extend his arms and kick his legs, he could push in a new direction. He stretched his arms to either side and immediately slowed to a float. Looking down, he saw Lisa almost at the black threads, which appeared thicker, more substantial, heavy ropes rather than threads. They trailed a considerable length, out to one of the white ships, churning into a mountain. Other black lines snaked from the developing mountain in all directions.

"What are you waiting for?" Lisa said. She had swum up to him. The expression on her face was not outright annoyance, but neither was it the bemused exasperation her voice was trying for.

"It's just—this is really something," he said.

"It is, isn't it? I'm forgetting this is your first time through. Sorry about that." She smiled an apology.

"What is all this?"

"Light," she said. "In here, light behaves differently. It's more," she waved a hand, "fluid."

"Huh." Pat pointed at the mountain, curling into a tsunami. "That's where Auld Glaikit is, in that…cloud?"

"At the moment." She caught his hand, his heart jumping at her touch. She tugged him toward the trio of black ropes, which had ceased their motion and were floating in place. He did not resist.

As they drew closer to them, he saw that his comparison of the appendages to ropes had been apt. Each was a braid of a half-dozen, a dozen, thinner strands, wrapped around one another in a pattern too complex for his eyes to unravel. The surface was coarse, bristling with tiny hairs; the end gathered into a slender barb the length of Pat's hand. The shape of each barb suggested the frilled head of some species of serpent. For a moment, Pat had the impression he was descending to a trio of blind snakes. Some part of him—the same bundle of phobias that caused him to leap back whenever he disturbed a garter snake while mowing the lawn—made him pull his hand free from Lisa's grip, pedal his feet to slow him.

"Patrick?" Lisa said, "What is it?" She drifted into the midst of the appendages, grabbing one of the ropes (*snakes*) behind the barb to arrest her motion.

"I'm sorry," he said, embarrassment flushing his cheeks. "These—I mean, Auld Glaikit—it's not what I'm used to, you know?"

"Let me show you something," Lisa said.

"What?"

Holding the black braid, she scissored her legs until she was beside Pat. "Give me your hand," she said.

He did. "What do you—"

Lisa stabbed the tip of the barb into his palm. So intense, so overwhelming was the pain that he did not feel it; rather, everything around him went blank. For an instant, it was as if he had been plucked from the strange space Lisa had disclosed to him and placed in a calm, quiet room. Then his nerves caught up to the pain, and he was hanging in the air, the sharp end of a long, black rope anchored in the flesh of his hand. His mouth was wide open, a high-pitched scream streaming out of it. Tears were spilling from his eyes. He wanted to move, to tear his hand free of the barb, but he was shaking, convulsed by the pain. When Lisa yanked the end of the barb from his palm, his screaming stopped, his body went limp. Without bothering to wipe the snot running from his nose, he shouted, "What the HELL was that for?"

"Wait," Lisa said, apparently unmoved by the ferocity of his question.

Through the pain, pounding up his arm, he felt something else, almost a tickle. He raised his injured hand and saw in the blood spilling scarlet out of it a darker liquid. It poured from the wound like ink, rolling through his blood, dimming it to sable. A fresh wave of tears fractured his vision. She'd poisoned him. Why had she done that? He was panting, his skin clammy.

"Patrick," Lisa said. "Patrick. I want you to listen to me. Patrick. You must listen to me. It's important. Listen to me, Patrick. Listen."

Mirror Fishing

Somehow, he found the breath to say, "Go to hell."

"Listen to me, Patrick. Listen to my voice."

"Get away from me." He kicked weakly, trying to gain distance from her. Lisa caught his leg easily and held him in place. He could not turn his eyes from the injury to his hand, from which (*blood*) liquid the rich black of used motor oil was welling up. There seemed to be something afloat in the substance, a pinpoint of brightness, which might have been a trick of the tears washing his eyes. He wiped his eyes with his left hand. No, there was something in the black, shining like a tiny star—

—and it was a star, hanging alone in a night sky. It was white, and it was close, far closer than the Sun. From its right hemisphere, flame trailed into space in a cone whose far end Pat could not see. He was squinting at the star from a ledge halfway up a narrow crystal spine, from whose height he saw a forest of similar structures rising from bare rock. The entire surface of the planet he was surveying bristled with these projections, he understood. This was the last planet, facing the last star, both of them inconceivably old, the final remnants of a universe whose entire remaining matter was compacting itself into an ever-smaller, ever-hotter space, a spot whose incredible gravity was stripping the star to nothing. As the star went, so would the planet, and with it, its sole remaining inhabitant, a being whose thoughts crackled among the crystal spires, trying to calculate some way for it to survive the imminent apocalypse. What there was to its body drifted among the bases of the projections, a trio of fleshy balloons tethered by black threads. The creature—Auld Glaikit—was frantically working at a set of equations so complex as to be a form of magic, which would allow it to leap from the ruin of its cosmos to the next universe to be born from its embers. But it was still far from having solved the most challenging subsets, and the star was bleeding mass at an accelerating rate, the planet shuddering as it listed in the direction of its inevitable end. Mixed with the thoughts flickering amidst the planet's spines, Pat felt a single, overpowering emotion: dread, at the prospect of the coming annihilation—

—which gave way to horror, as pure as the edge of a razor, as the scene in front of him collapsed into a chaos of color and form, everything rushing down a funnel to a place that was crushing to a point, dimensions bursting under pressure and heat, reason gone but not awareness, not horror—

—which was swept aside by a wave of triumph, of exultation, as that infinitely small spot erupted in fire and light, flinging its contents wide, and what had been and somehow still was the last creature from the previous universe became the first creature of the new one, riding a raft of light across unfolding space and time, speeding through clouds of gas condensing and kindling into stars, gradually realizing there was something wrong, something about its present state that was not as it should be, unforeseen consequence of those final, rushed calculations—

—and he was staring at the blood washing red over his skin. He lowered his hand to find Lisa watching him. "It isn't...solid," he said. "It made a mistake in the math. It can't hold onto...here."

"Not on its own," Lisa said. "It has to be connected to someone. If it can be tethered to more than one person, so much the better. In fact, the greater the number of tethers, the closer it can draw to our reality."

"Is that what I'm supposed to be?" Pat said. He waved his injured hand weakly.

"No," Lisa said; although she drew out the syllable enough for Pat to hear the gears in her brain turning. "That's not what I want. I brought you here because there was no way to tell you about any of it any have you think I was anything other than stark raving mad, was there?"

"I guess not."

"The poke with this," she held up the barb, its tip still smeared with his blood, "was the most efficient way to transmit Auld Glaikit's story to you."

"Well. What happens now?"

"That's up to you," Lisa said. "Since my grandfather introduced all of this to me, I've been on the lookout for new...connections for Auld Glaikit. It's what Grandfather did for years. It's more of a challenge than you might expect. You can't pick just anyone. You have to select a person whose absence won't be noted, or which can be explained readily. Still, it's astonishing what you can accomplish once you set your mind to it. My sister—Sara, the one I told you about, with the ring—was going through a particularly horrible spell at home. I mean, she was absolutely ghastly, and not only to me, but to my parents, as well. She was constantly threatening to leave home, run away. She'd even gone so far as to write a nasty letter to my mum and dad and me, to be discovered after she was gone. I found it tucked in her diary, which I read to keep up on her bad behavior. The moment I unfolded that letter, I knew I had the solution to two problems at once. I can't pretend my parents weren't upset at Sara's sudden departure, but honestly, they were much better rid of her. Grandfather agreed with me. After Grandmother's mind started going, and she took to wandering from the house, often quite far—well, there was nothing much for her to look forward to, was there? He understood."

"You want me to bring my family here?" Pat said.

"No," Lisa said, "your family's lovely. But I'm sure there are some kids you aren't too fond of, at school, perhaps? With a modicum of planning, you could be free of them, for good."

Pat started to protest, no, that wasn't true, he got along with all his classmates, but this wasn't his mom and dad, to whom he presented a front of normalcy, lest they learn the full extent of the catastrophe that was his social life. How often had he wished for Clark Figg and Joe Weisskopf to disappear, for their families to move, for them to transfer to another school, for a fate more drastic to befall them: struck by a car while out riding their bikes, chased and beaten by a band of marauding high-schoolers? He hadn't *prayed* for any violence to overtake them, but that was because he knew he was supposed to be working on forgiving his tormentors, not calling down divine wrath on them. Here he was, though, floating in a place that appeared to exist outside the framework of creation as he'd been taught it, treating with a being that didn't slot into the hierarchies of angels or the ranks of their infernal counterparts. Perhaps it was necessary to be more flexible in his attitudes.

"I guess there are a couple of kids I wouldn't be sorry to see the last of," he said.

"Exactly," Lisa said. "And I could show you a few tricks that would help you to bring them here."

"Yeah?"

"Have you ever looked in a mirror and been certain, for only a second, that there was someone standing behind you? That's called mirror walking. It allows you to peek in on all manner of places. With the proper instruction, you can step into one mirror in your house and step out of another, miles away."

"Wow." It was difficult not to be impressed. "Can I ask you something?"

"Of course."

"What happens to the people who become Auld Glaikit's tethers?"

"You can see for yourself," Lisa said, pointing at the clouds of light. A smaller mass the shape of a whale was rolling itself into the larger wave that housed Auld Glaikit. Flickering plumes rose and fell; shimmering waves rushed over the surface of the creature's dwelling. The black braids extending from that side of its domain recoiled at the collision, whipping their ends out of adjacent clouds. As they did, Pat saw attached to each a human form. Although the distance rendered them tiny and difficult to distinguish, Pat was pretty sure the bodies were thrashing with the agonized motion of fish hooked and dragged into the suffocating air. Was this a surprise? Hadn't he felt the creature's sentiment toward this new creation during his vision, a mix of disdain and disinterest? He glanced at Lisa. She said, "It uses the tethers as auxiliary sense organs, extra eyes and ears, to gather information."

"Through mirrors."

"Reflections," Lisa said. "You never know out of what puddle, what window, what doorknob one of its pairs of eyes might be watching you."

"Why?" Pat said. "I mean, I understand about it needing a way to keep itself here, but why does it want to spy on everyone?"

"It's studying us," Lisa said with a frown, "learning about us. For when it's finally able to cross out of this place into our world."

"And the more people we bring to it—you and I—the sooner that'll happen."

"There are others doing the same thing, but not many. As far as I'm concerned, that's better for us. Can you imagine? Once it's all the way in our universe, it's going to be extremely grateful to the ones who helped make that transition happen. Do you know what it'll do for us? Anything.

"That's why you use desire to draw it to you, because it knows desire the likes of which you and I can only dream. I wanted a ring, you wanted your robot, because we thought these things would make us more whole, somehow, as if they were parts of ourselves we hadn't known were missing. What I call Auld Glaikit wants to be whole, to be real, in the most literal of ways. Assist it, and reap the rewards."

Blood dripped from Pat's hand in long drops that plummeted past Lisa and the trio of black braids and continued to fall. He wondered if someone gazing into a mirror, a man shaving, perhaps, or a woman applying her makeup, would be surprised by a burst of red against the inside of the glass. He said, "Can we do something about my hand? I know you did what you

Mirror Fishing

had to do, but it's still pretty painful." He tilted his head back, sighting the dark, rectangular slot in the air that marked the route back to his room.

"What does that mean?" Lisa said.

"It means I need both hands in good working order," Pat said. "Those kids are bigger than I am."

"Wonderful," Lisa said. "I had a feeling about you."

"Thank you," he said, "for showing me all of this. It's incredible."

"You're very welcome," she said. "This is just the beginning. I promise you, you'll be amazed at what comes next." She released the black braid, which looped away from her, curving with its mates in the direction of Auld Glaikit.

Returning to the opening to his room was harder than Pat had anticipated. The mirror was further than it appeared, and it was more difficult to push toward it than it had been to descend into this place. His hand hurt with a deep pain, which ran straight through his arm to his chest, which was strangely hollow, as if the injury had emptied him. Below, Lisa called, "Would you like me to go first? It doesn't look as if you're moving very well."

"I'm okay," he said. "If it's all the same to you, I'd rather have you behind me, in case something happens and I fall."

"If that's what you want."

"Thanks," Pat said. "Thank you."

He swam past a school of shining ribbons, glimpsing in their silver lengths fragmentary images: a trio of boys his approximate age facing a painting; an old man asleep beside a stream, his fishing pole forgotten; a girl with short, platinum hair kissing a guy in a varsity letter jacket. Reflections—pieces of them, at least. He tried to picture what it would be like for Clark Figg or Joe Weisskopf to find themselves stuck here. Even if they weren't dangling on the end of Auld Glaikit's arms, Pat couldn't imagine either of them would go very long before losing his marbles. The thought was satisfying, deeply and frighteningly so. Would it be that difficult to bring Clark or Joe to this place, especially if Lisa followed through on her pledge to teach him how to approach them, unseen? Assuming what she had said was true (and why shouldn't it be? everything else she'd told him was), there would be no way to trace such an action to him. It would be a simple matter of waiting for either kid to stray close enough to the right mirror, opening the mirror, and hauling him through. No muss, no fuss, and no Clark or Joe to torment him. They wouldn't even be dead, technically speaking: they'd be part of something bigger, something greater.

He felt himself standing at the brink of a precipice, the edge of which was crumbling into space. Vertigo squeezed his stomach. What he was contemplating was far beyond agreeing to Lisa's proposal so she wouldn't trap him here. This was embracing what she'd put forward, opening himself to it because it evoked a sympathetic—an enthusiastic response from deep within him. He recalled this past summer's family vacation, a couple of weeks prior to Lisa and Carol's arrival. A late night conversation with his parents had soured into argument whose end had been Pat asking his father if he considered him a bad son, to which his father had answered, "Yes." *I could show him bad*, Pat thought, *I could show him bad like he wouldn't believe.*

Except he couldn't. He pictured his father's face, his expression fearful—eyes wide, mouth agape, skin pale—and the image filled him with terrible sadness, sadness and dread. He didn't feel nearly as bad at the prospect of similar looks on Clark and Joe, but he was aware of the imbalance of such a revenge.

He was almost at the opening to his room. Dangard Ace and Lisa's ring floated an arm's length from him. Through the mirror's shape, his nightstand, the headboard of his bed, was visible. He glanced at Lisa. She was at least a yard below him. She caught his look, said, "What? What is it?" He fumbled for an answer, still unsure of his exact plan, but while the words were rolling around in his mouth, Lisa's eyes hardened and he saw that she knew, had recognized his betrayal while he was still working through it. Her skin flushed. "You little shite," she said, the rest of the reproach she spat at him lost as he pulled and kicked for the exit from this space with all the strength available him. The fingers of his left hand touched the frame, but before he could grasp it, Lisa's outstretched hand caught his right ankle. She dug her nails into his skin. He screamed, striking at her fingers with his other foot. She swore, released his leg. Like a swimmer racing to the surface, he kicked, propelling his left arm and the top of his head through into his room. He flailed his arm wildly, clawing at the sheets on his brother's bed, slapping the carpet beside the mirror. He bent his arm, pressed down on it to lever the rest of his head and his right arm out of the mirror. Lisa was right behind him. She had not stopped trying to grab one of his legs, but the blood streaking his right foot and her palm hindered her efforts. She

Mirror Fishing

was shouting, her words distorted and diminished by his partial escape, but he didn't need to hear them to know the harm they promised. Ignoring the pain in his right hand, he placed it flat on the floor and pushed. White light flashed in front of his eyes. He brought his legs up, swinging the left and then the right out onto the carpet.

Relief flooded him. He couldn't rest, though. Already, Lisa's fingers were gripping the sides of the frame. Her threats burst into the room along with her angry face. Pat scrambled to his feet. "—you think that's the worst that can happen? You don't have a bloody clue, do you? I'll see you cored like an apple. I'll have you scraped out and used as a vessel for you-can't-imagine-what. I'll watch you drag the rest of your family to Auld Glaikit, and I'll laugh at their screams. I'll—"

Her voice stopped when she registered Pat, one foot on either side of the mirror, one hand on each of the fishing poles. She didn't waste time asking what he was going; instead, she released her hold on the frame and went to duck. As she did, Pat yanked the lures into the room.

There was a sound like a knife biting through a watermelon. The top half of Lisa's skull, from right below the sockets, sat on the suddenly-solid glass into whose depths Pat saw the rest of her body falling, blood trailing from the lower half of her head in a scarlet plume. He leapt back, dropping the toy and ring, which retained sufficient charm to pierce the mirror's surface. Eyes yet wide, outraged, the top of Lisa's head sank into the aperture, following the rest of her into Auld Glaikit's flickering domain.

***

Although Pat set the alarm on his clock radio for three a.m., he didn't need it. He had told his parents he was going to bed and had closed his eyes and faked unconsciousness to get Davis to stop talking to him and go to sleep, himself, but sleep had maintained its distance, which wasn't much of a surprise. His brain was overfull, brimming with the afternoon's events and their consequences that evening and night. His parents, siblings, and cousin had returned from the shopping trip to a scene of chaos: Pat, sprawled in the hallway outside his and Davis's room, his mother's silver hand mirror broken beside his head, pieces of its glass in his scalp, a deep wound in his right hand, scratches on his legs. Nor was his mother's mirror the only one shattered: every last mirror in the house had been cracked. Of neither Lisa nor her luggage was there any sign. The sight of him made his mother shriek, his sisters and cousin cry. His father hurried to his side, glass crunching under his sneakers, telling Davis to call an ambulance and kneeling beside Pat, asking him what had happened.

He kept his story simple. He had been reading in the living room. He had heard crashing from the other end of the house. He went to see what was happening, found Lisa using the handle of Mom's good mirror to smash the mirror in his and Davis's room, then the mirror on his sisters' bureau, then the bathroom mirror. He tried to talk to her, told her to stop, but it was like she was crazy. She kept saying that something in the mirror was after her; she'd thought she could escape it if she flew all the way to America, but she'd been wrong. Pat had put out his hand, and she grabbed one of the shards of glass and stabbed him in the palm. That was when he realized he was in real danger. He went to run away, but she cracked him on the head with Mom's mirror. After that, things were fuzzy. She dragged him into the hallway. He thought maybe he heard the front door opening and closing. He wasn't sure how much longer it took for his family to arrive home.

In the hours to come, Pat repeated his account of Lisa's frenzied actions several times: to the sheriff's deputy who was first to reach the house, to the paramedics who showed up shortly thereafter, to the town police officers who appeared next, to the detective they called in to interview him. He resisted the urge to embellish, to improve the narrative he'd arrived at before striking himself as hard as he could with his mother's mirror. No, he didn't know where Lisa had gone. No, he hadn't heard her phone anyone. No, he hadn't heard any cars pulling up outside. The cops were kindly, apologetic at having to ask him so many questions for so long. If we can catch her, they said, it'll prevent her from doing the same thing to anyone else. Pat said he understood. He cried frequently, in great sobs that shook his body. His parents, the police, patted his back and told him it was all right, he was safe, now. He couldn't tell them about the place on the other side of the mirror, the black braids lazing from Auld Glaikit's thicket of light, the barb piercing his hand. He couldn't tell them what he'd been shown by the creature, how the top of Lisa's head had rested on the mirror's glass, blood leaking all around its edges onto the glass. He could cry, so he did.

Eventually, the police left; though they said they'd want to talk to him

Mirror Fishing

some more, tomorrow. He nodded, thanked them. He wasn't worried about them finding out what had happened to Lisa, or what hadn't, for that matter. He had tipped her things into his room's mirror, tossing the fishing poles and their lures in after. Strangely, he'd felt a pang watching Dangard Ace plummet out of view. For a moment, the mirror continued to give a view of the other space, then it blurred into the flat plane of the ceiling overhead. He tested its surface with his left hand, and once he was satisfied of its solidity, turned it over and stomped on its backing. To that seven years' bad luck, he piled on decades more, running from room to room, breaking every mirror he could find, ending with his mother's hand mirror against his head. Now that a route had been established between his home and Auld Glaikit's, who knew if the creature or its agents might be able to access the house via another mirror. It was best not to take chances.

All the same, there were surfaces that gave reflections in every room, and he couldn't destroy them all. It might be possible to occlude a certain number, smear dirt on the basement windows, say, which were high and small and seldom paid attention to by his parents. He would have to work on the problem, as soon as he attended to his hand.

Shortly after the paramedic had cleaned, inspected, and bandaged it, the wound had started to itch. Just noticeable enough to distract him as he answered the assorted police officers' questions, the sensation persisted for the remainder of the day. Along with that itch had come a feeling of pressure behind his eyes, at his temples, which appeared to grow out of his memories of what Auld Glaikit had shown him, the bristling planet, the star draining to nothing, as if the images were swelling his brain. It seemed likely Auld Glaikit had left some piece of itself behind in him, as a hedge against betrayal. He was going to have to remove the bandages from his hand and examine the wound, but he was going to have to wait until the rest of his family was asleep.

Which they now were. He reached to the clock radio, clicked the alarm off, and slid from under the covers. Davis slumbered quietly in his bed. Pat crept to the door, opened it, and leaned his head into the hall. From his parents' room, his father's snores came steadily. His sisters' room was silent. The light in the living room, where Carol was sleeping (and where Lisa had been staying with her), was out. Moving slowly along floorboards whose creaks sounded extra-loud, Pat crossed the hall to the kitchen. His father had left the light over the sink on, for which Pat was grateful. The linoleum was quieter underfoot. He padded to the countertop to the left of the faucet, where the knife rack offered the handles of half a dozen blades of varying lengths and purposes. He withdrew one, another, searching for the long, slender knife his father sometimes used for slicing a roast thin. Once he had it in hand, he retreated halfway up the hall to the bathroom. He locked the door, set the knife on the edge of the sink, and opened the medicine cabinet. The tweezers were on the bottom shelf, the bottle of mercurochrome on the middle. He removed both and put them beside the knife. In the cupboard under the sink, he found gauze pads and a roll of medical tape. He placed them on the other side of the sink. He returned to the medicine cabinet for the slender surgical scissors on the top shelf. With the scissors, he cut away the bandages around his hand. He let the bandages fall into the sink. He swapped the scissors for the tweezers, which he used to peel away the pads with which the paramedic had layered his injury. The uppermost pad bore a scattering of rust-colored spots, and as he progressed down, the gauze squares turned dark red. The last couple adhered to the rent in his flesh in places; by the time he was done detaching them, sweat was tickling the sides of his face. But he had succeeded in confining his expressions of pain to a few sharp intakes of breath, so he figured he was doing all right.

It was a wonder, the paramedic who tended his hand said, that the injury had missed the tendons, avoided the bones. Looking at the raw, red cavity in his palm, still oozing blood and lymph, Pat did not feel especially wonderful. He lifted his hand, narrowing his eyes to peer into the wound. *There.* Right away, he saw it, a black fleck in the deepest part of the cut. Not much longer than the splinters he sometimes picked up running his hand along the rails on the back porch, it was a collection of points of differing lengths, like a sea urchin. Already, the longer points had dug into the surrounding tissue.

Panic surged in his chest. *It's too late,* he thought. *It's in too deep.* Tears wobbled his vision. He lowered his right hand, used the left to reach for a towel to wipe his eyes. *Okay. Okay. You have to do this. You don't have a choice.*

He didn't, did he? He took a deep breath. The tweezers weren't going to be any use: there was too much chance of them breaking off one of the

Mirror Fishing

spines, and then what would he do? He was going to have to cut the thing out, together with a sufficient margin of flesh to keep it contained.

Pat picked up the knife. He hoped its edge was sharp enough, his hand steady enough.

CAOINEADH

I

Bucksport

Growing up, I was sure I was my mother's favorite. Though I didn't disclose this belief to my younger brother or either of my younger sisters, I knew they did not share it. The standing family joke was that my brother was the apple of our parents' eyes. His report cards were crowded with excellent grades and laudatory comments from his teachers; he annually won the grand prize at the school science fair; he even received the silver medal for his age group in the CYO art contest. Next to his accomplishments, neither those of his older brother nor younger sisters appeared especially impressive. Our parents valued education above everything else except religion, so it made sense for the rest of us to assume he was their golden child. Sometimes, my youngest sister would declare, "Mom loves *me* best," but I don't think we took this as anything other than her performative brattiness. Occasionally, the same sister would tease my parents, together or separately, about our brother with a comment along the lines of, "He *is* the favorite." I don't remember Dad ever answering her, but without fail, Mom would respond, "I don't have favorites. I love all my children equally." "And the cat," I would say. "Yes," Mom would laugh, "and the cat."

Did we believe her? I have no doubt we wanted to. Speaking for myself, I didn't not believe her. But I also felt a particular bond with her I didn't observe with my brother or the older of my younger sisters. They gravitated to our father, with whom they had an easy relationship I never enjoyed. Only my youngest sister seemed to have a similar connection to Mom. Perhaps it was because we were the children at the opposite ends of the family, each of us something of a shock: me appearing after seven years of her and Dad trying to conceive; my sister showing up after my parents were sure they were done with having children. On more than one occasion, she said to Mom, "I was an *accident*, wasn't I?" Which question Mom met with the same answer every time: "You were a surprise." It never occurred to me then, but decades later, I would think, *I was a surprise, too.*

Asked for evidence of a special relationship with my mother, I would have cited the conversations we had. These were long, involved, and in retrospect, tended to consist in large part of me talking and Mom listening. She had a way of making you feel that whatever you were saying was supremely interesting, which she accomplished through a combination of nods, murmurs, and strategically placed questions, whose purpose often seemed to be to allow me to continue expounding upon the topic at hand. She never told me what I should be interested in or suggested my energies might be better focused on my schoolwork, two of the landmines talking to Dad might trip. I always felt comfortable with her, even when we weren't engaged in conversation. She kept the radio in the kitchen on from first thing in the morning until right before dinner, tuned to the easy listening station out of Peekskill, and would hum or sing along to whatever was playing. Her voice was full, clear, resonant, and I still recall her singing the Carpenters' "Close to You," which in her performance of it became about her and us, the children she had wanted and waited to have. (Funny—her singing was something of a legend among her and Dad's friends from Scotland, where they'd grown up, met, and married before moving to the States. There was one New Year's Eve when we went to visit friends of theirs who had also immigrated. While I was supposed to be asleep, I listened to everyone urging Mom to give them a song, a request she declined repeatedly, then gave

CAOINEADH

in to. I didn't recognize the tune she selected; all these years later, its notes have slipped from my recall. What remains to me is the utter silence that descended on the room prior to her starting, the anticipation and attention in the air.)

Our talks reached their peak in the early part of my teenage years, during the annual family vacation. Every summer, my parents took us on a trip, usually of two weeks. The first of these holidays—at least, the first I can remember—was to Lake George, in the Adirondacks. Mom and Dad rented a cabin on a nearby pond and we divided our days between swimming in that body of water and driving into the town of Lake George, where we toured Fort William Henry, took a ride on the Minnie Ha-Ha, a restored paddleboat, and walked Main Street wandering in and out of gift shops whose risqué T-shirts and towels scandalized and embarrassed me. We had a day in the local amusement park, Storytown, and another driving up to see Fort Ticonderoga, where the tour guides fired a cabbage out of a replica eighteenth-century cannon. All of us enjoyed the place well enough to return the following summer, and the next few after. One year old friends of my parents joined us for a week. They were former co-workers of Mom's, from her days at Marine Midland Bank, before she had me. Mount St. Helens had erupted the previous spring, and these friends had come into possession of a small clear medicine bottle full of ash from the volcano. They presented this to me and my brother (they gifted my sisters with something less ghoulish). The two of us were fascinated by the container of what appeared black soil. It was like a kind of sinister relic, not evil, exactly, but frightening. We never opened it; we didn't dare.

My family would have kept vacationing in that spot had the owners not sold it, forcing Mom and Dad to search elsewhere. In the pages of the local *Pennysaver*, Mom found an ad for a place in Maine. It was in Bucksport, which would turn out to be an eight-hour drive from our home in East Fishkill. The cottage they rented was even smaller than the small house in which we lived, but it was set on a square of green grass abutting the shore of the Penobscot River, at this point a wide estuary. When the tide was out, you walked to the edge of the lawn, slid down a three-foot incline, and were on a typical North Atlantic beach, gray-tinged sand studded with rocks of all sizes, their edges worn smooth by the water's motion. At its lowest, the river receded a considerable distance, allowing my siblings and I to venture far out on the exposed beach, where the rocks bristled with barnacles and were wrapped in rubbery seaweed, and tidal pools held tiny green crabs. We discovered mounds of translucent jelly, each the size of a saucer, which we realized were jellyfish and that I warned my brother and sisters away from, fearful the creatures might sting them. From the river, seals stuck their heads out of the water and watched us with interest. Usually hot and humid, the days gave way to cool nights during which fog might roll in from the Penobscot and hang around till morning, its appearance activating the foghorn in the lighthouse on the opposite shore, the distant call charming my siblings and me. All this part of Maine did, from the roadside blueberry pie we purchased from Nilda's farm stand, to picking our own blueberries from the bushes in the fields beside the cottage, to eating at Jed Prouty's, the upscale restaurant in Bucksport to which the family went for an end-of-vacation dinner. We attended Sunday mass down the coast in Castine, at a small church whose priest rode a motorcycle with a license plate reading NAZGUL, which in my eyes immediately made him the coolest priest ever. In the landscape of the state, from the beach outside our cottage to the rolling green fields ornamented with mossy boulders, my parents felt a powerful echo of their birthplaces in the southwest of Scotland, in a pair of neighboring towns, Greenock and Gourock, built on the southern shores of the River Clyde, a tidal estuary whose wide waters allowed the region to become a center for British shipbuilding. There was even a guy whose food truck specialized in fish and chips—wrapped in newspaper, no less—who parked on a turn-off overlooking the Penobscot not far from Bucksport.

The sole problem with the vacation was the size of our accommodations, which were too small for any of us to have much in the way of personal space, let alone privacy. The next year, Mom and Dad solved this by renting a new house from the daughter and son-in-law of the old Yankee who owned our first cottage. This house was considerably larger, with an open floor plan and a loft which ran the length of the house and had separate beds for my brother and me and a double bed for my sisters, plus a gray wool curtain hung between them and us. My parents slept in the big bed in the space directly below me and my brother, which had its own curtain, this one with a yellow floral print, for privacy. On cold nights, there was a metal stove with firewood stacked beside it at one end of the living room, near my parents' room. The house had no TV, but this was fine: we entertained

CAOINEADH

ourselves by reading, listening to Larry Glick's call-in show on WBZ on the half-sized boom-box I brought, or playing cards around the kitchen table (usually Gin Rummy and a game called Get Your Neighbor, whose name probably says more about the dynamics between my brother and sisters and me than I wish it did).

This house was set on a steep hillside, which allowed it to have a large deck with a fine view of the treetops below and the river beyond, but which also necessitated a climb down—and more importantly, back up—a long set of wooden stairs to access the beach. The aching thighs and calves were worth it, though, because this stretch of shore was better than our previous location. Here, the beach descended a long, gradual incline, so when the tide was out, a greater expanse of sand and rock was uncovered. Even when the water was coming in, it was possible to stay out on top of some of the larger rocks while waves splashed around you, then to escape by leaping to the next rock back. Long lines of rocks jutted out into the water, tumble-down jetties whose purpose was unclear to me. (Dad speculated they might be used to anchor lobster pots off the end of, which didn't sound more unlikely than anything I could think up.) Closer to the foot of the stairs, maybe thirty yards away, an enormous boulder rose amid its fellows. White and gray, it was taller than I was by at least a foot, so somewhere in the vicinity of seven feet. It was long, too, maybe four feet, and there was in its shape something which reminded me of the great blunt head of a sperm whale. The top of this mighty object was reached via a smaller stone at what I thought of as its rear. My siblings and I delighted in climbing onto it and surveying the beach from its lofty height, while whatever parent was with us told us to be careful.

A few feet away from this landmark was a smaller rock, whose flat top Mom liked to use as a kind of natural chair where she sat and read (generally Danielle Steel's latest). Sometimes, I would accompany her, ostensibly to read, too, atop the whale rock, but actually to engage in one of our wide-ranging conversations. Over the next four summers, the nature of our discussions changed, as Mom began to speak to me of her life as a girl in Scotland; of her older brother, with whom she had a complicated relationship; of the man to whom she was engaged before she met Dad; of coming to America, to stay with her mother's cousin in Brooklyn, and of the woolen dress clothes she and Dad wore during their first, astonishingly hot summer in the city. Some of what she talked about followed us up the stairs to the house, where she would ask Dad to fill in certain details she couldn't recall. (Not about the previous fiancé, though; never did I hear my father refer to this individual, who I later learned emigrated to Australia.) In turn, his memories would prompt more of hers, and together they would narrate to my siblings and me what life had been like when they were very small and the Second World War was raging; or, after lifetimes of living in towns and cities, what a change it was to settle into the house in which they raised all of us, where the lowing of the cows across the street could keep you awake at night. From here, Dad might recount some of the atrociously funny things he and his fellow soldiers had done to one another during his mandatory time in the British army, or Mom might tell us about going into Glasgow with her girlfriends for a night of dancing. Both my parents were great storytellers, having come from a time and place whose sources of entertainment were more limited in number, availability, and affordability, which meant the ability to recount an amusing incident or to sing a favorite song was encouraged and prized. Seated on the stones beside the river's broad flow, or on the couch and chairs around the wood stove whose fire was pleasantly warm on an unexpectedly cold night, we seemed to be knitted by our parents' stories into something larger than we were, to be joined into a narrative whose beginnings reached back into the time before we were born, and longer ago, still.

II

Greenock

A few of Mom's stories were new to me. One involved a bull breaking loose from the herd being walked from the docks near her apartment building to the slaughterhouse some streets away; his flight led the animal through the front door of her building, up the stairs, and outside her front door, behind which, she and her mother screamed and shouted for help. Another concerned a sledding accident she suffered one especially cold winter's morning, when an unexpected and unexpectedly heavy snowfall turned the streets scaling the hill up which the town was built into impromptu runs

CAOINEADH

for the sleds she and her friends improvised from whatever they could lay their hands on: discarded pieces of wood, crates, and boxes, the majority of which went only a short distance before coming to a halt; the bit of wood she chose, however, skimmed over the snow and down the street as if it were a proper sled, picking up speed, which was first exciting and then frightening as she realized she had no way to stop, even as the end of the street was rapidly approaching, not to mention, the larger thoroughfare it intersected, on which a large, horse-drawn delivery wagon was waiting, its rear wheel an obstacle she thought she could whip past but did not. Fortunately, her father had been watching her and the other children and before the corner of her sled caught the rim of the cart's wheel and sent her tumbling across the street, he was already running down the sidewalk full speed, heedless of the threat of slipping, arriving beside her while she was still lying on her back, dazed, watching the sky spin overheard, scooping her up in his arms and continuing his run, this time toward the local infirmary.

Though I had not heard them before, Mom would repeat them in the years to come; indeed, when I was in college, I would interview her and Dad about the sledding-accident incident, which I had conceived as a possible kernel for one of the stories I had been writing since my discovery of Stephen King's fiction at age fourteen locked my future into place and my more recent immersion in William Faulkner's work directed me toward the familial and the regional as sources of inspiration. In consultation with my parents, I drew an annotated map of the section of Greenock where Mom's sledding mishap occurred; although I would not write the story itself, as I could not figure out its parameters beyond the accident. Nor did I write down the ghost stories she recounted until later still, one of them in my first professionally published story and another in my first professionally published novel. And there was one story I never attempted to record, because she told it to me once only, on an overcast afternoon during our first stay in what I thought of as the second Maine house, in the long middle of our two weeks there. Still recovering from the pair of heart attacks that had almost killed him the previous September—though loath to admit it or have any of us mention it—Dad was going for occasional walks up or down the beach, sometimes accompanied by Mom, more often by one or all of us kids. If the tide was in, he would try to teach us how to skip stones across the water, a skill I had limited success mastering, but at which my siblings achieved a passable degree of proficiency. On this particular day, Mom opted to sit on her rock with her book, and I chose to remain with her as the rest of the family set out south along the sand. I wish I could remember the title of the novel she was reading, which concerned a nurse serving in London in the midst of the Blitz who becomes involved with an American who turns out to be a spy. Mom dismissed its plot with a laugh, but the descriptions of London when the bombs were falling fascinated her. "You know," she said, placing the open book face down on the rock beside her, "Greenock was very badly bombed during the War."

I was aware of this, in part because she had mentioned it previously. For years, she had repeated, "We were very badly bombed in the War," or a variation thereof so much that her utterance of it now prompted an almost automatic nod from me. Long after this day—decades—I would finally research the details of what was called the Greenock Blitz. It took place over two nights, May 6th and 7th, 1941, commencing around midnight each time. (Mom would have been a few months past her fourth birthday.) Much of the shore of the Clyde, with its extensive shipbuilding facilities and its deep ports, was a strategic target for the German war effort. Two months prior, on the nights of March 13th and 14th, the *Luftwaffe* had struck Clydebank, near Glasgow, in what was known as the Clydebank Blitz. Casualties and destruction had been substantial, so in early May, the German air force set its sights west, on Greenock. Three hundred and fifty planes, bombers guarded by fighters, crossed the North Sea. The bombers dropped explosive and incendiary bombs and parachute land mines. The fighters strafed anyone unlucky enough to be caught out in the open. Though deaths were fewer than at Clydebank (271), injuries were considerable (10,200). Those who could took cover in the train tunnels at the east end of the town; the rest of the populace hid in bomb shelters or, where those were not available, in cellars. Five thousand homes were destroyed, five times as many damaged. Despite the devastation, the operation ultimately was not a success, failing to achieve its objective, the destruction of Greenock's shipyards and the ships at anchor in the Clyde. But it left those who survived traumatized: in Mom's case, to the degree she refused to countenance Dad buying a German car. During our next family trip to Scotland, which would come the summer after my high school graduation, she would point out the building in Greenock whose side had been full of

CAOINEADH

bullet holes from when a family of three had been machine-gunned by a German pilot. The building's stone had been left unrepaired throughout Mom's youth and young adulthood, a staccato memorial.

At this point, however, my knowledge of the Greenock Blitz was considerably more rudimentary. To be honest, I didn't think Mom was going to say anything else; she had a distant, unfocused, I might have said dreamlike expression on her face. But she continued, "The first night was a surprise. My mother woke me in the middle of the night to hurry me into my shoes and coat. Uncle Bobby was already up and dressed. My father wasn't there. He was a warden, which meant he was in charge of making sure our neighbors were out of their flats. Everyone was supposed to go to the shelters. We had to take our gas masks with us, in case the Germans used gas. You carried them with you all the time, everywhere you went. I had a children's gas mask, which was made to look like Mickey Mouse. With the ears and all, so it would be less frightening, you know. I remember my mother asking where mine was. It had slid under the bed. We left before my father came back. My mother didn't want to, but we could hear the bombs falling. They made a whistling sound, then a great boom. Bobby and I held my mother's hands as we raced down the stairs. She was always telling us not to run on the stairs. Especially Bobby. But now here we were.

"Outside, the air was full of the noise of the planes, the droning of their engines. Like enormous bees. The sound was everywhere above us. The bombs whistled down from them. Our building was right on the water. When we came out the front door, we were looking up the hill the town was built on. There were explosions all over it, bursts of red and orange. Mixed in with the booms were other sounds. Buildings collapsing in a crash. Sirens whining. People screaming and crying. A fighter buzzed low overhead, tracer bullets shooting from its wings in green dashes. The anti-aircraft guns made a steady, coughing noise. Across the street, a car was on fire. In those days, cars were still rare. To see one wrapped in flames was strange. I could smell the fire, and other things burning besides. Wood and coal and petrol. My mother ran with us to the bomb shelter. Half our neighbors were inside already. They were wearing their gas masks. All together like that, they looked weird, frightening. My mother found us a seat and helped me put my gas mask on. The parent was supposed to put their mask on first and then help the child, but she took care of Bobby and me before she saw to herself. More people came into the shelter. My father wasn't with them. The sound of the bombs wasn't as loud, but the blasts shook the ground. I asked my mother where my father was. 'Where's Daddy?' I said. 'I want my Daddy.' I started to cry, inside my gas mask. My mother tried to hush me. 'Daddy'll be here any minute,' she said. 'Just you wait and see. He's on his way.'

"Another group of people jammed into the shelter. My father was with them. He wasn't wearing his gas mask. 'You see,' my mother said, 'there he is!' I kept crying, but it was with relief. My father made his way to us and lifted me up. I threw my arms around his neck and told him how frightened I had been. He shoogled me and said it was okay, he was with me. To my mother, he said he had been delayed by the Muirs. They were an old couple who lived at the end of the hall from us. My father had knocked on their door and told them we were being bombed and they had to go to the shelter. They refused. They had lived good long lives, they said, and if the Lord saw fit to take them to His bosom, then it was fine with them. He couldn't believe it. He tried arguing with them. There were bombs falling, he said. They were going to be blown up. No matter what he said, they wouldn't change their minds. Finally, he had to leave them, though he was very upset about it. I asked him if Mr. and Mrs. Muir were going to die, but he told me to hush.

"We stayed in the shelter until three in the morning. I fell asleep on my mother's lap. Wearing my gas mask, if you can imagine it. When they woke me to go out, I took it off. Without their masks on, everyone's faces looked bare, exposed. Uncle Bobby was a hurry to see what the bombs had done. My mother and father were anxious. They tried to hide it, but they must have wondered if we'd have any place left to return to. The Muirs, too: my father must have worried they'd be all right. My mother held my hand up the stairs out of the shelter. The sky was red, from all the fires, you know. Clouds of smoke hung over the town. You could hear fires roaring and crackling. People wailed. Men from the fire brigade shouted. All the smoke made it hard to breathe. My mother said to me, 'Don't look, Margaret, don't look.' But I did. How could I not? Uncle Bobby kept saying, 'Would you look at *that*,' so I would. I couldn't make sense of it. I knew what the street was supposed to look like. Some of it was the same. Then there were buildings that weren't there. They had been replaced by heaps of brick and

CAOINEADH

wood. Most of them were burning. There were already groups of men in front of them, working to put out the fires.

"Our building was still standing. A lot of the other buildings, even if they hadn't been bombed directly, had their windows blown in. From the force of the explosions. Our windows were fine. The Muirs were, too. My father was relieved. I saw him smiling and shaking his head.

"He had to go into work the next day. To help with the damage to the factory he worked in. Uncle Bobby and I should have been at school. But school was closed for the moment. My mother kept us inside. Bobby was not happy. He wanted to see the damage to the town up close. 'No!' my mother said, and that was that. End of discussion. So, the two of us sat at the living room window and he pointed out where the bombs fell to me. Parts of the town were still burning. Smoke rose high into the air in long black clouds. Buildings were gone, blown to bits. A few streets over from us, there was a row of apartments that ran the entire length of the street. Half of it was fine, and the other half collapsed, like an avalanche. You saw men everywhere. Some were putting out the last of the fires. Others were searching the wreckage for survivors. From our window, we had a view of the shipyards, with their big cranes, and the ships in the Clyde. Compared to the rest of the town, they looked okay. Uncle Bobby said to me, 'You know what this means, don't you?' I didn't. He said, 'The Germans'll be back tonight. They'll want another go at the shipyards.' When my mother heard him, she told him to stop talking rubbish.

"Bobby wasn't, but. That night, the planes came a second time. It was the same thing all over again. They started at midnight. My mother woke me and dressed me. She'd left Bobby's and my clothes by our beds. So that went a little quicker, maybe. I knew where my gas mask was. While my mother, Bobby, and I ran down the stairs, my father tried to convince the Muirs to leave their flat. God had protected them once, he said. To expect He would do so a second time was presumption. They wouldn't listen. He wished them well and left. He caught up to the rest of us outside the shelter. It was just as a bomb fell up the street. It was so close you felt the blast. The force of it. The noise was deafening. I screamed. My voice sounded like it was coming from far away. My mother and father just about carried Bobby and me into the shelter. We found seats and my mother helped me put my gas mask on. My ears were ringing. I couldn't hear anything else. Not really.

Everything was distant. I was frightened. I started to cry. My mother said something to me, but I couldn't make it out. I could only see her mask moving. She was softspoken, you know. Eventually, she gave up and settled for rubbing my back. The bombs shook the ground. I didn't know if they were worse this night, but they certainly weren't any better. I was exhausted. Even with the shaking, I started to fall asleep several times. The ringing in my ears wouldn't let me. For the three hours we were in the shelter, it improved a little. Enough for me to hear my mother and father's voices. They still sounded faint, muffled. The ringing didn't go away. Not exactly. It *sank* inside my ears. That was how I pictured it. The noise dropping into my head like a stone falling through the water.

"Eventually, the all-clear was sounded and we left the shelter. The sky looked like it was on fire. So many buildings had been bombed. There was glass all over the street. Pieces of wood sticking out of piles of bricks. A window frame with no glass in it. An alarm clock lying in the gutter. Sheets of paper floating in the air, pages from a newspaper. Someone's good cutlery scattered across the street and sidewalk. Uncle Bobby went to pick up a knife. My father said something and he left it. There were flames everywhere. Smoke and the smell of things burning hung in the air. People were screaming and shouting. To me, they sounded like they were under water. For the second night in a row, my mother and father must have been worried we would have no home to go back to. But no, there it was, waiting for us.

"This was years later, but Uncle Bobby told me, the reason our building wasn't hit was, we were so near the river. Most of the planes dropped their bombs too early. They missed the shipyards and they missed us. When really, they should have blown us to pieces.

"I didn't know this at the time. I was just happy to have my own bed to climb into. I was too tired for the ringing in my ears to keep me awake.

"The next morning, the sound was better. I could hear my mother tell me it was time to wake up without any problem. The ringing wasn't all the way gone, though. If I tried, I could still find it inside me. It was changed. Instead of a steady ring, it rose and fell. Almost the way a song does. My mother kept Bobby and me inside. He complained. She said there were bombs lying around that hadn't gone off. Not to mention, other things she didn't want us to see. 'Like dead bodies?' Bobby said. He thought he was

CAOINEADH

being cheeky. My mother said, 'Yes,' and there was something in the way she did that quieted Bobby. She had already heard about friends who had been killed.

"So, Bobby and I passed another day staring out the living room window. The damage to the town was worse. There was a distillery the bombs hit. It burned all night and through the day. There were streets where all the houses had been bombed. They were just heaps of rubble. A bomb had blown a car upside-down against the front of a building. A man was standing beside it. His hands were on his hips and his head was tilted to one side. It was as if he couldn't understand how his car had ended up like this. We knew we weren't supposed to laugh. There was plenty not to laugh at. But this was funny. We tried to keep quiet, but my mother heard us anyway. She stormed over to the window, demanding to know what we were going on about. Bobby pointed to the man and his car. My mother stared out the window, then made an exasperated noise and walked away. She didn't tell the two of us to move, so we stayed there, watching the man try to figure out what to do. When we were bored with him, we looked elsewhere. In what was left of some of the closer houses, you could see all sorts of things. A couch balanced on a heap of bricks. A China cabinet lying on its back in the sidewalk. The front door to a bombed house still standing upright. Bobby pointed to the shipyards and the ships on the Clyde. They'd taken very little in the way of damage. This time, when my brother asked me if I knew what this meant, I nodded. The Germans would be back.

"Except, they weren't. I don't know why. Maybe they thought they'd done enough. Or maybe there was another place they were due to attack. Whatever the reason was, they didn't return. We went to bed that night sure they would. We slept in our clothes. My gas mask was next to my bed. My father went through our building, making sure everyone's blackout curtains were drawn. It was like the whole town was holding its breath. But the night was quiet. So was the next. And the one after. And so on. The Germans never came back. Though we spent the rest of the War afraid they would.

"It was a couple of days before my mother let Uncle Bobby and me go outside to play. She wasn't happy about it. A lot of the town was in ruins. But Bobby and I were going stir-crazy. School wasn't back in, yet. Finally, my mother said Bobby and I could go out as long as we stayed right beside the building. We promised we would. There were other children standing around the building. Their mothers had told them the same thing as ours. Everybody compared the stories they'd overheard from their parents. Because our flat was on the top floor, Bobby described everything we'd seen. He was still predicting the Germans would be back.

"I wasn't interested in any of that talk. Or in what the rest of the kids had to say. I wanted to find out where the song I was hearing was coming from. The ringing in my ears, you know. From the explosion. I told you how it went from plain ringing to rising and falling. Well, during the next couple of days, the rising and falling changed. It became complicated, a melody. As I heard the tune more clearly, I could pick out words being sung along with it. They weren't any words I knew. Or any language I knew. It sounded like a girl doing the singing. At first, I thought I'd made a mistake and was hearing her on the radio. I asked my mother who that was on the radio. She gave me a strange look. 'The radio isn't on,' she said. 'Is she outside, then?' I said. 'Can't you hear her?' No, my mother said. There was no one singing. She put her hand on my forehead to check my temperature. I wasn't running a fever. 'Are you making up stories?' she said. I said I wasn't. She took my head in her hands and tilted it from one side to the other. To check my ears. 'There's no little girl in there,' she said and sent me on my way.

"There may not have been a girl in my ears, but her song was. I noticed it was louder whenever I was near an open window. This gave me the idea it was coming from somewhere outside. When Bobby and I walked through the front door, the song was stronger than ever. While he and the other children were comparing notes, I wandered around to the other side of the building. This was the one facing the river. It was a sunny day. A strong breeze was coming off the water. Standing facing the Clyde with her back to me was a girl. She was a few years older than I was. About Uncle Bobby's age. She was wearing a white, lacy dress. It was very fancy. It was also filthy, stained with dirt and grease and oil and blood. The hem was all ragged. So were the cuffs. Her hair was long, right down her back, and in a terrible tangle. It was blond, so light it was practically white. She was barefoot, which you never saw. Unless you were on the beach. But never on the hard pavement. I could hear the song clearly. It was all around me. I walked up to the girl and said, 'Is that you singing?'

"She turned to me. Her face was lovely. But strange, too. I couldn't say how, exactly. Just that there was something different about it. It was filthy,

CAOINEADH

too. She had been crying. Her eyes were red and shiny. The tears had made paths through all the dirt. She looked surprised. She said, 'You can hear it?' Her accent was strange. She pronounced her words carefully, like she wasn't used to them.

"I said yes I heard the song. I could see she wasn't the one singing. I asked her where it was coming from.

"'There,' she said, and waved her hand at the Clyde.

"'The water?' I said. I didn't see anyone out there singing.

"'Beyond,' she said.

"I thought maybe she meant the other side of the river. (Although my father had told me Ireland, where some of our family came from, lay across the water.) But I was more interested in finding out about the song. I said, 'What's it saying?'

"She told me I was hearing something. I couldn't understand the words she used for it. I said, 'I don't know what that is.' She said I could call it the road in song. The song road.

"I told her I didn't know what that was, either.

"'A path,' she said.

"'Where does it go?' I said.

"She used another word I didn't understand. This time, she translated before I asked. She said, 'To the place you go after you die.'

"I asked if she meant Heaven.

"She said if that was my name for it, then yes, Heaven.

"'How does it do that?' I said.

"She said, 'When the dead hear the song, it tells them what they need to know. But,' she said, 'it is very hard to hear. The dying, the freshly dead, need someone to sing it to them, so they can learn to listen for it.' This, she said, was her job. Except she didn't call it a job. She said it was her bond. I'm pretty sure this was the word she used. She was supposed to stand near someone who was at the end of their life and sing. To help them. To guide them.

"I said, 'Do you do this for everyone?'

"No, she said. Only certain people were to be sung to. They belonged to seven families—houses, she called them. Long, long ago, she said, these houses had come together to aid her people. A terrible monster had threatened her folk, she said. One so old, its name had been forgotten. Whatever it could get its hands on, it ate. Their queen had called for help, and the seven houses had heard her. Together, they sent their men to the queen's aid. There was a long and terrible battle. With the houses' help, her folk were able to defeat the monster. But even in defeat, the monster wasn't done. It lay in wait in the darkness of death, watching for the souls of warriors who helped the queen. And not just them: their families, too. If it caught them, it ate them. In this way, it would have its revenge.

"When the queen learned of this, she chose certain of her folk to aid the seven houses. It was their duty to sing to members of the families while they were dying. To assist them in finding the song road and avoiding the monster.

"None of this made sense to me. I said, 'Are you an angel?' The girl didn't look like an angel. But I couldn't think of anyone else who would do what she was describing.

"She shook her head. All that tangled hair. She said, 'I am not of their number. My kin are the—' She said another strange word. She said, 'We are the third host.'

"'Well,' I said, 'what're you so sad about? Is it all the bombs?'

"'Yes,' she said, 'all the bombs and all the people they have killed.'

"I said, 'My Daddy says it's a hundred. Maybe more.'

"She nodded. 'It is more. Almost three times. Of the injured, many will also die.'

"I said, 'Do you have to sing for all of them?'

"'Not all,' she said. 'But more than I have ever sung for. My sisters have attended to such scenes. They have walked on battlefields, in plague houses. Some of them have gone mad from the task, run screaming from all the death into the wild, to roam the countryside howling their misery. I could not understand why they did so. I am younger. I had not seen anything like this,' she said. She tilted her head at the town.

"'What happens if you don't sing?' I said.

"'Some souls will find their way,' she said. 'Some will not.'

"'The monster,' I said, 'will it get them?'

"'Yes,' she said.

"'Could I help you?' I said.

"She said, 'Why would you offer this?' She stared at me. She said, 'You are not of the seven houses.'

CAOINEADH

"That didn't make any difference. If anything, I was relieved. Having to face the monster the girl described frightened me. I couldn't stand the thought of all the people having to do it now. I imagined them in a group. Like on Sunday, standing outside church after Mass. I didn't know what the monster looked like. Just that it had a mouth. I didn't want to imagine it. I couldn't help myself. I pictured it as a giant. Made of brick and wood. Of all the rubble and ruin I'd seen out the living room window. The top of its head was a raging fire. The drone of German bombers came out of its open mouth. I didn't want anyone to be eaten by the monster. I said so.

"The girl didn't ask if I was sure. She started to sing the tune that had led me to her. She had a lovely voice. As she sang, I heard the song more fully. It was three notes braided one around the other. I didn't know if I could sing it. But I had said I would. I started following along as best I could. The words were weird, thick and lilting at the same time. I sang the sounds of them. They returned and I realized we were singing the tune again. That was what we did. The song wasn't very long. When we reached the end, we went back to the beginning. Over and over. I couldn't sing it the way the girl did. She followed the song as it climbed up to the sky and dove down under the earth. She knew the words to draw out and the ones to rush through. She held the notes it opened and closed with. I'd never heard anything like it. I couldn't understand the words, but I could feel what was in them. Sadness. Deep sadness at leaving life. Aching for everything around you. For how beautiful it was. Even the bad things were beautiful. Because they were part of the life you were sorry was over. They were strong, the feelings in the words. I'd never known anything so intense. Even during the bombing. It was difficult to bear. If I had understood what I was singing, I don't think I could have stood it.

"In the middle of all the sadness, though, there was something else. Like a thread. Running right through the song. I could just about see it. It was black. But shiny, too, like ink. Like it was a line of ink. It went all the way out from our singing, away over the Clyde. Into the distance. It seemed like, the farther it went, the bigger it became. Like our voices were joining something larger. What I'd been hearing since the explosion. That song. The song road. Like a stream flowing into a river.

"Around us, there was movement. Out of the corner of my eye, I saw someone. Not just one person, either, but a whole crowd. At the edges of both my eyes. I kept singing. I moved my head from one side to the other. If I looked straight at them, I couldn't see anything. If I looked away, there they were. Men, women, and children. Some wearing their work clothes. Most in what they'd gone to sleep in. When the bombs started falling. There were so many of them. My voice shook. But I went on with the song. The girl gave no sign she noticed them.

"The words I was singing—I could just about understand them. That was how it seemed. Like each time I went through the tune, they became clearer. *Closer.* They were about all the sadness of dying and the beauty everywhere. About it being the way from this place to another. About following the beauty as it left. I don't know. Maybe I was making it up.

"I was more sure about what I felt out over the water. In the distance, where our singing went. To join the bigger song. Something was waiting there. Standing next to the song road. Towering over it. Taller than any building. The monster the girl had mentioned. I could no more see it than I could the crowd of souls around me. Well, if I'd turned my head, maybe. Which there was no way I was going to. Hate was pouring from it, raging against me like a hurricane. It was freezing. I knew what was out over the Clyde looked far worse than I imagined it. I was so afraid, I almost stopped singing. I wanted to run away. But. I could see the people at the corners of my eyes. I didn't want to leave them to the monster. To its hate. Its freezing hate.

"So, I sang. Even though my mouth was dry and my throat was starting to hurt. I sang. Even though I was surrounded by ghosts. I sang. Even though a monster was blasting its hate at me. I sang. Even though the song was drawing on something inside me. My own soul, maybe. I sang and I saw the people to either side of me move forward. Until they were at the very edge of the tarmac. Then one of them—it was an older woman—stepped into the air. And kept going. I still couldn't see her. But I could, too, the same way I saw our song. The shining black heart of it. She was following it over the river. Walking beside the black thread. Another person, a man, went next. Then another man—just a boy, really. Now everyone was going. All of them walking one by one over the water. Into the distance. Right under the eyes of the monster. Which was furious. The people grew smaller. Like they were farther away than out above the Clyde. I kept singing. They reached the place where our song met the bigger song.

CAOINEADH

"The girl stopped singing. Just like that. I went on for another wee bit, then stopped. For a moment, it was like I was still singing. Still in the song. I could feel the song road. I could feel the monster and its hate. I thought I could feel what was at the other end of the song road. Then all of it was gone. It was just the girl and me.

"She thanked me. She said, 'You have done a great service.'

"I didn't know how to answer. I said, 'You're welcome.'

"Behind me, I heard Uncle Bobby yelling for me. I turned and shouted I was here. I turned back and the girl was gone.

"I told Bobby about her. He asked what she was doing. I told my mother and father about her, too. After Bobby repeated what I'd said to him to them. About the girl in the pretty dress I sang a song for all the dead folk with. My mother checked my temperature. I was already hot. For the next week, I was sick in bed. I ran a high fever. The doctor said it was probably from the strain of the bombings. Nobody believed my talk of the girl. Of the song road. They assumed I was already sick and hallucinated her. Though Uncle Bobby told me he'd overheard my mother and father wondering if I'd seen a ghost. I knew why I was sick. It was the song. Helping the girl with it had done something to me. The fever was because of that.

"After I was better, I didn't mention the girl. Or our song. Or any of it. There was the War going on, you know. A couple of my mother's brothers were in the Army. Like I told you, we were still worried the Germans would be back to bomb us. There were all sorts of ships in the Clyde. The Royal Navy. The Americans. The Free French, too. Sailors and soldiers were everywhere. School was back in session. Even there, the War was all everyone talked about. I never forgot the girl. Just, I didn't speak of her.

"I never did," Mom said, "until now." She laughed. "After all these years, you're the first one I've told this to. How do you like that?" She laughed again.

I didn't know how to answer. What I had been listening to seemed more of a piece with the fiction I was soaking in, with Stephen King and Peter Straub's novels and stories, than it did any of the other stories she and Dad had related. This wasn't the lives of the saints, either, or of more recent holy men and women. Mom's story came from some other source. I could feel my stunned expression. Mom was waiting for my reply, so I said, "You mean you never told Dad?"

She shook her head. "I couldn't find the right time."

In twenty-some years of marriage, it hardly seemed possible to me there hadn't been at least one moment Mom could have shared her story with Dad, especially in the seven years prior to my arrival. I wasn't sure what such an omission said about my parents' relationship, which had always appeared rock solid to me. But this was a question I had neither the words to phrase nor the bravery to ask. Instead, I said, "Do you remember the song? The one you and the girl sang? Any of it?"

Whatever question Mom had been anticipating, this was not it. Before she answered, she looked down the beach, to where Dad and my brother and sisters were faintly visible, heading in our direction. Her eyes still focused on them, she said, "The song never went away. It was harder to recall the specifics of it. The exact way the melody went. Sometimes I would hum a piece of it to myself. Only a little piece, though. I didn't want to make myself sick.

"The night Dad had his heart attacks—well. There was the one that put him in the hospital, then the one he had while he was there. The first was massive. The kind the doctors call a widow-maker. He was in so much pain. His face was gray. It was like he was dying in front of me. I wanted to call the ambulance. He said no, he didn't want to scare any of you. So, I phoned the Seymours and he drove us to Penrose while she sat with you."

I had been there for all of this, of course, which remained stamped in my memory with unsparing vividness. I had waited in the living room with Mrs. Seymour, with whom I had carried on a pleasant and empty conversation while the hours ticked past and we waited for news of my father. Every now and again, she would suggest I go to bed, a suggestion I politely declined, saying I preferred to stay up until my mother returned. To her credit, Mrs. Seymour did not insist.

"They took Dad back," Mom said. "Really, I don't know where they took him. One minute, we were in the Emergency Room. They had put Dad on a bed and pulled the curtain around us. He was in agony. Nurses were coming and going. The doctor, too. They asked him to describe his symptoms. I knew he was having a heart attack. Every time I heard him run through what he was feeling, I wanted to scream at then: 'He's having a heart attack! Can't you see that?' I suppose they had their procedures to follow. They drew his blood. They put him on an IV. They hooked him up to machines.

CAOINEADH

More nurses came and went. Another doctor walked in. He said he was a cardiologist. He asked Dad to describe his symptoms. He listened while he looked at some of the printouts from the machines. He said he was going to give Dad a shot of morphine for the pain. Then they were going to move him. I know the doctor said where to. I wasn't paying attention to him. I was too busy with the looks the nurses were passing back and forth. With the doctors, too. They reminded me of the looks the nurses gave when my father was dying of pneumonia. This was after the War. I was nine. They were looks that said my father wasn't going to live. I saw them again on the faces of those nurses around Dad. Of course, no one said anything. They didn't need to. I'm sure they thought I didn't notice anything.

"After they rolled Dad away, I went into the waiting room. Mr. Seymour asked me what was happening. I told him they took Dad for more testing. He asked me if the doctor had said anything. I said no. I said I needed a breath of fresh air. Mr. Seymour offered to come with me. I told him to call Mrs. Seymour and let her know what was going on.

"Outside the hospital, people were standing around smoking. I didn't want to be anywhere near them. Thirty years of cigarettes had brought Dad here. I walked past them. All the way to the edge of the parking lot. Near one of the lights there. The big tall ones. If I shielded my eyes from the glare, I could see the Hudson. There was barely any moon in the sky. Just a sliver. I stood in the light staring at all the dark. I was afraid. I could feel my life—everything Dad and I made together—teetering. I wanted to cry.

"Instead, I started to sing. The song the girl and I sang next to the Clyde. What I remembered of it. I didn't sing loud enough for the smokers to hear. I don't know what I thought I was doing. Dad wasn't a member of the seven houses the girl had mentioned. Not that I knew, anyway.

"A woman stepped into the light beside me. I hadn't heard her approaching. Because she was barefoot. She was wearing a white dress. All lace. Very fancy, but old-fashioned. Her hair went all the way down her back. It was pure white, and a tangled mess. She wasn't old—well, she didn't look it. You couldn't say what her age was. Her face was—there was something strange about it. Something I couldn't put my finger on. But which I recognized right away. This wasn't the girl I had sung with. This woman's dress was clean and whole. It was someone like the girl, but. She said, 'Why are you singing that?'

"I said, 'Please. My husband is in the hospital. I think he had a heart attack.' I didn't know what to say next. I was afraid to ask her the question I most wanted answered.

"The woman stared at me. Her eyes were a shade of green I'd never seen. So dark it was this side of black. She said, 'No.' Then she turned and walked into the night. I called, 'Wait.' She didn't answer. I shaded my eyes to see where she was headed. She was already gone.

"I wanted to run after her. Only, where was I supposed to run? I could sing the song again. Try to bring her back. But I had the feeling that would be the wrong thing to do. I had been out here too long already. I started toward the door and met Mr. Seymour coming to find me. He was worried I hadn't returned.

"The rest of the night went by in a blur. The minute I sat foot in the hospital, the woman and her, 'No,' went right out of my head. There was too much else to deal with. It wasn't too long until the cardiologist took me into a side room to tell me Dad had had a heart attack. It was a very grave one, he said. Very, very grave. I remember, the thought went through my head, *Does he think he's being funny?* The doctor wasn't, of course. He was trying to tell me how serious the situation was. Grave, but. He said he was hopeful Dad had gotten to the hospital in time. But he wasn't out of danger, yet. There was still a chance he wouldn't survive. I had to prepare myself in case this happened.

"I wanted to ask the doctor how I was supposed to do that. I didn't. I asked if I could see Dad. Yes, the doctor said., but only for a minute. A nurse took me to the Intensive Care. Dad was asleep. Or unconscious, from the morphine they gave him. There were all these tubes and wires coming off him. Machines beeping. I started at his chest, to make sure it was moving. The same way I used to study your chest, when you were a newborn and sleeping in your crib. Then I left and Mr. Seymour drove me home.

"Not until I was lying in bed did I think about what the woman said to me under the light. 'No.' Was it her way of telling me Dad wasn't going to live? Or that he wasn't going to die? Or was she saying she wasn't going to answer me either way? I spent a good deal of the night worrying over what she meant.

"I never figured it out. Not for certain. Dad came home from the hospital, thank God. He recovered. It took a long, long time. So maybe the

CAOINEADH

woman was telling me he wasn't going to die, after all. It would be nice if this was the case. If it was, though, you'd think she would have been less abrupt about it. So maybe she was just saying she wouldn't speak to me."

Mom glanced up the beach, to where Dad and my siblings had drawn nearer. I followed her look and saw Dad with his head inclined to my youngest sister, who was engaged in relating some story or opinion she accentuated with extravagant, sweeping gestures of her arms. "Now," Mom said, picking up her book, "I want to finish this chapter before your father gets back."

With that, our conversation—really, her narration—concluded. Nor would Mom return to it in the days, then months, then years, and finally decades to come. On many occasions, I weighed speaking to her about the events she'd disclosed while Dad and my brother and sisters took their walk beside the Penobscot. If nothing else, I wanted to ask her if she'd been telling me the truth for the time we sat on those rocks. Phrasing the matter so bluntly would be a mistake, I knew, one guaranteed to steer Mom's response away from answering me toward questioning my lack of trust in her honesty. I formulated more oblique versions of my query, of which probably the best ran something along the lines of, "Hey Mom? Do you remember the time on the beach in Maine when you told me about the girl you sang along with, after Greenock was bombed? Yeah, who," or sometimes, "what do you think she was?" I assumed I'd cue whatever came next off her reply. But even during what I knew were the most opportune moments, in the years after Dad died, when I was driving her the two and a half hours to visit my middle sister in college, I failed to broach the subject.

I have always loved, always treasured, the image of my mother as a little girl, standing facing the River Clyde, bravely lifting her voice to help sing a song for a group of the suffering dead. I've never asked her if she remembered it, let alone to sing it, to teach it to me. As a younger man, I was more nervous about its result than I cared to admit. As I grew older, I was less worried about its potential consequence than I was in interfering with what had become one of my favorite (private) stories of my mother.

Now, I wish I had revisited the narrative she shared on the beach, had convinced her at least to sing the song for me. I'm sure I could have remembered it. Now that Mom is old ("Say older," she corrects me, "not old"), and gray (but she keeps her weekly appointment with her hairdresser to have her hair cut and colored), and full of sleep (though she swears she barely sleeps at all, if I phone her after 10:30 at night, she's likely to be groggy), I would have driven down to the banks of the Hudson and sung that song, sung it over and over until it called forth from the shadows or the river a woman with long tangled hair wearing a white lace dress. When she asked me in her strange accent what I wanted, I would tell her.

And I would be satisfied with her answer, even if it was to say, "No," and walk away, back into the darkness or the water.

STORY NOTES

Starting with my first professionally published story ("On Skua Island") my fiction has drawn elements from my life. Indeed, "On Skua Island" opens with thinly disguised versions of myself, my wife, and several of our friends sitting around the living room of a real house on Cape Cod (long-sold but still-missed). I'm reminded of an interview Paul Tremblay conducted with Stephen Graham Jones at Readercon a couple of years ago, when Stephen was one of the guests-of-honor. Every time Stephen sent him a copy of his latest book, Paul said, he would inscribe it with words to the effect of, this is all true. What, Paul wanted to know, did Stephen mean by this?

Well, Stephen said, if he was writing something and arrived at a place where he didn't know what came next, he would insert something from his own experience. So, the facts of his life were part of his books in an ongoing way. In this sense, all of his fiction was true (or at least, truth-adjacent).

I knew what Stephen was talking about. Since that long-ago story, my fiction has been full of details taken from my life, sometimes in modified form, sometimes pretty directly. Page through the four collections I've published so far, and you'll find figures and situations lifted from my experience. (The story notes in each book offer specific details as to the individual instances.) On several occasions, I've been surprised to recognize something based in my life long after the story it appeared in was published. In this regard, I don't think I'm different from pretty much every writer I know. Speak to them about their work for any length of time, and you'll learn it's peppered with material drawn from their experience.

When exactly I had the idea to write stories dealing more directly with my autobiography, I'm not certain. (Though "Bor Urus," which is in *Sefira and Other Betrayals*, was an early effort. [As is "City of the Dog" in *The Wide, Carnivorous Sky and Other Monstrous Geographies*.]) I think it came gradually, as an outgrowth of the use I'd already been making of the personal in my fiction, a next logical step in my creative development. It's ironic: as a writing teacher, I've spoken often and at great length to my students about the wealth of material their lives and those of their families offer them, yet it took me years of my own writing to practice what I had been preaching.

At the same time I was coming to this realization, I was working on completing my second novel (*The Fisherman*). As I ventured further into the narrative, I began to see ways in which certain of its elements might feature in other things I was writing. Some of these connections could be subtle (the presence of streams of black water, of what I thought of as the primary trees), some more dramatic (the appearance of the black city, of its vampiric police force). I wasn't looking to create a tightly bound fictional universe; I had more in mind something along the lines of the shared context of the Robert E. Howard Conan stories I had read as a kid.

I'm pretty sure this development in my fiction owes something to conversations I'd been having with Laird Barron. (This would have been in the late 2000s/early 2010s.) By this point, Laird was already speaking about the different strands in his fiction: his Children of Old Leech stories; his Nameless Couple stories; his Jessica Mace stories; etc. Before he sat down at the computer, Laird said to me on more than one occasion, he would ask himself whether what he was going to type took place in any of these settings. If the answer was yes, then he had a certain amount of narrative armature already available to use.

Prior to this moment, I had thought of my stories in more localized ways, viewing them either by subject (this is my werewolf story; this is my Lovecraftian story) or approach (this is my letter story; this is my closet drama) or sometimes both (this is my screenplay story about a vampire). If there was any connective tissue among my stories, it was their location, my

Story Notes

fictionalized version of the Hudson Valley and its history. Occasionally, as in the stories collected in *Sefira*, I would realize I had been writing to a set theme, but this tended to become apparent to me only in retrospect.

Now, though, I was working on stories connected by their concern with the facts of my life and by their use of material related to *The Fisherman*. I wouldn't say the contents of this current collection constitute a direct sequel to my second novel, but they roam around a bit inside its imaginative territory. I find it fascinating that my decision to write with greater focus on the specifics of my autobiography coincided with my exploration of elements from *The Fisherman*. You could say I was employing materials drawn from the novel as a kind of frame for events taken from my life. Or perhaps it was the autobiography that was scaffolding the fictional elements. Or most likely, it was a combination of the two, my decision to explore my life facilitated by fictive elements that could withstand the weight of repeated visitation.

Given the admittedly autobiographical aspect of these stories, I realize story notes may seem almost redundant. But although they draw on my experiences, each story does so in its own fashion, and this seemed worth clarifying, as did some of the other elements at work in them. Your mileage may vary; if you feel like giving these a pass, no hard feelings, and I hope to see you down the road.

(Introduction by Sarah Langan: I don't usually comment on the introductions and afterwords to my works, except to thank their authors in the acknowledgments. I want to make a brief exception here because Sarah Langan has written a number of lovely blurbs for me over the years which I have passed along to my publishers and which have never been used. I assume this is because we share the same last name, and [the assumption is] must therefore be related, rendering any words of praise too suspect to be of use. I suppose we must be some kind of distant relations, cousins who-can-say-how-many-times removed, but those distant bonds matter much less than those of our membership in another group, the writers of a generation that includes Laird Barron, Michael Cisco, Gemma Files, Glen Hirshberg, Stephen Graham Jones, Victor LaValle, Livia Llewellyn, and Paul Tremblay. Some other time, I hope to write about the bonds I see among the lot of us. For the moment, I want to acknowledge Sarah's long-term support for my work and thank her for it.)

"Kore:" For a Halloween issue of the publication, *Shock Totem*, I was invited by Barry DeJasu to contribute a seasonal memory. The result was a story which is the nearest to an outright memoir of any of the pieces collected here. When my wife, Fiona, heard that there were kids in our son's elementary school class who didn't go trick-or-treating because their parents didn't feel their neighborhoods were safe enough to wander around in, she decided we would have them for a Halloween party at our house. For the next few years, between two houses, we hosted somewhere around a dozen of David's classmates and their parents for parties that culminated in what we called haunted walks, each based around a different theme. One of these did culminate in the younger brother of one of David's friends freaking out at the sight of my wife in a goddess costume. (At least, I'm reasonably sure it was my wife.) At various points, both my older son, Nick, and my friend, Laird Barron, joined in the fun, playing a Frankenstein's monster and a damned explorer, respectively. Our final event took place at the local fire house, and in addition to the usual group was attended by a host of local kids and their parents. I think it was a success, but Fiona and I were left exhausted, and the next Halloween, we decided to take the year off. And that was it for the haunted walk.

There still might be another story in it, though. Maybe two.

"Homemade Monsters:" Godzilla was *the* monster of my childhood. I loved the movies, which in those pre-cable, pre-VCR days were shown only once in a while at strange times and interrupted by lengthy commercial breaks. Although the man-in-a-suit special effects were not of the same technical level of accomplishment as the stop-motion achievements of Willis O'Brien and Ray Harryhausen, the imaginative energy driving the films more than compensated for this. Then, in 1977, Marvel comics began to publish a Godzilla comic, written by Doug Moench and drawn by Herb Trimpe. Over the course of twenty-four issues, they took Godzilla on a trip across the United States that began in Alaska and ended in Manhattan. Along the way, Godzilla wreaked havoc on such major American landmarks as the Golden Gate Bridge, the Hoover Dam, and (almost) the Empire State Building. He tussled with Marvel superheroes including the Champions,

Story Notes

Avengers, and Fantastic Four. There were also a host of new monsters for him to fight, including Batragon, Yetrigar, and the Beta-Beast, as well as a particularly aggressive New York City sewer rat. I had these comics, which I reread so much the images and dialogue remain burned into my memory, more than four decades on.

What I did not have, however, were Godzilla toys with which to reenact and extend the scenarios in the comics. It would be a year or so until I bought the Shogun-Warriors edition Godzilla, a two-foot-tall toy with a launching fist and a flame-tongue that extended when you pressed a lever on the back of its head. Around the same time, I found a six-inch Godzilla figure in the local Kay-Bee Toys. This was a reasonably accurate rubber figure whose wire skeleton allowed it to be positioned but which also had the tendency to poke through its flesh, particularly at the ends of its arms.

Though I treasured them, neither toy would have been suitable for the activities I envisioned. I took my old *Star Trek* Captain Kirk figure, stripped his Starfleet uniform from him, and set to work transforming him into the King of the Monsters. I used green watercolor paint to turn him green(ish), then cut out a tail, dorsal spines, and snout from a piece of cardboard, affixing them to the figure with tape. I borrowed one of my mom's brownie pans and recreated scenes from the comics in it using more cardboard and aluminum foil. I built the helicarriers S.H.I.E.L.D. used against Godzilla in the comics; I constructed the Golden Gate Bridge and San Francisco Bay. Not as well as I wanted, perhaps, but it was better than nothing. I worked at the dining room table, after I came home from school. I remember my mom preparing dinner in the kitchen and stopping in to check on my progress.

This—all of this was the first thing I thought of when Ellen Datlow invited me to contribute a story to an anthology of stories about dolls. The second thing was a couple of kids I had known growing up, one a neighbor a couple of doors down the street, the other a classmate. Each was, to put it mildly, mercurial toward me. My classmate, in particular, was as often cruel to me as he was kind, to the extent I wonder why I remained friends with him. Both kids moved away, the neighbor when he graduated high school, the classmate when IBM relocated his dad to Arizona. But the memory of both was not that far away.

It never is.

John Langan

(It also occurs to me that this story was the latest instance of me trying to fulfill a suggestion/request made to me by my older son, Nick, going on twenty years ago, namely, to write a story with a giant monster in it. "Episode Three: On the Great Plains, in the Snow," in my previous collection, was another attempt to answer this challenge. I'm still not sure I've done so to my satisfaction; no doubt, further attempts lie ahead.)

"The Open Mouth of Charybdis:" I don't know how old I was when my mom first told me that she had had a miscarriage between the births of my younger brother and the older of my two younger sisters. (I must have been in my early teens.) I remember not knowing how to process this information—this loss, I suppose, although it was more in the nature of a secret that had been kept from me. The knowledge of this lost sibling, or perhaps the question of what life would have been like had he survived, occurred to me at odd moments. (Yes, "he:" I knew this sibling would have been a brother, as I knew his name would have been Edward.) I can't claim to have come to any conclusions, but neither have I stopped thinking about the question.

When Lois Gresh invited me to contribute to an anthology of stories concerning H.P. Lovecraft's seaside town of Innsmouth, this missing sibling found his way into what developed. He joined a list of ingredients including: the attempts scholars of Lovecraft's work have made to locate the real-world inspiration for Innsmouth; the connections Lovecraft's story makes between Innsmouth and the South Pacific (and in turn the connection between the South Pacific and the paintings of Paul Gauguin); and some ideas about space and time Michael Cisco floated in his story, "Machines of Concrete Light and Dark." The lack of critical consensus as to the actual location of Innsmouth played into a notion that the town could not be found because it had been scattered by its inhabitants in ways that would preclude it being located in regular time and space. I put myself, my brother, and my lost brother into Innsmouth at the moment it's being excised from our physical and temporal space, the three of us on a mission to see the painting which (unknown to us) dramatizes this event. I know Gauguin's faults as a human being were profound, but I continue to love his art, and I enjoyed the opportunity to incorporate it into my story.

At first, I wasn't thrilled with the title I gave the story. There's a lot of

Story Notes

mouth/hunger references in my titles, and I felt I was settling for something a bit too easy. In the time since the anthology was published, though (during which, I've taught the *Odyssey* several times), the imagery of the whirlpool you must not sail too close to, lest it haul your entire ship down to its doom, has felt more appropriate. I like its sense of an accidental doom. I also note this story as one of two in this collection to feature the image of a spiral. ("Anchor" is the other.)

In the end, Edward remained lost to me. Any other outcome would have felt falsely sentimental. It was pleasant, if bittersweet, to have had the chance to visit with him, though.

"Shadow and Thirst:" I first learned of Robert Browning's great, strange poem, "Childe Roland to the Dark Tower Came," from discussions of Stephen King's inaugural "Dark Tower" book, *The Gunslinger*. I actually read the poem before I read the book, which in those days was available only in a limited edition beyond my means. My initial reading of the poem (which must have been in high school, maybe senior year) left me confused. A couple of years later, I asked my friend and then-professor, Bob Waugh, about it. "I think of its images of diminishment," he said, which wasn't much immediate help (but which I still recall).

As has so often happened with texts I find opaque, the poem became a minor obsession of mine. In the years and decades to come, I returned to it time and again, eventually teaching and writing about it. (There's a one hundred sixty page study of its relationship to three of H.P. Lovecraft's stories I really should complete [though who would publish such a thing?].) In part, my continuing interest in "Childe Roland" owed something to King's additions to the "Dark Tower" series. Even had King abandoned the story of Roland Deschain, I would have cycled back to Robert Browning's narrative of a (failed?) knight's quest across a broken (and yes, diminished) landscape. I'm not sure when, exactly, I decided I would write my own response to the poem, though it must have been pretty early on. But I didn't expect I would do so until I was much older.

How much older, I couldn't have told you. I had the sense of doing so as a kind of career-capping enterprise, as King was doing with the "Dark Tower" books. Yet when I sat down at the legal pad to write "Shadow and Thirst," almost the first image I saw was of the "round, squat turret" at the climax of Browning's poem. I pictured it at the foot of the hill behind my house, bathed in early morning light. Having put it there, I knew I was going to have to venture inside it. (As King had done in his series; as Lovecraft had in his short novel, *The Dream-Quest of Unknown Kadath*.) I also knew my tower was going to contain a vampire. This was because the story in which it appeared was being written for an anthology of vampire stories. Christopher Golden had invited me to contribute to it, his sole requirement that whatever I turned in be scary. No sparkly bloodsuckers need apply.

I suppose I might have made the tower itself the vampire, but I conceived of it more as the place in which the vampire would be found, and which therefore would be larger on the inside than it appeared on the outside. (You could describe it as a demonic TARDIS.) These kinds of spaces have appeared in other things I've written, including *House of Windows* and "Mother of Stone." I'm not sure what their appeal is for me. (Although in this case, you might see it as an oblique representation of the way the original structure of Browning's poem accommodates all manner of interpretive possibilities.)

Pretty early on, I made the connection between the vampire (imprisoned) in the tower and the sinister police force in *The Fisherman* (which, at the time, I had only recently completed). These figures patrol the black city on the shores of the black ocean, maintaining watch over its magical elements. I don't know if I was aware they were vampires (of a kind) while I was writing the novel, but by the time I came to the story, the detail had clarified itself to me. This made my imprisoned monster more interesting to me. Indeed, there are times I think I might have written this story in a different way, from the point of view of the dad, Tony, as he enters and becomes trapped inside the tower with the monstrous Edon Mundt. (I guess I still could. But it would be long, so long.)

The story I did write focuses on August, who has more than a little in common with my older son, Nick. He also became a police officer after dropping out of college. He's told me more than a few stories of his life in law enforcement, most of them comic, a few hair-raising. While I've had my issues with many of the things the American police have done (to put it mildly), I've felt that Nick is one of the good ones. This is not to say our relationship has always been easy, especially as we've both grown older—indeed, the labyrinth inside the tower might also be a trope for our

Story Notes

efforts to find our ways to one another. But I can't think of anyone I'd rather face down a vampire with.

Having responded to "Childe Roland" once, I wasn't sure if I was done with it. However, in looking over one of the other stories in this collection, "Anchor," I realized there's a trace of Browning's poem there, too. It looks like I'm not done with the tower—or it with me.

"Corpsemouth:" The title of this story came from some dental work I had done. A couple of root canals I'd had in adjacent molars failed, necessitating the removal of both teeth. The plan was for the oral surgeon who excised the teeth to replace them with dental implants. Before doing so, he wanted to build up the bone the teeth had sat in. He opened my gum, placed a piece of cadaver bone there, and sewed my gum up. The idea was, the corpse bone would graft onto my jaw and provide a more substantial platform for the implants to be screwed into. Not long after this, I was at a reading in the Strand Bookstore's rare books room. While talking to the writer, Kris Dikeman, I mentioned the procedure I'd just had done, closing my description of it with the declaration, "Just call me corpse mouth!" The instant the words left my mouth, Kris and I looked at one another, our eyes wide with the realization I had just uttered the germ of a story.

What the story was to be revealed itself when I started writing a story for Ellen Datlow's anthology, *The Monstrous*. I had the suspicion Corpsemouth was some type of mythological figure, one from the dim recesses of history. As the story unfolded, this became Scottish history. It's funny: by the point I told Ellen I would contribute an original piece to her reprint anthology, I had earned whatever small reputation I had as a writer of monster stories. Indeed, my second collection, *The Wide, Carnivorous Sky and Other Monstrous Geographies*, took this as its organizing principle. I very much liked the idea of coming up with a new(ish) monster for Ellen. Yet the story I wrote was intensely personal. I've written and spoken of my father's death before; it remains one of the axial incidents of my life. My grief over this loss and our fractious relationship has fueled much of my writing, indirectly and sometimes very directly. But I've never delved in such depth into the particulars of the last months before his death, as well as of the time following it, including the trip my mom, younger sister, and I took to Scotland the year after he died. Many of the story's details: the strange characters my father showed me after his surgery; my uncle taking my sister and me for a drive around town; my dream of my father in the van—are drawn pretty closely from my life at the time (though my uncle did not tell us about Merlin's visit to Dumbarton Rock). The monster I had named then called into existence featured in the resulting story, but as part of a larger supernatural context, which drew in part on pre-existing myth and legend, and in part on my own inventions (including a nod in the direction of *The Fisherman*—though it's quick! Blink and you'll miss it). It was also the most extensively I had written about what I guess you would call the religious tensions between my father and me, the extent to which his anxieties about me had a metaphysical dimension.

"Corpsemouth" also provided me an opportunity to write about some of the members of my extended family, especially my Uncle Lorrie, my father's brother-in-law. Every time my parents took me and my brother and sisters to Scotland to visit their respective families, we spent a great deal of time with Lorrie and his wife, Aunt Kathleen (Dad's second-youngest sister) and their kids and grandkids. I have very fond memories of all of them, and if there was anyone who would have been in a secret monster-fighting society, it would have been Uncle Lorrie.

In recent years, when I've been asked to name my favorite of the stories I've written, I've tended to choose "Homemade Monsters." Looking over "Corpsemouth" for this collection and these notes, however, I was surprised at how deeply moved I was by it, by the depth and honesty of emotion in it. I still miss my dad, and I wish things had been better between us before he died. Would he have liked this story? I can't say.

"Anchor:" This story had its origins in a couple of different conversations. The first, I had with editor and occasional writer, Justin Steele. We were talking about Jeff Ford's work, of which we are both great admirers, and Justin mentioned one story in particular, "The Manticore Spell," which he liked in no small part because of its use of the Manticore. It was such a cool monster, Justin said, but you didn't see very many stories about them. Right there and then, I told Justin I would write him a Manticore story. What the story was going to be about, I had no idea.

My promise remained in the lower levels of my brain, to be joined by the material of the second discussion. This one was with Paul Tremblay, follow-

Story Notes

ing Laird Barron's move east to live with me and my family, after his life out west had fallen apart. Paul and I were talking about how my younger son, David, had reacted to the addition of Laird and his faithful dog, Athena, to our household. (Short story: very well.) You should write a story from the point of view of a kid whose father's horror-writer friend comes to stay with them, Paul said. You could make it a young adult thing. I wasn't sure I necessarily wanted to write a young adult story, but the perspective of a more youthful protagonist was in keeping with the recent fiction I was now writing. (About which, more in the notes to the next story.)

The catalyst that brough these elements together was an invitation by Mike Davis to submit something to his anthology, *Autumn Cthulhu*. Mike was looking for pieces evoking the tone of the season—the reference points were as much the understated elegance of Charles Grant and the dreamy lyricism of Ray Bradbury as the cosmic hyperbole of the Lovecraft school. Of course, autumn is Halloween season, and this would have been an opportunity to write another, longer Halloween story. I kicked around a couple of ideas, but I found I wasn't interested in any of them. Instead, I was drawn to the cyclical dimensions of this time of year. Repetition and variation: that's what each season is, right?

At the same time, a couple of other elements came into play. The first was my affection for Richard Adams's great novel, *Shardik*, a fantasy which features an enormous, god-like bear as one of its central characters. I love bears. I've been thrilled at the couple of black bears I've seen locally. But they're also pretty intimidating creatures. I've never seen a Grizzly in the wild, the prospect of which evokes excitement and dread in me in equal measure. Ditto, polar bears. *Shardik* begins with the huge bear fleeing through a flaming forest; that image stuck with me.

The other detail that came into play was of making a stand, which comes from Stephen King's early novel, *The Stand*, and which recurs in the "Dark Tower" novels. To the best of my ability to discern, King drew the word from Bruce Springsteen's great early song, "Jungleland," off the *Born to Run* album, particularly its closing reference to "try(ing) to make an honest stand." It strikes me as an ethic derived from protestant Christianity and the American Western. In *The Stand*, the necessary act is for the book's heroes to stand in the face of terrible evil and the threat of horrible death. In the "Dark Tower" series, the necessary act is for the companions of the

John Langan

Gunslinger, Roland Deschain, to stand and be true against threats of no less villainy and magnitude, albeit, with a bit more firepower at their disposal. The idea of making a stand in the fashion of Stephen King (and perhaps Bruce Springsteen) has been important to my fiction for a while now—at least, as far back as one of my early stories, "Episode Seven: Last Stand Against the Pack in the Kingdom of the Purple Flowers," right through to *The Fisherman*, where it plays a role at a couple of key moments.

So there was all of that. Most important was my friendship with Laird. At this point, he's one of my oldest and truest companions. I've often described him as the other brother I didn't know I didn't have, a somewhat contradictory phrasing that gets at how close I feel to him as a writer and as a human being, despite us having grown up in environments about as different as you could imagine. When I started to write the story that would become "Anchor," I was still thinking about Laird as a traveler, as someone on a journey that had carried him from Alaska to Washington state, then from Washington to New York, and most recently, from living with me and my family to moving about ten miles west to settle with his girlfriend, Jessica. Given how important our writing has been to our friendship, I conceived of our fictional alter-egos as poets, his exemplary of the poets I know he loves, Dickey and Simic, and mine derived from the work of favorites such as Browning and Jorie Graham. During Laird's years with my family, I had joined David's Tang Soo Do school, beginning the process that would lead to my black belt. On more than one occasion, I floated the idea of starting my own *dojang* with Fiona, and while I never have, my alter-ego did. At this time, David spoke of his intention to become a fishing guide when he was older, so I gave him that future. It's funny: while I think of this story as being a reflection on my friendship with Laird, I realize writing these notes that it's also very much about my younger son, to an extent I'm embarrassed to admit I hadn't appreciated during its composition. In this regard, it pairs with "Shadow and Thirst" as another story about a father-son relationship told from the point-of-view of the son. (And indeed, this is the case with "Corpsemouth," too.)

A few years ago, during a question-and-answer session following a reading I did for the Lovecraft Arts & Sciences in Providence, Sean Patrick Bagley said he thought the subject of a lot of my work was time and asked what I thought of this. I agreed without hesitation, feeling that Sean had cut to the

Story Notes

beating heart of much of my fiction, and of this story, in particular.

"Outside the House, Watching for the Crows:" I wrote roughly the first half of this story around 2010, possibly a little before. Up until this point, I had studiously avoided writing about adolescents, in large part because so much horror fiction focuses on this age bracket (think *Something Wicked This Way Comes*, *It*, *Shadowland*, *A Boy's Life*, *Ghoul*, etc.) and I wanted to distinguish myself by doing something different. But I had an idea I would write about music, about a cassette tape whose songs come to inhabit the listener's consciousness.

In this, I was influenced by my (extremely) belated immersion in the music of the Velvet Underground. I had a passing acquaintance with and appreciation of Lou Reed's solo material (especially the *New York* album, of which I remain a great admirer) and I had heard a couple of his former band's songs ("Rock & Roll," "Sweet Jane"). Then, for reasons obscure to me (though I think they had something to do with hearing "Heroin" on the soundtrack to a PBS documentary [which one I'm not sure]), when my younger son was about four, I picked up a greatest hits compilation of the Velvet Underground. What I heard transfixed me. The CD opened with "Waiting for My Man," and from the first, staccato notes on the piano, and Lou Reed's aggressive whine, I was all in on these guys. There was in their music a blending of popular-leaning melodies with material from the urban underground. I don't know how much of it was informed by Bob Dylan's work; it felt more as if the Velvets and Dylan were running on parallel tracks. You could see in the Velvets' music certain family resemblances to what Springsteen would be doing a few years later. In any event, its melodious grittiness spoke to something deep within me, the same part of my soul that reacted so powerfully to grunge in the early nineties (and whose bands must also be accounted children of the Velvet Underground). I appreciated the use of a popular form as a vehicle for whatever you felt like talking about; it was my view of what myself, Laird Barron, Paul Tremblay, and other members of our writing generation were doing with horror. The songs on the greatest hits album, which I played constantly, conjured all sorts of fragmentary images for me, of a place (and time) both more fraught and more essential, of a life lived closer to the bone.

For reasons I'm not certain of (my twenty-year high school reunion, which I'd skipped but which was still in my mind?), when I started writing the story, it concerned the tail-end of my junior year in high school. I powered through the piece until the narrator attends his junior prom, then read most of what I'd written at that year's Readercon—after which, my friends who'd come to the reading asked me what came next. I told them I didn't know: I was still writing the story.

In fact, I would continue writing it for the next half a dozen or so years. Beyond what I'd already set down, I couldn't work out where the piece was supposed to go. I knew the weird tape the narrator was listening to, the music that had become his personal soundtrack, was going to lead him somewhere, but I could not work out exactly what the destination was. I left the story to percolate, returning to it every now and again to tweak a word choice or sentence, waiting for the Fornits to work out the rest of it.

This didn't happen until I finished *The Fisherman*. When Paula Guran invited me to contribute something to the *Mammoth Book of Cthulhu*, I thought about my unfinished story and realized the answer to its second half lay in the novel I had recently completed. In the novel, I had invented first a great, black ocean and then an ancient city located on its shore. I hadn't said much about the city, but a subsequent story ("Shadow and Thirst") had focused on a member of the city's vampiric police force. Now, I realized that the music on the tape was going to offer an avenue into the black city, one of whose names, the Spindle, I came upon while writing the rest of the story. Such an entry, however, would draw the notice of the city's undead guardians (who seem to me in some weird way descendants of the figures who guard Fritz Leiber's Nehwon in the Fafhrd and Gray Mouser stories). While it didn't occur to me at the time, I see that in Chris and his obsessive quest to gain entry into the Spindle, even at the cost of his own destruction, I was returning to a character type I had employed and explored in both *The Fisherman* and my first novel, *House of Windows*, as well as in a number of my stories. (It occurs to me, too, that there could be a sequel to the story which begins with the narrator opening his front door to find Chris standing there...) The figure of the obsessive over-reacher has its roots in my fascination with such characters as Melville's Ahab, Conrad's Kurtz, and Faulkner's Quentin Compson and Thomas Sutpen. The material of *The Fisherman* provided me a way to reflect on the desire—so strong in adolescence, but not absent from the rest of life—to break out of this

Story Notes

existence, to find a way to something else, something different, something (maybe) *more*. Sometimes, the answer to the (aesthetic) challenge you're facing now comes from something you haven't done yet.

"What Is Lost, What Is Given Away:" The anthology this story was written for began with a cover for a non-existent book. Its title was *What the #@!? Is That?*, the words positioned over a Mike-Mignola-esque drawing of Lovecraft's Cthulhu. There was a frantic (and fictional) blurb from Stephen King declaring he had no idea what was going on (presumably within the book's pages). The image made the rounds online every few months, and it never failed to make me laugh out loud. Eventually, it became the inspiration for an anthology edited by John Joseph Adams and Doug Cohen. The invitation to it I received gave me pretty much free rein to write what I wanted, as long as my story contained the exclamation, "What the #@!? is that?" or some variation thereof. While the obvious choice to employ the question would have been in regard to a Lovecraft-inspired beast, the first thing that occurred to me was the *Saturday Night Live* sketch I describe in the story, which a number of my friends and I imitated in the halls of our high school. On one occasion, we were joined by one of our teachers, though this is the limit of his similarity to the teacher in my story. None of my high school teachers behaved as Joel Martin does (to be fair, I should add, that I know of), but I've heard and read reports of other educators making less-than-inspired choices (to put it mildly). Although, at my ten-year high school reunion, someone did admit to having had sex with one of our teachers, a confession I found as shocking as does the story's narrator. (I have always been and remain among the most naive of my friends, if not the most.) It was only one of the things that made the occasion strange. Indeed, the way I describe the two days of the reunion in the story is fairly close to my experience of it, especially my surprise at how little it resembled its cinematic and television portrayals. The ending of the story came out of discussing it with Laird Barron, whose grim suggestions informed my eventual decisions.

The story is one of several to introduce a group called the Friends of Borges. (I can't recall if I came up with them for this piece, or for one called, "To See, To Be Seen," which I wrote around the same time and which is included in my previous collection, *Children of the Fang*.) I think it was the choice of Argentina as Joel Martin's destination for his flight with his son and as of the site of his (first) imprisonment that suggested the reference to Borges, which in turn led me back to his story, "The Aleph," which touches on such exotic mathematics as Poincaré's theorems. Borges was among a number of Spanish-language writers I discovered in my late teens and early twenties (Fuentes and Garcia Marquez the most significant with him). His stories continue to delight and inspire me, and I was quite tickled at the idea of a society of magicians named for the relationship with him featuring in a story written for a book that began as an imaginary text.

"The Supplement:" After *Autumn Cthulhu*, *The Mammoth Book of Cthulhu*, and *What the #@!? Is That?*, this story was written for the fourth Lovecraft-inspired anthology to which I was invited, this one Ellen Datlow's *Children of Lovecraft*. These were part of the wave of Lovecraft-related anthologies that dominated horror publishing during the 2010s, assuming the place zombies had occupied in the decade before. I was thrilled to have the chance to submit to Ellen's book, as I had missed out on contributing to her previous Lovecraft book, *Lovecraft Unbound*. (Although two stories had resulted from my efforts, "City of the Dog" and "Bloom.") The only instructions for this book were to avoid slavish pastiche: in Ellen's words, "No tentacles."

As it turned out, this wasn't much of an issue for me. (Which is not to say I don't have a few stories about tentacled beasts I'd like to write.) As I've gotten older, I've become concerned, if not obsessed, with the way our lives seem to pivot on certain moments. On the one hand, this makes me think of the Anglo-Saxon idea of *wjrd*, which means something like, "The way things are supposed to be because that's the way they are." On the other hand, I'm fascinated by the idea of alternate universes, of every possible decision you could make being made, and so on, into infinity. In some ways, you could see the story I wrote as a version of *A Christmas Carol*, one in which the supernatural mechanism allowing the characters to live an alternate life is not the intervention of one or several ghosts, but the titular book. The name of that volume originated in the writings of Jacques Derrida. In his conception, a supplement is something that stands outside a system of knowledge (whether philosophy, religion, aesthetics, etc.) and by its stable and to some extent unquestioned presence guarantees the system's overall coherence and stability. In my story, the book the characters lose

Story Notes

themselves in functions in a similar way by identifying the gaps in their lives, the places where their existences have broken down, and stabilizes them by allowing the characters an experience closer to their hearts' desires. Of course, there is a price for this brand of consolation (isn't there always?). The image of Minerva lost inside the labyrinth of her possible lives derives from Borges's story, "The Garden of Forking Paths," and is another instance of his enduring presence in my work. It occurs to me, too, that the story's title could apply to its relation to my larger body of work, as it's the place where elements from my novels, *The Fisherman* and *House of Windows*, meet with those from my stories, "Renfrew's Course" and "Mr. Gaunt." Here, the outlines of a larger fictional universe loom into view, if only slightly.

"Mirror Fishing:" I was sent two invitations to contribute to tribute anthologies for the great Ramsey Campbell. Both were inspired by the fiftieth anniversary of the publication of Campbell's first collection, *The Inhabitant of the Lake and Less Welcome Tenants*. The first invitation came from Brian Sammons and Glynn Owen Barrass, for a book inspired by Campbell's early creation, the monster Gla'aki. The second came from Joe Pulver and Scott David Aniolowski, for a more general response to Campbell's work. I was eager to contribute to both volumes. Campbell is one of those writers with whose work I've spent a great deal of time, both as a writer and a critic. (Indeed, I have a long, unpublished essay examining the use his novel, *The Darkest Part of the Woods*, makes of H.P. Lovecraft's influence.) Part of what I admire about his fiction is what he himself has identified in Lovecraft's stories, namely, its restlessness, its continuing effort to explore the possibilities of horror in terms of subject and form. (The same thing is true of Adam Nevill's fiction.) I came up with a story for each volume, but succeeding in finishing only the one for the Gla'aki volume. In part, this was because the comparatively narrow focus of the anthology gave me more to work with. The story of Campbell's Gla'aki involves him (it?) arriving from outer space and crashing into an English lake, where he remains trapped. Yet he is not without influence in his prison. He can communicate psychically with those who are amenable to his influence, and he can sting those who enter his lake with darts that transform them into his servitors. From this has come a volume, *The Revelations of Gla'aki*, full of information occult and sinister, Campbell's addition to the invented library that includes the *Necronomicon*, etc. The threat of him escaping his watery confines hangs over the stories. In the early stories, it's possible to detect the influence of Lovecraft's "The Colour Out of Space" and "The Call of Cthulhu;" Campbell would return to his creation much later with a novella, *The Last Revelation of Gla'aki*, which attempts to look at him through fresh lenses.

My first thought for my story was to have the monster trapped not in the lake, but in the reflection on its surface, thus confining him to a more interesting space, the world on the other side of the mirror. This promised to give him an accessibility that would allow my characters to interact with him without my having to fake the English location. I also thought of linking his name to the Scots word, "Glaikit," which means crazy. The similarity between name and word had occurred to me early on, and I liked the idea of the one as substitute for the other, in the way a figure such as the Devil has all manner of nicknames to allow people to avoid saying his name. During the summer between my seventh and eighth grade years at school, my older cousin, Julie, and her friend, Lisa, did come from Scotland to stay with my family and me for about a week. They were both glamorous and down to earth, and Lisa had the additional fascination for Catholic me of being a Protestant. This gave me the kernel for my story, but I feel I should clarify, my cousin's friend did not try to lure me into the service of an ancient entity. (Really.) The detail of the two rings derives from a pair of rings my younger brother and I had; though my parents did not obligate me to turn mine over to him. The toy sale was inspired by a trip to a local comic book store on which I tagged along with a couple of friends. (The friend whose mother drove us spent a considerable amount of money there [my memory says forty dollars, which would have been a lot in the fall of 1983, but I may be mistaken], for which his mother immediately grounded him when we returned to the car.)

Not until after the story was done and submitted did I realize I had written another story involving fishing (a form of it, anyway). Given that it's my younger son who's the fisherman in the family, I was both fascinated and a little flummoxed to find myself returning to this activity again. Clearly, it holds some imaginative appeal for me, so I decided to follow Laird Barron's advice and lean into it. I've since completed two more stories in which ice fishing features, one tangentially, the other more directly, and I have a surf-fishing story in the works. So much for not fishing.

Story Notes

The piece I wrote for the Gla'aki anthology reminds me less of Campbell's work than it does a mix of Robert McCammon and Stephen King's stories of children facing things that are too much for them, which are among the truest kinds of stories. It was not a place I expected to end up. It also was far more autobiographical even than I had intended, drawing on parts of my grade school experience I thought I had put behind me. Finally, it features connections to three other of my stories; I'll let you see if you can find them.

Not bad for something written to celebrate a writer's juvenilia.

(Oh, and the story for the other Campbell anthology: I'll get to it.)

"Caoineadh": After "Anchor," this is the second story in this collection to result from a request. As part of a fundraiser for the KGB Bar's Fantastic Fiction reading series, I agreed to contribute a story on the monster of choice for whoever selected my offering. This was Chris McLaren, with whom I've passed many pleasant hours over glasses of single-malt scotch at different conventions. Chris said he wanted to see what I could do with the banshee. During a brief email exchange, he shared a document he found in which a group of Irish gentry are waiting for one of their own to die while a banshee wails in the distance. When at last the wailing stops, a servant brings the news that Lord so-and-so is dead. The kicker was, the servant's name was John Langan. It was like finding myself in my own little weird tale. After a few more emails, Chris left me to write the story, which I spent the next four or so years trying to figure out how to do.

My problem was with Chris's choice of monster. In and of herself, the banshee is not a monster. In fact, in her traditional form, the banshee is tied up with notions of class, as she cries only at the dying/death of a member of one of Ireland's seven aristocratic families. Compared to other supernatural figures, she isn't particularly sinister; it's just that her appearance signals the end of all hopes for a loved one's recovery. I could have tried to make her into a monster, but nothing workable occurred to me.

What solved my problem was having to write an original story for this collection. In looking over its contents, I realized I had written a lot about my father—indeed, I have throughout my writing career. My mom, though, hasn't been a figure in as many of my stories, and even when she has appeared, has done so in more of a supporting role. In a collection whose focus was on autobiographically inflected stories, it would be nice to spend a bit of time with my mother. With that decision came the solution to my banshee dilemma. As I write in the story, my mom has always had a lovely singing voice. My memories of her singing to me and my siblings remain clear and vivid. Suppose, I thought, she had to sing the banshee's song, or to help a banshee in her task? Suppose you had a banshee who was overwhelmed at the number of the dead she had to cry to death, and Mom helped her? It wasn't long before I remembered my mother's references to her hometown of Greenock having been bombed during the Second World War, which a bit of online research filled out for me in more detail. Now everything came together, including a slightly oblique reference to Corpsemouth. Ironically, in the story I wrote about a more-or-less traditional banshee, I figured out a way to write about a more monstrous version of one. Another time, perhaps.

The finished story was suffused by my autobiography, organized according to the recurring image of a woman/girl beside a river. In the writing of it, I think I understood more about my mother than maybe I ever had before. In particular, I gained an appreciation for how traumatizing her childhood experience of the Greenock Blitz must have been for her, something I had never understood as completely.

So thanks to Chris McLaren for setting me a challenge whose solution turned out to be full of unexpected rewards. Funnily enough, as I was sitting down to begin the story, my mom did one of those Ancestry.com tests. While we've always known part of her family was Irish, she's always thought of herself as very Scottish. Turns out, though, that three-quarters of her ancestors hailed from the Emerald Isle.

As I said, like living in my own little weird tale.

ACKNOWLEDGMENTS

It's good to say thank you. It's good to acknowledge the people who have helped you in ways large and small to reach whatever point you've reached in your life and career. I try to thank everyone who has contributed to my writing as often as I can, but it's still good to have an opportunity to set down in black and white my gratitude for the family and friends without whom a book like this would not exist. So:

There's a reason I dedicate everything I do to my wife, Fiona. Twenty years in, our marriage continues to develop and grow in ways I never could have anticipated, and remains a source of deep and abiding joy to me. Thanks, Love.

I've benefitted, too, from the love and support of my younger son, David, with whom I've had long and wide-ranging discussions about writing and music as we've roamed the Catskills in search of fly-fishing spots. As a result, my musical education is now 67% more complete. (Who am I kidding? It's more like 23%. But I'm trying.)

In looking over the story notes for this book, I notice how often I mention fellow writers. I'm happy to have the friendships of Laird Barron, Stephen Graham Jones, and Paul Tremblay. Nadia Bulkin, Michael Cisco, Brett Cox, Gemma Files, Glen Hirshberg, Victor LaValle, Livia Llewellyn, S.P. Miskowski, and Kaaron Warren are pretty cool, too. Special thanks to Sarah Langan (who probably is a distant relative) for writing me such a terrific introduction.

John Langan

I count myself lucky in my agent, Ginger Clark, and her assistant, Nicole Eisenbraum. And in my editors: John Joseph Adams and Doug Cohen, Glynn Owen Barrass and Brian Sammons, Ellen Datlow, Mike Davis, Barry Lee DeJasu, Christopher Golden, Lois Gresh, and Paula Guran. This marks the third time Ross Lockhart has published me, and I continue to be grateful for his support and for producing such lovely books. (Scott Jones deserves credit for his contribution to the process.) Once again, Matthew Jaffe hit the ball out of the park with his cover illustration.

Finally, a sincere thanks to you, my reader, for picking up this collection. I'm grateful for the gift of your time and attention. You make books like this possible, and I thank you for it.

PUBLICATION HISTORY

"Kore:" originally appeared in *Shock Totem: Holiday Tales of the Macabre and Twisted*, Halloween 2014, edited by K. Allen Wood (Shock Totem Publications 2014).

"Homemade Monsters:" originally appeared in *The Doll Collection*, edited by Ellen Datlow (TOR 2015).

"The Open Mouth of Charybdis:" originally appeared in *Innsmouth Nightmares*, edited by Lois Gresh (PS Publishing 2015).

"Shadow and Thirst:" originally appeared in *Seize the Night: New Tales of Vampiric Terror*, edited by Christopher Golden (Gallery 2015).

"Corpsemouth:" originally appeared in *The Monstrous*, edited by Ellen Datlow (Tachyon 2015).

"Anchor:" originally appeared in *Autumn Cthulhu*, edited by Mike Davis (Lovecraft eZine Press 2016).

"Outside the House, Watching for the Crows:" originally appeared in *The Mammoth Book of Cthulhu: New Lovecraftian Fiction*, edited by Paula Guran (Robinson 2016).

"What Is Lost, What Is Given Away:" originally appeared in *What the #@&% Is That?: The Saga Anthology of the Monstrous and the Macabre*, edited by John Joseph Adams and Douglas Cohen (Saga 2016).

"The Supplement:" originally appeared in *Children of Lovecraft*, edited by Ellen Datlow (Dark Horse Books 2016).

"Mirror Fishing:" originally appeared in *The Children of Gla'aki*, edited by Glynn Owen Barrass and Brian M. Sammons (Dark Regions Press 2017).

"Caoineadh" is original to this collection.

ABOUT THE AUTHOR

John Langan is the author of two novels and five collections of stories. His second novel, *The Fisherman*, won the Bram Stoker and This Is Horror awards. He is one of the founders of the Shirley Jackson Awards, for which he served as a juror during their first three years. He reviews horror and dark fantasy for *Locus* magazine. He lives in New York's Mid-Hudson Valley with his wife and younger son, and is slowly disappearing into an office full of books. And more books.

CPSIA information can be obtained
at www.ICGtesting.com
Printed in the USA
LVHW101926061122
732500LV00003B/245